ALLIANCE BRIDE

ALLIANCE BRIDE

JAYE L. KNIGHT

CONTENT ADVISORY

This book contains themes of loss (including references to the death of a spouse, child, and parent), depictions of slavery, non-descriptive threats of sexual violence, and brief mentions of physical abuse by a parent. Please read with care if these are sensitive topics for you. While the story deals with these heavy subjects, it contains no explicit sexual content or strong language.

To Mom for sharing this special journey with me.

Pronunciation Guide

Names

Aevar (AY - vahr)
Alvir (AHL - veer)
Alys (A - liss)
Asfrid (AZ - frid)
Bened (BEH - ned)
Braan (BRAHN)
Dagr (DAYG - uhr)
Eadlyn (EED - lin)
Eydis (AY - diss)
Gorum (GOHR - uhm)
Gudrik (GOO - drik)
Halbjorn (HAL - byorn)
Heida (HIGH - duh)
Hiroc (HEER - ock)
Hjor (HYOHR)
Huginn (HOO - gin)
Ingvald (ING - vahld)
Jodis (YOH - dis)
Jorund (YOHR - uhnd)
Katla (KAHT - lah)
Kian (KEE - an)
Muninn (MOO - nin)
Njal (NYALL)
Oda (OH - duh)
Ranvi (RAN - vee)
Runar (ROO - nahr)
Staegar (STAY - gahr)
Tallak (TAH - lak)
Trygg (TRIG)
Vega (VAY - guh)
Viljar (VILL - yahr)

Places

Fjellheim (FYELL - hime)
Kjolur (KYOH - luhr)
Talta (TAHL - tuh)
Waelon (WAY - lahn)

Words & Phrases

All of the Nordric words and phrases within the book are a mix
of Old Norse, Icelandic, and fantasy equivalents.

Ást mín (OWST MEEN) = my love
Dunga (DOON - guh) = useless fellow
Ealdorman (AHL - dohr - man) = the lord of a shire
Fathir (FAH - theer) = father
Fífl (FEEF - uhl) = idiot/fool
Fjord (FYORD) = a long, narrow sea inlet
Góthan morgin (GOH - thahn MOHR - gin) = good morning
Grybba (GRIB - uh) = ugly hag
Gulrót (GOOL - roht) = carrot
Holmgang (HOHLM - gong) = a duel
Hórkona (HOHR - koh - nuh) = adulteress
Huskarl (HOOS - karl) = an elite household guard
Knattleikr (NAHT - layk - uhr) = a ball game with elements
similar to hockey, rugby, and lacrosse
Móthir (MOH - theer) = mother
Níðingr (NEETH - ing - uhr) = villain (a very serious insult)
Seax (SAX) = a single-edged knife/short sword
Tafl (TAFFLE) = a chess like board game
Tahk (TAHK) = thanks
Tahk fyr (TAHK FEER) = thank you
Veslingr (VESS - ling - uhr) = little wretch/runt

"Perhaps they will accept an alliance without us having to offer you in marriage."

Eadlyn dropped the tent flap to block her view of the fierce Nord warriors milling about their camp near the river that marked the border between Essix and Nordra. The ache in her stomach swelled into her throat, bitter and hot, but she swallowed it back down as she turned to her brother, Essix's so recently crowned king.

"God willing."

She didn't have the heart to dash Edward's fragile hope. She had prayed day and night for such an outcome, but the fact remained—Essix was weak and broken. They had little to offer in an alliance. Unless God intervened, a marriage proposal was their only hope, and even that was a slim hope.

Edward halted his persistent pacing, his jaw clenching as reality seemed to crash in. "What if they won't even consider an alliance?"

"They have to. You must convince them."

He dropped into a nearby chair, his brows gathering in a petulant frown he needed to banish if he wanted to be taken seriously as king. He was a man now and far too old for such childish dramatics. "How?"

Eadlyn held back a sigh. He was not ready for the responsibility that had been thrust upon him. And how could he be? No one had bothered to teach him. Their father would surely be remembered as one of the worst kings ever to rule Essix.

"By remembering Waelon may be preparing for war, and if this alliance fails, Essix will be doomed." She wasn't sure how much more clearly she could stress their dire situation. The kingdom to the west had long had its eye on Essix. Like it or not, Edward had to embrace his role as king and find the strength to be what their father was not.

He hung his head. "You're right."

She knelt before him and wrapped her hand around his arm. The path her life might take after today frightened her far more than she would admit to him, but her brother was the one who had to carry the weight of the crown. "God will not abandon us, and we have allies who will help us see this through."

As if summoned, a weathered figure ducked into the tent. Oswin had been around for as long as Eadlyn could remember, doing everything in his power to advise her father and temper the king's rash behavior. His once-black hair had turned almost entirely gray, and fatigue etched deep lines in his face. Yet, despite his worn appearance and heavy-lidded eyes, a closer look revealed they were sharp as flint, just like his mind. Without his counsel and influence, Edward might never have been crowned king after their father's sudden death, and the country would be in even greater turmoil. He was the one Edward had to rely on once she was gone.

"Your Majesty. My lady." Oswin gave them a respectful bow. "The pavilion is ready."

"So this is it." Edward's face turned a shade of green, and Eadlyn gave his arm another squeeze.

"I have faith you will go out there and be the king I know you can be."

This drew a weak smile from him.

While Oswin helped Edward slip into his royal robes, Eadlyn reached into a small chest and lifted the crown from its resting place. The cool brass pressed against her fingers, worn at the edges from generations of use. It served as a reminder of what was at stake. Their country's entire history might end here if they were unsuccessful in today's negotiations.

When Edward faced her, he dipped his chin, and she set the crown atop his head, tucking a few unruly strands of his dark hair beneath it. It had grown too long to be entirely respectable in Essix. She'd meant to trim it days ago, but time had slipped away. He needed a good wife. Someone to stand beside him and help him lead their people. If only she could be here to help him choose one.

He stepped back, holding his arms wide. "Do I look like a king?"

She smiled through the ache building in her chest. "Stand tall and proud. Then you will *be* one."

He took a deep breath, pulling his shoulders back, and Eadlyn did indeed glimpse the king she knew he could be. He just needed to work on his confidence. She prayed he would fake it well enough to convince the Nords to take their proposal seriously.

"All right, let's get this done."

He led the way out of the tent, shoulders square, his crown glinting beneath the overcast sky. Eadlyn followed behind, Oswin silent and steady at her right. To her left, Galen, commander of the royal guard, fell into step, tall as a tower and twice as unyielding. His grim expression rarely changed, always as though they were marching to war. Today, it suited the occasion. She took comfort in his stalwart presence. He and Oswin were two of the closest allies she and Edward had.

Ahead, the cream-colored pavilion stood as a symbol of neutral ground between the two camps, its scarlet trim fluttering in the chill breeze. Beneath the canopy, servants bustled, placing chairs and tables and arranging goblets and a cask of wine. The scene looked almost festive. But this was no celebration.

This was where their future would be decided. Her future.

Eadlyn's stomach twisted again, uncertain whether it should settle or rise. She forced the storm inside her to calm. She had to be strong for Edward and her people.

They stepped into the shadows beneath the pavilion. Three high-backed chairs waited, with a second set facing them. Eadlyn brushed her fingers along a polished armrest but did not sit. Her legs were too restless to stay still.

"The Nord king will join us shortly," Oswin said, glancing first at Edward, and then at her.

Edward's throat worked. "Any last advice?"

"We've gone over your words many times. Remain calm and keep a clear head. I will be here to counsel you if you need me."

This seemed to calm Edward because his shoulders loosened. Oswin always had that effect on him. If only it worked as well for Eadlyn.

He seemed to sense her unease. While Edward composed himself, Oswin stepped closer and placed his hands on her shoulders. His grip held firm, like a father steadying a frightened child. "Is there anything I can do to help you?"

Eadlyn blinked hard to keep an upwelling of tears at bay. She would not break down. "All I want is for this alliance to work…however that must happen."

"You do your people very proud, my lady."

She managed a weak smile. "Thank you, Oswin."

"My lord," Galen said suddenly.

Those two words cut through the air like a blade.

Everyone turned. Five Nord warriors marched across the field. The bear of a man in the lead must be the king. He was a generation older than the other four and carried himself with the proud confidence of a born leader. Eadlyn's breath grew shallow as they approached, and a shiver iced her spine. She'd heard so many stories of these savage northern warriors. They certainly looked the part in their abundant leather, furs, and long hair. No man of Essix ever grew his hair so long.

Each of them possessed at least one blade—a sword, an axe, or both. The way they carried the weapons said they'd practically been born with blades in hand. A shard of doubt pierced her. If things turned violent, could the royal guard truly protect them?

However, the dismissive way Galen watched them said they might as well have been flies waiting to be swatted. She drew from his confidence. Now was not a time to cow to intimidation. Essix had to show strength, or they would never rise from their weakened state again.

When the Nords reached the pavilion, a thick hush fell. For a moment, they faced each other like two armies meeting on a battlefield rather than diplomats attempting to secure peace. Eadlyn's heart pounded as the silence stretched. What if they hadn't come to negotiate? What if they meant to strike? Assassinate Edward and shatter Essix's last hope?

But no army followed them. The rest of their camp remained peaceful, and no blades were drawn.

With a nudge from Oswin, Edward stepped forward. "Welcome." His voice was steadier than Eadlyn had expected. "I am King Edward of Essix."

Their translator, a balding man with a permanent frown, repeated Edward's words in Nordric, the language sharp and guttural. The lead Nord's iron gaze traveled up and down Edward, not even glancing at the translator.

"I am Jarl Runar, King of the Nord clans." He spoke Aerlish, the language of the southern kingdoms, surprisingly well, though with a heavy accent.

After a glance at Edward, the translator stepped back, no longer of any use. At least this made negotiations quicker and more personal. All the better to make their plea.

"Thank you, Jarl Runar, for accepting our invitation. Please, sit." Edward gestured toward the second set of chairs.

The jarl gave him another long, appraising look before stepping into the pavilion. His men followed. Eadlyn took her seat at Edward's right hand, tracking each of the Nord warriors as they arranged themselves opposite. Two of the younger men claimed the seats on either side of the jarl. His sons? She gripped the armrests at that thought.

They were fairer-haired than the king, so it was hard to tell, especially with their beards. Each of the young Nord men wore their hair shorn close on the sides, leaving the top long and tied back. Such a savage appearance would have been scandalous back at the capital in Kenwich. The man to Runar's right had tattoos curling from each temple of a bear or wolf, inked in dark, winding lines. The other bore a jagged scar that ran down the side of his forehead and around one eye, lending him a fierce and wild air. Eadlyn suppressed a shudder, praying he wouldn't be chosen as her husband. Not that the thought of marrying any of them appealed to her.

One man among them stood out. He remained behind the jarl alongside the youngest Nord. His hair was cropped short, and his eyes were brown rather than the icy blue of the others. Most telling was the small brass tree pendant peeking out of his jerkin. A symbol of the kingdom of Talta to the northeast.

Had Edward noticed? They hadn't expected a Talt presence during negotiations.

She turned back to the Nords, and her focus snagged on the youngest. His hair was as dark as the Talt's, but his eyes were unmistakably Nord—a piercing blue that held her locked in place. Her breath hitched, her tongue dry against the roof of her mouth. But she held his gaze long enough to prove her resolve before turning away.

"May I offer you refreshments after your journey? We've brought our finest imported wine."

Eadlyn happily refocused on Edward, but the jarl dismissed his offer.

"That can wait. You said in your invitation you wished to discuss peace."

The words were blunt and without ceremony.

Edward blinked but recovered. "That is true. We wish to form an alliance with Nordra."

Silence followed. A long, stretching hush broken only by the rhythmic beat of a hammer somewhere in the Nord camp, and tension settled like a weight between them. Edward shifted and glanced at Eadlyn. She could tell he was trying not to fidget.

At last, Runar stirred. "What would be the benefit of such an alliance?"

"Trade, for one," Edward said, his voice sure. Good, he remembered Oswin's counsel. "You have vast forests full of timber. Essix has fertile farmland and plentiful crops. Through trade, we can each supply what the other lacks."

Runar's expression didn't change. If anything, his disinterest deepened. "Nordra has survived for generations without trade from Essix. We take what we need in raids."

"Yes, but with open trade, there's no risk to your men. I'm sure your people would welcome the grain we can offer to see you through your harsh winters. In turn, my people would value lumber and other resources. This alliance could end the raids both sides perpetrate along the border."

Again, Edward looked at Eadlyn. She flashed the briefest smile to let him know he was doing well.

Runar peered at him as if he were weighing Edward's worth. His hand rested on the hilt of his sword, tapping the hammer-shaped pommel. Was he thinking of using it? *Lord, only You can make this work. Please let their hearts be open. I don't know what else we can do.*

"Why come to us?" Runar's voice sliced through the stillness a moment later. "Why not Camria? Are they not your mother's people?"

The question showed more knowledge than she'd expected from him.

Edward nodded slowly. "They are, but that accord is broken."

Thanks to their father.

Runar raised a brow. "So you've burned one alliance beyond repair and now come to us in desperation. Why not go to the Talts?"

"Because we believe your people hold more sway than they do."

Eadlyn suppressed a wince. So he hadn't noticed the Talt. How many times had she told him to be more observant?

She eyed the man behind the jarl. His face creased with silent laughter as he exchanged a glance with the youngest Nord. Hopefully, in amusement and not ridicule. At least Runar appeared mildly entertained.

"It's true, isn't it?" Edward asked.

Runar shrugged. "To a degree."

He studied Edward again, calculating. If only Eadlyn could know how big a fool the jarl took him to be and whether he possessed even the slightest inclination to align with them. Edward sat straight and still in his seat, for which Eadlyn praised God. He was no doubt young and inexperienced, but at least he was putting forth his best effort, if he'd just stop glancing at her for reassurance.

"What is it you truly seek in this alliance? I know it is not trade."

And there it was. The question Eadlyn had dreaded from the start. She had prayed for a miracle, but deep down, she'd known trade alone would never suffice. Now came the moment they placed the fate of Essix in the hands of these fearsome warriors.

A flicker of discomfort passed over Edward's face, but he masked it. "As I'm sure you're well aware, the transition of power is a vulnerable time for any kingdom. We fear the kingdom of Waelon may declare war. In forming an alliance, we seek your assurance that, should we come under attack, Nordra will stand with us."

Runar gave a harsh snort. "So you want my warriors to die cleaning up your father's mess?"

"We ask only that you help us defend our borders. Essian soldiers would take the front lines. Neither of us benefits from Waelon gaining more power. And with your backing, it is our hope they won't even make such advances."

"In other words, you want us as your guard dogs."

Though Edward made an effort to be diplomatic, Eadlyn sensed the desperation creeping in. "We want a mutual agreement. If you help us defend against Waelon, we will likewise help you should Kalgora break your truce. We know how fragile that peace is."

Runar leaned back, studying them. Was he moved, or did he regret even meeting with them?

"How do we know you'll hold to this agreement? Essix is not known for keeping her word."

"I am not my father. As long as I am king, we will honor our terms. You have my word."

The jarl's eyes narrowed. "Boy,"—Eadlyn caught the way Galen stiffened at the jarl's blatant disrespect toward Edward, but he stayed his hand—"I don't know you. Your word means nothing to me. Trust is earned, not merely given."

The words stung, and rightly so. After all their father had done, no one in their right mind would offer Essix trust freely. That left only one option. Her heart gave a panicked lurch, but she held firm to her resolve. She looked at Edward with a single decisive nod. This was the cost, and she would pay it if it meant saving their people.

Edward's face fell. He hesitated for a moment longer and turned back to the jarl. "Then let us form a marriage alliance. I'm told you have three sons, and only one is married. I have a sister. Let one of them marry her. In doing so, our kingdoms will be bound not just by words, but by blood. I would never harm my sister, and once she is part of your household, I hope you will likewise guard her and, through her, Essix."

Eadlyn held her breath. The offer was made.

The jarl appeared genuinely surprised, judging by the lift of his brow. But what caught Eadlyn's attention most was the wordless exchange between the two men seated beside him. Maybe they were his sons. These rough, wild, heathen men. Her vision wavered at the edges. Then she caught the other Nord watching her again, his expression lacking any clue to his thoughts. Did he pity her? Or was he amused, laughing at her being bartered to them as if she, too, were only a trade commodity like the grain her brother promised?

No. She was not a commodity. This was her choice. She did this willingly for her people. Strength flowed into her chest, chasing away the cold in the pit of her stomach. She raised her chin and met the Nord's gaze, unflinching, until the jarl spoke.

"I wish to discuss this with my men before making a decision."

Edward nodded. "As you wish."

The Nords rose and left the pavilion. Once their backs were turned and distance stretched between them, Eadlyn sagged into her chair, the weight of fear and tension pulling at her limbs.

Edward, however, shoved up from his seat to face her and Oswin. Everything that churned inside of her raged on his face.

"I don't like this. Perhaps we should reconsider."

"Your Majesty," Oswin said in a cautioning voice. "You've seen for yourself. They will not even entertain an alliance without a marriage offer. I don't like it either, but we have no choice."

"There must be another way."

Eadlyn drew a slow, deep breath into her lungs, shoring up her resolve and drawing on the strength only God provided. "Oswin is right. This is the only way, and it's working. If Jarl Runar were uninterested, he would have refused outright. He's considering it. That means we have to stand firm."

Panic flared in Edward's eyes. "They're heathen savages. What if they hurt you?"

That question had haunted her for weeks, though she dared not speak it aloud. She couldn't answer it, not truly. Only God knew what lay ahead.

"I survived our father. I'll survive this."

"You weren't Father's wife. The most he did was hit you."

Eadlyn swallowed hard, her throat as dry as a grain field at harvest. Would she be used and abused? Her mother's silent suffering came to mind. These men inspired little hope, but war with Waelon offered her even less.

"We don't have a choice. If we rescind the offer, they will refuse us. And if Waelon conquers Essix, then I won't be a wife, I'll be a captive." Her voice faltered, then steadied. "Even if I married a man of Essix, there would still be risk. What matters is what this marriage can buy us. A chance at peace. A chance for unity. You must take that chance and make it count."

Edward's shoulders slumped beneath the weight of that truth. "You're braver than I am. You should've been born a man. You'd make a better king."

While that may have seemed true, Eadlyn knew better. "God made us exactly as we're meant to be. He knows what He's doing."

"I wish I had your faith."

"You can." She reached out to grip his arms. "You've heard the truth. You know what Brother Winstan and I have taught you. God isn't far off. He's waiting for you to come to Him. You'll need Him in the days ahead. Don't keep waiting."

Edward only responded with a brief nod, and that was all she could hope for.

She leaned back, staring out toward the Nords in the distance. The moment of decision was coming, and there was no turning back. Her only choice was to wait and trust.

evar trailed behind his father and older brothers, their boots crunching on the rocky soil as they strode away from the prying ears of the Essians. Kian stayed by his side, as usual. No one spoke, but Aevar sensed their thoughts turning, the tension rising like the bite of northern wind. Had they been alone, he might've wagered with Kian how long it would take before someone admitted what they were all thinking.

"That was surprising," Kian said, his Talt accent still thick despite his years in Nordra. "I didn't think they'd have the guts to offer a marriage alliance."

No doubt he felt the brewing uncertainty just as keenly.

The silence remained heavy until they reached the river's edge. Here, all eyes went to their father, who stared out across the water toward Nordra before he turned to them.

"What do you think?" Erik asked. As the eldest, he usually spoke first.

Aevar crossed his arms. Would their father address the obvious or circle around it?

"I think the king is weak and grasping for any alliance he can." *Fathir* leveled the pavilion with a stern glance.

So, a roundabout approach then. Aevar kept his silence.

Erik considered it. "She hasn't even spoken, but the princess seems to have a lot of influence with the king."

"Yes," Fathir muttered, "he hardly speaks a word without seeking her approval. I don't know if that is to our advantage or that we'd be fools to align ourselves with a king who does not know his own mind. A little of both, I fear."

"You'd think they would have sought a stronger union by the king asking for a bride instead of offering his sister."

Braan snorted, scratching the scar around his eye. "Maybe he's too much of a coward to take a Nord wife."

"Perhaps he would have if we had a sister to offer. At least this way none of us has to leave Nordra." Erik paused for a moment of loud silence. The final buildup to the real issue. "The question is…who will marry the princess?"

Aevar almost rolled his eyes. "There is no question. It has to be me."

Erik's attention snapped to him, that familiar protective edge igniting. "Hold on. Let's not get ahead of ourselves. It's still up for discussion."

Braan raised his brows, and his mouth tightened as if biting back a response.

As much as Aevar appreciated Erik's care, they were adults, and it was time they stopped treating him like he was glass, regardless of the past. "What is there to discuss? You're married, and Braan is betrothed. I'm the only one left." He turned to their father. "Surely you won't ask Braan to give up Heida."

Kian snorted. "Oh, she'd have a thing or two to say about that."

Aevar met his father's gaze. There it was again, that flash of protectiveness. The hesitation. But the truth was already on the table.

Fathir sighed as if in defeat. "You're right, I'm afraid. You're the only one who can do this. That makes the choice yours and yours alone. I won't force you into a marriage. I'd sooner send the boy king back home to sort out his mess on his own. We do not need their alliance."

Aevar let the words hang there as he stared out over the river. Marriage had been the furthest thing from his mind when they set foot in Essix. The last thing he'd been looking for.

He caught Erik watching him.

"Fathir is right. You don't have to do this. We can still discuss the alliance without marriage…" Erik glanced at their father. "Though I'd be less inclined to trust them without such an arrangement."

He, too, was right. The Essians couldn't be trusted, but they were not without their uses.

"The trade agreement would serve us well," Aevar reasoned. "More grain would ensure we do not struggle this winter, especially the northern clans. There is still plenty of rich land in Waelon and farther south to raid. Leaving Essix untouched will not hurt us. And if we're aligned with both Talta and Essix, it would reinforce our truce with Kalgora. They'd be foolish to attack while we have the backing of two other kingdoms." He motioned to Kian. "Would your uncle honor an alliance with Essix?"

Kian nodded. "Talta has no quarrel with Essix unless they make one. My uncle would likely even march alongside you to save their sorry backsides from Waelon should it come to that."

They might not like or trust the Essians, but a three-way

alliance was much more appealing than the possible alternative. Aevar focused once more on his father. "I know we do not need this alliance, but if what they say is true and Waelon invades, it might become our problem. If Waelon took over Essix and aligned with Camria against us, we could face a war on both our southern and northern fronts. You know Kalgora will break the truce the moment they see an advantage."

Fathir's expression darkened. "This is true."

There was no other choice then. "I'll do it."

Fathir stepped forward, placing a weathered hand on Aevar's shoulder. His firm grip instilled in him a sense of courage, like when he was a boy. "Are you sure?"

Unspoken grief hung between them. They all knew why he was the last one this duty should fall to. Yet perhaps it was also the very reason it should. He'd already had his chance at love and lost it. He had no expectation or desire to find it again. The least he could do now was aid his people.

"Yes. I will marry her."

His father's face softened, the edges of his resolve easing into reluctant acceptance. "Very well. We'll accept the marriage if their other terms are agreeable."

He eyed their camp set up in the grass that was still matted and brown from the recently departed snow. "I do not wish to linger here. We have the Gathering to prepare for. I will ask that the marriage take place tomorrow morning. That gives us time to break camp and cover some ground before sundown. The sooner we return to Fjellheim, the longer the princess has to adjust before the jarls arrive."

"Do you think they'll agree to such a swift union?" Not that it mattered to Aevar. He'd already accepted the marriage. Best not let it drag out. "It won't be time for a traditional ceremony, and I'm sure none of us have brought enough for any sort of usual payment exchange."

"If they are as desperate as I believe they are, they'll agree. It doesn't need to be traditional as long as it's binding. It's alliance agreements we're bargaining over."

At its core, this marriage was nothing more than a contract between Nordra and Essix.

"You know Staegar won't like it," Erik said, his voice low with warning. "He'll no doubt stir up trouble at the Gathering."

Fathir waved a dismissive hand. "Staegar doesn't like anything I do. He's welcome to challenge me again if he wants. Halbjorn and Gorum already support whatever I decide. The rest will follow them, especially when their storehouses are well-stocked this winter. This is another reason to have Aevar and the princess married immediately. It will be harder for Staegar to reverse an alliance than to stop it from happening."

Erik looked between them. "Well then, let's make sure this is an alliance worth fighting for."

Fathir clapped his shoulder.

Together, they walked toward the pavilion where Aevar's bride waited. He ignored the twinge in his gut at that thought. There were worse fates than marrying a stranger. A war that threatened his home and family was one of them.

"So…does this mean I'm your best man?"

Kian wore the impish smile he typically employed to draw Aevar out of a brooding mood. Under different circumstances, Erik would have had the honor of being best man, but nothing about this was normal.

"I suppose."

Kian grinned and leaned closer as they approached the tent. "If nothing else, at least she's easy on the eyes."

Trust him to make light of the situation. Still, he wasn't wrong. The princess *was* lovely. For a foreigner. But she was the complete opposite of the fair-haired beauty that still haunted Aevar's dreams and never let his wounded heart fully heal. Maybe that was for the best. Then she would not remind him of what he'd lost.

Before he could dwell on the past, his father's voice scattered the memories. "Let's see what this king is made of, shall we?"

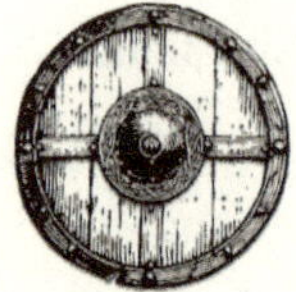

"They're returning."

Eadlyn lifted her head from prayer at Galen's grim announcement. The Nords were halfway across the field, marching toward the pavilion. She pushed to her feet to stand beside Edward and Oswin, who had been discussing the alliance terms should the Nords agree. She swallowed hard, though her throat remained bone dry. It would have been wise to fill a cup of water while she waited, but she was afraid it would have trembled right out of her hand or refused to stay down. She clenched her fingers to still the shakes. Why did it feel as though she were on her way to the gallows?

She forced a mask of composure into place as the Nord party reached the edge of the pavilion. Though she tried to read Jarl Runar's expression, it remained as impenetrable as before. This waiting wore on her. As much as she feared the verdict, she wanted to know her fate.

The jarl gave her a fleeting glance before focusing on Edward. "We have decided to accept your proposal of a marriage alliance, provided we agree with the remaining terms."

For one suspended heartbeat, Eadlyn's chest swelled with thankfulness while her stomach plunged like a stone. Essix would be saved, but her fate lay elsewhere.

"I am pleased to hear it," Edward responded, though the words were stilted. He cleared his throat, visibly collecting himself. "Have any of your sons accompanied you?"

Eadlyn's breath caught as she darted a glance at the two warriors who had flanked Runar during their earlier discussion. Which of them might she be joined to for the rest of her life?

But when the jarl motioned, neither of these men moved. Instead, the younger, dark-haired Nord stepped forward. Eadlyn's pulse skittered in a strange mix of relief and apprehension.

"My eldest are already taken," Runar said. "This is my youngest, Aevar. He has agreed to wed your sister."

Their eyes met again, and Eadlyn's heart now pattered like a frantic sparrow trapped in a window as the reality sank in that this was her husband-to-be. He stood with his hands resting idly on his weapons, feet set wide in the stance of a seasoned warrior. She'd seen that same posture in Galen countless times. If Aevar felt even a fraction of the uncertainty she did over this arrangement, he did not show it.

She searched his face for something—*anything*—to reassure her, but his expression was as unreadable as his father's. At least he didn't leer at her. Didn't assess her like a prize to be won or an object to be claimed or stolen. That had to count for something. She turned his name about in her mind, trying to become accustomed to it as the name of her husband.

That's when she realized Edward was staring at her. She switched her attention to him, reading the question on his face. She took a quivering breath and dipped her chin in a nod. What else could she do? She wouldn't back out now.

"We are in agreement then," Edward said, turning back to the jarl.

"Good." A glint sparked in Runar's eyes. One that set Eadlyn on edge. "There is an old tradition among our people. When a man seeks a woman's hand, he must first fight her father or her brother to prove he is worthy. Perhaps you should fight my son to see if he is worthy of your sister."

The blood drained from Edward's face. "F-fight him?"

"Don't worry. It's only until one of you yields, not to the death." Jarl Runar gestured to the open ground outside the pavilion.

Eadlyn looked between the two parties. Aevar studied Edward, a smirk playing at the edge of his mouth. A subtle challenge. He was every inch a warrior, armed and ready. Edward, meanwhile, wasn't even wearing his sword, a mistake, she now realized.

She squeezed her fists. This was barbaric and did nothing to embolden her hope that the stories of the Nords' brutish ways were exaggerated. Heat rose in her blood, and she stepped forward, facing down the jarl.

"My brother is the king. Essix cannot risk losing him." Even if it wasn't to the death, anything might happen.

The jarl didn't have a chance to respond before Galen's sharp voice cut through the tension. "I'll fight him, my lady. I'll judge whether he's worthy of you."

Of course he would step up in her defense, always prepared to stand between her and the fire. He had his hand on his sword, ready to draw it as he and Aevar took measure of each other. Galen was much taller than Aevar. If anyone could match and beat the Nord, it was him. But what was the point? Both would probably rather die than yield, and someone might get hurt for nothing more than a show of useless bravado. Eadlyn put her hand on Galen's arm to still him.

"No. The arrangement has already been made. A fight isn't necessary." Turning, she met Aevar's gaze. "Battle prowess does not determine the strength of a man's character anyway."

For a breath, no one moved. Then she caught it—a twitch of Aevar's lips—the barest hint of a smile and a slight nod. Whether in agreement or mere acknowledgment was a mystery. At least this confirmed that he, like his father, spoke her language. An inability to communicate would have made an already unthinkable situation even harder.

The charged atmosphere slowly abated. Galen stepped back, though his posture remained rigid.

Edward cleared his throat, still pale, his voice shaky. "Why don't we take refreshments while we discuss the terms of our agreement?" He motioned to the table at the rear of the pavilion.

This time, the Nords accepted. They moved to the table, pouring goblets of deep red wine. Aevar glanced at her as he passed an arm's length away. Her breath caught again, and a quiver stirred deep in her stomach. She held her ground, though every instinct screamed to step back.

Oh Lord, if this is truly Your will, please give me the strength to face it. If not, rescue me.

She turned to Galen, keeping her voice low. "Thank you for your willingness to defend me."

His attention remained locked on Aevar like one of the hunting falcons back home watching prey. "I'd gladly wipe the smirk off his face if you asked."

"I know." And not for the first time did she wish with all her heart he'd been her father instead. If he were, she wouldn't be in this position.

She looked over at Edward, who still appeared rattled by the prospect of facing a Nord warrior. Though Galen was working with him on his sword skill, they both knew he would never have stood a chance in a fight. Her soon-to-be husband would have made a fool of him. Still, it did sting that Edward hadn't been more willing to fight for her. She had witnessed her share of men, including these Nords, who possessed far more boldness than was good for them, but she didn't believe her brother's utter lack of courage was a good thing either.

No stars marked the heavy black sky, only orange sparks as Aevar stirred up their fire near the riverbank. Another blaze crackled a few yards away, surrounded by the *huskarls* they'd brought from Fjellheim. Their laughter rose and fell, mingling with the steady hush of the river's current.

He leaned back as the flames danced, then peered over his shoulder toward the Essian camp. A few fires glowed like beacons in the darkness. The princess was out there somewhere. She may have already taken to her tent, preparing for tomorrow. The aliance was secured. The marriage agreed upon, quick and reluctant as expected. All that remained was the morning ceremony.

"Your new woman's got more spine than her brother," Braan said, snapping Aevar back to the firelight. His brother's pale blue eyes gleamed with mischief. "You should've offered her a sword. She might have fought you herself to test your worth."

Aevar chuckled at the thought. It was almost appealing.

Erik tossed another chunk of wood onto the fire before adjusting the fur around his cloak. The night had a bite to it. "If the Essians had sense, they'd keep her and get rid of the king."

Braan, still grinning, turned back to Aevar. "Think you can handle her?"

Aevar scoffed. "Please. I've yet to hear you say anything to Heida but 'yes, dear.'"

Erik's laughter broke out, deep and full, joined by Kian's. This time, Aevar was the one smirking.

Braan shook his head. "Something wrong with keeping my woman happy?"

"Not at all," Kian chimed in. "Especially when she could take your head clean off your shoulders."

Braan snorted. "You're the only one in danger of that. You're always hiding behind one of us like your mother's skirts when you get her riled."

Aevar laughed as Kian feigned insult. *This* was comfort. His brothers. Their teasing. The easy camaraderie that had held him together when nothing else had. He wasn't sure what the last couple of years would've been like without them. Soon, Eadlyn would become part of it. If only he could see how that would change things. How much he might think back on this night and long for it.

He turned his head, scanning again beyond the glow of their fires. This time, he spotted a lone silhouette down by the river. His father had gone to check on the men but now stood still, attention fixed across the dark water. While his brothers continued heckling each other, Aevar rose and excused himself. He adjusted his own fur-mantled cloak as the icy wind rolled in off the river and walked away from the fire.

He came to stand beside his father, neither speaking. Together, they stared out across the darkened plains toward Nordra. Aevar missed the thick forests already. The freshness of pine and snow. These low, barren stretches were foreign and strange. He understood now why the Essians desired timber. They barely had enough wood for their fires from what they'd scrounged up along the riverbank.

Gravel crunched underfoot as Fathir turned to face him. Aevar couldn't make out his expression in the dark, but the weight of his father's gaze bored into him.

"I hope you're not doing this simply because you feel you ought to."

Aevar let out a long breath that clouded in front of him. In all honesty, he wasn't sure why he'd agreed to the marriage. Of course, he ultimately wanted to help his people, but whatever driving force lay beyond that he couldn't explain. Fate, possibly, if there was such a thing. He was not so sure anymore. The winding thread of fate he'd so eagerly followed in his youth had left his world shattered. He wasn't keen on trusting it again.

He shrugged. "The alliance will be good for Nordra. We all do what we can to make sure our people thrive."

His father sighed, long and low. "I only wish the responsibility did not have to fall to you."

"It's my choice, and I accept it. Besides, people marry for the sake of peace and alliances all the time. You and *Móthir* did. You did not know each other before you wed."

The shadow of his father's beard almost hid a smile. "No, we didn't."

"But it turned out well." Aevar offered the words like a quiet hope. He'd never once doubted his parents loved each other fiercely and passionately. He didn't expect or seek the same for himself, but perhaps peaceful companionship was attainable.

"Your mother and I were lucky. I pray to the gods you find the same luck."

Aevar didn't respond to that. Prayers hadn't done him much good in the past, but he appreciated them anyway. Maybe the gods might listen this time.

Rain pattered against the canvas above, steady and cold, as if counting down the final hours of her freedom. Eadlyn shivered, the chill sinking deep into her bones as her maid, Mildred, helped her dress.

What a wretched day for a wedding.

Not that she had expected sunshine. Hoping for something special now felt like a childish dream. It didn't matter whether she was married here in the mud and gray or weeks from now in the familiar stone hall in Kenwich. Either way, she would go north to a land she had never seen, bound to a man she did not know. No feast or fine silk would have softened that truth or quelled the roiling in her stomach.

She stole a glance at the bucket near her cot as her insides twisted again. Mildred had tried three times to coax her to eat something, but it was no use. Her nerves were wound too tightly to keep anything down.

As Mildred laced the back of her woolen overdress, Eadlyn ran trembling fingers along the pale blue fabric. It was the closest thing she had to a bridal gown, simple for travel. She hadn't prepared for a wedding. If this ceremony had taken place in Kenwich, she would have worn a gown fit for a princess. Part of her mourned the loss of a traditional wedding. However, except for God, nothing in her life had ever been as it should. This was just one more trial she had to endure with His grace.

Once dressed, she sat down for Mildred to brush out her long hair and pin back a little on the sides—an appropriate style for a maiden bride.

Mildred's voice broke the silence, hesitant and small. "I stepped out this morning to look for wildflowers for your hair. I thought…something to make it pretty. But they've not started blooming yet."

The thought warmed Eadlyn. "You're kind to think of that, and I appreciate the effort."

They both fell silent again. When Mildred finished her hair, Eadlyn rose from her seat, trying to settle her racing thoughts on what to do next. Jarl Runar had insisted the wedding conclude before midday. They apparently had no desire to linger on Essix soil. In a few brief hours, she would leave behind everything she knew—her home, her brother, her people—and travel with strangers to a kingdom she'd only heard and read about.

She'd hoped for a chance to speak with Aevar before they were bound in marriage. A moment to find something of the man behind the warrior's eyes. But she had not seen him since the tense negotiations had ended last evening. Still, part of her was relieved by the delay. Facing him meant acknowledging this was real.

Before she decided on her next course of action, Mildred caught her eye. The girl was wringing the life out of her hairbrush.

"Mildred, what is it?"

Her gaze faltered, too much moisture welling on her eyelids. "I know you shall leave with the Nords after the wedding. If you require it, I…" She gulped. "I will go with you."

Eadlyn's heart broke at the fear in her expression. Is that how she looked? Goodness, she hoped God gave her the strength to hide it better than that. She clasped her hands around Mildred's. "Milly, no. You will return to Kenwich with my brother. This is my path. I won't drag you into it."

A gust of relief left Mildred's lips as her shoulders sagged. "Oh, my lady…you're too kind to me."

Eadlyn squeezed her hands. "I would never take you from your home and your family."

Why did her own eyes have to water now?

Mildred's lower lip quivered. "I wish you didn't have to go with them alone."

"I won't be alone." Eadlyn lifted her chin with as much steadiness as she could summon. "God will be with me."

That truth anchored her trembling heart.

Mildred's eyes welled again. "And you'll have my daily prayers, my lady. I promise."

Eadlyn almost hugged her. "Thank you."

"My lady."

Galen's voice drifted through the tent flap. Was it time? But she wasn't ready. Not yet. Her composure shattered like glass across a floor.

Gathering what resolve she still possessed, she untied the flap and stepped outside. The rain had ceased, though the air remained heavy with dampness. Galen stood in the muddy grass. His dark hair plastered his brow, droplets of rainwater sliding down the hard lines of his face. It wouldn't surprise her if he'd stood guard there all night, in case the Nords snatched her away early. The thought made her skin crawl, but her attention snagged on the Talt just beyond him.

"Says he has something to ask you." Galen jerked his thumb toward the man.

The Talt stepped forward, glancing at Galen as if for permission. The scabbards on his belt were empty, so unless he had a dagger hidden somewhere, he wasn't much of a threat. When Galen didn't move to stop him, the man's gaze shifted back to Eadlyn.

A bright smile split his bearded face. "Morning, my lady. My name's Kian."

He seemed far too cheerful for a day like this. Then again, he wasn't the one marrying a stranger.

Eadlyn dipped her head in greeting.

"I was sent to see if any of these fit you." He opened his hand to reveal a small pile of silver rings. "We've been gathering them, hoping to find one suitable for the exchange."

The ring exchange, of course. They'd dispensed with so many traditions by holding this wedding so quickly she hadn't even thought of it. She stared at the collection. The rings were worn, tarnished, and engraved with foreign patterns, grime clinging in the crevices. A far cry from the delicate silver ring her mother had worn. Not that it had done her much good.

"It's only temporary," Kian added, as if reading her thoughts. "Proper ones will be made once we're home."

Eadlyn cleared her throat, a lump still hanging on. "Of course." She reached for a ring and slid it onto her finger, the metal damp and cool against her skin. It was too big, so she returned it to the pile. She searched for something to distract herself while she tried on the next. "You're a Talt."

"Aye. That I am." His grin had a calming effect, and his eyes sparkled with a genuine kindness that made him far less frightening than the Nords. Perhaps they should have made this alliance with the Talts after all. But she could not think that way. Not now.

"I figured as much during negotiations."

"You're observant."

"Well, you don't look much like a Nord."

Kian chuckled, a cheery sound in the gray gloom. "No, I don't."

If only Eadlyn could have had a conversation like this with her to-be husband. Then, possibly, she wouldn't feel as though she were going to throw up at any minute. She drew a chill breath into her lungs, glancing at Kian between rings.

"Do you know him well?"

"Aye, Highness, I do."

"May I ask…what sort of man is he?"

Kian paused, tilting his head. "A fierce warrior. Loyal. Honest. He's saved my skin more than once." He leaned in as if sharing a secret. "Honestly, I'd fight my own kin for him." His face crinkled with another smile, but it faded to a much more serious expression. "He's a good man. He won't harm you if that's what you fear."

Eadlyn searched his face for the truth in his words. Could she trust him enough to find comfort in them? *Lord, please show me.* While no answer was immediately forthcoming, she managed a nod. "Thank you."

She wiggled the ring currently on her finger. While still a bit large, it shouldn't slip too easily from her finger. From the looks of it, it was her best choice.

"I think this one will do." She pulled it off and dropped it into Kian's free hand.

"Good. I'll get these back to the jarl."

He headed off through camp toward the river, and it felt as if he'd taken the sunshine with him. Not that any could be found today, choked out by stifling gray clouds. A shiver worked its way through her, alerting her to the bitter bite in the breeze. Though spring had newly arrived, the frigid air suggested winter might have one final say in the matter.

She ducked back into the tent, rubbing her ring finger. The coldness lingered.

Mildred turned to her. "Is there anything else you need, my lady?"

Eadlyn shook her head. "No, Milly. I think I'd like a few minutes to myself. Once the ceremony begins, please pack the rest of my things for the journey."

"Of course." Mildred curtsied and grabbed her cloak as she slipped outside.

Alone with God, Eadlyn closed her eyes and pressed her hand to her fitful stomach. Now that she was by herself, it churned with renewed vigor. She took a deep breath to calm it, but light-headedness threatened instead, her heartbeat too loud in the quiet tent. Knowing she had to get a handle on her fears and emotions before the time came to face her fate, she stepped to her bed and sank to her knees on the sheepskin rug beside it.

Clasping her hands, she reached out to God. Any sort of elegant prayer jumbled in her head. Only a soul-deep desperation rose from her heart for God's strength and wisdom. For His deliverance. She did not want to do this, yet she must. She had prayed and prayed for a different way, but this was where she found herself. Yet even here, she prayed again. All she wanted was to go home, where she had finally found peace.

A tear escaped, sliding hot and unwanted down her cheek. She blinked hard, but the rest followed. A quiet sob soon slipped out, and she pressed a fist to her mouth to smother the sound. Galen's voice murmured outside, but she couldn't respond. Canvas rustled as he entered the tent. Only then did the crushing black tide that had risen around her recede. She drew in a long, shaky breath and pushed herself to her feet, wiping her cheeks.

For once, Galen's impassive face softened.

Sniffing, Eadlyn made a poor attempt at lifting her voice. "I don't suppose anyone would believe me if I said they were happy tears."

"I don't think anyone would expect them to be."

She let a long breath seep out, her shoulders sagging with it. "I just want to be strong and dignified. I don't want them to see me weak."

Galen's brow furrowed. "My lady, you are stronger and more dignified than any man I've ever served with or fought against. Certainly more so than your brother."

His mention of Edward was exactly what Eadlyn needed to summon the strength and purpose her fear had swallowed. He was the reason she was doing this. Both for him and for Essix. "He desperately needs someone to teach him how to be a man. You're the only one I trust to do that."

"I'll do my best." Galen's expression sobered again. "It would be better if you were here too. I'd stop this wedding here and now if I could."

"I know, but if Essix is ever to thrive again, I need to do this."

"Essix doesn't deserve you."

She always appreciated his candor. "Other women have been given in marriage alliances. I won't be the first or the last. At least I am the one making the choice."

Galen let out a weighty breath. Those facts didn't seem to help him as much as they helped her. He looked like he'd rather be out fighting the Nords than standing here as helpless as she was. His eyes blazed as he took a step closer and said in a low voice, "If he hurts you—if *any* of them hurt you—get word to me and I will get you out of there, alliance be hanged."

A smile rose to Eadlyn's lips.

"I mean it."

"I know, and that heartens me." Just knowing the option existed gave her a spark of hope. An ember to carry northward.

Galen shook his head, his expression burdened. "I did everything I could to protect you from your father and often failed, but I'll not stand by and let you suffer for the rest of your life."

Aevar tugged the laces of one of his arm bracers taut, the leather creaking beneath his fingers. He needed something to keep his hands busy while he waited for Kian. His father and brothers were already occupied with their own tasks, and the silence in the lean-to made the waiting worse.

A chill breeze swept in beneath the canvas. Not as biting as the river he'd bathed in at dawn, but sharp enough to draw a shiver. The icy plunge had shocked his thoughts clean for a time. But now the weight of what lay ahead settled in the forefront of his mind, heavy with the kind of uncertainty that made a man itch for battle. Better to face it head-on than circle it with dread.

Footsteps squelched toward the shelter, and Kian appeared, boots muddy.

Aevar straightened. "Did any of them fit her?"

Kian held up one ring while laying the rest on a pile of furs for the men to reclaim. They were generous to have offered them.

"Good, here's mine." Aevar handed the silver band to Kian. "Keep it safe, or Erik will have your hide."

"Will do." Kian tucked both rings deep into one of his pockets.

Aevar was honored Erik loaned him his own wedding ring. Though a hair too big, it meant far more borrowing it from him than from any of the other men. Maybe it would bring some of the good fortune Erik had in his marriage.

Kian took over on Aevar's half-laced bracer. "She asked about you, what sort of man you were."

"What did you tell her?"

"I told her you were a real bear. Grouchy all the time…"

Aevar rolled his eyes, though for half a moment, he wasn't sure he was joking. He was relieved when Kian laughed.

"No, I said you were a good man and wouldn't harm her. I think it helped settle her nerves a bit. I hope so anyway."

Good. Aevar had no desire to add fear to her burdens. He'd seen the wide-eyed way she regarded him yesterday. A princess from the soft South had every right to be wary. He didn't blame her.

"What's your opinion of her?"

"Well, not that we had much time to talk, but she seems like a nice girl. She wasn't all weepy or hysterical or anything. Like Braan said, she seems to have some guts, especially for a princess."

Aevar hoped they were right. A delicate southern woman would have a hard time of it in the harsh wilds of Nordra. "Do you think she'll be able to handle our way of life?"

"She'll have to. We all do."

He was right. Life didn't bend to comfort; it demanded adaptation.

Kian finished tying off the laces and slapped Aevar on the shoulder. "Maybe she'll surprise you."

In a good way, he hoped.

Kian had just tied off the second bracer when the others approached the lean-to. Fathir paused, taking him in. "Are you ready?"

"Nearly." Aevar reached for his belt holding his sword and seax knife.

Fathir shot a glance toward the pavilion where they'd negotiated yesterday. "We're about ready to start. I talked with the king and their priest. They'll keep the ceremony short and simple. Not a bunch of religious yapping. I've heard priests like to ramble."

Aevar nodded. They did not need to draw it out. It wouldn't have much effect on the marriage either way. That came only in the day to day.

Once he'd buckled his belt, he turned to Kian, who held his cloak for him. He shrugged it on and faced his father. Now he was ready. Fathir took a step forward and placed his hands on Aevar's shoulders. He said nothing at first. No words were needed at this point. Reluctance rested on his face, but this wasn't a death sentence, and Aevar wasn't the one leaving his home and everything behind.

Finally, Fathir just said, "Let's get this over with."

He led the way around the shelter. Erik, Braan, and Kian fell in around Aevar as they headed for the pavilion. The ten huskarls they'd brought with them milled about and offered him encouraging nods as he passed. They'd soon finish packing up camp. By the time he returned, it would be like they'd never been here at all.

As they neared the pavilion, his heartbeat elevated the way it did in the final moments before a battle. He hoped this wasn't the biggest mistake of his life. With something as significant as an alliance attached to it, he could not escape if things turned sour.

Gods, he prayed she wasn't an unreasonable sort of woman he'd have to contend with for the rest of his days.

When they stepped into the pavilion, the princess was not yet present. Only the priest and a handful of Essian soldiers, including the man who had challenged him yesterday. Their eyes locked, and if only a look could kill, Aevar would have been on the ground bleeding out. That glare hadn't softened overnight, and he held the piercing stare for a long moment. He would have enjoyed testing himself against this warrior had the princess not intervened.

He shifted his attention to the priest. Before today, he'd only ever seen a dead one, face down in the Talta mud after a Kalgoran raid. That man had worn simple brown robes. This one, however, wore fine white linen trimmed in gold. A large, jewel-encrusted cross hung heavily on his chest. He might have made an impressive sight where he came from, but here, mud spattered the robes from hem to knees, marring the image.

The man's long face pinched as he peered down his nose at Aevar. At least as best he could, given they were the same height. Erik would have accomplished the feat much better, standing as tall as the scowling Essian warrior who still tried to kill Aevar with his gaze. Aevar couldn't help himself and gave the priest a slow, insolent smirk. The one he used to annoy his brothers. Sure enough, the priest recoiled, lips curled in contempt. So much for Christians loving their enemies.

Beside him, Braan stifled a snort, and Erik let his gaze drift over the priest in the cool and dismissive way he'd perfected as the eldest. Aevar contemplated leaning over to ask Kian if all priests were like this. After all, the Talts were Christian, or so they claimed.

"Stand here."

The priest's thin voice drew Aevar's attention back to him. The man pointed at a spot to his left as if Aevar were a wayward child. Aevar stepped forward, raising an eyebrow. The priest huffed. What did he have to be so uptight about?

As much fun as tormenting the man turned out to be, the mood changed in an instant when the priest straightened and focused on something beyond the pavilion. Aevar turned to find the king approaching, his sister on his arm. Their smooth-talking adviser followed behind. All thoughts of mischief flew out of Aevar's head as his heart gave a heavy thump. He never thought he'd see another woman as his bride. She kept her head bent as she approached, though stole glances his way. She walked with a steady, accepting pace, not like she was being dragged to the ceremony. If anything, her brother's steps marked reluctance.

A shame the heavy woolen cloak she wore hid her shapely figure he hadn't failed to notice yesterday, but he stopped his thoughts there. Best not to go down that road until he knew what sort of relationship theirs would be. He wasn't sure he was ready to acknowledge the draw of another woman anyway.

He did notice the way her dark hair fell long and soft around her shoulders, tempting him to bury his fingers in it. But the thought of that and the memories it stirred cut painfully into his chest, bringing such observations to an end. Today they were bound only by political arrangement. The future was something he had no desire to consider right now.

The princess and the king crossed the remaining distance, and when they reached the gathering, she faced her brother. He clasped her shoulders, and a silent exchange passed between them. She attempted a smile before they parted. The king and his adviser took a stand with their men while the princess turned and took the spot in front of Aevar.

Here she met his eyes but broke away almost immediately. He caught each shallow, deliberate breath she took. Though her face was dry, moisture clung to her lashes. He supposed that was to be expected. She showed her courage by hiding her tears here.

He let his gaze wander over the rest of her face. He'd spied them yesterday, but now that he studied her more thoroughly, he counted three light scars skimming the soft flesh of her cheek and another threading down through her lips toward her chin. They didn't detract from her beauty, but how might a princess have come by such wounds? Maybe she'd tell him one day.

The priest cleared his throat, interrupting Aevar's perusal of his bride.

"You will join hands." The man didn't even work up the decency to hide the disgust in his voice.

Aevar freed his hands from the folds of his cloak and held them out to the princess. She moved more timidly, and her fingers came to rest in his, cold and trembling a bit. He almost folded his hands over hers to warm them but caught himself.

Reflex. Nothing more.

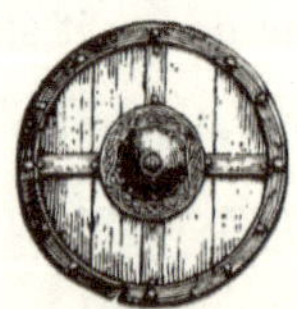

Tingles raced through Eadlyn's chilled fingers, all the way up her arms, sending a twinge to her middle. It wasn't as if she hadn't held a man's hand before, but something about this was far more intimate. Aevar's hands were warm to the touch—rough, worn, strong.

She swallowed, though it was nearly impossible to do without gulping. His thumb brushed over her knuckles, shooting another shiver straight up her arm.

She forced her gaze back to him. He still watched her intently, and she wished so much she knew what he was thinking. They were standing so close, only their linked hands between them. Close enough for her to notice a scar under his cheekbone she had missed before, and another peeking from the dark hair on his chin. So many scars between these Nord men, and those were only the ones she could see. Not that she was one to be put off by scars, but they told stories. Of battles fought. Of a life that likely looked nothing like her own. Just what kind of world was she stepping into?

She tried to imagine him as an Essian man, clean-shaven, hair trimmed short, and without the scars. To her surprise, she came to the conclusion that he might have caught her eye under different circumstances. Not that it completely helped, but she acknowledged she could be marrying a much older man. Perhaps she should count her blessings.

Father Bened began the ceremony, his nasally voice thick with the contempt he harbored toward her husband-to-be. He'd made no secret of it since negotiations had ended. Though he'd been the royal priest for over a decade, it had brought little good to the palace at Kenwich. He spent far more time counting coinage and drawing attention to his outward piety than doing any actual work for the Lord.

If only Brother Winstan were here instead. Eadlyn craved his spiritual guidance and counsel. He was the one who had taken up where Bened failed and helped guide her to true faith in Christ. But he had his small church to tend to back in Kenwich, and

Father Bened was expected to travel with them. He was one person Eadlyn did not regret leaving behind.

He had complained for half the evening last night that they should have insisted on Aevar being baptized as part of the marriage agreement. Thankfully, they had not. It would no doubt have led to a pointless debate and ill feelings with their new allies. They couldn't risk that. Getting dunked in the freezing river by Bened would not have made Aevar any more Christian than the other Nords anyway. That could only ever come through a change of heart and true faith. She should have prayed for such an outcome more than she had. It seemed so impossible, but she was ashamed of such a lack of faith on her part.

Lord, if I can be a light and witness in Nordra, guide me and use me. Give me the courage to be so.

Except for such prayers, she found it hard to focus with Aevar's solid presence so near and overwhelming and missed most of the ceremony. His attention remained fixed on her. Of that, she was very aware. She wasn't sure what sort of unnerving sensation it sent to her already tangled stomach. She'd seen men leer at her before, but this was not that. Dare she believe there was some honor in this man when she knew so very little about him? She recalled what Kian had said and prayed yet again for it to be true. She didn't need for a husband to love her, just for him to be kind. That was all she asked.

Before she even knew it, they had come to the vows, and she fought to concentrate. Her heart raced as she forced herself to hold Aevar's gaze while Bened recited the words.

"Do you, Aevar Runarsson, take Princess Eadlyn as your wife, for better, for worse, for richer, for poorer, in sickness and in health, forsaking all others until death do you part?"

Eadlyn held her breath, but only a heartbeat passed before Aevar answered, "I do."

And she realized this was the first time he had spoken in her presence. The first time she had heard his voice. It was deep yet warm, and she wanted for all the world to believe he'd meant his vow.

Tremors threatened her limbs as Father Bened's attention shifted to her.

"Do you, Princess Eadlyn, take Aevar Runarsson as your husband, for better, for worse, for richer, for poorer, in sickness and in health, forsaking all others until death do you part?"

Eadlyn stared into Aevar's eyes. If only she could see the future in them. Yet, whatever it held, she was here for a purpose she would not abandon. *Lord, I'm laying my life down at Your feet. You brought me here, and I will trust You.*

"I do."

Fear still thudded in her chest, but at that moment, she found a strange sort of peace in the knowledge she had made her choice. She had followed through despite the unknown. At the same moment, Aevar's hands tightened around hers, and she wanted very much to believe it was his way of saying, whatever happened now, they were in this together.

There were no congratulations. No celebratory applause or cheers. The ceremony simply ended with the exchanging of the rings and Father Bened pronouncing them man and wife before God. Not that Eadlyn had expected more. This was, after all, a transaction, not a celebration. One that now left her standing awkwardly beside her new husband outside the pavilion, where they had followed his father and the rest of the men.

The jarl turned to them and settled his attention on her. "Are you packed, Princess? My men have finished with our camp."

Eadlyn forced herself not to shrink, since he hadn't spoken harshly. "Yes. If my maid has finished, I should be ready."

"Will she be accompanying you?"

"No, I will go alone."

Saying it aloud sent a chill down her spine. The jarl—her father-in-law, she realized with a jolt—raised his brows. Likely they'd assumed she would bring at least one person to serve her.

"And do you have a stout horse for the journey?"

"Yes." Her gelding, Hiroc, was no gangly creature.

"Good. We'll leave as soon as you're ready."

Though he phrased it as a courtesy, Eadlyn doubted he would appreciate delay.

She inclined her head. "I'll retrieve my things."

She flicked her gaze to Aevar, uncertain whether she needed his blessing to leave. Was she a partner now? Or property? Would she need to seek his permission for anything she did? But he made no move to stop her or follow, so she turned and walked away, the rain-soaked grass squishing beneath her feet as she headed back to her tent.

Alone for a breath of a moment, she lifted her eyes toward the gray sky, not even sure what prayer to offer. Her thoughts jumbled too much for her to form words. She looked down at her left hand, where the ring shone dully in the dim light. It was done. The agonizing, the waiting, the planning. Over. There was no going back now. Maybe the finality left her numb, but she prayed it lasted long enough to survive the goodbyes.

She ducked into her tent, where Mildred waited.

"Your things are all packed, my lady."

"Thank you, Milly. You've served me so well. I've asked Oswin to see if you might stay on at the palace."

"It's been my honor, my lady. You've always been very kind."

The girl curtsied, and Eadlyn nodded, her throat swelling as she turned to her two travel bags. She crossed to the bed and opened one, sliding her hand inside, not to double-check Mildred's work, but to assure herself a particular treasure was still there. Her fingers found the familiar leather cover, and she drew it out enough to glimpse the old parchment pages inside.

Biblical manuscripts, her most cherished possession. She'd found them hidden away in the palace library years ago, once belonging to her great-grandmother. That they'd survived her father's scorn for faith was a miracle. Had he known she possessed them, he might've destroyed them out of spite.

Father Bened had objected, of course, when she asked Edward for permission to take them to Nordra, but her brother had granted it without hesitation. It would have devastated her to leave them behind. She needed the strength they had provided all these years, now more than ever.

She tucked the bundle between the folds of her dresses and secured the ties. The numbness she'd hoped to keep wrapped around her heart was already beginning to fade, and pain crept in. Leaving this tent was harder than the wedding vows.

Steeling herself, she stepped outside. Galen stood waiting with a stocky dun horse.

"I brought Hiroc for you."

The pain in her chest dug deeper at the subdued tone of his voice. She fought to keep it from summoning tears. "Thank you."

He took her bags and attached them to the saddle in silence. Eadlyn ran her hand down Hiroc's warm, rain-damp face, smoothing his dark forelock. She glanced toward the Nords near the pavilion, then at her brother and Oswin, standing apart from them.

When Galen finished, his eyes met hers in an exchange that nearly broke her. Other than God, this man had been the most steadfast thing in her life, and right now, that strength seemed shaken. When she left, part of his life's purpose would leave with her. She had to turn away otherwise she would lose the composure she fought so hard to gain.

Gripping Hiroc's reins, she began walking toward the others, savoring the comforting, protective shadow of Galen's presence as he walked alongside her one last time. He'd given her a sense of safety and security when her world had been dark and lonely. Now she had to let that go and trust God to face the unknown.

They joined the gathering, and Jarl Runar stepped forward to speak with Edward.

"We'll begin cutting timber. I expect a shipment of grain to arrive soon."

Edward met his gaze with resolve. "It will."

It steadied Eadlyn to see him standing tall, speaking like a king.

Satisfied, Runar mounted his horse, and most of his men followed.

Eadlyn turned to Oswin first.

"You've done your people proud, Your Highness," he said. "All of Essix will be grateful."

"Thank you, Oswin. For everything."

He nodded solemnly, and she turned to Edward. Her voice caught. So many words unspoken. But maybe they didn't need saying.

She placed her hands on his shoulders. "You'll be a great king, Edward. I know you will. Just seek God."

He swallowed hard. "I will."

And oh, how she prayed he truly would. She wrapped her arms around his neck and drew him into a tight embrace.

"I will miss you so much, but I will write to you. I hope you will do the same."

Edward's arms squeezed around her. "Of course."

She did not want to relinquish her hold, but after a long moment, she loosened her arms, and they parted. Actually saying goodbye was too hard, so she turned to Galen. It had been easy to stay strong with Edward. Instinct. Something she had always done. But with Galen, it was the opposite. He was the one who stood strong. So, when she met his solemn gaze again, her resolve faltered.

She'd never hugged him before. It wouldn't have been seemly back in Kenwich for the princess to hug a guard, but here she cast propriety aside. In one step, she put her arms around him, resting her face against the cold chain mail cowl that hung around his neck. Chain links jingled as he placed his own mail-encased arms around her.

"Thank you," were the only words she managed. She gritted her teeth, but despite her fierce struggle to fight them, a couple of tears dribbled down her cheeks as the pain overwhelmed her. She clung to his armored jerkin while it passed through her in a breath-snatching wave before forcing herself to let go.

Galen gripped her arms before releasing her and met her eyes. "Remember what I told you."

She nodded, though they both knew she couldn't accept his offer. Not if she wanted peace for her people. Swiping at her cheeks, she took a shaky step back and looked between him and Edward. They were the only family she had. Just the two of them—her protector and her brother. This may be the last time she ever saw them, and for one suffocating, heart-thrashing moment, her entire being screamed for her to run. To beg her brother to annul the marriage, to seek Galen's steadfast protection, and to go back home to Kenwich. It ripped like claws through her chest, seeking release, but she choked it down. In front of her was her family. Behind her were strangers. Strangers she must leave with if she were to save Essix.

Tears blurred her vision as she forced herself to turn away from her family. Only a couple of paces behind her, she found Aevar waiting with Hiroc. She blinked him into focus and found understanding on his face. He knew the pain she suffered for this alliance, and in that she found some comfort. She stepped toward him, and he kept Hiroc steady and even held her stirrup for her as she mounted. She straightened her skirt and cloak and took up the reins, catching his eye once more before he turned to his own horse, a tall pale gray.

Without a word, Jarl Runar urged his horse toward the river, the men falling in behind him. Clutching the reins, Eadlyn cast one last look at Edward and Galen, committing them to memory. In a final acceptance of her fate, she touched her heels to Hiroc's sides and rode forward, into the unknown, with Aevar at her side.

Tiny ice pellets pattered against Eadlyn's cloak, creating a shushing sound that muffled even the persistent thump of hooves. It lulled her into a strange, uneasy numbness. Nightfall must be close.

They'd crossed the river hours ago, swallowed since by a dense gray forest. Last year's leaves carpeted the ground, damp and silent underfoot. Patches of snow clung in shaded heaps. Eadlyn had never seen a forest without leaves before. She'd hardly seen any forest at all, only the scraggly trees near Kenwich, which passed more for oversized bushes than woodland. Here, sharp, skeletal branches reached skyward like clawed fingers.

She shivered, tugging her cloak tighter. The cold here hit differently. It seeped through the layers of her clothing and into her bones. What she wouldn't give to be back at the palace, curled up by the hearth. She exhaled, her breath rising in a white plume, and another tremor ran through her.

Eadlyn startled when Aevar's voice shattered the hush, commanding and foreign. The group halted, and Jarl Runar turned in his saddle to look back but said nothing. From beneath her hood, she watched Aevar turn his horse around and ride farther down the line to one man leading a packhorse. Leaning over the animal, he dug through the bundle on its back and pulled out a fur pelt. He then guided his horse once more toward the front. As he approached again, he nudged the horse alongside hers, so close their legs brushed. Her breath caught as he leaned toward her and draped the thick pelt around her shoulders.

"Fur is the best way to keep warm out here."

He had noticed she was cold. That small, unexpected kindness stirred an odd, yet grateful sensation within her, and the thick fur began working immediately. No wonder they all wore mantles like it.

"Thank you."

He glanced down at her wool-lined boots. "Are your feet warm enough?"

"For now." They were a little chilled but not unbearable.

"We won't be riding much longer. We'll need to make camp before dark."

The group moved on in silence, but now that it had been broken, the stillness fell heavier than before. Surely Nords weren't such silent creatures all the time. It would go against what most written accounts said of them. Not that she was inclined to believe such things now that she was among them.

With a breath for courage, she shifted in her saddle to face Aevar. She still struggled to wrap her mind around the fact that he was her husband now. "How far do we have to travel?"

"If the weather does not delay us, we will arrive the day after tomorrow."

Two nights. Her first two nights as a married woman. A shiver traced down her spine, though not from the chill this time.

She pushed the thought aside and reached for something more comfortable.

"What is it like where we're going?"

This time, Aevar smiled faintly. "Fjellheim sits at the head of a fjord that winds west toward the sea. A river flows into it from the north and provides access to some of the other clans."

Eadlyn tried to picture it. She was not well-traveled and had nothing to draw on, though she had read a little about the northern fjords in her hasty research. "It sounds beautiful."

His smile grew with fondness. "It is."

Kian, riding ahead beside the Nord with the scar near his eye, turned in his saddle and grinned back at her. "Especially later in spring when the trees turn green. It's quite a view."

Despite the weight pressing on her, Eadlyn smiled. However small, a spark of curiosity lit within her. All her life, she'd lived within the confines of Kenwich. Her journey to meet the Nords had been the farthest she'd ever traveled. For the first time, she realized she was eager—just a little—to see what lay ahead.

They lapsed into silence again, though not as heavy this time. The tight coil of tension that had gripped her throughout the afternoon loosened, and they traveled companionably for another hour.

When the forest grew dim, Jarl Runar raised a hand and called a halt. "We'll camp here."

Eadlyn was grateful to dismount. Her legs ached from the long day's ride. At least the freezing rain had ceased. She shook out her cloak, dislodging the icy pellets that clung to it, and looked around, unsure what she was supposed to do.

Aevar stepped around his horse and approached her. "Let me take your horse for you."

"Oh. Thank you." She handed over Hiroc's reins, acutely aware she didn't know the first thing about unsaddling a horse. There had always been someone around to handle such things.

Aevar led Hiroc away to where the other horses were gathered, leaving her standing alone. Around her, the men fell into their routines, some tending the animals, others collecting wood and clearing a space for a fire. Eadlyn would have liked to help, but she had neither an axe nor the skills to be useful. So, she did the only thing she knew and stayed out of the way.

A few minutes later, Aevar returned, carrying her bags. He set them near a tree close to where the first fire crackled. Another group was working on a second one. Eadlyn hesitated. She was used to being surrounded primarily by men, but what was she to these warriors? Was she welcome among them or more of an inconvenience? A means to an end?

Before deciding how she wanted to proceed, Aevar approached her. Her breath grew shallow in his presence. She did not know what to expect from him or what he might want from her. Even now, hours after being married, they'd traded but a handful of words between them. While he'd been kind and made sure she was warm on the trail, he'd also cared for the horses. Even livestock was well tended before being slaughtered for food.

"You should warm yourself by the fire," he said, gesturing to the flames.

Asking God to change her cynical thoughts, Eadlyn accepted the invitation, and he joined her at the fire. While the fur mantle had helped, the heat from the flames to her chilled fingers and face was welcome. It chased away and dried out the dampness of the weather her cloak did not fully ward off.

Her thoughts drifted to Edward. He would be on the road too. Perhaps already sitting around a fire with Oswin and Galen. She imagined their voices and laughter, and her heart squeezed. How strange to know life in Essix went on without her.

Aevar's voice broke into her thoughts before they dragged her into melancholy.

"I realize there haven't been proper introductions."

She turned her gaze toward him as he gestured to his left.

"Kian you've met, though he no doubt failed to mention he's King Toryn's nephew."

Kian gave Aevar a playful smack on the arm. "*Favorite* nephew, thank you."

Eadlyn never guessed him to be related to royalty. But then, in their rugged gear, she wouldn't have taken Jarl Runar or Aevar for royalty either had they met under different circumstances. "You're the king's nephew, but you live here? In Nordra?"

Kian grinned. "I do."

"May I ask why?"

"More peaceful. Don't get me wrong, I love my family, but they are…a handful." He tossed a teasing grin at Aevar. "And someone's got to keep this one out of trouble."

Aevar rolled his eyes. "Speak for yourself."

He turned, motioning across the fire to the tall Nord with the animal tattoos. "This is my eldest brother, Erik."

The man inclined his head. "Princess."

"And my other brother, Braan," Aevar continued, gesturing to the scarred man, who gave a single, silent nod.

So she had been right. They were the jarl's sons.

"You've met my father," Aevar added. "The rest are our warriors."

He introduced each of them. She did her best to remember the unfamiliar names and offered a polite smile and warm greeting as her governess had taught her. She was still a princess, even out here in the wilderness, and if she wanted to be a light for God in this strange land, she had to start now, no matter how fear lingered. These men were no less loved and made in God's image than she was. That thought helped ease the tightness in her chest.

Now she needed to get to know them better. Left up to them, she would never learn anything.

She shifted her attention away from Aevar, who still made her stomach constrict in strange ways, and turned to Erik instead. "Do you have any sisters? Or other brothers?"

Though they'd only heard of the three sons in Essix, information between kingdoms was often lacking. They'd discussed asking Jarl Runar if he had a daughter for Edward to marry, but Oswin had counseled that bringing a foreigner into Essix when things were so unsettled might not sit well with the nobles. Eadlyn had agreed. Better she marry than risk more unrest.

Erik shook his head. "None who survived infancy."

"I'm sorry," Eadlyn responded, hoping to convey her genuine regret.

He gave a shrug. "It's life." His eyes darted to Aevar, something passing between them before he focused back on her. "What about you? Is it only you and your brother?"

"Yes. Our mother died before she had more children." She considered saying no more, but if she wanted to become part of this family, she must find the courage to speak more freely among them. Timidity wouldn't get her very far. "It's just as well. My father didn't deserve more."

Her frankness seemed to amuse Braan because he snorted, and it raised a smirk to Erik's face as he said, "Given his reputation, I'd agree."

Eadlyn chanced a peek at Aevar and found a smirk tugging at his mouth as well. At least she was engaging with them.

Once both fires blazed in the gathering gloom, the group sat close and passed around pouches filled with dried meat, berries, and various nuts. Not a feast, but after the long day, Eadlyn welcomed it eagerly.

Between bites, she looked across the fire at Jarl Runar. "During negotiations yesterday, you mentioned an upcoming gathering. What is it exactly?"

"Once a year, in spring, the clan leaders gather to share how they've fared through the winter. We prepare together for the season ahead and celebrate the return of warmth and plenty."

"So all of them will be there?"

"Yes. The jarls, their families, and some warriors."

That explained his urgency to return. Such a gathering in Kenwich took weeks to prepare. "That sounds like quite an event."

"It is a good time. Feasting. Competitions. For many, it's the only time we see each other all year."

She could see how families looked forward to the Gathering, and it surely carried great political importance, especially now. "Will the other jarls support the alliance?"

Eadlyn watched for any uncertainty, but Runar seemed confident when he said, "Most will. That is all that matters."

Hopefully, he was right. She had placed her entire future and the future of Essix on that hope. She knew what a delicate job it was keeping the lords happy in Essix. Pleasing everyone was no simple task.

"How many jarls are there?"

"Ten clans and ten jarls across Nordra, including myself. Long ago, we fought each other for land and power. Then the Kalgorans invaded from the north. One jarl was chosen to unite the clans and drive them out. Since then, we have fought to remain united."

"Unity is never easy," Eadlyn murmured. "I hope this alliance helps us both grow stronger."

"Indeed."

After eating her fill, she accepted a waterskin from Aevar. The water was frigid but refreshing. She passed it back as a deep, haunting howl pierced the darkness. Another followed, then another, until the forest echoed with their chorus. Goosebumps rose on her arms. She peered into the black beyond the firelight. The howls faded, leaving only the crackle of flames and a silence that hung thick.

"Are those wolves?"

Aevar nodded without alarm.

"Don't worry," Kian said from his place on the other side of Aevar. He leaned forward to see her. "As long as we keep the fires burning, they'll not come near."

Good to know. She edged closer to the flames and drew her cloak tighter. She'd only been with these men for half a day, but already she saw how little she knew of life and survival outside the palace and city where she'd grown up.

"Do you not have wolves near Kenwich?"

She looked back at Kian. "Not that I've heard. We don't have many true forests in Essix, except in the far south near the border of Camria. Our wildlife is not as plentiful as in Nordra. Leastwise with large predators."

This led to a brief conversation about the creatures she might encounter in Nordra. When Braan mentioned the great brown bears roaming the forest, she very much hoped she would never run into one. At least not without several armed men with her.

After a time, she grew uncomfortable with the need for privacy. She'd gone all afternoon without the opportunity to relieve herself. She'd noticed the men stepping away from camp, presumably to tend to similar business, but the thought of making her needs known was a bit embarrassing. It was unavoidable by this point, however, and they still had two days of travel ahead of them.

Trying to swallow down the discomfort that brought a little heat to her face, she leaned toward her new husband and spoke so only he would hear her. "I need to…step away for a moment."

He stood and gestured for her to follow. She gathered her skirts and trailed him into the trees, the firelight fading behind them. The thought of wolves sent a chill slithering down her back. No doubt that was why Aevar hadn't let her wander off on her own, but how much privacy would he give her?

Once far enough from the fire that the men's voices grew muted, Aevar gestured to a fallen log tipped into a small hollow that allowed for some privacy depending on where he planned to stand. Eadlyn hesitated for a moment, but Aevar turned his back to her and walked several more yards away, keeping her safely between him and camp. It showed consideration, though whether it came from any genuine care or was simply to protect their new alliance was impossible to guess.

Either way, Eadlyn didn't waste time. So far, Aevar didn't seem to be given to impatience, but she wouldn't test him. A couple of minutes later, she made sure her skirts were righted and stepped up out of the hollow. Aevar was a solid dark shape standing guard against the black forest, his back still to her.

"I'm finished."

He shifted and walked back to her, his face hidden in darkness until he was standing right in front of her. That's when it occurred to her they hadn't been alone together since meeting yesterday. If he was thinking of taking any liberties as her husband, now was the time. Her heart thumped and caught in her throat. She should have gone straight back when she finished instead of waiting for him to catch up. Now, however, her feet froze to the ground. She caught the glimmer of his eyes but couldn't read what expression rested on his shadowed face.

When he moved, she tensed, but he only gestured toward the camp, inviting her to make her retreat. She tried not to let her breath all rush out at once as she turned to walk back toward the comforting light, though her legs wobbled. Glancing at the ink-black sky through the branches overhead, she reached out to her Savior. *Oh, Lord, help me. I said "I do" knowing what that meant. But I don't feel ready. Give me strength. Give me peace.*

Back by the fire, she sat again, working to calm the way her pulse raced. Aevar didn't join her right away. Instead, he moved around the group toward the supplies. A short time later, he returned with an armful of furs. He dropped them beside her, spread a bearskin on the ground, and layered it with blankets.

"You should rest," he said. "It will be another long day tomorrow."

The mention of sleep had her fighting a yawn. Her eyelids had grown very heavy while staring at the fire, and her shoulders ached with a plea to lie down. However, she eyed the makeshift bed with trepidation, trying to comfort herself with the fact that it was only big enough for one person. What else could she do?

Without meeting his gaze, she moved from the fire and crawled into the nest of warmth he'd made. The fur cushioned her from the frozen earth, and the blankets offered a welcome escape from the chill air. Lying there, she listened to the rustle of Aevar making a second bed behind her and tried not to wonder how close he would settle. Around them, the others prepared to sleep as well. Eventually, her body overpowered her nerves, and her eyelids closed as sleep took her.

After passing by the horses to make sure they were calm and settled, Aevar worked his way back around camp to Erik, his watch companion. Braan had offered to take his turn on watch, but as tired as Aevar was after the long day, he wasn't ready to sleep yet. Besides, Eadlyn might fall asleep better without him next to her. She and everyone else lay under their furs around the fire and had been quiet for an hour now.

When Aevar reached Erik's side, they both stared out at the night-cloaked forest. Neither had said much since their watch began, but then Erik looked over at him.

"How do you feel about your new bride?"

Aevar shrugged. Could he even answer that question after less than a full day? "How am I supposed to feel?"

"Your guess is as good as mine."

Aevar still didn't know who she was or even how to talk to her. He rarely found conversation difficult, but he suspected they both struggled to figure out how to interact now that they were joined for life. Kian was doing a much better job of it than he was, and he hoped that the more comfortable she became with his family, the more comfortable she would become with him.

His mind flashed back to standing with her in the trees. "She's terrified of me."

"Can you blame her? She's a woman surrounded by strange men. No one would feel safe in this situation."

"I don't like being the one to cause her such fear."

"She just needs to get to know you. Once she does, things will change."

"I hope you're right."

Aevar looked over his shoulder at the lump of furs where Eadlyn slept, or at least seemed to be sleeping. He had to admit it surprised him she hadn't broken down at least once during the journey, but she hadn't shed a single tear since trading goodbyes in Essix. That alone took strength he had to admire.

adlyn woke from another night of surprisingly sound sleep considering she was not only sleeping on the ground but surrounded by men she still knew precious little about. The camp was quiet. Unlike yesterday morning, when she'd awoken to the sounds of bustling movement and conversation, now only stillness surrounded her. Gray light seeped through the canopy above, and somewhere close behind her, she caught the whisper of slow, steady breathing.

She hadn't ever been aware of Aevar sleeping beside her the first night, but he was there now, and her entire body hummed with awareness of his presence. At first, she lay still, trying to pretend she was still asleep, but curiosity grew, silent and insistent. Finally, she turned her head and rolled onto her back.

He lay less than a foot away, his expression relaxed in sleep. She let herself examine the details of his face to a degree she never had when he was awake and might catch her. His dark lashes against his skin, the pale ridges of his scars, the dark hair edging his strong jawline and getting a little longer and thicker at his chin. She studied the fine stubble along the sides of his head and the long dark hair at the top. It had seemed so wild and foreign to her at first. Now she found herself oddly drawn to it. Perhaps because it was so unlike anything back in Essix.

He shifted beneath the furs, drawing a deeper breath, and his eyes blinked open, startlingly blue in the dim light. She stifled a gasp and rolled back to her side, heart hammering her ribs. Had he seen her watching? She clamped her eyes shut, willing her pulse to slow, and feigned sleep once more. Only after he rose did she breathe properly again.

She waited until the camp stirred with movement before sitting up. The furs fell away as she adjusted her cloak and glanced around. Her gaze snagged on his. Aevar stood near the supplies, his face unreadable, but something in his eyes twinkled as if he knew she'd been watching him. Heat flushed her cheeks. She ducked her head and focused on smoothing her skirt with unnecessary care.

Like the day before, they ate a quick, cold meal and packed up camp. Eadlyn tried to be helpful, but her muscles were already sore from the previous day's ride. Before long, they were on their way again. The terrain had grown more rugged, no longer the straight, grassy paths of her homeland, but a winding, climbing journey through dense woods and deep ravines. The trees had changed too. Now evergreens towered above them, their dark boughs blocking much of the sky. They were beautiful in a stark, powerful way, so unlike the rolling grasslands and bogs of Essix.

Conversation had become easier, at least with Aevar's family and Kian. Erik had a quick wit, and Runar's dry observations added unexpected levity. Kian especially made a point of including her in discussions, and she appreciated that. But Aevar...he remained quiet and distant. And though she wanted to bridge the space between them, she didn't know where to begin.

It was as if the fact they were married meant they should have some sort of relationship, but they didn't, and she had no sense of what their future life together might hold. Marrying an Essian lord would have made expectations much clearer. Other than no doubt being expected to produce and care for children, she didn't know what day-to-day life was like for a Nord wife.

Starting a family with a man she hardly knew was the last thing she wanted to think about, so she forced her mind on her surroundings instead.

A couple of hours after breaking camp, they encountered the steepest climb yet. Eadlyn braced herself in the saddle, Hiroc working hard beneath her, his hooves scraping over stone and root. Ahead, the trees thinned out. Without warning, they crested the incline and emerged onto a rocky plateau.

Her breath caught.

To their left, the land dropped away steeply, and far below, water spread like a sheet of polished sapphire, rimmed by jagged mountains. On the near side of the fjord, buildings roofed with thatch and sod nestled between the shore and the sloping, wooded hills. Though barely visible, she spotted docks jutting out into the water and longships moored alongside them.

"There she is," Kian said, turning in his saddle with a grin. "Your first look at Fjellheim."

Her new home.

The words hung in the chilly morning air. She glanced at Aevar. He sat with a smile, not forced or formal, but one of comfortable ease. The expression of a man returning to the place he belonged. If only Eadlyn shared that feeling. She turned her thoughts heavenward before the ache in her chest intensified.

Lord, I've entered a completely strange land and do not know my place in it. Guide me the way You did the Israelites, and help me be much more attentive to Your leading than they were at times. Show me where and how You can use me. Please grant me peace and protection, as well as courage in facing the unknown.

The descent toward the fjord was long and winding. The path narrowed in places, forcing them single file. Eadlyn focused on her horse's movements, the cool wind brushing her cheeks and tugging strands of her hair. The sharp freshness of pine gave way to damp, mossy earth and a hint of salt as they drew nearer the fjord.

When they broke through the trees again and onto the beach, the world opened wide. The fjord's shoreline curved, waves lapping against dark, coarse sand. The breeze off the water was sharper here, and Eadlyn pulled her cloak tighter.

Ahead, Fjellheim stretched before them, and she caught the sounds of village life. Boots scuffed packed dirt, hammers rang from the smithy, laughter and shouting rose from children as they dashed between homes, chasing one another and scattering chickens in their wake. A goat bleated from a pen near one house, and beyond it, a pair of men sparred with wooden staves, their grunts and strikes echoing over the sounds of labor.

The villagers turned as their party rode in. Most called greetings to Runar and the others, but their attention lingered on her. Eadlyn sat straighter, trying to return their stares with an open, calm expression, neither too proud nor too timid. Still, her pulse quickened under their gaze as if she were an exotic bird perched in the middle of a wolf pack.

The women especially drew her eye. They moved with quiet

strength, their practical woolen dresses and braided hair both beautiful and rugged. A couple wore trousers like the men, and one striking woman even had her pale blonde hair shaved on one side, braids adorning the other. Several carried knives or axes on their belts. They might have been for utilitarian purposes, but it appeared even the Nord women were prepared to fight, or at least defend themselves should the need arise. The most lethal thing Eadlyn had ever wielded was a pair of embroidery snips. She let out a quiet breath. Hopefully, Aevar hadn't always dreamed of a warrior wife.

As they passed deeper into the village, the group thinned. The men who had accompanied them split off with waves or brief goodbyes until only Aevar's family and Kian remained. They followed a wide path that angled toward the far side of the village, where the forest pressed close once more. There, at the edge of the trees, stood a structure so large it stopped Eadlyn's breath all over again.

It rose like a barn, but larger and more refined, clearly built for more than animals. Its massive roof arched steeply, heavy with thatch. The wide door stood open to reveal dancing firelight and the shadows of a vast interior.

"This is our longhouse," Aevar said from beside her.

Our. The word rang louder than it should have.

This was it. Not just a destination, *the* destination. The place where her new life would truly start. It didn't help that her mind chose that moment to remind her she'd heard Nord families lived and slept all together in one hall, not in separate, private chambers. That meant anything and everything about her and between her and Aevar would be on display in front of his entire family. For the first time since the morning of their wedding, she thought she might be sick.

Before the feeling overwhelmed her, the others dismounted. She followed their example, focusing on the small motions of slipping from the saddle, straightening her skirts, and adjusting her cloak. One thing at a time.

A sudden flurry of high-pitched voices drew her attention. Two children—a dark-haired boy of about six and a golden-haired girl no more than three—burst from the longhouse. They ran straight to Erik, who caught them both in strong arms, kissing their cheeks and grinning at their eager chatter.

Behind them came two women. One, not much older than Eadlyn, was slender and dark-haired, a young toddler perched on her hip, his plump cheeks rosy and his thumb planted in his mouth. She approached Erik with a soft smile. Still holding both older children, he bent to kiss her, setting off a loud protest from the boy.

Despite herself, Eadlyn smiled. For all their strange customs, this was familiar. A man who loved his wife. A family unashamed of affection. Maybe not so different from Essix after all.

She shifted her attention to another, no less affectionate, reunion between an older woman and Runar. Clearly his wife and Aevar's mother.

Eadlyn's new mother-in-law.

The woman was taller than Erik's wife, with strength in the set of her shoulders and a calmness in her manner. Not a warrior, but not someone to be underestimated. Eadlyn shrank a little. Would she be accepted here? Welcomed?

Suddenly, Aevar stood at her side, closer than she'd realized. His presence was solid, yet uncertainty weighed on his stance and in the slight tilt of his brow. Maybe he didn't know what to do either. His mother greeted Erik and Braan with upbeat, rapid words Eadlyn couldn't hope to understand, but then the woman turned and spotted her. The smile on her face shifted to one of curiosity. A question followed in that unfamiliar tongue.

For a heartbeat, no one answered. Then Aevar's hand rested lightly against Eadlyn's back, the first intentional touch since they had held hands during their wedding. She wasn't sure if it steadied her or made it harder to breathe.

At last, Aevar spoke in Aerlish. "This is Princess Eadlyn, King Edward's sister." A pause. "My wife."

The change in the women's expressions was immediate, surprise rippling across their faces. Smiles faded, and Eadlyn fought the urge to flinch beneath their stares. If her brother had returned home unexpectedly married, she wouldn't know what to think either.

Aevar's mother turned to Runar with a questioning look. He rested a calming hand on her shoulder, also speaking in Aerlish.

"We made the alliance with Essix. To bind it, we agreed to a marriage between Aevar and Eadlyn."

Eadlyn wasn't sure what emotions flickered across the woman's face. Distress? Resignation? Hope? They came and went too quickly to name. Eadlyn glanced at Erik's wife, who met her husband's gaze. He shrugged, lifting his brows.

Aevar's mother turned back to Eadlyn, and a smile bloomed once again, softer than before. Gentler. "Princess Eadlyn, I'm very pleased to meet you. I'm Inga, Aevar's mother."

Her Aerlish was slower and less practiced, but Eadlyn sensed the sincerity beneath the careful words.

The younger woman stepped forward. "I'm Ranvi, Erik's wife. These are our children. Alvir," she bounced the toddler on her hip, "Trygg, and Katla."

Eadlyn greeted them each, though she wasn't sure the children understood her words. Trygg eyed her with tentative curiosity, while little Katla was more shy, hiding her face against Erik's neck.

Before anyone said more, a third woman slipped into their midst as if she'd materialized there.

"I hear congratulations are in order."

She stood at Braan's side, her dark hair falling to her waist and ornamented with small braids and silver beads. Her eyes were darker than most Eadlyn had seen among the Nords. Like a few of the other women, she wore trousers and a leather coat trimmed with fur. Two axes hung from her belt. This woman *was* a warrior. There was no doubt about that. While her Aerlish was fluent, Eadlyn detected a subtle difference in her accent.

Braan draped an arm around the woman's shoulders, and Aevar motioned toward her.

"Eadlyn, this is Heida, Braan's betrothed."

She greeted her politely. Heida nodded in return, watchful and quiet. Eadlyn did not know what the other woman thought of her, but she detected no hostility. Only a reserved, mysterious air. The kind that no doubt drew Braan's attention in the first place. She hoped her instincts were right. So far, no one seemed to harbor any outright dislike toward her. It was as good a start to her new life as she could have hoped for.

Inga took over, slipping into what Eadlyn recognized as hostess mode. "Let's get everything inside."

The men turned back to the horses to unload their supplies. Before Eadlyn even realized it, Aevar had her belongings in hand. Kian, Braan, and Heida led the horses away, and Eadlyn followed the others into the longhouse. Trygg scampered ahead, a bundle of excited chatter.

Giant pillars carved in winding patterns rose overhead, drawing Eadlyn's attention upward to a vaulted roof that curved like the hull of an overturned ship. A wide balcony lined each side of the hall, likely used for storing food and other household goods. Wood smoke clung to the air, mingling with something savory.

When she lowered her gaze again, she studied the layout of the longhouse. Two long tables stretched parallel to a central hearth, their surfaces scarred and marked by many years of use. At the far end, atop a raised dais, rested a third table—a place of honor. It wasn't the palace in Kenwich, with its stone halls and gilded fixtures, but it held its own kind of majesty.

Colorful tapestries hung along the walls, their bold, swirling patterns softening the rough timber with comfort and artistry. To the left, two broad platforms were built against the wall, raised a little off the ground. Cushions dotted the surface, and a pair of standing looms sat nearby to create a space for working and for resting.

Near the hearth, a trio of women worked. One, older and gray-haired, stirred a blackened pot that released the mouth-watering scent of meat and vegetables. The younger two sat with spindles in hand, wool twisting between their fingers. They wore clothing like the Nords, but their hair was cut short. Slaves, most likely, taken in raids.

Eadlyn's attention shifted away from them as Aevar veered toward the left wall, disappearing with their things through one of several wooden doors that broke the line of the hall. Four on the left and four on the right.

Private bedchambers.

Eadlyn exhaled long and low, the tension in her limbs loosening.

Thank you, Lord.

The rest of the day passed in a whirlwind, with Eadlyn at the center of many questions and curiosity. Her first impression of Aevar's family was one of genuine warmth. They were louder and more rambunctious than anything she had ever known, their laughter bouncing off the smoke-darkened beams overhead, the children always running about. The chaotic nature was a stark contrast to the hushed, brittle formality and constant dread of her childhood. She suspected this was what a true family was like. The kind she had only ever glimpsed from a distance.

The evening meal of venison stew cooked over the hearth had been everything she hoped for. Though not as fancy as a dinner prepared by the cook at Kenwich, after days of cold trail fare, it tasted heavenly.

Eadlyn said little as they sat around the table, and the family often slipped back into Nordric before catching themselves. She didn't mind. Weariness clung to her, and she was content to listen and observe. Apparently, she wasn't the only one ready for rest.

"Well, I'm going to call it a night," Erik announced, pushing back from the table with a stretch of his arms. "After all those days on the trail, I am looking forward to sleeping in my own bed tonight."

His declaration began a chain reaction. They exchanged good-nights, and one by one, the family disappeared into the small rooms branching off the longhouse.

Everyone except Eadlyn and Aevar.

Unsure, Eadlyn remained seated, folding her hands tightly in her lap. Her heart drummed her ribs, each beat growing louder as the inevitable approached. She couldn't bring herself to look up, afraid of what might already be written across Aevar's face.

Without a word, Aevar took a small soapstone oil lamp from the table and rose. His voice, when it came, was low and unreadable. "Come. I'll show you our room."

Eadlyn stood, her legs wobbling beneath her, and followed him. They entered the room she had seen him carry their belongings into earlier. The dim circle of lamplight illuminated a bed set against the far wall, piled with blankets. Aevar moved about the room without haste, lighting a few more lamps placed in the corners. The glow spread across the timber walls, softening the harsh lines of the room into something almost welcoming. Almost.

Then he closed the door behind them. The lump in her throat climbed higher, choking her. Now her heart hammered so violently it was a wonder he did not hear it. She locked her hands together to keep them from trembling.

Silence stretched between them, heavy and uncertain. Eadlyn forced herself to face him and found him watching her with a slight furrow to his brow. Her cheeks flamed. Surely he read every frantic thought as clearly as if she had spelled them out.

Then, at last, he spoke. "I will sleep on the floor."

For a moment, she thought she must have misheard him over the wild pounding in her ears.

He continued, and his tone softened almost gently. "You may take the bed. I will not force you to share it. That is by your invitation alone."

A shuddering breath left her lungs, and she sagged. In one way she felt she had failed in her duty as an alliance bride, but a bigger part of her was so thankful she could have cried. She'd never expected this kindness from him. Blinking to keep the tears in check, she met his gaze again.

"Thank you."

He nodded, a simple gesture that somehow made her feel as though he truly understood the level of her gratitude, and turned to a pile of furs in the corner she hadn't even noticed before. He must have carried them in during the day, which meant he'd had no intention of sleeping with her tonight. Her respect for him deepened, twining itself through the wary knots in her chest.

As he busied himself arranging a bed on the floor, Eadlyn gathered her frayed composure. Only now did she realize how badly she trembled. She pressed a hand to her stomach, drawing slow breaths until the tremors eased.

Watching him, she hesitated, then took a tentative step closer. "This is your room. You should keep your bed. I'll sleep on the floor."

He peered over his shoulder, one corner of his mouth quirking upward. "No. You are a lady. You will have the bed. My mother would skin me alive if she found out I let you sleep on the floor."

Despite herself, a small, breathless laugh broke free. "Your mother seems to be a very formidable woman. I suppose she would have to be, to raise three sons."

He smiled—not the tight, guarded smile he usually wore, but one touched with genuine fondness. "She is." He paused as if contemplating, something like regret taking over his expression. "I would have prepared you a room of your own, but if this alliance is to work, we must at least give the appearance you and I are fully joined in marriage. Not all the jarls will be pleased my father agreed to the alliance. If they think there is any weakness in it, they will exploit it."

His words caught her off guard. Not the warning, but the candid way he shared it with her. They'd said so very little of anything important to each other since meeting, and she realized she had even less knowledge of what sort of man he was than she'd imagined. And he'd given their situation much more deliberation than she'd given him credit for.

"Yes, of course, I understand." She knew full well what sort of political ramifications might result in opponents having reason to believe their marriage wasn't binding. It could jeopardize the whole alliance. So, for her foreseeable future, she would share this room with him, the man who at this time was her husband in name only. But she would not complain. The situation could be far, far worse, like it had been for her mother. The agreement might be awkward, but at least he treated her with respect and far more honor than she'd expected considering the Nords' reputations.

"You can change for bed if you want," Aevar said, his voice lighter, almost teasing. "I won't look."

Heat spread into her cheeks again. Yes, this was an awkward arrangement indeed, but she had to get used to it. At least now she knew he posed no danger.

She retrieved a linen shift from her pack by the bed, hardly fresh after the journey, but better than the one clinging to her now. Casting a glance at Aevar's broad back, she turned her own and changed swiftly. True to his word, he did not so much as peek her way. Not quite comfortable with him seeing her in only a shift, she crawled into bed and pulled the blankets up to her chin.

When Aevar finished, he glanced at her. Though she did not fear he'd change his mind, having him see her in his bed made her squirm. But he said nothing and doused the lamps, plunging the room into darkness. Eadlyn lay and listened as he rustled around in the corner before settling.

And there, in the hush of the strange room, with her heart finally slowing, she lifted a prayer of gratitude, of hope, and a plea for the strength to meet whatever tomorrow brought.

The distant crow of a rooster woke Aevar. Dim light seeped through the oiled cloth covering the window across the room. He lay still, listening. In the hush, he picked out the sound of Eadlyn's deep, even breathing.

He pushed aside his blankets, the chilly air prickling his bare chest and chasing away the last remnants of sleep. Though he couldn't see much in the dimness, he didn't want to disturb her with a lamp. Groping for yesterday's tunic and jerkin, he slipped them on and tugged on his boots.

When he stood, he let his gaze drift to the bed. In the faint light, he made out the gentle rise and fall of the blankets draping Eadlyn's body. His throat squeezed, a deep ache tightening in his ribs. He could far too easily imagine a different woman lying there, and for one torturous moment, he let himself do just that.

Giving his head a sharp shake, he blinked away the sting in his eyes. He couldn't dig up the past. Not now. That life and the longing that came with it had to stay buried where he had fought so long to put it. He wouldn't survive this otherwise.

With a deep breath, he slipped from the room. The low murmur of his brothers' voices by the hearth helped dispel the lingering ache. He crossed the hall and dropped into a seat across from them. They nodded in greeting.

"How was your night?"

Aevar narrowed his eyes at Braan's question. His brother just stared at him, and Erik, for his part, did a terrible job of hiding his curiosity.

"Not that it's any of your business," Aevar said dryly, "but I slept on the floor. I will not force her to be a wife. If I'm going to be married, I want it to be pleasant for both of us at the very least."

He had seen the panic on her face last night and the way she'd fought to resign herself. Even if he'd wanted to, he couldn't have ignored it. Other men might not care they were strangers, but he did. And if he was honest, part of him would have felt unfaithful even if only to a memory. Judging by the way his chest still ached, that wouldn't change any time soon.

Braan bumped Erik with his elbow. "Look at that, our little brother has wisdom."

Heida appeared behind him. Aevar hadn't noticed her approach, as usual. She had an uncanny way of slipping in without anyone ever seeing her coming. An ability he suspected was natural more than learned.

She leaned into Braan's shoulder. "Something you could learn from."

Braan glanced up at her, then leveled Aevar with a cool stare. "Yes, dear."

Aevar smirked, but his attention returned to Heida as she slid onto the bench beside Braan.

"You're doing right by her, Aevar," she said, her voice lower now. "It's not easy leaving everything you've ever known behind. It will take her time. She doesn't just have to learn to trust you; she has to trust all of us."

Eadlyn startled awake, blinking against the light that filtered through the window above her. Beyond the door, muffled voices drifted across the room. Laughter. A child's shriek. The sounds of a family already deep into their day.

She sat up and looked to the corner of the room. Aevar's bed of furs lay empty. She let a slow breath seep out and sat there a moment longer, the coolness of the air biting against her skin. Today was the first day of her new life. Not as a guest, but as part of this household, somehow. She had to find her place here, and she could not do that by hiding.

Shivering, she slipped out of bed and lit a lamp, the small flame flickering. She rummaged through her packs. There wasn't much. Far less than she would have brought had she known she would not return to Kenwich. Edward had promised to send more of her belongings, but that might take weeks, perhaps months. For now, she had to make do.

She pulled out a red gown; one Aevar had not yet seen her wear. Not that it mattered. Until her things arrived, she would have to cycle through the couple of gowns she had.

Once she'd laced up the dress, she brushed out her hair. She wasn't sure what more to do with it beyond pulling some of it back. Ranvi and Inga wore their hair braided into beautiful, intricate styles, but that was a skill she had never learned. This was one small moment she wished Mildred were here to help.

Tucking the rest of her clothing back into her pack, she ran her fingers over the bundle of Scriptures at the bottom. She hesitated. There had been no time for reading on the journey. It tugged at her now, a longing for the familiar comfort of the words. But she didn't know the household's routines yet, nor the hour. She didn't want to keep anyone waiting on her.

Instead, she closed it away again and bowed her head for a brief prayer. She thanked God for His grace last night with Aevar and for the kindness shown to her here. When she whispered *amen*, she blew out the lamp and walked to the door.

Stepping into the hall, the central hearth drew her attention. A bright fire crackled there, the smoke curling up to the smoke hole in the roof. Voices rang more clearly now. She turned toward the tables and found Aevar's family gathered, their laughter and conversation filling the space.

Aevar straddled a bench, laughing as little Trygg clung to his back. The boy shouted something triumphant and wrapped his arms around Aevar's neck like he was trying to wrestle him to the ground. Aevar twisted, feigning a struggle, and a grin lit up his face, wide and unguarded. She had never seen him like that—truly smiling, eyes bright and full of life.

A knot of uncertainty tightened low in her stomach. Everyone was kind to her yesterday, but kindness to a stranger was easy. Where did she fit once the novelty wore off? She lingered near the doorway, unsure whether she should approach or wait. Aevar looked up, catching her eye. He was hard to read, as always, except for last night, when he'd let something real slip through.

"Good morning."

The simple words caught the others' attention. A handful of cheerful greetings followed, and just like that, they drew her into their circle.

Inga and Ranvi bustled near the hearth alongside the other women, who were tending a large pot.

"I hope I haven't kept you waiting," Eadlyn said, her voice a little too formal in her own ears.

"No, we are just finishing," Inga assured her.

The woman turned to give the children quick instructions. Trygg hopped up from where he was still half-hanging off Aevar. Then, rather than walking around, he scrambled over the tabletop, earning a scolding word from Erik.

Aevar's brother sent an apologetic glance toward Eadlyn. "Excuse him. He can be a bit wild."

"Like his father at that age." Inga sent him a wry smile as she set the pot on the table.

Erik shook his head, sighing. "As you so often remind me."

Laughter rippled as everyone settled into their seats.

Eadlyn slipped onto the bench beside Aevar, accepting a bowl of porridge and berries he passed to her.

"Did you sleep well?" he asked.

"I did, thank you." And she had. Once she had fallen asleep, she hadn't stirred all night.

Before she took a bite, she hesitated. Would it offend them if she prayed before she ate? She knew so little of the customs and beliefs here. Regardless, she bowed her head and silently thanked God for the food and the protection He had given her. When she finished, she lifted her spoon and blew across the steaming porridge. The heat spread through her with the first bite, chasing away some of the morning's chill.

Around her, the family fell into lively conversation, mostly in Nordric unless they addressed her directly. She listened, trying to catch the shape of the words, but everything still felt strange.

As soon as Aevar emptied his bowl, he shifted toward her. "After you finish, we should visit the silversmith and see if he can craft our rings before the Gathering."

Rings. She had almost forgotten since she'd returned the borrowed one during the journey, not wanting to risk losing it. She nodded and scooped another spoonful of porridge, eager not to keep him waiting. By this time, most of the family had finished, and Trygg had already wriggled free of his seat, chattering at Heida. Aevar exchanged a few words with his father, then rose and turned toward the entrance. Eadlyn gathered her cloak before following him outside.

The sky was overcast, thick fog swallowing the peaks of the mountains in the distance. A damp, chill breeze blew off the fjord, sweeping through the streets and setting Eadlyn's teeth on edge. Still, she drank in the strange, beautiful sights around her. The rugged tree-covered slopes vanishing into the mist, the sheer cliffs along the fjord, and the sturdy timber houses braced against the cold. So different from the stone halls and crowded, dirty streets of Kenwich.

They passed several villagers along the way. Aevar offered short greetings, receiving nods or brief words in return. Eadlyn caught curious looks darting toward her as they passed. No doubt word had already spread among Runar's people. Aevar had brought home a foreign wife.

Near the center of the village, they stepped into a low, broad building. The hot, acrid air inside made her blink. The forge at the heart of the workshop glowed, its smoke leaving the space thick with burning coals and hot metal. Along the walls, sturdy work-benches bristled with hammers, tongs, molds, and other tools Eadlyn could not name.

A large man stood at one bench, shaping a piece of metal with careful strikes. He turned at their entrance to reveal a long blond beard braided with tiny silver beads that caught the forge-light. His wide mouth lifted into a friendly smile, and he seemed to inquire about the visit.

Aevar responded and motioned to Eadlyn. The man seemed surprised but intrigued. Aevar turned to her and said, "This is Tallak, our silversmith."

Eadlyn offered a soft hello, hoping her tone bridged the language gap if her words did not. Tallak responded with something that sounded pleasantly close enough. Aevar spoke again, and the man nodded. With quick, sure hands, he took measurements of both their fingers. Once finished, Aevar said a few more words, and they stepped back out into the misty morning.

Aevar walked in silence at first, his strides easy and unhurried. Eadlyn lengthened her own to keep pace, watching the village life unfold around them.

"How many people live here in Fjellheim?" she asked.

He scanned the buildings. "About five hundred. We have two more clan settlements east of here, and one to the southwest. Farming villages and homesteads too, scattered between."

She absorbed that, picturing the rugged wilderness dotted with small communities clinging to the mountains and forests.

"Are there other clans nearby?"

"Yes. Jarl Halbjorn's clan is just north of us. He's a good man and a friend to my father. He holds a lot of sway with the other clans. And Jarl Staegar is farther down the fjord." He jerked a thumb over his shoulder. "He would be king himself if he could. I expect he'll have plenty to say about the alliance at the Gathering."

Eadlyn committed the names to memory. Halbjorn, friend. Staegar, potential threat. The knowledge settled uneasily. There would be allies here, but also enemies. She could not afford to be naïve.

Near the longhouse, movement captured her attention. A woman stood at a corner, watching them. Eadlyn recognized her at once—the striking woman she had glimpsed from horseback yesterday with the shaved hair. She wore a tunic and trousers like Heida, and a sword hung from her hip with casual ease. Her pale eyes, rimmed in black, locked onto Eadlyn, and the open hostility that burned there made the hair on the back of Eadlyn's neck prickle. They didn't just hold suspicion but smoldering anger. Eadlyn drew closer to Aevar, but before she could speak, a building rose between them, and the woman vanished from sight.

Back at the longhouse, none of the other men were around. Inga and Ranvi stood at the table with two of the young slave women. Festive banners and garland lay in a heap on the tabletop between them, creating a tangle of bright colors against the worn wood.

Inga paused from sorting through the pile and addressed Aevar. "Your father and brothers went to help set up for the competitions."

Aevar turned to Eadlyn. In that moment, he hesitated, as if he wasn't sure whether he should leave her or stay.

"Go." She motioned to the others. "I'm sure there's plenty I can help with here."

With a quick nod, Aevar turned and left the hall again.

Eadlyn crossed over to the table. "What can I do?"

"We need to untangle these so Alys and Nesta can decorate."

Inga gestured to the two young women.

Eadlyn went to work, disentangling a length of blue wool garland from the pile. When she finished, she handed it to one of the waiting girls. Before long, the hall took on a festive air as they strung garlands and banners from the balconies and wrapped them around the pillars.

As she worked, Eadlyn noted how easily Alys and Nesta interacted with Inga and Ranvi, laughing and exchanging comments. Sometimes, when they spoke amongst themselves, Eadlyn caught snatches of Aerlish, confirming her suspicion they were from one of the southern kingdoms.

When they finished the decorations, she moved to the hearth. Burning pine filled her nose as she extended her hands toward the flames, the heat prickling at her fingertips. She let it soak into her skin, trying to push back the chill that had sunk deep since she arrived. One of the slave girls appeared a moment later with two pieces of wood cradled in her arms. She crouched to lay them on the fire.

"You're Alys?" Eadlyn asked.

The girl dipped her head. "Yes, my lady. Nesta is my sister."

"Are you from Essix?"

"No. We came from a small village on the coast of Waelon."

"How long have you been here?"

"Seven winters now."

Eadlyn hesitated. She wasn't sure if she should speak so freely, but Alys seemed open, even eager to talk. Her heart ached at the thought of the two girls torn from their home. Not that things were any better in Essix. Though she'd tried to befriend the slaves kept at Kenwich, her father's mistreatment of them had left them too withdrawn to respond. She prayed Edward did better.

They had discussed it at length before she'd left.

"Are you happy here?"

Alys offered a smile that was far more genuine than those back home. "I am, my lady. When our village was raided, it was terrifying. But Jarl Runar bought us and gave us a home here. Truly, I feel blessed. My father…" She faltered, a shadow drifting across her face. "He was not kind."

Eadlyn understood more than she wished she did.

"We are better off here. We are well-fed and sheltered. Jarl Runar does not force us to entertain his guests like I've heard others do." Alys's smile turned shy, almost glowing. "And he is allowing me to marry."

"Really?" This came as a surprise, yet it fit with everything Eadlyn had observed of Runar's family. "To who?"

"Alrik. He is a shipwright. He's building us a house right now. We will wed once he finishes it."

Warmth seeped into Eadlyn's heart despite the lingering chill in the hall. "Congratulations."

"And to you as well, my lady," Alys added. She spoke tentatively, her voice holding an unspoken question.

While Eadlyn missed Edward and Galen, all things considered, her first few days as a new bride were far more pleasant than she had expected. "Thank you."

By nightfall, the longhouse had been transformed. Woven garlands draped from the beams, colored cloths adorned the extra tables, and carved wooden ornaments caught the firelight, casting dancing shadows across the walls. Eadlyn had spent the afternoon working with the women, her hands busy kneading dough, stirring pots, and learning little by little the rhythms of their life. Laughter had been easy between them, their stories blending with the crackle of the hearth.

The sound of voices near the doors caught her attention. She turned in time to see Aevar among the men, laughing as he gave Erik a playful shove. He said something she didn't hear, and the others burst into hearty laughter. This was the most relaxed she'd ever seen him, grinning, shoulders loose, completely at ease with his brothers and Kian. She liked seeing him like this. She wanted to know this side of him better.

As the men approached the tables, Runar gave the hall a sweeping glance, nodding with approval. "Everything looks good."

Inga smiled in satisfaction. "Yes. Now we just need our guests."

Everyone gathered for supper, the family filling the hall with easy conversation. Runar spoke of the final preparations for the Gathering, while Aevar and his brothers swapped stories of past competitions and old rivalries they hoped to settle. Eadlyn listened, smiling at their lively banter. She didn't know what the contests involved, but she suspected there would be no shortage of weapons.

After the meal, no one hurried away. They lingered over the fire, talking and laughing in low voices, their faces lit by the soft flicker of the flames. But, one by one, the day's fatigue caught up with them, and the family drifted away into the quiet.

Eadlyn rose with a sleepy sigh and headed toward the room she now shared with Aevar, her thoughts drifting toward the warmth of the bed waiting for her. Even with a full belly and pleasant company, the chill had clung to her all day. Yet before she could sleep, she had one important task to accomplish.

Aevar followed behind, carrying an oil lamp. He moved around the room to light a few others like last night. While he straightened the furs in the corner, Eadlyn opened one of her travel packs and pulled out the bundle of Scripture. The leather cover was worn and scuffed, the pages inside as familiar as an old friend.

She hesitated before turning to Aevar. "Would you mind if I read before we put the lamps out?"

He gestured at the bundle. "Go ahead."

Thanking him, she settled at the small table near the bed. After unwrapping the bundle, she turned through the delicate parchment until she found the Psalms. Closing her eyes, she bowed her head, whispering a soft prayer. Behind her, the blankets rustled as Aevar settled down, and the room fell into peaceful silence.

Some time later, his voice cut across the stillness, low and curious. "What is it you're reading?"

She turned halfway in her chair to face him. "Scripture. God's Word, written long ago and passed down so we can know Him."

He said no more, and she shifted back to the pages but hesitated again, a thought stirring inside her. "I'd like to be up with the rest of the family in the morning. Would you wake me when you rise?"

"If that is what you want."

"It is. If this is to be my home now…" She looked down at the pages in front of her, then back to him. "I want to learn the routine of it. I want to do my part."

Aevar met her gaze across the lamplight and gave a small nod.

9

evar woke early, as he always did. The light through the narrow window was dimmer than yesterday, and the steady drum of rain pelted the roof. For a moment, he stayed still, listening to it, letting the soft grayness of morning wrap around him.

His thoughts turned to Eadlyn. Móthir had spoken well of her yesterday, of how she had worked without complaint, eager to help and willing to learn. Admirable traits and not what he had expected from a southern princess.

He swept his blankets aside. Best to get moving. He dressed and lit a lamp, its small flare of light chasing the gloom from the corners of the room. He had hoped the noise or brightness would rouse Eadlyn, but she only shifted once under the covers, sighed, and settled again.

Aevar glanced at her. And regretted it.

Her dark hair spilled across the pillow and over the blankets, a few fine strands resting across her face. It would be far too easy to reach out, brush that hair aside, and let his fingers trace the curve of her cheek…

No.

He clenched his jaw. This was not what he wanted.

He took a step closer, forcing himself to focus. "Eadlyn."

She didn't stir.

Frowning, he hesitated a moment before reaching out and resting his hand on her shoulder. Warmth seeped from her skin through the linen of her shift, soft and inviting beneath his touch. It ignited something in him he didn't want to name.

He shook her gently. "Eadlyn."

This time her eyes fluttered open, widening in momentary confusion. She stiffened under his touch, and he withdrew his hand at once, stepping back as if burned.

"It's morning."

With a yawn, she pushed the hair from her face and sat up, her expression soft and vulnerable from sleep. For one reckless moment, he let himself look—really look—at her. The way her hair now draped over her shoulders, the lamplight turning her skin to warm gold.

He tore his gaze away before the pull deepened. Having fulfilled his promise, he left the room, closing the door behind him to give her privacy. And to give himself the space he needed.

Eadlyn brushed through her hair, managing a simple braid despite how the morning chill stiffened her fingers. Outside, rain beat against the thatch. Though she had hoped for signs of spring, the morning felt no different from the last—cold, gray, and biting.

The hall was quieter today when she entered. The men sat together at the long table, voices low in conversation. Inga stood near the hearth, giving instructions to Alys, Nesta, and the cook. Ranvi and the children were absent for the moment.

Drawn to the fire, Eadlyn made her way over and held her hands toward the glowing embers.

"Good morning," Inga said kindly.

Eadlyn echoed her and asked, "Is there anything I can help with?"

Inga shook her head. "The girls have everything well in hand."

Before long, Ranvi entered, ushering in the children, who tumbled through the doorway like a gust of fresh wind, their bright laughter filling the hall. Breakfast was a lively, if brief, affair. Afterwards, the men slipped outside into the rain and mist, leaving the hall to settle into its pattern of chores and conversation.

Eadlyn busied herself where she could, but despite the heat of the fire, the chill stuck to her bones. By midmorning, she found herself once again at the hearth, teeth chattering no matter how she tried to hide it.

Ranvi appeared at her side, Alvir perched on her hip. "You're not used to the mountain air."

"No." Eadlyn offered a thin smile.

Ranvi eyed her gown. "Come with me."

Eadlyn followed her across the hall to a private chamber. While it resembled Aevar's, it had a softer, more feminine touch. Woven hangings adorned the walls, and a cradle sat tucked into a corner where Ranvi now settled Alvir, handing him a pair of wooden rings to play with. She then opened a large chest and pulled out various garments.

"Put these on instead."

Without hesitation, Eadlyn shed her gown and pulled on the brown dress Ranvi handed her—simple, practical, and lightweight. A second dress followed, heavier and made of deep red wool. Then came a dark blue apron dress, fastened in place with two round, brass brooches. She let out a soft breath, the heat returning to her limbs.

"These will help if you need them." Ranvi draped a thick coat and a woven shawl across the chest. "We'll make you new dresses soon. Until then, we'll share."

"Thank you. I truly appreciate it." Eadlyn smoothed her hands down the sturdy fabric. "Had I known I wouldn't return to Kenwich, I would have packed more appropriately."

Ranvi gave her a sympathetic smile and opened a small wooden box on a shelf. From it, she withdrew a strand of silver and red jasper beads, which she fastened between the brooches perched near Eadlyn's shoulders.

"There. Now that is more befitting a princess."

Eadlyn brushed her fingers over the smooth stones. "They're beautiful."

She glanced at the twin strands Ranvi wore, and at the intricate braids adorning her head. Without quite meaning to, she asked, "Maybe you could show me how to do my hair? Though I don't think I'll ever manage anything as lovely as yours."

Ranvi's answering laugh was light. "Of course. Come, sit."

She guided her to a chair and loosed Eadlyn's simple braid, brushing out her hair with a bone comb. Her fingers worked swiftly, weaving and twisting strands, explaining each step with patient clarity. Eadlyn tried to memorize the pattern, though she anticipated many mornings of tangled fingers before she could recreate it on her own.

As Ranvi worked, curiosity welled up inside Eadlyn. "When did you learn Aerlish?"

"Shortly after I married Erik. As the wife of a future jarl and king, if the gods will it, I should know, especially since the Talts primarily use it now. Most of the jarls learn it."

To learn another language, and so well, took far more discipline than southerners gave these people credit for. How little they knew.

"I know that if I want to communicate well, I must learn your language," Eadlyn said. "I admit, though, I don't even know where to start."

"Don't worry. We will help you."

Aevar shook the rainwater from his cloak as he entered the longhouse for a brief respite from the downpour. Behind him, Kian hurried in, his own cloak waterlogged and leaving a trail.

"Every year," his friend muttered, shoving his hood back, "it dumps rain right as we prepare for the Gathering."

Aevar gave a low grunt of agreement. "Could be worse. At least it's not snow like last year."

The blizzard had delayed the Gathering by nearly a full week.

"I'll give you that."

They stepped farther inside, and Aevar was about to say more when movement near the hearth caught his eye. He blinked. Was that…?

He had to look again to be sure. It was Eadlyn.

She stood by the fire in conversation with Móthir. At first, he didn't recognize her. Gone was the elegant southern gown, so at odds with the chill and wilderness here. Instead, she wore a simple layered dress in rich tones and an apron pinned with brass brooches. Her hair, too, had been transformed, woven into fine, intricate braids.

She looked…right. As if she belonged in this hall. As if she belonged to them.

Something shifted uncomfortably inside his chest. She caught sight of him, and their gazes met. Her smile was tentative, as if unsure whether he would welcome it. Aevar forced himself to nod, brisk and impersonal. He didn't even realize he'd stopped walking until Kian had already reached her.

"Look at you!" His friend grinned. "Only three days here, and you already look more Nord than I do."

Eadlyn laughed, tipping her head. She'd never smiled like that at Aevar. He told himself to turn away, to go back to work. But he didn't. He stood and watched her—the ease with which she spoke to Kian, the way the firelight caught in the braid over her shoulder. For one selfish moment, he wished she'd interact with him in such a manner, but he shook it off. He could admire her resilience and her willingness to adapt, but letting his guard fall was not an option.

"She's made quite a transformation, hasn't she?"

The voice beside him made him flinch. Ranvi had joined him, her eyes sparkling as if she knew his thoughts.

"She wears it well," Aevar said after a pause, keeping his voice low.

"She'll need more clothes. Her gowns aren't suited to the cold."

Her voice held a question, unspoken but palpable. Aevar didn't answer, and after a moment, she said, "Inga and I will make her some."

She turned to go, but Aevar stopped her. Eadlyn was his wife and his responsibility. Whether by alliance or not, as her husband, it was his job to provide for her needs.

"I'll take care of it," he said at last, the words rougher than he meant for them to be.

Ranvi studied him, something unreadable in her eyes, before she moved toward the hearth.

As soon as she was gone, Kian reappeared at Aevar's side and elbowed him, grinning like a boy who had caught him in a secret. "I hope you've noticed how beautiful your wife is."

He had.

That was the problem.

He turned away. "Come with me. I need your help."

They crossed the hall to a ladder that led to the upper balcony. Aevar climbed first, the wood slick under his wet boots. At the far end, pushed deep into a dark corner, sat the chest. He hadn't touched it in three years. Hadn't even looked at it. But he always knew it was there.

He cleared his throat. "Help me get it down."

Kian didn't ask questions. His usual easygoing manner faded into something more careful as he helped Aevar heave the heavy trunk toward the ladder. The wood groaned under the shifting weight. They wrestled it down carefully and carried it into the room Aevar shared with Eadlyn.

Once they set it down, Kian straightened. He studied Aevar for a moment, a flicker of understanding passing between them.

"I'll leave you to it," he said.

The door closed behind him.

Aevar stood there, staring at the chest. Lamplight caught on the worn iron hinges. Shallow scratches marked the grain of the wood, like fingerprints from a different life. He curled his fists at his sides.

Finally, he knelt and lifted the lid. The must of old wool mingled with lavender hit and wrapped around him like the hands of a ghost. He closed his eyes against it, but it was too late. The memories rushed in. A musical laugh, a flash of golden hair caught in the wind, a gentle hand brushing his cheek.

Bright colors met his eyes when he opened them. Dresses, shawls, woven belts she had loved. All of it folded and preserved with deliberate care. For a moment, he didn't move. The weight of it pressed on him, stealing the breath from his lungs.

He reached out and let his fingers brush the fabric. Soft. Familiar. He found himself tracing the pattern of woven trim on the edge of a dress, the thread worn slightly loose in places. His throat tightened. He had thought—hoped—time would make this easier.

It hadn't.

Gritting his teeth, he closed the lid again, pressing it shut. He sat back on his heels and scrubbed a hand across his face, forcing the tide of memory down, shoving it deep into the same locked place where he kept everything else he didn't dare touch. This wasn't about the past anymore. This was about what came next, and whether he was ready or not, Eadlyn was there.

The rain continued into the afternoon, a persistent drumming that blended with the low murmur of voices inside. While the slave women tended to other household chores, Eadlyn worked alongside Inga and Ranvi at the table, preparing ingredients and organizing bunches of herbs for the evening meal and for the upcoming feasts during the Gathering.

She found it impressive that they planned such feasts, given winter stores must be running low. But Inga explained that feeding their guests during such a lean time was a matter of honor and pride. It proved that, as king, Runar could provide generously for his people.

Slicing vegetables, Eadlyn was surprised by how much she enjoyed this simple act of preparing food and learning the names of things in Nordric as she went.

"*Gulrót*," Ranvi said, handing Eadlyn a thick, purple-skinned carrot.

Eadlyn repeated it, the unfamiliar word thick and clumsy in her mouth.

A draft of frigid air swept through the room as the door creaked open. Heida stepped inside, carrying a string of fresh fish. The sight of her brought a change of atmosphere, the sharp scent of fish replacing the smokiness in the air.

"You're just in time," Ranvi said, smiling at her entrance. "We're educating the princess in Nordric."

Heida glanced at her as she set the fish down on the table and drew a blade from her belt. With the practiced ease of someone who had gutted countless fish, she made a clean cut behind the gills and sliced down the belly. The guts spilled out onto the table with a squelching sound. Though the smell was far from pleasant, Eadlyn didn't turn away. She found something fascinating in the way Heida moved—efficient and unfazed. Nothing like the noblewomen of Essix.

"How's the learning coming along?" Heida asked.

"Slowly," Eadlyn admitted with a sheepish smile.

"You'll get there." Heida continued working as she spoke, her voice lilting with a different cadence compared to the others. "It's just a matter of repetition and patience."

Eadlyn studied her effortless movements. "You don't speak quite like everyone else does. Your accent…it's different. Are you from a different clan?"

Heida barely paused. "I'm from Kalgora."

Eadlyn blinked, a jolt of surprise running through her. The Kalgorans had an even more savage reputation than the Nords. "Really?"

Heida nodded once, laying aside a slice of pale fish. "Jarl Gudrik and his hunting party found me when I was a child. My *family*—" she put icy emphasis on the word, "—was about to sacrifice me to their gods and made the mistake of crossing into Nordra. Gudrik rescued me and brought me back to his village to raise me alongside his own sons."

A chill gripped Eadlyn despite the warmth of the hearth. "How old were you?"

"Eight. Old enough to know what was happening."

The weight of Heida's words settled in the room. Eadlyn's own childhood had its fair share of darkness, but nothing as horrific as that. "That's terrible."

Heida shrugged, rinsing the fish in a bowl of water and slicing it into chunks for the stew pot. "It was a long time ago. I'm better off here." She picked up another fish and began working on it.

"So you must have known Braan for a while."

Heida's lips lifted into an affectionate smile. "Yes. Since we were children. During the Gatherings, he threw hazelnuts at my head and feigned ignorance."

Laughter bubbled up from the group.

"Then, the year I turned seventeen, he gave me this." Heida tugged at the leather cord around her neck, pulling out a carved wooden eagle. The edges were worn smooth. "Didn't say a word. Just handed it to me and walked off toward the sparring ring."

Though Eadlyn was still getting to know everyone, that did sound like Braan.

Heida tucked the pendant back into her tunic. "I think I knew then we'd marry one day. But tensions with Kalgora kept me home for years. Now, there's enough peace to move forward."

Eadlyn reached for another carrot, her curiosity piqued. "When will the wedding be?"

"Autumn. Braan will speak to Gudrik during the Gathering and make the arrangements."

Eadlyn considered what that wedding might be like. Her own ceremony had been so short and somber. What would it have been like to have had a wedding filled with love and celebration? The thought put a small, unexpected ache in her heart.

Eadlyn stifled a yawn as she and Aevar stepped into their room, the door closing behind them. The long days of preparing for the Gathering had left her body aching and her feet sore, but she found a quiet satisfaction in the weariness. It felt good to be useful and to be part of the household activities instead of lingering on the edges, uncertain of where she fit.

She pulled her shawl tighter around her shoulders, the weight comforting against the cool air in the room. Her attention drifted to the table where she had left the Scriptures. She wasn't sure she had the energy for more than a few verses, but even a little brought comfort.

Her muscles protested as she took a step toward the table, but Aevar's voice, low and steady, stopped her.

"This is for you."

She turned, finding his attention fixed on something. He motioned toward a chest at the foot of the bed. It hadn't been there this morning. A momentary spark of curiosity flared amidst her exhaustion, and she found herself drawn to it.

She lifted the lid, the iron hinges creaking as if they hadn't been disturbed in some time. Inside rested neatly folded stacks of women's clothing—apron dresses, underdresses, woolen shawls, and other items like those Ranvi had lent her.

Eadlyn reached out with tentative fingers, brushing them over the fine stitching. "They're beautiful." She glanced up. "Thank you."

He responded with a brief nod, his face unreadable in the shifting lamplight. For a moment, he didn't move, standing as if lost in thought. His focus shifted back toward the chest, and something flickered in his eyes. Something distant. Before she could dwell on it, he turned away and began unbuckling the wide leather belt at his waist.

Eadlyn's curiosity surfaced again, this time stronger than before. She looked down where her fingers still lingered on the edge of the fabric. The garments were well made and kept with care. These weren't cast-offs or spares from the household stores. Someone had once worn them. Someone important. She considered asking him, but something in his movements made her hesitate. The way he avoided her gaze, the way his back remained turned, the careful distance he placed between them. It all made her pause.

Instead of asking, she closed the lid and moved to the table to read, leaving the chest a mystery for now.

The longhouse buzzed with a constant undercurrent of movement and purpose as Inga issued final instructions to Alys, Nesta, and the other household slaves. Eadlyn moved among them, offering help where she could. The first of the jarls and their families were expected by midday, and the entire household stirred with a barely contained anticipation.

The atmosphere was infectious, everyone caught up in the rush of the coming festivities. Yet a slight thread of apprehension tightened inside Eadlyn. The Gathering was a time of celebration—a reunion of families, a chance to strengthen bonds—but she couldn't shake the memory of Aevar's warning about Staegar. What if others shared his view? What if her presence brought unrest? She pressed her fingers against the fabric of her apron as she moved, a silent prayer rising in her thoughts. Hopefully, it wouldn't come to that.

As she helped Ranvi arrange a crate of drinking horns, someone called her name. A low, distinct call that cut through the chatter, drawing her attention. She turned as Aevar made his way across the room, his stride steady and purposeful despite the swirl of activity around him. She had seen little of him over the last few days, except at meals and when they retired to their shared room for the night. Even then, their interactions were minimal. He quietly settled into his furs, and she read. Once the chaos of the Gathering had passed, maybe they would find time to get to know each other better.

As he drew near, she caught his gaze lingering on her—on the cream dress and the red apron she'd chosen that morning. A fleeting change crossed his features, leaving her guessing. She couldn't quite place it. Not attraction—of that she was sure—but something flickered in his eyes. Wistfulness, perhaps? Longing? It disappeared before she recognized it, vanishing behind his usual mask.

He reached into his coat and held out a hand. Resting in his palm was a small silver object. "Tallak finished our rings this morning."

Eadlyn took it from him, turning it over in her hand. The intricate vine and flower designs crafted into the band caught the light at every angle. She let out an admiring breath. "It's beautiful."

"I asked him for his finest work." Aevar's tone was surprisingly gentle, as though the act held weight beyond simple craftsmanship.

She looked up. Such fine work must have been costly. "You didn't have to do that. A simple silver band would have sufficed."

Aevar's expression softened a fraction, a rare glimpse of openness slipping through his guarded demeanor. "You are a princess and my wife. You should have the best."

The words settled inside her, warm and unexpected. She smiled and slipped the ring onto her finger. The silver gleamed against her skin, completely different from the ring she had worn at their wedding ceremony. This one felt…personal.

"Thank you," she murmured.

Before he could respond, a horn rang out from beyond the walls. He turned toward the open door. "Sounds like someone has arrived."

Inga swept past, already heading for the door. "Probably Halbjorn and Gorum. They always race to be first."

Ranvi joined them a moment later, herding the children ahead of her. Together they stepped outside, where the spring sun had pierced the stubborn grip of winter. Though the air remained brisk, bright sunlight bathed the village, seeping into Eadlyn's dress.

Runar and Inga positioned themselves at the head of the gathering. The rest of the family formed a semicircle behind them, creating a show of unity and welcome. Eadlyn stayed close at Aevar's side and fixed her attention on the path winding toward them.

Then they appeared.

A line of riders rounded a corner, the sun glinting off polished helms and spearheads. Some forty or fifty strong, they made an imposing sight, cloaks streaming behind them, round shields painted in vivid colors hanging from their saddles. Though they came in peace, they appeared ready for war, armed and alert.

At their head rode a man who could have passed for a giant in any southern tale. As tall as Galen and twice as broad, his thick auburn hair and beard blazed like fire in the sunlight. His booming laugh echoed ahead of him as he pulled his horse to a halt.

"Runar!" he bellowed, flinging himself from the saddle.

He strode forward with arms outstretched and seized Runar

in a bear-like embrace that ended in a thunderous clap on the back.

Runar grunted but grinned through it. "Halbjorn."

A second rider dismounted more quietly. Younger by a decade, he had coal-dark hair and a neatly trimmed beard. His eyes, sharp and assessing, flicked over the gathering with the kind of caution born of experience.

"Gorum," Runar greeted, clasping forearms with him.

After a few brief words exchanged in Nordric, Halbjorn turned toward the assembled family. He swept his gaze over them until it landed on Eadlyn. His thick eyebrows lifted.

"You must be Princess Eadlyn," he said in heavily accented Aerlish.

She dipped her head. "I am."

"Ha! I expected some shy little thing." He barked a laugh and turned to Gorum. "But look at her! Already seems like one of us."

Eadlyn glanced down at her apron dress. "I've been doing my best."

Gorum's eyes lingered on her for a moment, appraising, and then he gave a quick nod. No grin, no theatrics, just a glimmer of approval before he turned back to the others.

More of the riders dismounted behind them, and the area filled with the rise and fall of voices greeting each other in Nordric. Though Eadlyn understood little of the language yet, she didn't need to. The energy in the air—the laughter, the clasped arms, the slaps on the back—spoke of long-separated friends reunited. She met each curious gaze with a welcoming smile. Though her nerves stirred beneath the surface, she kept them hidden. Poise under pressure had been trained into her long ago.

Within an hour, Halbjorn, Gorum, and their entourages pitched a cluster of tents in the wide field Runar's men had cleared at the edge of Fjellheim. Bright pennants fluttered from tall stakes, each bearing the colors and symbols of the visiting jarls. Laughter and the hammering of tent stakes filled the air, creating a festive bustle.

Though the language barrier made it difficult for Eadlyn to offer direct help, she stuck close to the other women, mimicking their movements, hauling supplies, and doing whatever she could. It was easy to be swept along by the busy energy of preparation.

By the time they finished, word came that more of the jarls were approaching. This time, the gathering moved toward the edge of the fjord. Eadlyn stood behind Ranvi and Inga and scanned the water's northern horizon as dark shapes glided into view.

Several longships slipped over the glittering fjord, sails billowing in the breeze. Some were plain cream colored, while others bore bold stripes of crimson, black, or deep blue. The sight was magnificent. And chilling. She could too easily imagine how such ships had terrorized the shores of Essix over the years. The stories of raids she'd grown up hearing came vividly to life in her mind.

Throughout the afternoon, more jarls came ashore or arrived on horseback. The once-quiet village swelled with the clamor of warriors and shouting children. By the time the sun dipped toward the snow-capped peaks to the west, Eadlyn had met eight jarls, which meant someone was still missing.

A sharp blast of a horn cut through the noise, and a strange hush fell. Every head turned toward the fjord.

Runar's mouth tightened into a grim line. "Staegar."

"The last to arrive, as usual," Erik muttered.

A current of unease rippled through the family.

Runar exhaled heavily. "Let's go greet him, shall we?"

Halbjorn and Gorum flanked him at once. Eadlyn wasn't sure whether it was in unity or a silent show of force.

As they moved, Aevar fell into step beside her, his voice pitched for her ears alone. "Stay close until we know where Staegar stands."

"Is there danger?"

"Maybe."

When they reached the shore, a dark ship cut across the water, its sail a harsh slashing of red and black against the deepening sky. Shields lined its sides, the warriors behind them silent and grim. When the longship scraped against the dock, the men disembarked in rigid lines. No one said a word, the group quiet save for the hollow clatter of boots and armor.

The man at the head drew Eadlyn's attention. He was tall and sinewy, not broad like Halbjorn or even Runar. He wore his brown hair pulled back tightly, and his plaited beard formed a point that made his long face sharp and angular. Black ink marked his skin in a row of dots beneath each eye and a winding knot of a tattoo across his brow. Though his eyes were blue, the kohl lining his lids gave them a darker appearance.

Runar called out a greeting as they neared. No one responded, and when they halted on shore, Staegar's dark gaze swept over the group before landing on Eadlyn.

"This is the Essian princess?" His Aerlish was smooth but bitten off with disdain.

Runar spared her a quick glance before replying. "Princess Eadlyn. Aevar's wife."

Halbjorn stepped forward, raising his voice in a hearty tone. "Doesn't look much like an Essian lady to me. More like one of ours, eh?"

Staegar didn't laugh or soften. His stare sliced through her, disgust written on the hard edges of his face. Eadlyn forced herself to meet it, spine straight, chin high. If she'd learned one thing about Nords in the last couple of weeks, it was that they valued strength and courage.

Beside her, Aevar shifted, his hands inching toward his weapons. Staegar caught the motion and sneered, the contempt in him dark and palpable. Without a word, he snapped a command in Nordric, and a group of slaves rushed forward, burdened with chests and supplies.

As Staegar's men passed, a younger warrior with Staegar's same lean build and cruel mouth locked eyes with Eadlyn. A long scar cut across his nose, twisting his expression into something savage. His slow, leering smirk made her skin crawl.

She turned her face away, though her heart thudded.

When Staegar and his men disappeared into the growing sprawl of tents, the group seemed to breathe again.

Halbjorn gave a low chuckle, though it carried no real amusement. "Well, that could have gone worse."

Runar remained focused on the distant camp. "We'll see. I doubt we've heard the last from him."

Laughter rolled through the longhouse, echoing off the timber beams overhead. The fire crackled in the hearth, orange light dancing across flushed faces and casting long, restless shadows against the walls. The air was thick with roasting meat and the warm bite of ale that wrapped the night in a heady haze. Aevar dunked his drinking horn into a brimming barrel, the cool ale sloshing over the sides as he pulled it free. Around him, voices clashed and tangled with boasts, bawdy songs, and drunken stories, the hall already alive with the spirit of the Gathering though the official meetings did not start until tomorrow.

As he turned back toward the heart of the hall, he found Eadlyn. She sat near the fire, her face aglow with the flickering light. Gorum's wife had taken to her, even with the language barrier, and Halbjorn's daughters seemed fascinated by her. Eadlyn smiled with that quiet, composed grace he was coming to admire. Even in a foreign hall, surrounded by strangers speaking a tongue she did not understand, she held her own.

Heida stood nearby, always lingering at the edges but never far from Eadlyn. She caught Aevar's glance and gave a barely perceptible nod. That small exchange steadied him. He appreciated that Heida had taken it upon herself to watch over Eadlyn during the Gathering. With Staegar prowling around—and worse, his good-for-nothing nephew and heir, Sig, slithering in his shadow—Aevar needed eyes on her at all times.

He drifted back to where Kian and a group of other young

warriors were drinking just in time to catch the tail end of a raucous story about a skirmish against Kalgoran raiders. Heida's brothers from the north were the loudest, their hands weaving wild shapes in the air. One of them mimicked a fleeing raider tripping over his own spear, and the group roared with laughter.

The lightheartedness made it easy to believe all was well. But the atmosphere soured the moment Sig appeared and swaggered into the group like he owned it. His reddened nose said he was well into his drink, and his voice already grated on the frayed edges of Aevar's patience like a dull blade.

"Sounds harrowing," Sig slurred, "but let me tell you about a real battle."

The circle cooled like a doused fire. Aevar shared a glance with Kian. The group passed around their own silent exchanges, both of annoyance and disbelief as Sig launched into some outlandish tale. He rambled on, drunk and desperate for attention. When he realized none would be given freely, he switched tactics. Elbowing Aevar hard enough to spill ale down his hand, he barked out, "That's quite a bride you snared."

Aevar wiped his fingers on his tunic, forcing his face to remain neutral. He refused to be baited. Not when this was supposed to be a night of celebration.

Sig, clearly unsatisfied with the lack of response, swept his gaze over the hall until it landed on Eadlyn. "Who knew an Essian could look like that? A shame about the alliance. Might've been worth marching on Kenwich myself if I'd known the spoils."

He jabbered on, his words turning filthier and fouler. Aevar locked his jaw as heat climbed the back of his neck, and he tried to focus on his ale instead of the tightness building in his chest. A few warriors turned away, and others stared at their cups, unwilling to be drawn into the brewing storm.

Aevar didn't really hear the rest until Sig asked, "How does she compare to Thora?"

For a moment, the red rage blinded him. By some miracle of the gods, he kept himself from smashing his drinking horn right into Sig's face. The temptation to knock his teeth in remained a deafening roar as all eyes settled on him.

"Sig, if you don't stop wagging that tongue of yours, I swear I'll cut it out and gag you with it. Now get out of my hall and crawl back to your uncle before I lose my restraint."

Sig straightened, faking injury, but his eyes glittered with nasty satisfaction. He licked spilled ale from his beard like a mutt. "Is that any way to treat a guest? What would your mother say?"

Aevar took one lethal step forward, settling his hand on the hilt of his knife. "She'll be the one holding you down."

From behind him, Kian's voice snapped through the tension, cold as ice. "And she won't be alone."

Sig looked between them, weighing his odds. He drained the last of his ale in a single messy gulp, wiped his mouth with the back of his hand, and sized Aevar up one final time before turning toward the door. The hall's energy didn't resume until the night swallowed him. Aevar stayed rooted for a moment longer, breathing deep, forcing himself back under control.

Kian gave him a sidelong glance. "There'll be blood between you two before the week is done."

Aevar didn't respond right away. He'd let his attention wander back to Eadlyn, who still sat with the other women. Still smiling peacefully, unaware of the wolves circling.

Kian was probably right.

adlyn blinked against the sudden flare of the oil lamp as it hissed to life. She stretched, rubbing the sleep from her eyes, still heavy with exhaustion from the day before. The ache of yesterday settled into her limbs like a slow bruise. After all the greetings and visiting, another hour or two of rest would have been welcome, but this was only the first day of the Gathering. Ranvi had said it would go on for six more.

She slid out of the bed to gather her clothing, and Aevar kept his attention averted. He always left shortly after waking her, allowing her to change in private. They never said much, but after all the mornings like this, she was getting used to the routine and to sharing the room with him. The awkwardness lingered but was softer now, wrapped with a strange sense of comfort. With so many new men in the village, especially Staegar, she found it reassuring to know Aevar was there at night.

He turned to go, one hand on the door, but hesitated. "How are you handling all of this?"

She thought for a moment before answering. This wasn't so different from the celebrations back at Kenwich, though the rowdiness here was on another level. "I'm all right. Not knowing the language makes it difficult sometimes, but I'm managing. I've enjoyed getting to know some of the women. They've treated me kindly."

A small, fleeting smile tugged at his mouth, so brief she might have missed it if she hadn't been looking. "Good."

"So what happens today?"

"Everyone will have the morning to rest after their travels. This afternoon, my father will call the jarls to council. They'll speak about the clans, the alliance, and whatever disputes need settling. After that—" a note of anticipation colored his tone "—we feast."

Feasting meant drinking. Likely more than last night. A knot of unease wound tight beneath Eadlyn's ribs, but she pushed it aside.

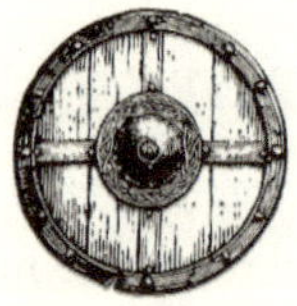

The morning slipped by faster than Eadlyn expected as she met more of the visiting women. Few spoke her language, and once again she leaned on Ranvi or Inga to bridge the gap. Some women were warmer, others more distant, but none hostile. Not like the crackling tension in the air whenever Staegar passed within sight.

By late afternoon, movement stirred at the far end of the hall. The scrape of chairs dragged across packed earth pulled Eadlyn's attention toward the dais, where Aevar and his brothers worked. They placed one chair atop the dais, draping it in a thick bearskin.

Runar's seat of authority. The others they arranged in a semicircle below, leaving a path open to the center.

This must be the council.

The jarls filed in, some with sons at their heels, a few with wives who drifted to the edges. Warriors filled the remaining space. Eadlyn hesitated before following the other women, unsure whether she should stand with them or somewhere else.

The hall thickened with silence as Runar climbed the dais and took his place. Erik stood beside him, and when he spoke, his voice cracked like a whip against the walls. Though Eadlyn didn't understand the words, the weight of them was unmistakable.

"He's calling them forward to swear their oaths of loyalty," Aevar's voice murmured beside her, low and close. She startled, not having noticed him at her side. "And to offer their tribute."

She glanced up at him, grateful for the translation.

One by one, the jarls stepped forward, each kneeling before Runar, offering oaths and chests heavy with tribute. Aevar named them quietly, translating when needed. It moved with solemn precision, the ceremony steeped in honor and tradition.

Until the final jarl.

Staegar strode down the aisle, his nephew Sig trailing. Neither carried a chest nor a sign of tribute. Only the heavy, dangerous air of a challenge. The hall seemed to shrink around them, the light itself dimming. Halfway to the dais, Staegar ripped an axe from his belt.

Eadlyn's breath seized. Beside her, Aevar's hand jumped toward his own weapon, body snapping taut. But Staegar didn't attack. Instead, he drove the axe into the packed earth at the foot of the dais with a brutal thud. Straightening, he spat out a string of words so sharp and venomous Eadlyn didn't need a translation to understand their threat.

The hall held its breath.

Runar stood and descended the dais, each step deliberate. When he reached the axe, he tore it free and stepped nose to nose with Staegar. He bit out a short couple of words and offered the axe back. Staegar snatched it and turned on his heel, stalking from the hall. Murmurs rose behind him, a rumble of unease and speculation.

Eadlyn spun toward Aevar. "What just happened?"

His jaw clenched, his focus fixed on his father. "Staegar challenged his position as king."

Eadlyn's heart stumbled inside her chest. "He can do that?"

"Anyone can if they have the will. He's invoked the right to fight for the crown."

"To the death?"

Aevar shook his head, yet uncertainty lurked. "It's meant to end when one yields. But Staegar…if he sees a weakness, he won't stop. So far, he's never been given that opportunity."

So far? She stared at him. "This has happened before?"

"Once. Years ago. My father won the challenge."

His words brought little comfort. Years could change a lot. She swallowed hard as the crowd advanced toward the doors. The heavy stench of sweat and smoke hung thicker now, pressing on Eadlyn's lungs.

Outside, the longhouse emptied like floodwaters breaking through a dam. Eadlyn followed, legs stiff, blood pounding in her ears. Runar's men moved swiftly, clearing a space in the yard. Already the crowd pressed in, breathless with expectancy.

She stuck close to Aevar as they wove through the growing throng toward one side of the ring. There, Erik was helping Runar into a shirt of mail, the heavy links catching the sunlight that broke through the clouds. Across the clearing, Staegar strapped on hardened leather, his glare molten with unmasked hatred.

Erik spoke clipped words into his father's ear. Runar nodded once, grim and resolute. Inga approached, resting her hand on Runar's arm and whispering something only for him. For one aching heartbeat, Eadlyn saw the man behind the king. The husband, the father, the one with everything to lose in this fight.

When Erik finished securing the armor, he passed Runar a round shield, deep blue and white with a black eagle emblazoned across its face. Runar took it without ceremony. He turned to Inga, pressed a brief kiss to her forehead, then strode into the ring. His sword hissed free of its sheath. Across the space, Staegar stepped forward, every movement coiled with menace.

Erik barked an order to a nearby slave boy and turned back to the ring. His voice was low with restrained anger. "If Staegar wins, his first act as king will be to face me."

Aevar flicked his gaze toward the crowd's edge. "Halbjorn might not wait that long."

Eadlyn followed his glance. The other jarl already stood armed, shield ready, sword drawn. He looked like he was just waiting for an excuse to jump in.

Erik's face remained hard. "As long as one of us puts him down."

Eadlyn wanted to believe it wouldn't come to that. Erik and Halbjorn would both uphold the alliance, but it didn't feel right. Not when the agreement had been made with Runar. And it had only been a couple of weeks, but she cared for her father-in-law. She did not wish to see him defeated or, worse yet, killed.

Lord, he may not be one of Your children, but I pray for his protection, and that You would give him the strength and guidance to defeat Staegar. So much relies on it. Please keep him safe. Don't let Staegar succeed.

Across the ring, Staegar let out a guttural shout that rang of challenge. Runar gave no reply. He only lifted his shield, shifted his sword into a ready guard, and advanced. Their blades met with a crash that echoed against the longhouse, rattling the air itself. Eadlyn flinched and clenched her hands tight against her skirts.

The two men circled, swords flashing, each strike reverberating like thunder as the crowd roared, a wild, wordless sound that surged and dipped with every movement. Splinters burst from their shields with every savage blow. Runar's shield split halfway down, a jagged gash cutting through the eagle's wing. Still, he pressed forward.

The brutality of it turned Eadlyn's stomach. This wasn't some staged duel for sport or practice. This was pure survival. She couldn't imagine either of them walking away whole if they walked away at all.

Staegar feinted left, swinging hard right. Runar blocked it but stumbled. Staegar hammered at him in a brutal assault that forced Runar into a hard defensive rhythm. Shield up, blade flashing, struggling to keep pace. For a breathless moment, Eadlyn feared he might fall.

With a roar, he countered. One brutal slash clipped Staegar's arm. Blood flowed, dark against his leathers. Yet Staegar didn't even flinch. He charged like a wounded bear, swinging harder and faster. Their blades locked, and they strained against each other in a test of strength. Inch by inch, Runar shoved Staegar back.

And then a slip. Barely a misstep but enough.

Runar lunged. His sword bit into Staegar's thigh. The man snarled. Runar's sword and shield worked in a furious tandem, battering Staegar's defenses. Their feet tore up the dirt, their faces contorted with effort. Staegar rallied and launched a brutal swing at Runar's head only to have it blocked and answered with a shield to the shoulder.

Staegar reeled, and Runar pressed his advantage. He slammed the damaged remains of his shield against Staegar's sword hand. With a clatter, the blade spun from Staegar's fingers, landing a few feet away in the dirt.

A roar erupted from the crowd.

Desperate, Staegar clambered sideways, reaching for his sword, but Runar slammed into him with his shield. Staegar crashed to the ground, the breath punching from chest. His shield snapped up, but Runar was already there, knocking it aside and planting the point of his blade at Staegar's throat.

Silence swept over them.

Runar stood, unmoving, his sword held steady. One thrust would end it. But he waited. The two men stared at each other, breathing hard, locked in a silent war of wills. Moments dragged. Every heartbeat boomed against Eadlyn's ribs and in her ears.

Finally, Staegar spat out a word, and Runar withdrew his blade. The crowd exploded in wild, triumphant cries. Relief flooded Eadlyn so fast she swayed a little, but only as Runar approached his family did she feel as though she could breathe again. He had won and, for now, the alliance remained safe. *Thank you, Lord. Thank you.*

As quickly as they'd exited, everyone streamed back into the longhouse. Runar took his place on the dais again, and the other jarls settled into their seats. Staegar returned, wounds hastily bandaged, pride hanging off him like a tattered cloak. He limped toward the dais and paused. Slowly and painfully, he lowered himself to one knee. His voice came thick with resentment, but the oath of fealty was unmistakable.

The moment the last word left his lips, he hauled himself upright, the intensity of the fight still evident in his staggered movements. He limped to the vacant seat in the semicircle of jarls, his presence now marked by defeat. The oppressiveness that had gripped the hall since his challenge seemed to melt away with his submission. The council resumed, and Eadlyn realized Aevar had once again settled at her side.

She turned to him, keeping her voice low. "How exactly does someone become king? I thought it passed from father to son, but if anyone can challenge…"

Aevar's attention didn't leave the dais. "It passes down by blood, yes, but the other jarls have to agree, and anyone with enough strength or ambition can fight for it."

She swallowed hard. "It must be difficult knowing anyone can challenge your father."

Aevar shrugged, the motion detached and almost cold. "If a man isn't willing to fight for the position, he doesn't deserve it."

Eadlyn's thoughts shifted to Edward. Men like Galen held the responsibility of fighting to ensure her brother's position as king. She couldn't see her brother ever being willing or able to fight for it himself.

Mead flowed freely, filling the air with laughter as the evening stretched on. Alys and the other thralls wove through the crowd to refill horns and mugs. Aevar kept a watchful eye, ensuring no one forgot themselves. No hands straying, no roughness, or harassment toward the girls. Some might grumble, but everyone knew Fathir's thralls were off-limits.

Satisfied for the moment, he took a long drink from his horn, savoring the sweet mead Móthir and Ranvi had prepared. It settled warmly in his chest and chased away the chill that lingered from the tense council meeting earlier.

He scanned the hall, finding Staegar sulking in a corner with those who tolerated him. His expression was all hard lines and bitter resentment. He had made his objections clear, but the majority of the jarls had agreed the alliance was in the best interest of Nordra. Those less favorable ultimately decided to give it a chance. Staegar's acceptance—or lack thereof—no longer mattered.

Aevar found Sig next. The *dunga* lurked across the hall, worming his way into a group that no doubt wished he'd find somewhere else to spoil with his presence. At least he was well away from Eadlyn. Aevar looked to where she sat beside Ranvi at the head table reserved for family. Satisfied she was under no immediate threat, he worked his way toward the front of the hall, weaving through the noisy crush of bodies. Near the doors, a loud group of men had gathered around a barrel of ale. Kian and Braan stood by, watching with amusement as Ulf and Skolli—two of Aevar's cousins—prepared to square off in a drinking contest.

The moment Ulf spotted him, he waved Aevar over, sloshing ale from his mug. "Join us!"

Aevar shook his head. He'd had enough of the rowdy games tonight. Better to stay sharp, especially with so many guests—and grudges—packed under one roof.

He leaned against a pillar, watching as Ulf's opponents, Skolli and a jarl's son, downed their ale with reckless speed. Skolli's face flushed crimson as he choked mid-swallow, while the jarl's son, already swaying, collapsed in defeat. Ulf threw back his head and roared in triumph, arms raised like a conquering hero. Aevar chuckled under his breath but let his gaze drift again toward the tables.

The seat beside Ranvi was empty.

Prickles crawled along the back of his neck, and he swept the hall. The tables, the hearth, the clusters of men by the walls held no sign of her. His heart picked up pace. Sig was still making himself unwelcome where he'd been before. Staegar remained slouched in his corner, brooding into his drink. Neither seemed in a position to cause trouble, but where was Eadlyn?

A band of unease pulled tight across his ribs. He squeezed back through the crowd to Ranvi and bent low to speak to her over the din. "Where's Eadlyn?"

She looked up with a knowing smile. "She asked if she could retire to your room for the night."

Aevar breathed out, the knot in his chest easing but not vanishing entirely.

"She's all right?" he pressed, scanning Ranvi's face for any hint that might betray otherwise.

"She's fine. Just tired, I think. It's been a long day. A lot for her to take in."

Aevar straightened. Though there was no true cause for concern, the strange, persistent pull to check on her remained, gnawing at the edges of his mind.

The hum of voices and laughter from the feast still seeped through the walls, but the closed door softened the noise enough for Eadlyn to focus on the Scriptures. She'd done her best to withstand it, but the crowded hall and the rowdy behavior had left her suffocating. She hoped stepping away helped, though a small part of her still worried she had made a mistake by withdrawing so early. Ranvi had understood, at least.

Now, as she read, the tension in her body loosened. Her breathing steadied despite how the dull roar from beyond the door still left her on edge.

The door creaked open, and her heart jumped into her throat. She spun in her seat, but relief flooded through her when Aevar stepped inside.

He paused, scanning her face as if searching for something unseen. Concern darkened his eyes. "Are you all right?"

Eadlyn nodded, offering a small, apologetic smile. "Yes."

"Were you not enjoying the feast?"

She hesitated, weighing her words. After seeing how much effort went into the festivities and what it meant to the Nords, she didn't want to offend anyone, especially Inga and Ranvi. "I just needed space."

Aevar's expression softened, as though sensing more beneath the surface. "I'm sorry if you noticed anyone talking about you or looking at you oddly. Most are only curious. They mean no offense."

"That's to be expected. It doesn't bother me." At least not much. Even back in Kenwich, she was used to whisperings behind her back. Coming from her own people cut deeper than it did here. "That's not why I left."

He tilted his head. "May I ask why?"

Eadlyn drew a slow breath. Though she had reconciled with the past, the sight of drunken revelry still stirred something in her. "The drinking…it makes me uncomfortable."

Aevar shrugged, a small, matter-of-fact gesture. "Drinking is part of feasting."

"I know." She paused. Though they were still strangers in so many ways, he was her husband. He deserved the truth. "It's just that…my father drank more than he should have, and when he did, that's when he was at his worst."

She caught herself touching the scar on her lips.

Aevar must have too. He stilled, his jaw tightening. "He did that to you?"

"Yes." She kept herself emotionless, refusing to let the memories hold power over her.

"Then he is lucky he is already dead." His voice held a protective, almost vengeful edge. The tone surprised her, an unexpected shift from the distant and controlled mask she was used to.

Aevar pushed away from the door and crossed the room to lean against the wall opposite her, arms folding across his chest. "How did he die?"

The memory of that day came to her. It had been snowing—the first snow of the season—and she'd returned from a walk in the courtyard. Her father had ambushed her on her way in, shouting drunkenly about something she didn't even recall now before storming off. She'd heard his stumbling steps echoing down the hallway, followed by a loud crash.

"He'd been drinking all morning. He fell down the stairs at the palace and hit his head. He never woke up and died three days later."

Aevar absorbed the information in silence.

A sudden roar of laughter from the feast outside broke the stillness, and Eadlyn flinched despite herself.

"So that's why," she said, gesturing toward the door, "I prefer to leave when the drink flows too freely."

"I understand." Aevar's voice was quiet now, an anger still simmering beneath the surface. He glanced at the Scripture pages. "Does your Holy Book say anything about drinking?"

Interesting he asked that. "It does. '*Be sober, be vigilant; because your adversary the devil, as a roaring lion, walketh about, seeking whom he may devour.*' How can you oppose evil if you're too drunk or distracted to notice it?"

"There is wisdom in that." Aevar paused for a moment, then asked, "What else does it say?"

"More than I could tell you in an evening." She smoothed her fingers over the delicate pages before her. "There are thousands of years of history within Scripture, and this is only a portion of it."

"Will you read it to me?"

She snapped her attention back to him. "You want me to read the Scriptures to you?"

He shrugged. "Perhaps I am curious why so many follow your God."

"You're not returning to the feast?"

"The guests think I have left to be with my wife. If I return, they will wonder why."

She studied him. Was it the alcohol making him more open to her, or was he truly curious? He didn't seem intoxicated, at least not to any discernible degree. Regardless, if he wanted to hear God's Word, she wouldn't deny him.

"All right."

She shifted back to the parchments and turned to the front. She would start at the beginning with the story of Creation, and if he still wanted to hear more, they could go on to John and Romans.

Across the room, Aevar settled into his furs, getting comfortable as if he really meant to listen. She had not expected such a response, and she prayed this moment—this small opening— might be the beginning of something more.

Aevar finished buckling his belt, adjusting the sword and knife at his waist. There would be no violence today outside the competitions, but he would not go unarmed. Not with Staegar's bitterness still hanging heavy in the air and Sig's predatory glances trailing Eadlyn like a wolf sizing up prey. Better safe than sorry.

Behind him, Eadlyn gathered her clothing. He looked over his shoulder at her. His mind drifted back to last night. The soft cadence of her voice as she read, the way her words wove a thread of calm even through the chaos beyond the walls. He had not expected to be so intrigued, and yet…

He didn't know what to make of her God, but curiosity tugged at him nonetheless. Maybe they would read again tonight. If she was willing.

Still, her devotion to her faith posed a complication. He turned toward her. "After breakfast, everyone will gather to offer sacrifices to the gods."

She stilled mid-motion. Her gaze lifted to meet his, and hesitation tinged her voice. "Sacrifices?"

Aevar nodded, watching her closely. Unease crept into her features, but this was part of his world. He didn't know how to navigate it any other way. "Animal sacrifices. Not human ones. Kalgora is the last to practice those."

Some of the tightness eased from her posture, but uncertainty lingered thick between them. Her fingers curled around the fabric she held. "May I stay here?"

The question caught him off guard. He had expected her to protest, but this was different. She wasn't asking to avoid the sacrifices out of rebellion or disdain for his people's ways. Her request came from conviction, from a discomfort rooted in her faith. For some reason, he couldn't ignore that.

Still, he hesitated. He didn't trust Staegar's dark mood or Sig's wandering eyes. Luckily, he had a solution.

"Yes, you may stay."

Genuine relief flashed across her face, softening her features into something more open and grateful. "Thank you."

Aevar inclined his head and left to give her privacy to finish dressing.

As he stepped into the main hall, the sounds of the morning drifted through the air. The revelry from the night before had quieted, but the warmth of mead and food still lingered. His father and Halbjorn were already awake, Halbjorn's voice filling the hall even without him having to raise it. His brothers sat nearby, occasionally joining the conversation, while Ulf and Skolli lay sprawled near the door, snoring loud enough to wake the gods themselves.

Kian met him halfway across the room. At least he appeared none the worse for wear.

"I see you didn't join the drinking games." Aevar waved his hand toward the men on the floor.

Kian snorted. "Against Ulf? Not a chance. I prefer to keep my wits about me."

Aevar chuckled. "Wise choice, since you'll need them this morning. I'd like you to stay here and keep an eye on Eadlyn. She won't be attending the sacrifices." While Kian usually tagged along, he'd never taken part, so he wouldn't mind missing it.

Kian's expression shifted into something more serious. "Of course. I'll keep her safe."

Aevar dropped his voice lower. "Keep a close eye out for anyone who might linger behind."

"Don't worry. No one will try anything and live to tell of it."

The idea of the sacrifices left a sour taste in Eadlyn's mouth, stealing whatever appetite she might have had. She had no desire to witness bloodshed, especially not in the name of pagan gods. It still surprised her that Aevar had respected her wishes and allowed her to stay behind. As her husband, he could have forced her to attend. For that mercy, she silently whispered a prayer of thanks.

And possibly, she dared hope, the Scriptures she had read to him the night before had planted a seed. That he had listened with genuine curiosity still felt like a small miracle. Even Edward had never shown such interest, swayed by the likes of Father Bened—who viewed faith as a source of power and wealth—into believing that moral superiority was enough.

She was still mulling over these things when Aevar pulled her aside as the others prepared to leave. "Kian will remain behind so you won't be here by yourself."

Being alone in the longhouse had not occurred to her until now. She wasn't sure where the sacrifices took place, but probably far enough away that no one could help her if trouble arose. She was grateful Aevar took her safety seriously.

The hall emptied, leaving only her and Kian behind. He leaned against one table, a half-eaten hunk of bread in his hand. His smile was easy and reassuring. "So, how are you settling in? I imagine it's been overwhelming, what with the Gathering so soon after your arrival."

"A little. It's been better than I anticipated, though. I think the hardest part is being unable to communicate. Especially now, with so many guests."

"You'll pick it up quicker than you think. Besides, half the people here barely speak it properly themselves." Kian winked, and she laughed.

Her attention drifted to the *tafl* board left abandoned nearby. She picked up the king piece, studying its strange design. It seemed to be carved in the likeness of one of the Nord gods with its serious, imposing expression rather than an Essian king.

"Do you play?" Kian asked.

She set the piece back on the board. "Yes, I played quite often with Galen, the commander of our royal guard. He's the one who taught me."

Kian's eyes gleamed with recognition. "Tall fellow? Looked like he was deciding whether to murder Aevar at your wedding?"

A bittersweet smile surfaced as she recalled that morning. "That would be him. He's always been very protective of me. We tried teaching Edward to play, but he never had the patience for it."

Kian chuckled, low and easy. "I'm no Galen, but if you want a game to pass the time, I'm your man. I warn you though, I cheat shamelessly."

"I'll keep that in mind." Eadlyn settled on the bench across from him. As they arranged the pieces, she asked, "Where do the sacrifices happen?"

"Old shrines in the forest, about a mile from here. Nice hike if you like mud and midges."

Eadlyn laughed and then paused before asking, "Do you think Aevar would ever be open to Christianity?"

Kian's expression was unreadable as he considered the question. "Hard to say. He's not the sort to change his mind easily. But I've seen him do impossible things before."

Hope flickered in Eadlyn's chest. She studied Kian for a moment. Talta considered itself a Christian kingdom, but she didn't know how seriously they practiced their faith. "What about you? Where does your faith lie?"

"My parents dragged me to church more than a few times as a boy. Taught me my prayers. I believe I'd be dead right now at the hands of the Kalgorans if God hadn't brought Aevar along when He did."

So, a surface-level belief. "I'll keep you in my prayers. And Aevar and his family."

Kian's grin returned. "I'll take all the prayers I can get."

They played for a while, exchanging light-hearted barbs and friendly conversation. Kian was a clever opponent, though he made exaggerated groans and wild accusations of sabotage every time she foiled one of his attempts to capture her king.

"You're clearly cheating," he accused at one point, squinting at her. "I can see it on your face."

"I assure you I'm not," Eadlyn said, laughing.

"You smile too much for an honest player," he grumbled, though the twinkle in his eye gave him away.

But the light mood fractured when he stiffened, his attention on the door. Eadlyn followed his gaze. Sig sauntered toward the longhouse with all the arrogance of a cat who thought he owned the world.

"Just what Aevar was afraid of," Kian muttered under his breath.

He moved swiftly, slipping the seax knife from his belt. He pressed a finger to his lips, motioning for her to stay quiet, and ducked behind a pillar. Eadlyn remained seated, her heart thudding as Sig entered the hall. His eyes swept the room before locking onto her.

"Hello, Princess. Here all alone?" His Aerlish was clumsy, and his voice oozed false charm.

She pushed up from the table without answering the question. Her stomach recoiled as he drew closer, invading her space. However, she stood her ground. "You should not be here."

"Come now, a guest should be welcomed warmly."

Eadlyn's pulse quickened, but she wouldn't show fear. "You should leave before Aevar returns."

He stepped closer still and lifted a hand as if to brush her hair. That's when Kian made his move, slipping out behind him. The point of his blade pressed into Sig's neck.

Sig froze.

"I believe the lady asked you to leave," Kian said, his voice low and dangerous.

Sig snorted, too calm for having a blade at his throat.

Kian leaned in. "You know, Aevar's still liable to take your tongue, if not your head, when he finds out you came into the longhouse uninvited looking for his wife."

Sig raised his hands as if innocent. "I meant no harm. Just wanted to see if the princess needed any company."

"She's got company enough. Now you best be going before I decide to save Aevar the trouble and gut you myself."

Sig took two steps backward, casting one last lingering look at Eadlyn before retreating from the hall.

She exhaled. Her hands shook, but she steadied them on the table.

Kian turned to her, slipping the knife back into its sheath with a flourish. "Well," he said brightly, "wasn't that a lovely visit?"

Eadlyn laughed, relief bubbling out with it. "Thank you. For everything."

"My pleasure." Kian flashed a grin. "Saving princesses from idiots is my second-favorite pastime."

She tilted her head. "And your first?"

He winked. "Winning at *tafl*. Which I was about to do before we were so rudely interrupted."

The air buzzed with unrestrained excitement. Shouts and cheers, the heavy thump of wood against wood, and the sharp clash of weapons rose around Eadlyn in a chaotic chorus. The crisp spring breeze cut through the crowd, laden with water, sweat, and the raw bite of damp earth. She had watched Galen and his men train many times back home, but never had she seen anything to match the fervor and fierce determination that coursed through the warriors here. This was not mere practice but a celebration of strength and skill. A test of pride and honor.

The ferocity was almost frightening. Yet the current of enthusiasm pulled at her, and she was caught up in the thrill as she stood at the edge of a ring. Within it, Aevar, his brothers, Kian, and Heida stood in a tight line, shields locked, wooden swords ready to face off against a group from another clan in a mock battle. While their group comprised only five, across the field she spotted clusters of ten or more preparing to engage.

At the signal, the two sides charged forward and clashed with a roar. At first, it was just a chaos of bodies and swinging weapons, but soon, Eadlyn caught the subtle signals passed between Aevar and the others. A nod, a shift of stance, a shouted command she didn't understand. They moved not as individuals but as a single living creature, outmaneuvering their opponents with swift, practiced efficiency. She didn't know the rules or how they counted a "kill," but when one of the opposing men limped out of the ring, clutching a bruised arm, she understood enough.

Though Heida was fascinating to watch since she was the first woman warrior Eadlyn had ever encountered, she found her gaze kept slipping back to Aevar. She knew little of warfare, but even she recognized the ease and skill with which he fought. He moved as if born to war, ducking low beneath a swing, pivoting on the balls of his feet, striking with swift, decisive blows.

Her breath caught once when he spun and slammed the edge of his shield into an opponent's shoulder, sending the man sprawling. Though this was only sport, the clash had a dangerous edge to it that made her heart pound against her ribs.

When the dust settled, only Aevar, Erik, and Kian remained standing in the ring. However, the two sides came together again, laughing and clapping one another on the back. Despite Braan's bloodied knuckles and another man's bleeding nose, a sense of camaraderie, not bitterness, filled the air.

A thrill of pride welled in Eadlyn's chest. *Pride.* For a man she had once feared marrying, and now she found herself drawn to celebrate his victory. Across the ring, he caught her gaze. She offered him a smile, hoping he would see how she felt. He didn't grin like he did with his family, but he did return it, and something warm flared in his stern face.

Before she could savor it, someone slammed into her shoulder hard enough to jolt her sideways. Turning, she caught sight of the woman with the shaved head moving through the crowd. Eadlyn might have brushed off the collision as an accident, but the woman glanced back with a look cold enough to freeze stone. When Eadlyn turned back to the ring, she found Aevar also watching the woman with a stormy expression.

Eadlyn shifted closer to Ranvi and Inga, seeking the comfort of familiar faces. Together, they observed several more skirmishes as the competitions carried on. Aevar fought four more times and won all but one when he was left to face three men alone. Even then, he had made them fight hard for their victory.

Later, they moved to another ring, where single combat took place. Here, warriors stood alone, challenging whomever they wished. They watched two matches between strangers before a swell of excitement passed through the crowd. Heida stepped into the center of the ring, sword and shield in hand, her stance relaxed but alert. From the sidelines, Jarl Gudrik, a grizzled warrior, and his sons bellowed their support.

Heida called out a name—Oda Jokulfsdottir—and a murmur drifted through the crowd. A moment later, the woman with the shaved head stalked into the ring, glaring at her. Apparently, Eadlyn wasn't the only one Oda held a grudge against.

The two women faced each other. Heida murmured something too quiet for Eadlyn to hear. Oda's lip curled in response, and she snarled something back before charging.

Their wooden swords crashed together in a blur of strikes and parries, the sharp crack of wood ringing out. Unlike the earlier matches, this fight seethed with hostility. Each blow was meant to wound and humiliate, not just to win. The fight appeared even at first, each woman matching the other's strength and speed. Yet, the differences soon became clear. Heida remained calm and composed, measuring each strike, while Oda fought with raw anger, her movements sharper and less controlled.

With a furious yell, Oda lunged, but Heida sidestepped, shield up, letting Oda's momentum carry her off balance. Then, in a smooth, brutal motion, Heida slammed her shield into Oda's, catching her square in the face. Blood blossomed from Oda's lip.

She howled in rage and attacked wildly, but Heida was ready. She parried, dodged, and waited. As soon as Oda's anger burned itself out, Heida pressed in until the other woman stumbled. Losing her footing, she fell to her knees. Before she could rise, Heida pressed her sword to Oda's chest, and the crowd erupted into cheers.

Heida said something low and harsh before turning her back on her defeated opponent. As she strode from the ring, she exchanged a nod with Aevar. Eadlyn wasn't sure what it communicated, but they both appeared pleased. Behind her, Oda threw down her shield and sword with a clatter and stalked away, blood dripping from her chin.

Aevar clapped Erik on the shoulder, the weight of another victory settling between them with easy pride. His brother had yet to lose a single bout, proving not only his strength but his worthiness as a future king. Hopefully, the gods granted their father many more years on the throne, but it was good for Erik to carve his place now.

With Erik's match finished and Braan still locked in a bout with one of his future brothers-in-law, Aevar was up. He lifted his shield, adjusted his grip on the worn wooden sword he had chosen, and stepped into the ring. He searched the crowd, not looking for just anyone. Heida had handled Oda. Now it was his turn to answer the insult dealt that morning.

He raised his voice above the murmur. "I challenge Sig Sigvidsson."

A ripple passed through the spectators. Conversations fell into a tense hush, as if everyone sensed this bout was not just for sport. Across the ring, a pair of men stepped aside to reveal Sig, grinning like a wolf scenting blood. He swaggered forward, and Aevar let the tension coil in his limbs. He would end that grin soon enough.

Aevar raised his shield and braced himself. As the one challenged, Sig would strike first. However, he took his time, strolling a few paces closer and sweeping the crowd before locking on Eadlyn.

"You sure you want your new wife seeing this? She might wonder if there were better warriors she could've married."

Aevar snorted. "What she'll see is me putting a loud-mouthed *fífl* in the dirt where he belongs."

Sig's smile faltered, rage flaring in its place as he sprang. Aevar caught the blow on his shield, and the jarring impact jolted up his arm. He answered with a quick swing of his sword, striking Sig's exposed ribs. Not a hard hit, but enough to sting. Laughter bubbled from the sidelines, and that would wound Sig deeper than the blow.

They circled, boots grinding into the churned dirt. Sig attacked repeatedly, but his strikes were sloppy, his shield drooping as frustration ate at him. Aevar let him wear himself out, conserving his own strength. When the next opening came, Aevar struck with a jab to the chest that sent Sig stumbling back with a grunt.

Reckless now, Sig tried to shoulder into him with a wild roar. Aevar sidestepped and tripped him with a sweep of his sword. When Sig crashed into the dirt, Aevar planted a boot against his chest to keep him down. Pressing the tip of his blade into the hollow of Sig's throat, he leaned in close enough to see the rage and humiliation battling in the man's eyes.

"Stay away from my wife," Aevar growled low enough only Sig would hear, "or the next time you face my blade it will be a real one."

He gave a slight push with the sword, making Sig wheeze, before straightening and turning away. The crowd erupted around him, voices blending into a rough, roaring cheer. Erik and Kian were grinning as he approached, yet his gaze drifted to Eadlyn. She stood near Ranvi, a smile blooming on her face, something unexpectedly proud and fierce.

But then her expression shifted. Her eyes went wide, her mouth parting in alarm.

A shout tore from somewhere nearby. "Look out!"

Instinct roared through Aevar. He spun around. Sig charged at him, sword raised high. It slammed into the side of Aevar's head. Pain exploded in his skull. The world tilted. He staggered but forced his body to obey, raising his shield to block the next vicious blow.

Hot, blinding fury crashed through him. The roar in his ears was no longer the crowd. He wrenched Sig's sword aside, their shields colliding with bone-shuddering force. This was no competition now. This was a fight for honor. Sig fought like a cornered animal, wild and dirty. Aevar dodged the clumsy swings and drove him back step by step.

With a crack that rang across the ring, Aevar slammed his sword into Sig's knee. Sig let out a strangled curse, but Aevar was already following with a jab to his stomach, cutting off his breath. Sig stumbled, shield sagging. Aevar knocked it out of his hands and sent it spinning to the dirt. Discarding his own shield, Aevar gripped his sword two-handed and advanced.

He struck again and again until Sig struggled to raise his sword fast enough. Then Aevar landed a vicious blow to his ribs that made him cry out and crumple to his knees. Sig gasped, dropping his sword and holding his side. He raised his hand in weak surrender. Aevar stood over him, chest heaving. Every muscle screamed to strike again, to make him stay down, but he forced the urge away. Let everyone see Sig shamed like this. Broken, bleeding, beaten.

Without a word, Aevar turned his back. Something trickled into his eye. He swiped it away with his wrist and scowled when his hand came away slick with red. Around him, voices swelled— Erik, Kian, his mother—all speaking and reaching for him at once. He tried to brush them off, not needing their fussing, but Erik grabbed the back of his head to hold him still and peered at the wound.

"Looks worse than it is," he pronounced, clapping him on the shoulder.

Móthir fretted about getting it cleaned, but Aevar barely heard her. His attention had already found Eadlyn again. Her face was pale as she eyed the trail of blood, yet she held herself steady, not appearing to grow weak at the sight of it like some women might. He met her eyes, and in them he found genuine concern. Perhaps only because their newly formed alliance could so easily collapse, but something told him it was more than that.

Strangely moved, he offered her the reassurance he had not given anyone else. "I'm fine."

Eadlyn waited until most of the guests were well into their cups before excusing herself for the night. Hopefully, this way, no one noticed her early departure and started to whisper. Aevar's family did not seem to mind, but she didn't want to stir any gossip that might suggest she didn't respect the hard work and traditions of the Gathering.

Closing the door behind herself and muting the commotion from the hall, she let out a breath and yawned. Though she had not taken part in any of today's competitions, simply watching had exhausted her. Especially the bout between Aevar and Sig. Her stomach still knotted at the memory of Sig attacking while Aevar's back was turned. A blow like that might have killed him.

She changed into the heavy linen shift she'd been sleeping in and wrapped a thick shawl around her shoulders. Gently, she opened her Scripture pages to where she'd left off before Aevar came in last night. He had appeared to be enjoying the night with his brothers and Kian, so she didn't expect to see him again until morning.

But not ten minutes later, the door opened, and he slipped inside. Last night he'd come to check on her. What might have brought him in early tonight?

"Is everything all right?" she asked.

"Yes." He hesitated a beat, as if even he wasn't sure why he was here. "Everyone's getting drunk. With more competitions tomorrow, there's an advantage to staying sober." He shrugged, something almost like a chagrined smile taking hold. "Like your Holy Book says."

Eadlyn couldn't dampen her own smile as she watched him cross to his corner, unbuckling his sword belt and shrugging off his leather jerkin. A brief wince crossed his face. After seeing the day's brutal matches, she had no doubt the soreness was fierce tonight.

He wandered to the small shelf holding a polished mirror and inspected the cut along his brow. Though he'd washed after the competitions, traces of dried blood still clung to his skin and streaked down his neck. He wet a cloth in the basin and started cleaning up, missing the flecks of blood around his eye that were hard to see in the dim light.

"You still have a little blood on your face."

He frowned, trying to find it, and she pushed to her feet. "Here, let me help."

She stretched out her hand for the cloth. Aevar hesitated for a moment before handing it over, and she stepped closer. Carefully, she dabbed the cloth around his eye, loosening the dried blood. Without realizing what she was doing, she raised her other hand to tip his chin down so she could see better.

Their eyes locked.

Eadlyn's heart did an odd flip. Not even during their wedding ceremony had they been this close. Something flickered across his face before he blinked and stepped back. She dropped her hand and retreated just as quickly, heat rising to her face. Clearing her throat, she managed a breathless, "I think I got it."

Aevar only nodded before striding back across the room. She was still trying to calm the sudden swirl of emotions when he tugged his tunic off. She averted her gaze, but not before glimpsing the well-defined muscles of his shoulders and back. Her face burned hotter.

Against her better judgment, she glanced back. This time the muscles didn't hold her attention, but the dark splotches already blooming into bruises and a long, pale scar slashing from his shoulder to halfway down his back.

Curiosity got the better of her. "How did you get that scar?"

He turned toward her, fresh tunic in hand, and she fought not to blush yet again. He, however, didn't seem as flustered to catch her watching him.

"Last spring we were ambushed by Kalgorans while hunting up north. One of them dropped from a tree with a knife. If he'd been a grown man instead of a boy, I'd probably be dead."

Eadlyn winced, fighting to keep her eyes on his face rather than his bare torso, though she did notice the hammer pendant he wore. She'd seen the darkened metal amulet peeking out of his tunic a time or two before and had learned it was a symbol of their god Thor. "I thought you had a truce with them?"

"We do. But it doesn't stop raiders from crossing into Nordra to cause trouble." To Eadlyn's relief, he slipped on the clean tunic. "Their so-called king claims ignorance. Says they're rogues. Maybe they are. But dealing with a few raiders is better than open war."

"How long has the truce been in place?"

"Three years."

"And how many battles have you fought?"

"Five major battles." His voice was matter-of-fact. "Many more skirmishes."

Eadlyn marveled to think of him surviving so many. "How old were you when you started fighting?"

"I was fifteen the first time I rode with my father and brothers to defend the northern border."

Fifteen. She thought of Edward at that age and couldn't imagine him in that position even now. She prayed Galen could turn him into the strong man he needed to be to lead Essix successfully. He had so much to learn, and pressure squeezed her lungs not to be there and help him find his way. The sudden longing for home was so strong it constricted her throat.

Her thoughts snapped back to Aevar as he settled onto his furs.

"We can read again if you'd like," he said.

At those words, the bout of melancholy lifted, and a fresh hope bloomed in its place. It was as if God were giving her a quiet confirmation that she belonged here in Nordra, not Essix.

adlyn observed as Inga worked the loom with practiced hands and explained each step along the way. The upright frame, as tall as Eadlyn herself, leaned against the wall on one of the platforms, stone weights at the bottom holding the warp threads taut. A half-finished length of woven wool stretched across it, destined to become someone's new dress or tunic. Beside it, another loom stood with the beginnings of an exquisite tapestry. Ranvi sat there, bent over her work, her shuttle weaving in and out of the jewel-toned yarn. Someday, perhaps, Eadlyn would learn to weave such intricate beauty. For now, she was content to master something simpler.

After passing the shuttle, wound with wool, through the vertical warp threads, Inga picked up what looked like a wooden comb and tamped the new row into place with a few sure strokes. "There. Now you try."

She stepped aside with an encouraging smile, and Eadlyn traded places with her. Mimicking the movements she had watched, she guided the shuttle through. It took more effort to settle the weft evenly, not pulling too tight or letting it sag, but when she finished, Inga gave a small nod of approval.

"Good. Keep at it, and you will soon find it comes naturally."

She remained near as Eadlyn repeated the process, the soft whisper of thread the only sound between them. The quiet work soothed something in Eadlyn, especially after the chaos of the Gathering a week ago. The jarls had departed with as much fanfare as they had arrived, leaving everyone to go about their everyday lives.

Once again, Eadlyn rarely saw Aevar, save for mornings and evenings. Yet, to her astonishment, he still allowed her to read the Scriptures to him each night. It had become such a habit that last evening, she'd simply started reading without asking if he wished to continue, and he hadn't objected. He spoke little, but now and then, he asked a question. While he may only be humoring her or listening for entertainment, she prayed every day the words would lead him to faith. If nothing else, his curiosity gave her hope she did not expect to find here.

Still, a cloud hovered over that hope.

Almost a month had passed, and yet a wall remained between them. His family welcomed her as one of their own, their kindness easing many of her early fears. But Aevar remained distant most of the time, as if unsure where she fit beside him. She might have believed it was just his way, or the way of Nord marriages, if not for the open fondness he displayed toward his family and the affectionate way Runar and Erik treated their wives.

A prickling sense of disappointment needled at her, and she fought to smooth it away. He treated her with consideration and respect. That was enough. What more could she ask for?

Still, the question stirred in her mind and, after a moment's hesitation, she turned from the loom and spoke. "I love how close your family is. It's something I've never experienced before." She paused before forging ahead. "It's clear how much Aevar loves all of you. I know I'm still new, and we are still learning one another, but…do you think he might ever let me in like that? Or, because I am Essian, will he always be more reserved in our relationship?"

For a heartbeat, something drifted across Inga's face. Something like sorrow. She reached out, resting a warm, calloused hand on Eadlyn's arm. "It isn't you, dear. My son…he carries a lot of pain. He was married once, to a girl named Thora. She was his life. She died almost three years ago, bearing their daughter. The babe lived but a few hours herself. And with them, something in Aevar died as well. He's spent these years guarding the pieces of his heart too closely to risk breaking them again."

The words struck, echoing in Eadlyn's mind. No wonder Aevar kept his distance. She had believed she'd been the one to sacrifice for her people and this alliance, but Aevar had made his own sacrifice, marrying a stranger while still mourning the loss of his wife and child.

Another, more terrible, realization struck, seizing her with icy fingers. She clutched the string of beads at her chest. "These clothes…they were hers." It all made sense now, the wistful, aching looks Aevar had given her.

Inga nodded, her smile sad but tender.

"I shouldn't wear them," Eadlyn whispered, already turning toward the bedroom to change at once.

But Inga stopped her. "It's all right. Aevar gave them to you."

Even so, guilt twisted in Eadlyn's belly. "I don't want to cause him, or any of you, more pain."

"You aren't. You needed clothing. And Thora herself would have wished for her things to serve the living, not gather dust."

Eadlyn wavered until Inga gave her arm a comforting squeeze.

"As for Aevar," she said, "I cannot promise he will love you, but I can promise he will take care of you and guard you with his life. We all will."

The words wrapped around Eadlyn like a cloak against the cold. Tears smarted in her eyes. "That is already more than I ever hoped for."

"I win!" Trygg's triumphant shout rang through the hall, drawing a few amused glances from the others.

In his excitement, he scattered half the *tafl* pieces across the table. Aevar chuckled, snatching the king piece before it tumbled off the edge. He didn't let his nephew win every time, but tonight he'd been inclined to indulge him.

Trygg hopped off the bench and rushed off to brag about his victory to anyone who would listen. Still smiling to himself, Aevar reset the game board, gathering the scattered pieces into neat rows in case someone else wanted a game before bed. He found his gaze drifting to Eadlyn, who sat on the other side of the hearth with Ranvi, Katla, and Alvir. Everyone would turn in before too long. He was tired after a day of hard labor, preparing the fields for planting, but not enough to skip their nightly reading. He wouldn't admit it aloud, but he found himself rather enjoying the tales.

Missing a piece, he leaned over to check under the table. He spotted it beneath the bench and retrieved it. When he straightened, his mother had joined him.

"I introduced Eadlyn to weaving today," she said, keeping her voice low enough to stay between them. "She's picking it up quickly."

"Good."

"I told her about Thora."

A familiar, sharp ache lanced through his chest, the kind that never dulled with time. He drew a calming breath through his nose. Perhaps he should have told Eadlyn himself, but it was better this way.

"I expected you would."

His mother watched Eadlyn for a moment before studying him again. "It is good for her to know why you treat her the way you do."

Aevar frowned. Her words prickled under his skin. She made it sound as though he'd mistreated Eadlyn. "I've treated her kindly. I've done everything I can to make her comfortable."

"Kindly, yes, but at arm's length and certainly not like your wife."

"I barely know her."

His mother hummed, unimpressed. "And whose fault is that?"

Aevar twisted the *tafl* piece between his fingers, focusing on the small weight instead of his mother's words. He'd provided for Eadlyn's needs, made sure she was safe. What more did Móthir expect?

"I like her," she said quietly.

Aevar gave her a sidelong look. He didn't like the sound of where this was headed, but he knew better than to stop her.

"I think," she continued, "if you gave it a chance, you two could be very happy together."

He bit back a sigh. "I married her for the alliance."

This drew a smirk to Móthir's face. "I'm sure your father thought the same thing. At first."

"That's different."

"Is it?" she asked, a glint in her eye.

He didn't answer. There was no point.

Móthir rose from the bench. As she passed him, she bent down, kissed his temple, and murmured near his ear, "You two would give me beautiful grandchildren."

Aevar snorted under his breath, shaking his head. That wasn't likely to happen any time soon, if ever, considering their current arrangement. He glanced back toward Eadlyn. Trygg was chattering to her now. Despite her inability to understand anything he said, Eadlyn offered him her full attention, smiling patiently. The children, even Alvir, who was shy with newcomers, had really taken to her.

Some small, traitorous part of him wondered what life might look like if things were different and he and Eadlyn had a true relationship. But as his mother's words lingered, cold sunk deep into his chest. He couldn't bear to lose another wife or child. Couldn't bear even taking the chance.

Soft goodnights echoed across the hall as everyone drifted to their rooms. Eadlyn remained by the door as Aevar moved around their chamber, lighting the lamps. Shadows danced across the walls as the flames caught and flickered across his features. Her mind centered on the conversation she'd had with Inga that morning. It had changed how she saw him and their situation. Even just sharing this space with her must be agony.

He turned and caught her staring. His brows drew together, puzzled.

Eadlyn hesitated, then stepped closer, gathering her courage. Some things needed to be said. "I'm sorry if my being here and wearing these clothes has caused you pain. I didn't know."

For a moment, he said nothing, and his gaze dropped away from hers. Unguarded suffering crossed his face. It stole her breath to witness it so plainly. She couldn't change the fact that they were married or the necessity of sharing this room, but one thing was within her power.

"I will stop wearing them." An ache squeezed her throat, but she kept her voice steady. "I will make something for myself."

Aevar's mouth tightened, not in anger, but in a way that betrayed grief. The loss shadowed his expression before he locked it down again. When he lifted his eyes to hers, they were resolute.

"No. You don't need to. You are welcome to them."

Eadlyn held his gaze a moment longer. She needed to be sure. "Are you certain?"

"Yes."

Compassion swelled, sharp and helpless. She felt it between them—the shared grief and the sacrifices neither of them had asked for but both carried. "I'm very sorry for your losses."

Aevar dipped his chin in acknowledgment, but she caught the shimmer of moisture in his eyes before he turned his head away. This was the most vulnerable she had seen him.

"Thank you," he said, his voice roughened.

A long silence stretched between them, broken only when he cleared his throat. He looked at her again, his face composed, the mask back in place. His voice seemed lighter. "So, what are we reading tonight?"

Relief and sadness tangled inside her. "Tonight, I get to read you one of my favorite stories. Joseph."

They finished preparing for bed and settled in for their nightly reading. When Eadlyn reached the part where Joseph's brothers sold him into slavery, Aevar let out a low chuckle.

"These people in your book are as devious and vengeful as the gods."

Eadlyn suppressed a grin. He *was* listening. "Yes, but they are just people, flawed and sinful, prone to making terrible choices and mistakes. We all are. That's the amazing thing about God. Even when we fail or rebel, His plans don't. And even more incredible, He still loves us in spite of it." She paused, then added, "Have you heard about Jesus?"

Aevar shrugged. "A little. He died and came back, supposedly."

"He did." She shifted, setting the parchment aside for a moment. "Do you know why?"

"A sacrifice of some sort?"

"Yes, because sin can only be covered by death and blood. It's part of why Abel's offering was acceptable and Cain's was not. We are all born sinners because we have a sin nature that has been passed down by our fathers ever since Adam. Elsewhere in

Scripture it says the wages of sin is death. That debt is on us, but Jesus, who is fully God, gave up everything to become human and die to pay that debt for us. He offers salvation and forgiveness of sin freely to anyone who will accept and trust His sacrifice."

Something flickered in Aevar's expression, but he remained silent.

"It's simple," she continued. "The Bible says, *if thou shalt confess with thy mouth the Lord Jesus, and shalt believe in thine heart that God hath raised him from the dead, thou shalt be saved.* Nothing complicated. Just faith."

Aevar didn't reply, but she didn't expect him to, and she prayed the seeds would take root. For now, she was simply content to be here, sharing these quiet moments and trusting that God was at work in ways she did not yet see.

The sun shone outside the hall, the air much warmer than Eadlyn's first couple of weeks in Nordra. A welcome change. It pulled at her, awakening a familiar yearning. Back in Kenwich, she had loved her morning walks through the gardens when the weather allowed. She missed that, especially now with the first green of spring creeping across the land.

Leaving the hearth, where she had helped the women prepare breakfast, she walked over to the table and sat down beside Aevar. "If you have time today, could you show me around the village?"

Though she had seen parts of it, she had never had the chance to explore it properly. It was time she learned more about the place that was now her home.

He turned to her. Something about him was different this morning. She hoped she wasn't imagining it, but the steady way he met her gaze gave her hope. Maybe speaking of Thora last night had shifted something between them. Maybe acknowledging the pain had begun to heal some of it.

"I'll take you after we eat," he said.

She smiled in thanks as Alys and Nesta brought breakfast to the table. The rest of the family gathered and served themselves enthusiastically. Eadlyn paused to bow her head in prayer before eating. No one ever commented or objected, and she appreciated the silent respect. Another Nord family may have opposed, but God had blessed her in this situation.

Mealtime had become one of her favorite parts of the day. The camaraderie, the teasing, the sheer life that pulsed around the table. So different from the tense, formal meals she had grown up with. Here, love permeated every glance and offhanded jest. It gave her plenty of opportunities to work on her Nordric. Like Kian had said, understanding it came faster than speaking it. While she still couldn't follow an entire conversation, she picked up more words and phrases each day, the language gradually becoming less foreign to her ears.

When breakfast finished, she retrieved her shawl in case she needed it, and together she and Aevar stepped out into the morning. Sunlight warmed her face, the crisp air sweet with budding leaves. She drew a deep breath, and something within her lifted.

Aevar led her through the village, pointing out the different craftsmen and important locations. He introduced her to several people along the way. She remembered seeing a couple of them in passing at the Gathering. One was Alrik the shipwright, Alys's betrothed. He was a big man with strongly muscled arms from his work. Eadlyn understood now why Alys was so smitten.

They conversed with him for a few minutes before continuing. At the edge of the village, they came to a large wooden structure. Outside, a man leaned on a staff, his shoulders hunched, and his long gray beard touching his waist. His blue-green eyes fixed on them with clear, alert interest. Aevar introduced him as Hjor, keeper of the messenger ravens.

Eadlyn tried to keep up with their conversation, catching a few words about food that made Aevar chuckle. He then led her inside.

Dusty wood, straw, and the musk of feathers lingered in the air. Tall wooden cages were built into the walls and housed sleek black ravens. They shifted and flapped, their sharp eyes following every movement.

"This is how we communicate with the other clans," Aevar said, leading her down the center aisle. "The ravens carry messages across Nordra and sometimes to Talta."

He opened one cage, and a raven hopped onto his arm. Up close, its feathers gleamed like polished obsidian. Aevar stroked its head, and it croaked low in its throat.

"I used to sneak in here as a boy. There were two ravens named Huginn and Muninn, after the ravens said to wander the earth and report to Odin what they have seen. At that age, I thought they really were Odin's messengers, so I'd ask them to take my requests to the Allfather. I even bribed them with treats." He chuckled at the memory. "One day Hjor caught me and told me I had to stop because I was making them too fat to fly."

Eadlyn laughed, imagining a young Aevar with a fistful of treats and grand ambitions. "What kinds of requests?"

"The usual things a boy of seven asks for. A sword, a horse, to outgrow my brothers."

Another laugh trickled between them, thinking of Erik's towering stature.

Aevar shrugged, and his humor faded. "But the gods have never seen fit to answer any of my requests. I do not know if they even hear me."

Eadlyn's heart ached for him. How many prayers had he offered—not just childish ones, but desperate ones—that seemed to fall on deaf ears? "At times I've felt like God didn't hear me either. But He does. Always. Even when the answer is no, even when we don't understand, He hears. And He loves."

Aevar didn't answer, his attention fixed on the raven, but she hoped some part of her words found a place in his heart.

After a moment, he returned the raven to its cage, and they stepped back into the bright morning. Circling the edge of the village, they reached the fjord and paused on the beach. Eadlyn drank in the sight. The water glittered under the sun, and lazy waves lapped against the shoreline. Farther down the fjord, sheer cliffs rose along each side, dark gray and green. It was wild, beautiful, and so unlike the muddy river she had grown up near.

"You like the fjord?" Aevar asked.

"It's beautiful. So much larger than anything I've seen."

"I couldn't imagine living far from the water."

Though he'd lived here his whole life, she still sensed his deep appreciation for what lay before them. She breathed in deeply. The cool breeze coming off the fjord, laced with fish and pine, tickled the hair at her neck. Standing here, she felt…peaceful.

"Would it be all right if I came here on my own sometimes?"

Aevar looked back toward the village, then nodded. "The people know you are my wife. If anything happened to you, there would be consequences."

She smiled, experiencing a strange sense of freedom she had

never known before. Galen had accompanied her everywhere outside the palace. He wouldn't be comfortable knowing she didn't have the same watchful presence here, even with Aevar's assurance, but she was happy to accept it.

After a few more minutes of standing at the water's edge, they turned toward the village, walking in companionable silence. But as they rounded a corner, a familiar figure emerged, shattering the peace.

Oda's mouth curled into a sneer the instant she spotted them. Eadlyn glanced at Aevar. He eyed the woman dismissively, but she detected tension in his posture. As they drew near, he placed his hand on her back as if to guide her around the woman without acknowledging her. However, Oda's voice spoiled the morning air. Eadlyn caught the word *Essian* but did not understand the others strung along with it. She was probably better off not knowing, judging by the woman's caustic tone.

Aevar stopped and turned, maneuvering Eadlyn so she stood behind him. Whether or not for her benefit, he spoke in Aerlish, his words clipped. "Oda, do not treat my wife with such disrespect."

"Your wife." She sneered the words as if they tasted of bile. "So you defend the decision that forced you to marry her?"

"It was my choice. No one forced me."

"And is it worth it, being stuck with the *grybba* for the rest of your life? Everyone knows we have no need of an alliance with Essix."

"Oda," he spoke her name harshly and with a tone of warning. "You will not insult her again. Leave politics to those who know what they are talking about and stay away."

She seemed ready to keep arguing, but Aevar cut her off. "I mean it. I will not tolerate any continued harassment. I thought Heida already made that clear."

So that had been the purpose behind the contest between Heida and Oda.

Oda's thunderous look shifted from Aevar to Eadlyn, the loathing enough to send a chill to the blood. But Eadlyn refused to cower. She'd faced far more daunting foes, including her own father. She took a step forward, putting herself at Aevar's side instead of behind him, and lifted her chin slightly. Tall and proud, like she'd instructed her brother.

With a snort, Oda glared at Aevar before turning on her heel and marching down a side path. Aevar didn't move until she disappeared around another corner. Then he turned to Eadlyn, regret tightening his expression.

"I apologize. I thought the matter settled after the Gathering."

Eadlyn drew a deep breath to calm the quiver in her stomach. She'd never liked confrontation, but it was often unavoidable. "Who is she?"

Aevar sighed and rubbed the back of his neck. Clearly, the two shared a history.

"She was my sister-in-law, Thora's half-sister. She was always jealous of Thora, and now it seems she is jealous of you."

"Oh." An envious rival was not something she foresaw.

"If she continues to harass you, let me know and I will put an end to it."

Eadlyn nodded, but uncertainty rose. "Will I still be able to walk to the fjord in the mornings?"

Aevar peered down the road where Oda had gone but seemed confident when he spoke. "Yes. She will not dare harm you. Not physically. Like I said, if she speaks to you again, I will handle it."

After seeing Eadlyn safely back at the longhouse, Aevar strode across the village toward the training field. He half hoped he'd come across Oda again. If he did, he'd be sorely tempted to drag her to the ring for a *holmgang* for disrespecting Eadlyn and settle things the old way. Publicly and unmistakably.

She should have learned her lesson after the match with Heida, but Oda had never been one to back down. Memories returned of how she had skulked around before his wedding to Thora, full of half-hidden bitterness. Thora had taken her to the ring herself, but it was up to Aevar to see Eadlyn did not have to deal with her.

He reached the field and spotted Kian with the huskarls. A bout was underway with the youngest and oldest of the men facing off in the center, weapons clashing and shouts rising around them. It would've been a good fight to watch another day, but Aevar wasn't in the mood. He caught Kian's eye and nodded him over.

Kian lingered a moment before leaving the others and meeting Aevar at the edge of the field. "What's going on?"

"Oda's up to her old ways."

Kian shot a look toward the village. "That woman's got the persistence of a blood gnat. Want us to swat her, or just keep her buzzing out of reach?"

"I already made myself clear to her." Aevar crossed his arms. "Eadlyn wants the freedom to walk down to the fjord. I want it known that she's to be protected at all costs. If anyone, especially Oda, bothers her again, they're to be brought directly to me."

"I'll let the men know. They'll spread the word and keep watch." Kian gave a dry snort. "Honestly, it's like watching someone try to start a fire in the fjord. The obsession with you is almost impressive."

Aevar grunted, jaw tightening. What had once seemed like petty sibling rivalry between Thora and Oda had twisted into something darker. Now Oda seemed bent on claiming what was denied her. He remembered too well the day she had come to him, so soon after Thora's death, thinking in his grief he would welcome her offer of comfort. The memory made his insides turn. He had refused her outright, and she'd slunk back into the shadows. But now, Eadlyn's arrival had stirred her up again like hornets from a broken nest.

A hard smack landed against his shoulder.

"You look like you need to hit something," Kian said, grinning. "And I'm feeling particularly generous today. I'll let you take a swing at me."

Aevar didn't argue. His hands itched, and his blood flowed too hot beneath his skin. Kian was right. He did need to hit something.

The ring cleared once he and Kian stepped inside. The huskarls knew better than to interrupt when Aevar was like this—the kind of storm that needed letting out before it struck elsewhere. Kian tossed him a wooden sword and shield, and Aevar caught both without breaking stride.

"No blades," Kian said, grabbing his own gear. "You look like you might be in the mood to *accidentally* break something."

"I'll aim for your head. Wouldn't damage much."

"Generous as ever."

They circled once. Wooden swords felt slightly unbalanced compared to iron but familiar. The grain of the grip bit into Aevar's palm, the shield solid against his forearm. Kian struck first, a light, quick swing toward Aevar's shoulder. Aevar blocked it and returned with a downward strike that Kian deflected with ease.

"I've missed this," Kian said, shifting his stance. "You, angry. Me, being useful."

Aevar didn't answer. He let the rhythm of the fight take hold. Each strike gave him something to focus on, drowning out thoughts of Oda. Of Thora. Of Eadlyn standing tall beside him.

Kian pressed forward, shield low, sword swinging fast. Aevar stepped aside, caught the strike, and countered with a quick combination. The final strike landed squarely against Kian's ribs.

He staggered back with a hissed breath, laughing despite it. "You're a menace when brooding."

"You asked for it."

"I *offered*, actually, out of friendship. This is gratitude, apparently."

Aevar shook out his shoulders. Sweat clung under his collar, but the heat in his chest was starting to bleed away.

Kian circled again, more cautious now. "You ever going to tell her?"

Aevar tightened his grip on his sword. "Tell who what?"

Kian raised a brow. "Eadlyn. That you're half in love with her already."

Aevar swung hard and fast in a brutal arc that slammed into Kian's shield with enough force to send him stumbling two steps back. The crack of wood rang out sharp and final.

Kian blinked, regaining his balance. "Right. Noted."

Aevar reset his stance, measuring each breath. He was *not* half in love. He struck again. Kian blocked and tried to counter, but Aevar stepped inside the swing and shoved him back with his shoulder. Kian stumbled, turning it into a dramatic fall and landing on the dirt with a loud *oof*. He stayed there, staring at the sky until Aevar offered him a hand.

Kian took it, groaning as Aevar hauled him up. "Next time I bring armor."

"You'll need more than that."

Kian grinned. "Maybe a priest."

That night, Aevar settled in to listen to Eadlyn read and massaged his arm where one of the men had struck him during their training bouts after he and Kian had sparred. It still throbbed beneath the skin, a clean hit and well-earned.

Eadlyn's voice filled the room, enthusiasm coloring her tone as she told him of how her God had sent plagues down on the land of Egypt because the king refused to let God's people go free. It was a dramatic tale—water turned to blood, locusts darkening the skies, the sun blotted out—and Aevar had to admit he found it more gripping than he'd expected.

But his focus wandered.

He kept drifting back to the moment earlier when she had stood at his side so boldly, facing Oda's sneering hatred without flinching. She was quiet, and gentle, and poised, as one expected from a southern princess, but she carried a deeper hidden strength. He'd seen it from the first day they'd met, and it had revealed itself again today. And with that strength, he suspected she had a spark of fight as well. He'd caught a glimpse of it when she'd stepped in to stop the match between him and her Essian guard when they'd first accepted the marriage proposal. He hadn't forgotten the spark in her eyes. It made him wonder, idly at first, but with growing interest, what else lay buried beneath that calm and grace. What would it take to get her ire up?

He shifted and looked over at her, that question turning into temptation. "Are you sure this story isn't about the gods?"

Eadlyn paused mid-sentence and lowered the parchment. "No. It's definitely about *the* God. The whole point of the plagues was to show that the gods Egypt believed in were not real and had no power."

Aevar nodded as if mulling it over. "Still sounds like the gods to me."

"But you see, this reveals God's power over all of creation. He is the God of gods. More powerful than any created thing."

"'God of gods.'" He lifted an eyebrow. "So there *are* others."

She blinked. "What? No!" The first thread of exasperation slipped into her voice. "That's not what it means." She adjusted her shawl and sat straighter. "It means He's God over everything, including man's attempts at creating their own gods."

"How can you be sure?"

She stared at him as if he'd sprouted antlers. After all, he had never questioned her like this. Not directly. Not in this tone that always annoyed his brothers. She thought through her answer for a long moment and drew in a breath. One of those slow, deliberate ones people took when they were keeping calm.

He fought a smile, but not well enough, apparently.

Her eyes narrowed. "You're trying to irritate me."

He shrugged, letting a grin break free. "I wanted to see if you could get irritated."

She reached behind her and snatched a pillow. The throw was quick and clean. He laughed as he caught it just before it smacked him in the face.

"I'll have you know," she said with exaggerated dignity, "I can get plenty irritated. Edward would tell you that."

Her face held his gaze, the amusement tilting her soft lips and sparkling in her dark eyes. It struck him how happy she looked, sitting there on his bed as if she had always belonged, her hair spilling over her shoulders in sharp contrast to the light blue shawl she'd wrapped around herself. Something sparked deep in his chest, and he forced himself to look away.

Without speaking, he tossed the pillow back at her—not too hard—and caught a feminine scent of lavender. It hit him without warning, bringing the past colliding with the present. Warding off the memories, he lay back down and stared at the ceiling. Eadlyn continued reading, but the words grew lost in a confusing sea of longing for what once was and the way his heart tugged at him now.

The morning air held a keen edge, thick with fjord salt and the promise of adventure. It hummed in the sounds of boots over planks, the shouts of orders and farewells, and the dull thud of crates and chests loaded into longships. Nearly all of Fjellheim had gathered at the docks to see the raiders off to seek their fortunes outside Nordra.

Eadlyn stood amidst the bustle and observed as men carried bundles of supplies onto the waiting ships, while others held their wives and children in long embraces. There was excitement, but also somberness in it all. The kind that came from knowing some of these goodbyes might be the last.

She had grown up hearing the dreadful tales of Nord raids along Essix's coast. Of ships landing without warning, villages set ablaze, and people dragged away from their homes. How strange to stand on the other side now, watching the same ships depart under the blessing of people she had come to care about. Because of the alliance, Essix was now spared such horror. She found grim relief in that.

She scanned the crowd and found Aevar near one of the docks, clasping forearms with one of the departing warriors. He wasn't among those leaving. Thank God for that. She approached him as he stepped away from the man, his expression unreadable.

"Where are the men headed?"

"Waelon. We figure if they are dealing with raids, they will be too busy to think about invading Essix, and we will not have to march to your brother's aid. It benefits both sides of the alliance."

A tangle of mixed emotions knotted inside her. Relief, yes, but also guilt. Waelon might be an enemy of Essix, but the ones who suffered most were the farmers, the villagers, the children. She offered a silent prayer for them. For those with no warning or say. The people around her might not approve, but she couldn't pretend she did not care.

She let her attention drift over the raiders themselves, many faces she now recognized, and prayed for their safety too. This was her home now, and though she didn't condone their violence, she didn't wish grief on their families either.

She turned her attention back to Aevar. "Have you ever been raiding?"

"A couple of times. Years ago. My family usually stays here in case Kalgora breaks the truce. There's no guarantee year to year, and we must keep a strong enough force to hold them off."

She didn't ask whether he had raided Essix. She didn't want to know. Not now, when things between them were easier.

He caught her eye. For a moment, something lingered in his gaze. A glint of understanding. Maybe even regret. He didn't speak, but it felt like an apology just the same.

When the final longship pushed away from the dock, a chorus of farewells followed. Dozens of oars dug into the fjord in unison, churning up the water. Soon, a wide sweep of ships dotted the horizon, their long hulls cutting west toward the sea. The crowd dispersed, and Eadlyn spotted Oda farther down the beach, arms folded, her expression stony as she stared at her.

She wasn't the only one who noticed.

"Perhaps we should've ordered her onto one of the ships," Erik muttered.

Braan motioned toward the water. "Some of the northern clans haven't passed by yet. We can still toss her aboard."

Kian raised his brows. "Sounds like a dangerous endeavor."

"I'll do it," Heida said, settling her hands meaningfully on her twin axes.

Braan's chuckle was low and dark. The brothers and Kian joined in. Oda's face darkened further when she caught their eyes, and she spun around, storming away from the beach. Eadlyn might have felt sorry for her had she not brought it on herself.

Back at the longhouse, the mood was lighter. The sun shone across the village, hinting at the summer soon to come. With the men occupied and chores finished, the women gathered outside with their various projects. Alys and Nesta arranged chairs in the grass, and the children played nearby.

Eadlyn joined the women, careful not to tangle the threads of her tablet weaving as she sat. She tied one end of the trim to a short pole Alys had driven into the ground and the other end to her belt to keep tension on the warp. She passed the shuttle through, tamped down the row, and turned the tablets as Ranvi had shown her. For the thread, she had chosen blue, gray, and white—colors of the fjord—and while not as intricate as Ranvi's work, it was the first piece she'd done on her own. Each row brought quiet contentment and pride.

"You're getting good at that," Inga said, leaning over to examine her progress.

"*Tahk fyr.*" The thank you still felt new on her tongue, but she used every opportunity to practice.

She wasn't sure which meant more, the compliment or the genuine tone behind it. Her governess growing up had been strict. Not cruel but never kind. And when the noblewomen of Essix offered praise, it was often sugar-laced flattery. A bargaining tool more than the truth.

As they worked, the conversation drifted toward a few budding romances in the village, light laughter shared among the women. This sparked Eadlyn's curiosity. She glanced toward Inga. "How did you and Runar meet?"

A fond smile creased Inga's age-lined face. "Much like you and Aevar did."

Eadlyn paused, shifting her full attention to her mother-in-law.

"I'm from one of the western clans. Jarl Skaldar is my brother," Inga said, setting her work in her lap. "There was bad blood between my father and Runar's, like between Runar and Staegar. Enough that the other clans feared a war would split us all. So Runar's father proposed a marriage between Runar and me."

Another alliance bride.

"My father brought me here to the Gathering when I was seventeen. Because of the strain between our clans, I had never attended before, so I had never met Runar." She peered out toward the fjord, a faraway look in her eyes. "But I still remember seeing him for the first time, standing on the dock, so strong and handsome."

Eadlyn shared a grin with Ranvi and caught a giggle from

Nesta where she and Alys worked on spinning a little farther away.

Inga just smiled.

Ranvi leaned toward her. "I'm sure he was equally smitten."

Inga nodded in happy agreement.

"Were you afraid?" Eadlyn asked, thinking of the terror she had lived with before coming here. The uncertainties must have been just as great for Inga, especially with the tension between their families.

"Yes, but he treated me kindly, and I soon found myself at ease with him."

Like Aevar. "And you fell in love?"

"We did."

The warmth in her voice stirred something in Eadlyn. She had not married for love or even companionship, yet a corner of her heart still desired it. Was it possible for her and Aevar to share the same story as Inga and Runar? Of course, they had more to overcome in their vastly different backgrounds and the scars Aevar carried from the past. Yet, like a tiny ember kept sheltered in a jar, she lifted the hope up in prayer.

Aevar smiled at the way Trygg's laughter echoed through the air as he approached the longhouse. His nephew's voice rose in a tangle of words loud enough to reach halfway across the village. He didn't know anyone as enthusiastic about life as that boy. It was infectious. Untouched. Aevar reached for the Thor's hammer amulet resting against his chest, a habit so familiar he hardly thought about it.

The weight of it pressed against his palm, and for a moment, he considered sending up a silent prayer. A simple wish that the world wouldn't crush the boy's spirit.

But he hesitated. Would the gods even acknowledge him if he made a request on behalf of his nephew?

Eadlyn's words whispered in his mind. *God always hears and answers prayers.* He brushed them away. Even if it were true, he was not Christian. Her God would not hear or answer him.

As he drew near the longhouse and took in the peaceful scene outside, he slowed to a halt. His mother and Ranvi were sitting in the sun. Nearby, Eadlyn knelt beside Trygg and Katla in the grass, her hands resting in her lap as Trygg showed her a rock he'd found. Eadlyn listened with full attention, as if he'd discovered a rare gem. She tried to answer something he'd said and butchered it.

Trygg doubled over in giggles, prompting Katla to do the same. Móthir and Ranvi joined in the mirth, gently correcting Eadlyn's mistake. A few paces away, Alvir wobbled forward on unsteady legs, determined to be part of the moment. Eadlyn straightened as he raised his arms toward her. She lifted him up without hesitation and settled him on her hip.

The sight hit Aevar square in the chest as if his pendant had turned into Thor's true hammer. She looked so natural and comfortable standing there with a child in her arms, the other two at her skirts, almost as if he were seeing a vision of what the future could hold. He tried to take a breath, but his lungs struggled to expand at the ache that grew in his heart.

And yet, icy dread pooled in his stomach. The two battled each other until something brushed his shoulder. He jerked his head around, finding Braan at his side. He banished the tumult within him.

His brother observed the scene, arms crossed. "She'd make a good mother."

Aevar fought a wince, unable to disagree with him. "She would."

Braan said nothing. Only watched until Aevar felt his attention shift to him. "Well, there's only one way to make that happen. Maybe stop treating her like a guest and start treating her like your wife."

The words hit a raw nerve. Aevar straightened his spine. "I won't do that. Not without her consent."

Braan's brow lifted. "Have you asked her lately?"

Aevar shot him a sour look. His brother needed to mind his own business.

Braan held up his hands in surrender. "Fine. Be miserable."

"I'm not miserable."

Braan let out a dry laugh. "Could've fooled me."

Without waiting for a reply, he turned and walked off, muttering something under his breath that Aevar didn't bother trying to catch.

Aevar remained behind, jaw clenched, the weight in his chest morphing into something harsher. Frustration. Shame. Maybe even grief, though he didn't know what for. His attention drifted back to Eadlyn as she bent to hand Alvir over to Ranvi. He sucked in a hard breath, banishing any remnant of the longing that had arisen so fiercely, and forced his gaze away.

He didn't want a wife, and he didn't want children.

The arrangement with Eadlyn worked just fine. She may never have her own children, but at least she could enjoy Erik and Ranvi's. That was enough for both of them.

It had to be.

Mist shrouded the mountains, and a pale light filtered through the clouds as Eadlyn stepped out of the long-house. She adjusted her shawl, breathing in the damp air. The trees had burst into bright green in recent days, spring fully arrived, but the cool, rainy weather had kept her indoors. She'd missed her morning walks.

The clouds overhead still lingered, but they didn't appear heavy with rain, and the faintest glow behind them suggested the sun might yet win the battle. She stepped onto the path toward the fjord, her spirits lifting. As she walked through the village, she exchanged soft smiles with the women tending to their animals or carrying pails. A group of children came dashing up the road, full of shouts and wild energy.

"*Góthan morgin*, Princess!" they chorused as they swept past.

She laughed at their exuberance, and her thoughts drifted as she walked. What would life have looked like if she and Edward had been born in a place like this, children of a smith or a weaver? Would they have been freer? Happier?

But no. Her life was not a mistake. God had crafted her specifically for the time and situation in which He had placed her.

The fjord greeted her like an old friend, the surface glassy beneath the gray sky. Rain had left the sand damp and soft, squelching under her shoes as she stepped to the water's edge. A gentle stillness met her. No wind, no waves, just the slow inhale and exhale of the fjord against the shore. She breathed in the air, cool and clean, and the calmness of the water settled in her soul.

She loved it here.

And not just the fjord, but the village. The longhouse. Her home. In a little over a month, she had settled into her new life. She recalled the anxious days and nights leading up to the alliance. The fear that had clawed at her from the inside. She never imagined finding peace here, and she praised God for the miracle.

After a time in prayer, she turned back toward the village, eager to return to her weaving project. But as she passed the first cluster of buildings, someone stepped into her path. She opened her mouth to greet them, but the words died on her tongue.

Sig.

He stood too close, a gleam in his eye that turned her stomach. Though only the same size as Aevar, he seemed especially large and menacing, blocking her path to the longhouse.

She gripped the edge of her shawl. "What are you doing here?" Though she kept her voice steady, her pulse kicked into a faster rhythm.

He was supposed to be gone. He and his uncle had left weeks ago. Aevar would never have let her walk alone if he'd known this.

Sig shrugged as if his presence were no more alarming than a change in the weather. "I wasn't ready to leave yet."

She darted a glance left and right. The path was empty. "I have work to do."

When she sidestepped to pass him, he shifted, matching her move.

She straightened and lifted her chin. "You need to step aside."

He chuckled, a cruel sound that sent prickles along her arms and neck. "What's the rush? Surely it can't be for Aevar. I doubt he's even thinking of you." He stepped closer, and Eadlyn's breath grew shallow at the way he eyed the entire length of her like a hungry dog. "Everyone could see how much he loved Thora. He couldn't keep his hands off her. You? I haven't seen him touch you once."

Had he been watching them?

He took another step. Too close. She had to back up to keep the distance, her heart pounding now.

His voice slid over her like cold mud. "It must be lonely being married to a man who doesn't want you."

Something hot sparked in Eadlyn's chest, and she glared at him. "I am not lonely. Aevar has been nothing but kind and honorable toward me."

"Oh, I'm sure he's been honorable. So honorable he hasn't treated you as a wife should be treated. I can fix that."

He reached for her.

She bolted, but his hand caught her arm and yanked her forward like she weighed nothing. Her heart lurched as she stumbled into him. His chest hit hers like a wall, solid and unmoving, the rough leather of his jerkin scraping against her palms as she shoved against him.

"You will release me right now. When Aevar finds out—"

"I'm not afraid of Aevar."

Considering what Aevar had done to him during the competitions, he should be. "It is Jarl Runar you should fear. I am under his protection, and he is your king."

For a moment, hesitation wavered in Sig's eyes, but it didn't last. The hungry look returned as he leaned in. She turned her face away from him and fought to gain space to kick him, but he laughed at her efforts.

Then came footsteps, fast and heavy.

Sig shoved her aside just before someone grabbed him from behind. Eadlyn stumbled, catching her balance in time to see Aevar throw Sig to the ground. A fist connected with bone. Aevar dragged Sig up by his jerkin and drove his knee into his ribs. The breath went out of Sig in a sharp wheeze. Before he could draw it back in, Aevar threw him against a wooden pillar with a thud. Holding him there with one hand, Aevar yanked his long seax from his belt and pressed the blade to Sig's throat.

"You *dare* touch another man's wife?"

Sig gasped, his lips curling into a pained smile as if this were all a game to him.

Aevar's voice dropped to a low growl, thick with fury. "I should kill you right now."

"Do it," Sig spat. "My uncle—"

Aevar's hand twitched, and the knife bit. A thin red line appeared on Sig's neck, a drop of blood trailing downward.

Eadlyn shook herself out of the shock that had frozen her to the spot. She didn't know what kind of trouble might come of Aevar killing Staegar's heir, but she did not want any of them to find out. An act like that might set the clans at odds and risk the alliance. Staegar would seize it as the perfect excuse to go to war against Runar. She could not let that happen, even just for the safety of Aevar and his family.

She stepped forward, trembling, and laid her hand on Aevar's arm. Beneath her fingers, his muscles were taut with the grip he had on his knife. "Aevar, no."

His eyes, dark and dangerous, flicked to her. In that moment, she realized she had never seen him truly angry before. Her mouth went dry, but she stood her ground. "It's not worth killing him."

He pinned his fiery gaze back on Sig. His hand tremored as if it took every ounce of strength to stay the blade.

She held her breath.

Then, slowly, he pulled the blade away and stepped back, reaching out his free hand to draw her back with him. Sig slumped against the pillar, blood oozing into his collar.

Aevar pointed the tip of his blade at his face, his voice ice-cold. "Come near my wife again, and I *will* kill you."

Sig swiped at the blood, glancing at the stain on his fingers. His gaze flicked to Aevar, then to her. The way his attention lingered chilled her to the core. Then he shoved away from the pillar and sauntered off as if nothing had happened.

Only after he'd disappeared around the corner did Aevar turn to her. His face was a mask of fury, and his chest rose and fell in sharp breaths. He didn't speak for a moment, just stared at her, his hand still clenched tight around the hilt of his blade.

"Did he hurt you?" The words were low and sharp.

She almost flinched. "No."

"Are you sure?"

"Yes. What you saw is all he did."

He didn't relax. His jaw twitched, and he shot another glare in the direction Sig had gone that burned with the kind of rage that stole the moisture from her throat. What if he somehow blamed her for what had happened?

"I swear to you," she said quickly, "I did not invite or welcome his advances."

His eyes snapped back to hers. Something unreadable rested there, hot and dangerous and heavy with unspoken things. She couldn't tell what it meant. He gave a single stiff nod and slid his knife back into its sheath, the snap echoing too loudly in the stillness. Then he gestured for her to walk ahead of him.

They moved in silence. With every step, the tension rolled off of him like a storm barely held in check. He didn't look at her. Didn't say a word. And that, more than anything, weighed on her. She didn't know what he was thinking. Didn't know if he was angry only at Sig, or if he reserved part of that wrath for her. He wasn't like her father. She knew that. But the silence made her doubt. Just a little.

By the time they reached the longhouse, the uncertainty had stretched her nerves thin. Inga and Ranvi looked up from the hearth when they entered, and their conversation halted at the sight of them.

Inga rose. "What happened?"

"Sig is here." Aevar spat his name like a curse.

Inga's face changed in an instant. Her gaze darted to Eadlyn, but Aevar spoke again.

"Take care of her." He ground the words out and turned, marching out of the hall.

Eadlyn stood frozen, afraid of what he might do. A gentle touch on her arm brought her back. Inga was watching her now.

"What did he do to you?" The whisper of ice in her voice suggested she endorsed any violent actions Aevar might take.

Eadlyn swallowed hard. "Nothing beyond grabbing me, but he threatened worse."

Just saying it caused her stomach to lurch toward her throat. She wrapped her arms around herself as the chill crept back in.

Inga's jaw flexed, but her voice softened. "Come. Sit by the fire."

Flames still smoldered in Aevar's chest, ready to ignite the moment he laid eyes on Sig again. Every part of him burned with the need to hunt the man down and finish what he had started. Had Sig harmed Eadlyn or laid more than a hand on her, Aevar would not have hesitated to take his head off right there in the street. However, since he'd stopped him, simply killing him was not within the law.

Challenging him to a *holmgang* to the death was his next option. A challenge he would have already issued if Sig had been any other man. But the fact that he was Staegar's heir twisted justice into something far more complicated, and Aevar knew better than to make a decision when his blood still roared in his ears.

He strode toward the training field. Kian, his father, and his brothers were there with the huskarls. Ingvald, who had alerted him that Sig had been spotted in the village, lingered nearby. They all turned as Aevar approached.

"Sig put his hands on Eadlyn." The words ripped from his mouth.

Fathir's face darkened. "Just now?"

Aevar nodded.

"Did he harm her?"

"No. But he would have if I hadn't gotten there in time."

Fathir's eyes went hard. "Where is he?"

"I don't know. He slunk off."

"Then we'll find him."

They moved together, a wall of fury cutting a path through the village as Fathir questioned every person they passed. Finally, someone pointed them toward Oda's house. Aevar ground his teeth together. Of course. The *niðingr* had been hiding with her this entire time, nursing his injuries from the Gathering. With the way Aevar's blood pulsed with heat, he was ready to challenge them both.

As they neared the small house Thora and Oda had inherited from their father, they spotted Sig standing outside with Oda. She didn't react when they arrived, but Sig straightened, lifting his chin in bold defiance.

Fathir motioned to Ingvald and Njal. "Seize him."

Sig reached for his weapons but was too slow. The men were on him in a moment, wrenching his arms behind his back and dragging him to face Fathir.

"You assaulted the princess of Essix, *my* daughter-in-law, in my village?"

Sig snorted. "I did nothing. I was only offering what her husband clearly isn't." He sent Aevar a sneering grin. "Before he showed up, the *hórkona* clearly enjoyed it."

Aevar lunged. His fist collided with Sig's face, snapping his head back with a satisfying crack. He reared back to hit him again, but someone grabbed his shoulder. Erik. Though he'd stopped him, his brother's expression said he'd rather take a swing himself. Aevar stepped back, breathing hard in the struggle to keep his anger in check.

Sig spat blood, laughing breathlessly. "My uncle will love hearing about this."

Fathir stepped in, seizing Sig's tunic and pulling him in close. "You think you're safe because your uncle's a jarl? I am *king*. You crossed a line."

Sig didn't blink, his expression holding steady and defiant.

Fathir turned to Aevar and drew him a few steps away. His voice dropped. "If you wish to challenge him, I will back you and deal with Staegar. Eadlyn is your wife. I will let you decide."

Aevar's pulse thundered in his ears. The fire in his lungs demanded vengeance. Demanded blood. But through the fury, reason broke in like an icy wind. One wrong move and Staegar would turn it into a justification for war. Aevar wasn't willing to put Eadlyn, or his people, at the center of that.

He dropped his head, each breath hard and bitter in his throat. "I won't start a war, but I want him gone. Banished from Fjellheim."

They may not be able to keep the banishment in place forever if Sig became a jarl one day, but hopefully, that would be many, many years in the future. With any luck, and if the gods had any sense of justice, he would meet a well-deserved end before that even happened.

Fathir nodded, something proud and grim in his expression. He gave Aevar's shoulder a brief squeeze before turning back to Sig. "You're lucky my son's a better man than you. You'd be meeting the gods otherwise. You are banished from Fjellheim. You're never to set foot on my land again. Unless you'd like to swim home, I suggest you find a boat."

Sig's face twisted, but he said nothing.

"Understood?" Fathir snapped.

"Understood," Sig muttered.

Ingvald and Njal released him. He shrugged his shoulders and straightened his tunic, pausing at Braan's chill voice.

"You better be gone by nightfall, or I'll come drag you to the fjord myself."

"We all will," Erik added, tone deadly calm.

Fathir turned to the huskarls. "Ingvald, watch him. I want confirmation when he's gone."

He dismissed the rest, and they returned to the longhouse. Heida stood at the door, waiting. She scanned their faces as if checking for signs of blood.

"Is he dead?"

Aevar couldn't answer. The fire still lingered in his chest, burning a hole straight through.

Fathir answered for him. "Banished from Fjellheim."

Heida shared a glance with Aevar. Her expression suggested she was thinking of paying a visit to Sig in his sleep. Aevar wouldn't stop her.

Inside, they found Eadlyn sitting by the fire with Móthir and Ranvi. She appeared unhurt, but her eyes…her eyes held fear. That alone nearly unraveled Aevar all over again. Just seeing her. Remembering her held in Sig's grip. Powerless. The rage surged, and he balled his fists.

Fathir spoke first. "I apologize. That should never have happened."

Eadlyn shook her head. "It's not your fault. You didn't know he was here."

"It won't happen again," Fathir assured her. "He's banished and will be gone by nightfall. My men will see to it."

The relief was visible, the tension easing from her shoulders.

But for Aevar, the fire didn't burn out.

He spent the rest of the day at the training field, battering every man who stepped in to spar with him. After a while, Kian suggested he should take a break, but he didn't listen. It was the only thing that kept the anger from driving him to hunt down Sig. Even after Ingvald returned and confirmed Sig had left the village, the fury still clung to him like a second skin.

Night fell, and everyone returned to the longhouse. By now, exhaustion weighed on Aevar, and every muscle ached. But his mind wouldn't settle. When he and Eadlyn retired to their room for the night, he stripped off his gear and went through the motions of bedtime in a daze.

"Would you like me to read tonight?" Eadlyn asked.

"If you want." He realized how cold he sounded, but he had no real desire for her tales tonight.

She paused, a small hitch in her breath.

When he dropped onto his bed, he caught the frown on her face before she turned away, gathering a few parchment pages like she did every night. Guilt pricked at him.

She read softly, her voice barely above a whisper. He tried to listen, but her words were nothing but a distance hum. She didn't read long. After a murmured goodnight, she blew out the lamps and climbed into her bed, leaving Aevar to lie in the dark and stare at the ceiling. His body was heavy, his thoughts heavier. And now, with no sword in his hand and nothing to fight, he couldn't escape the truth.

He had begun to care.

Not just for her safety. Not just for the alliance.

For *her*.

Eadlyn.

Care enough that the threat of harm to her left him barely in control. For the first time in three years, something he had thought long dead surged inside him. It was terrifying, because caring meant he had something to lose again, and he couldn't survive another loss.

A slow breath dragged through his lungs. He forced his eyes shut and reached for the armor he'd spent years building. Maybe if he rebuilt it fast enough, he could pretend this had never happened.

The warm spring air beckoned, fresh grass and damp earth mingling with the bright songs of birds from the forest behind the longhouse. Eadlyn stood at the entrance, gazing out across the village, and a heavy sigh pressed against her ribs. She missed walking to the fjord.

Several days had passed since Sig's banishment, but the thought of venturing out alone still sent a chill creeping up her spine. Everyone assured her Sig was gone, but what if he secretly returned? He'd been in the village for a month without their knowledge. She didn't trust him to abide by the banishment. Not when he had acted as though no consequences would befall him for his actions. Such arrogance was dangerous.

"Is everything all right, my lady?"

She startled, snapping her gaze toward Kian. She hadn't noticed him approaching. The men rarely lingered around the longhouse during the day.

She gave a small shrug. "I miss my morning walks. But ever since…everything, I haven't wanted to risk it."

"Ah. Well, if you'd like, I'd be happy to escort you wherever you'd like to go."

Her heart lifted. "Are you sure? I don't want to take you away from anything important."

Kian grinned with a familiar boyish light in his eyes. "The men will survive without me. Might do them some good, actually. I'm starting to think they fight better when I'm not around to show them up."

A small laugh escaped her, lighter than she'd felt in days.

Together, they set off through the village. Though later than her usual walks, many of the villagers were still tending their chores, and she returned smiles and nods along the way. Children dashed between buildings, and a dog barked nearby. For a few precious minutes, all was normal.

But near the edge of the village where Sig had stepped into her path, a prickle crawled over her skin. She rubbed her arms without thinking.

Kian noticed, and his pace slowed. "This where it happened?"

She nodded.

He peered around, sharp-eyed despite his easy manner. "Good thing Aevar came looking for you when he heard Sig was still around."

Eadlyn hesitated. "Did he say anything? About me welcoming the attention?"

Kian stopped and turned to face her, frowning. "What? No. Of course not. Why would he?"

She let her shoulders sag under a weight she hadn't meant to voice. "He's hardly spoken to me since it happened. I've never seen him so angry. And I can't tell if it's just at Sig...or partly at me too."

They had reverted to those awkward post-wedding days, but even worse. Not only did he not speak to her, he hardly even acknowledged her. She thought of the night he'd teased and tried to rile her. The way he'd looked at her in that moment had almost made her wonder if, perhaps, there was something between them. That night had fed the fragile hope she'd carried, but Sig's assault had snuffed it out like a flame in the wind.

Kian's face softened, his voice low and certain. "We know you're not that kind of woman. Aevar knows it too. It took every scrap of restraint that day to keep him from tearing Sig's head off. He's not angry at you. He's stewing over not being able to finish what he started."

She swallowed hard, praying that was true.

"And," Kian added, "I think…he doesn't know how to be with you. Because of what he's been through."

"Inga told me," she whispered. "About his wife and his daughter."

"I don't think he's ever fully gotten over that."

Eadlyn exhaled, and the ache of it settled deep inside her. She couldn't compete with the memory of a wife he'd loved so dearly. She didn't know why she had let herself hope. It had been foolish. She drew a breath and forced herself to let the longing go or at least shove it back down where it didn't hurt as much. She had so much more than she once dared hope for. Aevar had given her respect, safety, dignity. It had to be enough.

They continued, and the fjord came into view. At the sight of the water, the heaviness in Eadlyn lifted, breath by breath. They walked down to the edge where the wet sand clung to their boots, and the breeze stirred the skirt of her dress. Eadlyn closed her eyes and stood there, letting the peace soak into her soul.

Kian stayed beside her, silent and giving her space with no need to be told. For a few long minutes, they stood like that, the stillness between them easy and companionable. Eadlyn offered a silent prayer of thanks, lifting her heart to God for this moment. For this strange, hard, precious new life He had given her.

When she opened her eyes, she turned to Kian. "Do you ever miss home?"

He smiled, a bit crooked. "No. Not since coming here to Fjellheim. What about you?"

Eadlyn considered it, tucking a strand of hair behind her ear. "I miss the people who made it home." Her thoughts shifted to Edward and Galen. She'd really missed them these last few days. "But no. I don't miss the place itself."

"That's the thing, isn't it? Home's not wood and stone. It's people. And if the people are stubborn enough to adopt you, like these lunatics did with me, well…you're stuck."

A laugh broke from her, light and unforced. "I could think of worse places to be stuck."

"Same," he agreed, nudging a stick with the toe of his boot. "There are far less entertaining places to nearly freeze to death in winter. Fjellheim's a good place with good people."

"It is." She studied him for a moment. "I never asked before, how did you come to be here? You said once that Aevar saved you from Kalgorans."

"Ah. Well, a few years back, the Kalgorans were pushing hard into the north, hitting Nordra and Talta. I headed up there with my uncle's army to help beat them back." His grin turned sheepish. "Thought I was very brave and important at the time."

Eadlyn glanced to the north. "I've heard of the Kalgorans' cruelty and sacrifices. The fighting must have been fierce."

"You have no idea," he said with a half-laugh. "They fight like demons loosed from the underworld. Whatever you've heard, believe it. Anyway, we were ambushed early one morning. The fog was so thick you couldn't see your hand in front of you. I got knocked flat during the fighting. Some big brute of a Kalgoran was ready to run me through."

He shrugged casually, but Eadlyn caught the flash of memory in his eyes. "And then Aevar showed up. He and a few others. Jumped right into the thick of it like madmen. We fought side by side until it was over. We've been brothers ever since. Saved each other's skins more times than I can count."

A wistfulness whispered through Eadlyn. If only she could know Aevar that way. *Truly* know him. Not from a distance. Not with walls between them.

Aevar ran his hand over the horse's ebony coat and bulging midsection. Movement from the foal inside rolled against his palm. Any day now. The mare turned her head and nudged his shoulder, her breath hot through his tunic. He reached up and rubbed the white star on her forehead, and she sighed, leaning into him. Vega had been Thora's horse; one she'd raised from a foal.

She had loved horses. She'd dragged him out here to the stable almost daily. This had been their place. A quiet escape where they talked and dreamed and stole kisses. It smelled the same as it always had—sweet hay, oiled leather, and the earthy musk of the horses— but the memories thickened the air and made it hard to breathe.

A door creaked. Aevar blinked, brushing away the sting in his eyes, and dragged himself back to the present. Edgar, the old thrall who oversaw the stables, joined him at Vega's stall. He had been here for as long as Aevar could remember, as much a fixture of the stable as the worn wood beams and the leather tack hanging on the walls.

"How's our girl?"

Ever since Thora had died, Edgar had become as attached to Vega as Aevar was. Edgar had been the one to teach Thora everything she knew about horses.

Aevar rested his palm against Vega's side one more time. "She's doing well."

Edgar reached in to stroke the mare's shoulder. "I'll keep an eye on her, as always."

"Let me know if anything changes."

Outside, Aevar headed toward the fields. Halfway there, he spotted Kian strolling from the longhouse. "Where have you been?"

Kian gestured back the way he'd come. "Off being useful, as usual. Took your wife for a walk."

Aevar frowned. "A walk?"

"She's wary of going alone now. Figured someone ought to keep her company." He considered Aevar for a long moment. "You know, she'd probably appreciate it if *you* offered to take her in the mornings."

Aevar fought not to wince. The idea of spending more time alone with Eadlyn—hearing her laugh, watching her smile, feeling everything he couldn't afford to feel—made his defenses strain at the seams.

Kian watched him too closely. "Listen, I get it. You've got your reasons, and I know it's painful, but I've got to tell you, I think you're missing out on a real good thing with her."

Aevar gave him a sidelong glance and remained silent.

Kian shrugged. "Just saying." He turned away, but Aevar caught the words muttered under his breath. "I can't stop you from being a *fifl*."

Aevar shot a look at his back, grinding his teeth. First Móthir. Then Braan. Now Kian. He didn't need everyone ganging up on him like this. What happened to all the protectiveness when he'd agreed to marry Eadlyn in the first place?

When he returned to the longhouse that evening, he steeled himself. The women worked together near the fire, preparing the meal as the children darted between benches. Eadlyn met his eye. He held her gaze only briefly, but long enough to catch the uncertainty in it. He turned away, fixing his attention on Erik and Fathir's conversation.

A few moments later, he heard her approach before she appeared. Her expression was tentative, searching his face as if for reassurance. Nothing like the way she'd smiled and interacted with him just over a week ago. The change punched something deep in his chest that ached of longing layered with guilt.

He quickly buried it. He couldn't let himself want what he could not afford to lose.

When she realized he would give her nothing more, resignation claimed her expression. The voice that usually held so much optimism was dull.

"If it's all right with you, I'm going to ask Heida to teach me how to defend myself. I'm tired of feeling defenseless. I've felt it my whole life, and I don't want to live in fear of another confrontation like the one with Sig."

Her tone carried a determined undercurrent.

Aevar nodded. While it would always be his duty to protect her and the alliance, life here did not suit those who could not put up a fight. "That is a good idea."

"*Tahk.*" She dipped her head and walked away without saying another word.

He watched her go. It was what he wanted. Distance. Detachment. Safety. Yet something hollow gnawed at him. He dragged a breath into his lungs, trying to steady the ache, and caught his mother's disapproving look from across the hall.

Eadlyn stirred at the sound of Aevar's voice, low and brief, followed by the soft thud of the door closing. She blinked away sleep and lifted her head, but he was already gone. A sigh slipped past her lips.

At least right after they'd been married, he seemed to tolerate her. Now he couldn't seem to get away from her fast enough. Despite Kian's reassurance, she couldn't shake the nagging suspicion Aevar blamed her for Sig, as if something she had done had made the encounter possible. Everything had changed that day, and no matter how she turned it over in her mind, she found no other explanation.

She sat up and bowed her head, folding her hands in her lap. Her whispered prayers tumbled together, not polished or poetic.

Just a tattered hope tangled with confusion. She wasn't even sure what to ask when it came to Aevar anymore. Only that he might one day stand the sight of her again.

After several minutes, she got up and reached for the long tunic and trousers she'd found in Thora's chest. Heida had said training would be easier in something less encumbering than a dress. A leather jerkin laced over the top, snug but comfortable. She glimpsed herself in the polished metal mirror on the wall and released a soft laugh. Edward would have teased her relentlessly, and Galen would have frowned but then offered to show her how to hold a sword.

After tying her hair back in a quick braid, she left the room, drawn into the usual morning routine. Aevar seemed to notice her from where he was talking with Kian, but his gaze did not linger. A sting bloomed behind her ribs. She scolded herself for it. Since when had she started longing for his attention anyway?

She turned toward the women instead. At least his family had not withdrawn from her. They greeted her as lovingly as ever, and she lost herself in the familiar comfort of practicing Nordric over breakfast.

When the meal finished, she followed Heida outside to the grassy patch along one side of the longhouse. The morning was cool but clear—the kind of air that filled her lungs with crisp freshness. Here, Heida handed her a knife the length of her forearm. It settled into her palm, heavier than it looked, but not unmanageable. She turned it in her hand. The edges had been dulled for training.

"We'll start with this," Heida said. "Once you are comfortable with that, I'll show you how to use an axe."

Eadlyn tightened her grip. The blade pressed against her palm, its weight shifting with each small adjustment of her fingers. She'd never be a warrior like Heida, but if she could walk through the village without fear, that was enough. She had always wanted Galen to train her, but her father hadn't allowed it. At least Aevar had given his blessing despite whatever issue he had with her.

"I appreciate you taking the time to do this," she said.

"You're the princess of Essix and Aevar's wife. It's in my best interest to make sure you don't get killed." Heida gave her a lop-sided smirk. "That, and we all like having you around."

Eadlyn laughed under her breath. Aevar might be an exception. "I'll try not to embarrass you too badly."

"Good." Heida nodded approvingly. "Confidence is the first lesson." She stepped back and motioned. "Show me how you hold it."

Eadlyn adjusted her grip on the knife.

Heida raised a brow and strode over. "We'll work on that."

The crack of training swords rang across the sparring field as Aevar drove Rollo backward in a relentless flurry. The boy, just thirteen, had recently joined the huskarls in training and was learning, but not quickly enough. His shield sagged again, leaving his ribs wide open.

"Keep your shield up," Aevar snapped, the words landing harsher than he'd intended. "It's no use flopping at your side like a broken wing."

Rollo flinched but adjusted, sweat streaking down his flushed face. Yet within minutes, the shield drooped once more. Aevar halted the bout with a sharp breath through his nose and gestured toward the sidelines.

"Ingvald, take over."

As the other warrior stepped in, Aevar strode away, tension knotting his shoulders like rope twisted too tight.

Nearby, Kian leaned on his shield, arms folded and one brow lifted in silent judgment. "Rollo is doing his best. You know he hates to disappoint you."

"Which is why I had Ingvald step in." Rollo was a good kid. He just needed more practice, but Aevar did not have the patience for training today. Better to let Ingvald handle it.

Kian gave him that I-know-you-too-well look. "He's not the only one you've been short-tempered with lately."

Aevar clenched his jaw. The truth of it scraped too close to the surface, and he didn't trust himself to respond. The fact that he was short-tempered only fueled his dark mood. He knew full well it was uncalled for but wasn't keen on too closely examining the cause.

Without a word, he handed his sword and shield off to Kian and strode away from the practice field. Kian called after him to ask where he was going, but he waved him off. He needed to clear his head. Maybe a swim would help. Though the days had warmed, the fjord was still cold. Hopefully, cold enough to shock him back to his senses.

At the beach, he walked to one of the docks. The water stretched before him, dark beneath the midmorning sun. Wind moved across its surface, scattering the reflection of the sky. He pulled off his outer garments and walked barefoot to the edge of the dock, the wood rough beneath him.

The cool breeze gave a taste of what was to come. With a deep breath, he dove in. The icy water struck him like a fist, and he surfaced a moment later with a gasp. The cold clutched his chest, coiling around his lungs and limbs, stealing the air from his body. Each breath burned, but he forced his muscles into motion, treading water and letting it pull the heat and frustration from his blood until the worst of the tightness in his chest loosened. As soon as he could breathe more fully, he struck out toward the middle of the fjord as if his thoughts would stay behind if he pushed far enough.

But they followed.

Eadlyn's soft voice reading at night. Her fingers smoothing her apron dress. The confusion in her eyes.

He swam hard, out past the shallows, into the deeper chill where the water turned black beneath him. His arms ached, and the cold burrowed down to his bones. Only then did he turn and cut back toward the dock, breath coming in harsh pulls. His limbs dragged with effort, and his whole body had numbed. His mind not as much as he'd hoped.

When he reached the dock, Erik waited there, crouched like a cat and grinning. "Cold?"

Aevar huffed a breath, not dignifying the question. Erik offered a hand and hauled him up onto the sun-warmed wood. Water streamed off him, dripping from his hair and limbs. The sun was hot on his skin, but it only made the chill more apparent, a contrast that prickled and burned.

He swiped the water away and reached for his clothes. "What are you doing here?"

"I was passing by and saw you swimming." Erik settled on one of the pilings and leaned over to peer at the water. "I thought about joining you but remembered I like my bones not frozen."

Aevar dragged his tunic over his head, fighting back shivers. "You're going soft."

Erik shrugged and glanced up as a gull flew over them, shrieking. "So how are things with Eadlyn?"

Aevar narrowed his eyes, trying to decide if he was prying or just casually asking. He bristled at the question, his walls going up, but then they crumbled. All the tension and irritation he'd been carrying drained out of him, leaving a sort of heavy uncertainty in their place. With a sigh, he sank down on the post across from Erik. He did not want to talk about Eadlyn, but the truth slipped out anyway. Maybe the cold had cracked something open.

"It's harder than I thought it would be."

Erik studied him, curiosity in his gaze. "How so? She has taken to life here remarkably well. Better than I expected. I've not heard her complain once since we met her. Considering the circumstances, I'd say you are very fortunate."

"That's the problem. I didn't expect her to integrate so well into our family." Aevar lowered his voice. "I didn't expect to be so drawn to her."

Erik's lips twitched as if he found the confession humorous. "Is that not a good thing?"

"I…" A burn at the back of Aevar's throat caused his voice to die as the truth he'd been battling rose to the surface. The words grated, raw from long denial. "I'm afraid to care for her, Erik. I'm afraid that if I let my guard down, I will lose her like I lost Thora."

He swallowed hard. What if the gods heard and made it so? But according to Eadlyn, there was only one God, and He cared for His creation. Could that be true? He banished the thought, unsure of where it had even come from. Now was not a time to tempt fate.

Erik's smile had disappeared, understanding coming to rest heavy on his expression. "We're all afraid of loss. Loving Ranvi and the children terrifies me sometimes. But what's the alternative? A life with no love at all? Just keeping her at arm's length, going through the motions, and growing old in silence? Is that really what you want?"

Aevar winced at the question, not sure he could answer it honestly.

Erik stared out at the fjord as the wind rippled the surface before shifting his focus back to Aevar. "For me, the risk is worth it. Was the time you had with Thora not worth it? Would the time you could have with Eadlyn not also be worth it no matter when or how it ends?"

Pain bloomed sharp and sudden, but Aevar forced himself to sit with it. Forced himself to remember Thora's laugh, the way her eyes had crinkled when she smiled, the tender moments together. He wouldn't trade any of it. Even knowing the end, he would do it all again.

He let his shoulders sag in a kind of surrender. "You're right."

A twinkle returned to Erik's eye. "Of course I am. I'm older than you. I'm always right."

Aevar managed a laugh before Erik's expression turned serious again.

"She's a good woman, Aevar. You've been given a second chance at happiness, and I would not waste it. It would not only rob you, but her as well."

Aevar let that settle, heavier than the frigid water. He had been punishing Eadlyn for his fear. Protecting himself but condemning her to a loveless marriage right alongside him. She didn't deserve that. He could change it if he took his brother's advice.

But would she even be receptive? What if any advancement scared her off?

"What if she is not interested in anything more?"

Erik chuckled, standing. "I do not think you have to worry about that. Woo her, and she will respond. I'm sure of it."

Aevar released a long breath. How did one go about wooing a woman who was already their wife? Whether she welcomed his interest or spurned it, they were still married. That would not change, which meant he had to tread carefully and slowly. Had to keep the feelings that had been building inside him from growing into a heartache that would eat him alive if she did not reciprocate.

Erik crossed the dock to clap Aevar on the shoulder as if he knew what he'd been thinking. "Go, find your wife. Start by showing her you care."

He walked away, the dock creaking as his footsteps faded. Aevar remained sitting, the breeze cutting through his damp clothes. The fear he'd carried for so long wanted to resist his brother's advice and left a cold reluctance at the thought of going to find Eadlyn. But he was tired of it dictating his life. Pushing to his feet, he left the dock and headed toward the longhouse.

He spotted the women in the garden when he arrived, and his pulse thumped harder than seemed reasonable. Eadlyn worked there among the rows, sleeves pushed up, dirt on her fingers. In his fog of agitation this morning, he'd failed to notice the golden yellow dress and red apron she wore. Her braided hair was especially dark and rich against the bright linen.

At the edge of the garden, his mother straightened. "Aevar. A little early in the day for a swim, isn't it?"

He glanced at the wet splotches on his clothing. Typically, the men waited until later in the day after working or sparring to cool off in the fjord.

He shrugged. "I had things to figure out."

He shifted his attention back to Eadlyn. She remained focused on pulling weeds from their sprouting vegetables and didn't acknowledge him. Not that he blamed her after how steadfastly he'd ignored her lately. Guilt pricked his conscience.

"Eadlyn."

Her eyes darted to him, the surprise on her face driving the guilt deeper.

He cleared his throat, his heart trying to choke him with a final protest of fear. There was no going back if he took this step. He swallowed his hesitation. "Have you taken a walk yet today?"

She shook her head.

He gestured to the village. "I'll take you if you'd like."

She hesitated long enough that he braced himself for the polite refusal he deserved and looked at Ranvi. No doubt the two of them had done a lot of talking about his recent behavior. The surprise in her expression shifted to something softer, almost cautious, like the moment before stepping out onto thin ice.

"I would." She straightened and brushed the dirt from her hands as she stepped from the garden.

It left Aevar strangely winded, as if he'd just run a race he hadn't known he was in. He caught an approving nod from his mother. One less weight on his shoulders.

They walked side-by-side back toward the fjord, their steps falling into a rhythm, but neither said anything. The silence pressed between them, making each footfall echo in Aevar's ears. Finally, he asked, "How is your training coming?"

"Well, Heida is intense but a good teacher. She's very inventive when it comes to ways to incapacitate a man."

Aevar gave a low chuckle. "She's a dangerous woman."

Eadlyn smiled, though more slowly than she had with him a couple of weeks ago. "She is that."

"The more you can learn from her, the better."

Her smile faded. "Do you think I'll ever have need of her training?"

Aevar hesitated, the fear of something happening to her trying to snatch his breath. "I hope not."

Down at the shore, they stopped. Eadlyn's gaze swept across the water, the breeze lifting strands of her hair. There was something reverent in the way she viewed it. The way she breathed in the air and the peace that washed over her expression as if all worries disappeared when she saw the water. Despite everything she had left behind, she had found contentment here, never complaining, just as Erik had said. Aevar had never known anyone with that kind of resilience.

She turned to him, and he averted his eyes so she wouldn't catch him staring. She didn't speak right away, but he felt her studying him now.

At last, she said, "I don't know how to swim."

He turned back to her. "You never learned to swim?"

"I never had the opportunity. Or permission."

"Then I will teach you."

Her brows shifted ever so slightly upward. "You would?"

He gave a firm nod, hoping for a day when the doubt he'd created in her healed. "Yes. But not right away. The fjord still has teeth."

They shared a smile, hers tentative but warmer. Aevar let out a slow breath. It was a beginning—a cautious one—but one he'd fight to protect.

evar lit the lamp, its glow spilling across the room as he turned toward the bed. Eadlyn lay still beneath the blanket, her eyes closed, and her face soft in sleep. He watched her for a long moment. His feelings for her had grown in the last few days, faster than he was ready for. It scared him. But he kept choosing to stay the course. If he pulled back now and didn't show her how he felt, she'd never trust him again.

A lock of hair lay across her shoulder, and he found himself reaching for it. He paused but gave in to the desire that had lingered within him since their wedding day and brushed it aside. Soft as silk, just as he'd imagined. He let his fingers rest on her shoulder and traced his thumb over the curve of it.

She stirred beneath his touch, and he said her name. Her eyes blinked open, slow and unfazed. She didn't startle anymore. A sign, he hoped, that she felt safe here now.

"*Góthan morgin,*" he murmured.

She echoed him in sleepy Nordric, and he smiled at the way she formed the sounds. She was getting better at it. He withdrew his hand, but the warmth of her skin stayed with him. As she yawned and sat up, he left the room as was their routine.

When she joined the family a little while later, she wore a pale cream dress and green apron. She'd left her hair long and loose, tempting him more than ever to run his fingers through it. Ranvi had been braiding it for her in the mornings. She took her seat, and Ranvi joined her, fingers weaving the strands. Katla climbed onto the bench beside them, pointing and chattering as Ranvi worked in beads and tiny ornaments. Eadlyn listened patiently, smiling as the little girl spoke.

Aevar didn't realize how long he'd been watching until someone bumped his arm. He whipped his head around to find Kian beside him, grinning like an idiot.

"Enjoying the view?"

Aevar shoved him away. "Quiet."

Kian chuckled, undeterred. "Don't let me stop you."

Aevar ignored him as he turned back to watch Ranvi finish the braid.

After breakfast, Aevar and Eadlyn left the longhouse for their morning walk. This was fast becoming Aevar's favorite part of the day. They spoke more now, sharing about their childhoods and lives before the alliance. But the more she revealed of her past, especially her father, the deeper Aevar's anger burrowed. The man had stolen so much from her. Dying in a drunken stupor, while not an honorable or glorious death, had been far too merciful a punishment. He'd deserved to suffer more. Especially since it sounded like Eadlyn had been more prisoner than princess before his death.

He hoped she did not feel that way now. She'd given up her home, her brother, and her friends to come here. Had there been more?

"Did you have any suitors? Anyone you left behind because of the alliance?"

Eadlyn smiled, though a sad sort of one. "None who saw me as anything more than a political advantage. My father made personal connections difficult."

A complicated mix of relief and sadness warred in Aevar's chest that she'd never had that connection before, but something in her expression shifted, wistful and faraway.

"There was this one ealdorman's son. I met him when I was thirteen and was smitten. I used to imagine him rescuing me from the palace." Her expression changed to something more of amusement and old embarrassment. "He married not long after. I was heartbroken. However, when I saw him again a few years later, I realized what he possessed in outward appeal he sorely lacked in character."

Aevar sent her a playful grin. "So no lingering torch for the dashing ealdorman's son?"

She blinked as if caught off guard by his teasing, but another slow smile pulled at her lips. "Not even a flicker."

Down at the fjord, they fell into silence. Eadlyn often prayed here, quiet and contemplative, her face turned toward the breeze. Aevar let the stillness stretch between them, watching her take in the view, peace softening her features. He'd have to bring her out on the boats someday. But first, he should teach her to swim.

After a time, she asked, "How far are we from Staegar's village?"

He moved beside her, following her gaze toward the far distance where the fjord disappeared around a bend. A dip in the cliffs marked the beginning of a valley where Staegar dwelt. "He has outbuildings for trade and shipbuilding at the shore too far to see from here. Ormvik, his main settlement, is a couple of miles inland."

She rubbed her arms, unease creeping across her face. Aevar stepped closer, tempted to reach out in reassurance, but he held back.

"You don't have to worry about Sig. He would be a fool to come back. It does not matter who he is, the consequences would be severe, and the whole village knows to be on the lookout."

And if he did return, Aevar would kill him.

Eadlyn's shoulders relaxed a little.

Wanting to lift the weight entirely, he gestured back toward the village. "Come. I want to show you something."

They walked to the far side of the village, where the stable sat. Aevar had debated the idea of bringing her here because of the memories, but if he wanted to build something real with her, he couldn't keep avoiding the past.

Inside, he led her to the stall where Vega had birthed her foal, a dark brown filly, just over a week ago. "This is Vega and Eydis."

Eadlyn's face lit up as the foal bounced to the front of the stall, ears twitching as she sniffed at her hand. With a sudden burst of energy, Eydis leaped back and tried to buck, drawing a musical laugh from Eadlyn. The little animal had spunk. It was as if she'd inherited Thora's spirit.

Vega stepped forward, nudging her offspring aside with maternal grace. Eadlyn stroked the mare's neck. "They're beautiful. Are they yours?"

Aevar ran his hand down the length of the horse's face. "Vega belonged to Thora."

Eadlyn went still. The silence between them shifted, uncertain yet respectful. But Aevar let himself smile, finding that talking about Thora was not as hard as he'd expected.

"She loved horses."

"There is much to love." Eadlyn scanned the other stalls. "Is Hiroc around? I haven't seen him since I got here. Back at Kenwich, riding was one of my few escapes."

"He's out in the pasture and doing well. I'll take you riding sometime, if you'd like."

Her face lit up at the offer, and he held her gaze until she turned away shyly.

"Thank you. For bringing me here." The sincerity in her voice held an understanding that this wasn't the easiest decision for him.

They spent another few minutes enjoying the horses before leaving the stable. Near the longhouse, they parted ways—her going inside to join the women while he headed toward the training field to find his brothers and Kian.

When he arrived, Aevar found his father watching the warriors spar. He joined him, focusing on Rollo, who was finally learning to keep his shield up.

"You and Eadlyn seem closer," his father said, still facing the ring.

Aevar glanced back toward the longhouse. "I hope so. But I don't want to rush her."

"You care for her then?"

"I do." He let out a slow breath. "I don't even know when or how it happened. But when Sig threatened her…" He trailed off, the memory igniting a familiar flame. The fierce protectiveness he'd experienced that day was not something he had felt since Thora.

Fathir turned to face him. "I'm glad you are pursuing her. She is a good woman."

"Erik said the same. You're both right." He took a breath as the weight of it all came to rest in his mind. "There are still times I fear I'm going to lose her."

Fathir's expression held understanding. "You were too young to remember, but we almost lost your mother one winter. She came down with fever that kept her in bed for many days. There was nothing I could do but wait. I did not think she would pull through." He sighed, his voice lower. "The fear never truly leaves, but it teaches you not to waste the time you have."

Aevar took that in, letting it settle in his mind. It was a hard lesson, but he was learning.

"Speaking of not wasting time," Fathir's eyes had taken on a sly glint, "your mother mentioned they were taking the children out to gather strawberries. Might be wise to give them an escort. In case of bears."

Aevar grinned. How could he say no to an excuse to spend more time with Eadlyn?

Basket in hand, Eadlyn walked alongside Ranvi and Inga outside the village as sunlight streamed down on the path before them. Trygg and Katla raced ahead through the grass, Trygg brandishing his wooden sword. Katla let out a high-pitched squeal when he lunged at her and shouted something about a troll. Eadlyn shared a laugh with the women as the little girl dashed back to join them, away from her brother's antics.

At the edge of a wide meadow, they fanned out to look for strawberries. Trygg, his troll battle forgotten, grabbed berries by the handful and stuffed them into his mouth. In contrast, Katla was precise and proud of her task, carefully dropping each berry into one of the woven baskets.

Eadlyn knelt next to a small patch, tasting a few herself. They were sun-warmed and bursting with sweetness. She'd never had them fresh from the plant before.

Alvir toddled over a few minutes later, his lips stained pink. He reached for Eadlyn's basket with sticky fingers, but Ranvi caught his hand before he snatched more.

"Wait until he and Trygg are both running," she said, guiding Alvir back toward her. "There won't be a single berry left for the rest of us."

Inga laughed, her voice light with memory. "When my boys were small, they'd sneak off to gorge themselves and ruin their appetites. There were entire summers we struggled to fill a basket."

Eadlyn smiled to imagine Aevar as a mischievous boy shadowing his brothers, mouth stained with berries.

As if her thoughts had summoned him, Trygg's voice rang out across the meadow. "Aevar!"

Eadlyn wasn't sure why, but something in the way he strode toward them captured her attention. Confident yet relaxed, the sun gleaming on his weapons and somehow making his gray-blue tunic more vivid than earlier. She considered the men in Essix she might have married, and none of them held the same appeal.

Catching herself staring, she dropped her attention to her basket. But Trygg raced past, bringing her eyes up again. When the boy reached Aevar, he jabbered about the troll. Aevar knelt to meet him, responding with mock gravity and praising his courage.

"A great warrior," he said, tousling the boy's hair.

Trygg puffed out his chest, sword raised to face the invisible foe.

Inga grinned up at him. "Come to eat our berries, have you?"

Aevar chuckled. "Not this time. I came to keep watch for bears." He glanced at Eadlyn as he said it, lingering for a beat longer than necessary. Then he turned back to Trygg and switched to Nordric, telling the boy how bears loved strawberries, especially the ones already in a person's belly. He poked Trygg's stomach.

The little boy released a shrieked giggle before waving his sword in the air. "I'll kill the bear!"

He ran off, grunting as he waged imaginary battle. They watched and laughed, though Eadlyn noticed Aevar's gaze slip toward her again. She got the distinct impression his excuse about bears was only that. Even so, she darted a wary look at the trees rimming the meadow. Excuse or not, she welcomed the safety he brought. A couple of months ago, she might have laughed at the notion that she would equate his presence with safety.

The women returned to gathering while Aevar remained nearby, entertaining Trygg by growling and stomping around like a great beast. At one point, when Eadlyn laughed at their antics, Aevar sent her a smile that stopped her breath. It was the unguarded, carefree smile she had been longing for this whole time. Something had changed since the morning he found her in the garden. She didn't know what, but the difference in him was obvious.

When Katla tired of the berries, she tugged on Eadlyn's hand and asked to go pick flowers instead. Happily, Eadlyn followed, helping the girl gather white, yellow, and orange blooms from the edges of the meadow. The children's acceptance of her—running to her, pulling her along—meant more than she thought it ever would.

Aevar stayed near, walking a loose circle around the outer edge of the meadow and eyeing the tree line. Protective and quiet. Bending to help Katla reach for a tiny yellow flower, Eadlyn sensed his presence behind her even before he spoke.

"I don't think you have any of these yet."

She straightened and turned, startled to find him so close. He held out three delicate wildflowers with long blue petals and golden centers.

Her breath caught. "They're beautiful."

"They usually bloom higher in the mountains," he said. "It's rare to find them here."

She reached out to take them. Their fingers brushed, and the contact sent a small, bright spark along her skin like the one she'd experienced on their wedding day when they'd first held hands.

"*Tahk*," she said softly.

His eyes were steady on hers, serious in a way that made her stomach flutter.

She dropped her attention back to the flowers.

"Pretty!" Katla gasped, reaching for the petals.

Eadlyn knelt again, letting the girl admire them while she collected herself. When she lifted her gaze again, Aevar had already turned away, retreating with the same easy stride. She let her focus linger on his back. She wasn't a naïve young girl to be undone by a simple flower. And yet...

She shook her head to clear it. She didn't even know if Aevar meant it as anything more than a friendly gesture, despite how he'd looked at her. Despite how her own heart had reacted at his gaze. He might still distance himself from her. She should not leave herself vulnerable. Not yet.

adlyn stepped out of the bedroom to find the air in the longhouse unusually charged. Trygg's words blended together so quickly she struggled to catch the meaning of them. That wasn't unusual, but the men were also energized.

She made her way to the table where Ranvi was waiting, comb in hand. While Eadlyn had tried braiding her own hair some mornings, she still struggled to create a style on her own. She greeted her sister-in-law and sat, letting Ranvi work.

Out of the corner of her eye, she noticed Aevar watching. She'd caught him doing that more often. Watching her from across the room, during meals, while she spoke to the children. Ever since the day in the meadow, it had happened more and more frequently. And every time, her heart fluttered in a way she didn't fully understand yet.

But this morning his attention was divided.

She glanced at Ranvi as she finished brushing. "What's going on? Everyone seems restless."

Ranvi sighed as she separated a section of Eadlyn's hair. "The men have decided to set up a game of *knattleikr*."

"*Knattleikr*?" Eadlyn repeated the unfamiliar word.

Erik answered from farther down the table, his voice brimming with enthusiasm. "A ball game. A test of strength, and wits, and skill."

Ranvi tugged on Eadlyn's hair as she braided a portion of it. Though Eadlyn could not see her face, exasperation tinged her voice as she replied to her husband, "Try not to break anything this time."

Eadlyn raised a brow. "Break something? As in…bones?"

While the men acted as if it were of no consequence, Ranvi answered plainly, "Yes."

Eadlyn gave Aevar a look, but he waved it off.

"Don't worry. It has been years since anyone has been killed during one of our games."

Killed? "Is that supposed to comfort me?"

He shrugged, unbothered. "I'll make sure I don't die."

"I certainly hope so. How do you expect me to explain to my brother that the alliance collapsed because you were killed playing a ball game?"

He chuckled, that familiar rumble softening the tension in her chest. "It won't. I promise."

She wasn't sure how he could make such a promise, so she whispered a silent prayer for his protection.

They ate breakfast, though Eadlyn found herself too unsettled to enjoy it. Across from her, Trygg couldn't sit still long enough to chew, excited beyond control at the idea of seeing his father play. Erik egged him on with boasts of how he was going to defeat everyone.

After a while, Braan rolled his eyes. "You do remember it's a team sport, right?"

Erik grinned. "He doesn't need to know that."

When the meal ended, the men filed out of the longhouse to prepare for the game, goading each other along the way. Trygg scampered after them. The silence they left behind made the hall seem strangely hollow.

Ranvi rested a reassuring hand on Eadlyn's shoulder. "Don't worry. When it's just the men of the village, it usually doesn't get too violent. It's when visiting clans are involved that things get wild."

Eadlyn did her best to release the nervous energy building inside her.

Once they finished morning chores, the women gathered baskets with weaving and spinning, though Eadlyn didn't know how she would focus on a project. In the same open field where the earlier competitions had taken place, the men were assembling in groups—Runar's huskarls alongside villagers like Alrik and Tallak. The women took seats in the shade of an awning someone had set up. Ranvi spread out a blanket for Katla and Alvir, who settled into their own little world of dolls and wooden animals. Trygg joined them, still chattering.

A moment later, Eadlyn spotted Aevar and Erik striding toward them. Before they reached the shade, they stripped off their tunics. She averted her eyes.

Ranvi leaned toward her, voice low and mischievous. "He's your husband. It's your right to admire."

Eadlyn's cheeks flamed. She ducked her head, praying Aevar hadn't noticed. He didn't say a word as he approached, just dropped his tunic beside her chair and slipped off the hammer pendant he always wore, placing it on top. Still flustered, Eadlyn only glanced at him.

On the other side of her, Erik hooked an arm around Ranvi's waist and gave her a solid kiss. "Wish me luck."

"Good luck."

Eadlyn, trying to look anywhere but at them, found Aevar again. He was watching her. Intently. And when her eyes met his, his gaze dropped momentarily to her lips.

Her heart tripped over itself.

And then, just like that, he gave her a quick smile and turned to walk back to the field. A slow breath leaked from her lungs in relief. Or was that disappointment? Because she had the oddest urge to call him back. Instead, she whispered another prayer for his safety.

They all sat down, and Eadlyn reached for the rumpled pile Aevar had left by her chair. The linen was still warm against her fingers from his body heat. She set the pendant in her lap and neatly folded the tunic. Then she nestled it back down in the grass and laid the pendant on top.

On the field, two separate teams had formed, facing each other.

Next to her, Ranvi said, "Looks like we'll be cheering for opposite teams." Her eyes sparkled with friendly competition.

Eadlyn scanned the players. Erik and Braan stood on one side. Aevar and Kian on the other. A spark of competitive fire lit inside her. "So it does."

Near the edge of the field, Runar stood watching.

"Not playing?" Inga called from her chair.

"I think I'll watch."

Her face said she didn't quite believe him.

A moment later, Heida joined them. She had Braan's tunic with her and draped it over the back of the empty chair on the end as she sat down. Focusing once more on the men, Eadlyn found each carried a sort of club-like stick. Erik stood at the center of his team, facing Aevar. Eadlyn didn't even realize he had a ball in hand before he hurled it at Aevar. Lifting his bat, Aevar struck the ball and sent it flying over the other team's heads. Every man on the field charged for it as if the fate of their gods depended on it.

From that moment on, chaos reigned as both teams fought for possession of the ball. Tackles, shouts, curses, flying mud and flailing limbs—all of it a blur. Eadlyn flinched as they crashed into each other and hit the ground with hard thuds. It looked more like battle than sport. At times, she peeked through her fingers, unable to fully watch.

But as the game progressed, as Ranvi and Heida shouted encouragement, as laughter and roars echoed across the field, Eadlyn's hesitance melted into something else. When Aevar scored a goal, she found herself standing and cheering, letting her voice join the others without shame.

At the end of the first hour, one man from Aevar's team left the field clutching his shoulder. Another limped off not long after. Runar sighed. Wordlessly, he stood from where he'd sat down by Inga and shed his layers.

As he strode onto the field, Eadlyn caught the way Inga's face glowed with appreciation. Ranvi noticed as well, and they shared a giggle.

Inga lifted a brow at them. "What? Admiring your husband is not just for young women."

When Runar joined Aevar's side, Erik called it cheating. Aevar shouted back that they were still down a man, and the game continued.

It stretched into the afternoon, the sun arcing overhead. More players hobbled off, none seriously hurt, but not unscathed either. Alys and Nesta brought a basket of cheese and berries, which the women shared under the shade while the men paused only to drink from a water bucket before returning to the fray. Eadlyn never touched her weaving, unable to tear her attention from the field.

By the time the sun began brushing the mountaintops with gold, Aevar's team pulled ahead by a single point, ending the game with cheers and laughter and more than a few bruises. Eadlyn clapped, breathless as she sank back in her chair. Her heart pounded as if she'd played right alongside them. As the men grouped together in a sweaty, muddied cluster, she scanned the crowd and found Aevar. He caught her gaze and sent her a grin—one that said *see, I survived*—and then vanished into the others as they headed for the fjord.

Inga rose. "Well, we best go prepare the bandages and salves so we're ready when they get back."

Eadlyn bent to gather Aevar's tunic, making sure his hammer pendant did not fall. She ran her fingers over the knotwork ridges and breathed a prayer of thanks to God for His protection over Aevar today and asked that one day he would seek the truth. Putting them in her basket, she joined the women as they walked back to the longhouse.

Along the way, Ranvi leaned into her. "You enjoyed that."

"No." The denial sprang from Eadlyn's lips. The people of Essix would be scandalized to think of their princess enjoying such a violent sport. And yet, she couldn't deny that her own blood still thrummed with the thrill of watching Aevar play. She tried to stifle a smile, but it broke out anyway. "Well, maybe a little."

Back at the longhouse, Alys and Nesta fetched fresh water while Inga set baskets of healing supplies on one table. Though it took a while for the men to arrive, their rowdy voices reached the hall before they did. It sounded like Braan and Kian still argued about whether it was cheating for Runar to have joined mid-game, but they were grinning as they came through the doors.

Eadlyn eyed them now that they'd washed the grime away. Bruises and abrasions darkened their skin in places, along with some fresh blood. Aevar's hair was wet, and a thin line of blood traced down from a cut near his hairline. She tried not to stare at the way water beaded on his chest. However, she remembered what Ranvi had said and allowed herself a longer look.

The men took seats along the benches for the women to examine them. While Eadlyn had never cared for any serious wounds, she had tended both herself and Edward many times after their father's drunken rages, so she knew what to do for simple cuts and bruises.

When Aevar sank down, a wince crossed his face. She could only imagine how sore and exhausted he must be after so many hours of intense game play, but he gave her a sort of lazy smile that made her insides flip. She reached for a bowl of water and a clean cloth.

Across the table, Kian heaved a loud sigh. "I guess I'll languish here with no wife to tend me."

Inga lightly cuffed him on the side of the head as she passed. "Be patient. I'll get to you."

Everyone laughed, and Eadlyn focused her attention on Aevar. She started with the blood on his face, memories returning of when she'd done the same during the Gathering. Had there been something between them even then?

"So all these heroic scars I thought came from battle, are they actually from playing *knattleikr*?"

He chuckled. "Not all. But this will be the second one Braan's given me."

His brother snorted. "He had the first one coming."

Eadlyn scanned the collection of scars on Aevar's face. "Which one?"

He touched a scar on his chin.

She glanced over at Braan. "And how did that happen?"

"Well, this *veslingr* tried to creep up behind me while I was practicing and got a sword to the chin."

"I was eight," Aevar muttered.

"Old enough to know not to sneak up on a man while he's practicing."

"Not sure I would have called you a man."

"I was thirteen. Close enough," Braan shot back.

More laughter rose from the group, and Eadlyn kept working. She moved to a patch of raw skin on Aevar's shoulder, cleaning it gently before reaching for a small jar of salve. As she smoothed it over the wound, his fingers skimmed along her arm.

She froze. Her heart skipped a beat and fluttered on. This was the first time he'd touched her affectionately. When she looked up, he was watching her, waiting. There was no mistaking the intent this time. The flowers, the attention, the way he'd interacted with her lately—they weren't just friendly gestures. He was seeking more. While she had harbored the fragile hope that someday they would share a deeper relationship, this new possibility of it caused butterflies to erupt in her belly. She felt a tentative smile slip out and dropped her attention back to her work, though she found it much harder to focus now.

From the corner of her eye, she caught the pleased smile that spread across Aevar's face, and deep in her chest, something unfolded, warm and new.

The echoing call of a horn cut through the air, halting Eadlyn's work. She looked up from the garden, her fingers still tangled in the roots of a stubborn weed. Around her, the other women paused as well. Trygg, who had been galloping up and down the rows swinging his wooden sword, stopped midbattle cry.

"That's from the southern lookout." Ranvi shielded her eyes and scanned the horizon.

Inga squinted toward the trees. "Might be travelers from one of our other settlements."

Eadlyn, too, peered out over the village but found nothing amiss. "Is it cause for concern?"

Inga shook her head. "No. If it were a threat, the signal would have been different. And everyone would be armed by now."

The moment settled back into weeding and chatting, but Eadlyn kept glancing toward the road with growing curiosity and maybe a little apprehension despite Inga's reassurance. The air carried a faint tension, like the hush before a storm. Whatever group warranted a signal horn would surely bring some excitement.

Several minutes later, the sound of riders approaching rose above the hum of the village. Shouts echoed. Eadlyn stood and followed Inga and Ranvi out of the garden as a group appeared. Aevar, Runar, and a few huskarls marched at the head, guiding them toward the longhouse. Eadlyn scanned the strangers behind them, realization striking her. These men were not Nords; they were Essian. Then the man in the center captured her attention.

She gasped, her heart leaping. "Galen!"

Aevar and the others parted to let her pass as she rushed to meet him. Galen was already dismounting, and she flew into his arms the moment his boots hit the ground. His embrace wrapped around her in an instant, strong and familiar. Worn leather and the tang of mail enfolded her like home. For a moment, she pressed her face to his shoulder and just breathed, fighting back an onslaught of tears.

When she stepped back, Galen's piercing gaze swept over her from head to toe as if expecting bruises or heartbreak. No doubt he noticed the moisture still pooling in her eyes, but she met his examination with a smile.

"You've turned into a Nord," he said at last. She couldn't tell whether he was impressed or dismayed.

She laughed, brushing the garden dirt from her apron. "I guess I have." She took in the other riders—Essian guards and a line of wagons behind them. "What are you doing here?"

"We brought some of your belongings from Kenwich, as well as the first shipment of grain." He gestured to the wagons, and his attention shifted to Runar standing close by. "There are also merchants interested in trade now that an alliance has been established."

"Your merchants are welcome. My men will show them where they may set up."

Runar issued instructions to two of the huskarls. As the main caravan rolled away, his attention returned to Galen and the remaining guards. "You may stay with my huskarls during your visit. Ingvald will show you to the men's quarters. We have thralls to tend your horses and unload the wagons."

At the mention of his name, Ingvald stepped forward. At least he was one of the few who knew passable Aerlish.

As the men prepared to follow, Eadlyn turned to Runar. "If it's all right, I'd like Galen to stay here at the longhouse as my guest."

He nodded without complaint. "Of course."

But Galen hesitated. "Oh, that's not necessary."

He always grew uncomfortable with anything that elevated him above his station as a guard, yet Eadlyn insisted. "I'd really like for you to be here and get to know Aevar and his family."

He relented with a grunt. "Very well. Thank you."

Once everything was settled, they led him inside the longhouse, where Inga welcomed him with the graceful hospitality Eadlyn had come to admire. Galen scanned the interior, his focus drawn to the carved pillars and rafters before snagging on the weapons displayed near the entrance.

"It's impressive," he said.

They showed him to a chamber across the hall from the family rooms. Meanwhile, Aevar and his brothers carried Eadlyn's things inside from the wagon. Galen watched them closely, and his eyes narrowed when they brought the chests into the room she shared with Aevar. His fingers twitched at his sides, as if he wanted to step between them and the door.

As soon as they finished, Eadlyn made formal introductions. Leeriness lingered on both sides, but she had confidence it would fade with time. Once that was done, she turned to Galen and motioned to the doors.

"Would you like to take a walk with me?"

"Of course, my lady." She sensed his shared eagerness for a chance to talk privately.

They turned to leave, and Eadlyn traded a glance with Aevar. Something protective rested on his face. His gaze shifted, growing more guarded, and Eadlyn realized Galen was giving him the same impenetrable glower he reserved for untrustworthy nobles and overeager suitors. She stifled a laugh. These two would take work.

Outside, she led Galen along the path she and Aevar often walked in the mornings. The familiar crunch of gravel beneath their shoes mingled with the low murmur of village life. Now that they were alone, Galen's shoulders relaxed, and his stride eased as the tightness in his jaw faded. Still, his eyes flicked from face to face as they passed, a familiar habit of measuring threats. A woman tending dyed wool paused to eye them curiously, her hands stained crimson to the wrists. Galen offered a polite nod, though his fingers brushed instinctively toward the sword at his side.

"Any word or threats from Waelon?" Eadlyn asked, drawing his attention. So much could have happened in the weeks since she'd left her brother and Essix behind.

"Not a peep, and our spies haven't reported any suspicious activity. Sounds like they're too busy trying to fend off Nord raids." He gave her a pointed look.

A quiet confirmation settled deep inside Eadlyn. "So the alliance was the right choice then."

Galen's expression remained keen. "Was it?"

"Yes." No doubt or hesitation tugged at Eadlyn, only a comfortable surety in her answer.

He continued to watch her as if waiting for her to break down with the truth. She didn't blame him. She'd spent so many years putting on a brave face when things were hard. But being able to share the truth of her life here brought deep joy and thankfulness.

"I hardly dared hope for such an outcome, but I am happy here. Truly. Happier than I ever was in Kenwich."

A fisherman passed them, a bucket sloshing at his hip, and the pungent odor hit them both. Galen wrinkled his nose but refocused on her, clearly not convinced.

"And your husband?" He said the word as if it left a foul taste, shooting a glance over his shoulder like he expected to find Aevar skulking in the shadows behind them. "How is he treating you?"

"Very well. Honestly, I think he's treating me better than most Essian lords I might have married would have." She paused, trying to be delicate. "He has not forced me into the role of a wife. He's been nothing but honorable since we wed. We are friends right now…becoming more."

She thought of Aevar's growing affection toward her, and the way his fingers had traced along her arm after the *knattleikr* game the other day. Her heart fluttered even now and drew a smile to her lips. She tried to dampen it, Galen's gaze resting heavily on her, but failed miserably.

After a long moment of observation, his brows rose, shock edging his tone like an accusation. "You're actually falling for him."

Heat crept into her cheeks, and she ducked her head. "Yes."

He appeared caught between relief and disappointment. "So I don't need to find a way to sneak you out in the night?"

"No, you don't."

He grunted somewhat unhappily. "I was looking forward to that."

She laughed. "Sorry to disappoint."

They rounded a bend in the path, the fjord becoming visible.

Galen sighed in resignation. "Well, I guess I'm glad to be disappointed and proven wrong in this instance. I did not think you would find such care."

"A lot of notions we had about Nords back in Essix I've found to be wrong, at least here amongst Aevar's family and people. There have been those who've shown opposition to the alliance and to me, but the majority have treated me kindly and with respect. Aevar's family has been wonderful from the start." Happiness welled up in her chest. "And Aevar even lets me read Scripture to him every night."

Galen's brows shot up. "How did you convince him to do that?"

"I didn't. He asked me to. I think it was idle curiosity at first, but now…I hope he is at least intrigued by it. It has given me much hope that God is working in his heart. So, I would like you to give him a chance and get to know him while you're here."

He hesitated, though Eadlyn could tell it was more for show. "We shall see."

Now that she'd assured him of her wellbeing, Eadlyn shifted the conversation to other important matters. "How is Edward?"

If only her brother were here too. For a brief heartbeat, a dart of pain pierced her. There would likely never be a reason for Edward to visit Nordra, so unless she traveled to Essix, she would probably never see him again. But she pushed the thought away. Now was not the time to mourn such things. Not with Galen here.

"He misses you. That much is certain. Oswin keeps him busy with matters of state. He balks at the responsibility...but he'll get there."

Though not the glowing report she had hoped to receive, as long as he was well, she was thankful. After all, she'd only been gone a couple of months. He still needed time to adjust to her absence and his throne.

"Did he send any letters?"

Galen's mouth twitched in something like a wince. "Sorry, no."

"Oh." Disappointment sank into her, though she shouldn't have been surprised. Edward had always hated sitting still long enough to write anything. "Well, I'll write a letter of encouragement for you to take back to him."

He needed it more than she did at this point.

"I'm sure he'll be eager to read it. He did send along silver for you. Since there was no agreed-upon bride price, he wanted to make sure you had something should you need it. It's hidden under a false bottom in the largest chest."

Though she did not need the silver, she appreciated the gesture. "Make sure to thank him for me."

"And—" Galen reached into his jerkin and pulled out a thick bundle of folded and sealed parchment. "I know it's not from Edward, but I do come bearing a letter."

When he handed it to her, she recognized the script on the outside, and her earlier disappointment faded. "Brother Winstan!"

"He said it was a long one. Full of blessings and wisdom and all that."

She laughed. "That sounds like him."

She held the letter close to her chest. It might not be her brother's words, but these would be even more encouraging.

earty laughter and good-natured insults echoed through the hall as Eadlyn stepped from the bedroom, drawn by the cheerful din. The men were gathered around the tables awaiting breakfast. Even Galen, who had seemed so stiff and wary only yesterday, stood among them, listening to Kian exaggerate a story with dramatic gestures while the others jeered and laughed.

Eadlyn paused for a moment to watch, smiling to herself. The slow melting of mistrust over the past day and night had taken time and effort, but the results spoke for themselves. The alliance wasn't just holding; it was growing roots.

A chorus of good mornings greeted her as she joined them, standing next to Aevar. His fingers grazed the back of her hand. She found his smile warm and relaxed. His gaze settled on the long, simple braid over her shoulder. He wouldn't get to watch Ranvi fix her hair this morning. But he didn't seem to mind as he reached up and took the end of her braid between his fingers, running his thumb over the woven strands.

Heat rose in her cheeks, and she looked away to hide it only to find Galen watching them. His expression was unreadable, though less severe than the day before. Maybe grudging acceptance was the best she could hope for. At least for now.

Just then, Trygg clambered onto the table and brandished his wooden sword at Galen like a tiny warlord. "You look like a troll!"

Laughter erupted, and Galen eyed them suspiciously before focusing on Eadlyn.

"What did he call me?"

She coughed into her hand to hide a grin. "He said you look like a troll."

Galen considered Trygg for a long beat and turned to Erik. "Well, you can tell him he looks like a baby rat."

Erik's laugh boomed out, and he relayed the insult with great delight.

Trygg's eyes rounded, his mouth falling open. "I do not!"

Erik smirked, tousling his son's hair. "You kind of do. Now off the table."

Trygg hopped down in a huff, muttering about trolls and rats and promising vengeance. He was still giving Galen dirty looks when they sat for breakfast, much to everyone's amusement. The men dominated the conversation, and Eadlyn was happy just to listen. If Galen grew to trust and see Aevar and his family the way she did, he would take that understanding back to Essix, and that would only strengthen the alliance.

Then, inevitably, the conversation shifted to combat. Sword styles, sparring mishaps, the time Aevar's cousin had knocked himself out by tripping over a chicken.

Eventually, Galen leaned across the table and pinned Aevar with a steady look. "You know, we never established whether you were worthy of Eadlyn."

Aevar sent him a lazy smile. "Is that a challenge?"

"Maybe."

"Very well. Challenge accepted. Swords and shields?"

Galen nodded.

Eadlyn set her cup down and shook her head. At least this time, she didn't have to worry they'd actually try to maim each other. Hopefully.

Braan slapped the table. "Ten pieces of silver on the Essian."

Aevar gaped at him as if wounded. "Betting against your own brother?"

"He's bigger than you."

"And older and slower." Aevar smirked at Galen.

"Keep talking, Nord," Galen responded with a scowl as the others chuckled.

Kian leaned toward Braan. "If Galen wins, I'll eat my belt."

"I hope it's well-seasoned." Braan turned to Erik. "What about you? Where are you putting your money?"

Erik sighed as if the entire exchange pained him deeply, but Eadlyn knew him well by now. He was just as invested as everyone else. "I suppose I'll be the supportive older brother and bet on Aevar." He pointed a stern finger at him. "Don't lose my money."

"I won't," Aevar replied, casting Galen a dismissive glance.

"I'm in," Kian said. "My silver's on Aevar."

"This is going to be fun." Braan grinned like a man already counting his winnings.

Eadlyn wasn't sure what to make of it. She'd seen both Aevar and Galen spar before. Both were fierce, competent warriors.

The moment breakfast ended, the men filed outside to prepare for the match. Eadlyn lingered behind with the women as they cleaned up the children and turned to her sister-in-law.

"What is it with men trying to beat each other senseless to prove something?"

Ranvi laughed. "You'll get used to it. They're all just overgrown boys."

Once the children were wrangled and wiped down, they headed out to the training field. The morning sun filtered through the drifting clouds, casting a soft light over the packed earth. Huskarls and Essian guards had already gathered in a wide circle, exchanging coins and grins. More wagers. Hopefully, no bruised egos followed.

As the women drew near, Aevar stepped away from the crowd. He already carried his shield and a wooden sword and met Eadlyn's eyes, searching her face.

"Who will you be cheering for?"

She glanced at the ring, then back at him. "I've never cheered against Galen before."

He nodded with a look of resignation, dropping his gaze, and something in his posture seemed to droop. Before he turned away, she reached out, letting her fingers rest on the leather rim of his shield.

"But you're my husband," she said softly. "I want you to win."

A smile broke across his face, wide and boyish. He stood taller in that instant, pride straightening his spine like armor. That her words and support held such power over him thrilled her.

They rejoined the others, and Aevar and Galen stepped into the ring. Cheers rang from both sides. Eadlyn stood beside Ranvi, her pulse quickening as the men circled each other. It didn't seem right to pray for one to win over the other, so she prayed neither would get hurt. At least they were using wooden swords.

The match began at a measured pace. Aevar shifted his weight from foot to foot, watching Galen's stance with a practiced eye. Galen moved as he always had, efficient and calculating. No unnecessary movement, no wasted energy. They traded light strikes at first. Taps meant more to test and provoke than to land.

After a minute or two, Kian called out, "You two going to fight or just flirt with your swords a while? Remind me to bring a chair next time."

Laughter rippled through the spectators.

Galen aimed low. Aevar knocked it aside and went high. Galen stepped back. Their shields clapped together with a jarring thud, then separated. Neither of them smiled now.

Then, as if by silent agreement, the pace shifted.

Swords sliced through the air, meeting and hammering each other's shields. The crowd gasped as the tempo surged. They fought like warriors used to the chaos of actual battle, not the rules of sport. Eadlyn's breath caught as they locked shields, twisted, and broke apart again, the smack of wood-on-wood echoing off the houses nearby.

Aevar landed the first real blow, striking Galen's shoulder with a solid thunk. Galen grunted but didn't falter. He responded with an attack aimed at Aevar's ribs, but Aevar caught it with his shield. The shock of it jarred his stance, and he staggered half a step before regaining control. Eadlyn's heart pounded, adrenaline rising even though she wasn't the one fighting.

They circled again. Aevar lunged and shifted at the last moment to strike Galen's side. Galen turned with him and met the blow head-on, driving it away with a grunt of effort. He pressed forward. Aevar parried and stepped back under the force of Galen's attacks. They were both sweating now, breathing hard, faces flushed with exertion and focus. Around them, the crowd shouted and cheered, urging them on.

Galen slammed his shield forward, harder than before. Aevar slipped in the loose dirt. Galen didn't hesitate. He swept Aevar's legs from beneath him and drove him to the ground with a thud. Even as Aevar tried to scramble up, Galen followed through, planting his shield against Aevar's chest. His knee dropped onto Aevar's arm to pin his sword hand, and he pressed his blade to Aevar's throat.

Silence fell.

Eadlyn raised a hand to her throat. She had never seen Aevar bested in single combat before. Would he be angry? Humiliated? She struggled to read his face at first. He lay still for a moment, chest rising and falling with harsh breaths. Then he let his head fall back against the earth with a breathless laugh.

"You're faster than you look."

She exhaled in relief.

Galen gave a crooked smile, tucking his sword beneath his arm and offering a hand. Aevar took it without hesitation, and Galen hauled him up in one smooth pull. They stood shoulder to shoulder, sweat-streaked and breathing hard.

Aevar dusted off his tunic and rolled his shoulder. "I guess Essix does have warriors after all."

"It does indeed. I make sure of it."

Aevar sent a glance toward Eadlyn. "So, am I worthy of your princess?"

Galen looked at her too, and she dipped her chin.

"I suppose. For now. Just keep it that way or next time I'll bring a real sword."

"Fair enough."

Down the line, Braan smacked his hand against Erik's chest with a smug grin. "Pay up."

Erik rolled his eyes but slapped a handful of coins into his palm.

Braan turned to Kian next. "You too. And you've got a belt to eat."

Kian grumbled something about not eating his favorite belt, but Eadlyn barely heard. Aevar approached her, still catching his breath, his expression sheepish.

"I hope you still consider me worthy even in defeat."

A fierce warmth swelled in her chest. "It was how you handled defeat that proved you're worthy. Like I said back in Essix, battle prowess does not determine the strength of a man's character."

He leaned in close, tracing his eyes over her face as he spoke in a low voice. "You showed your own strength that day. I've never forgotten it." His gaze dropped to her lips…

"All right," Galen's voice rang out. "Who's next?"

Eadlyn jumped, peering past Aevar. Galen still stood in the ring as if he hadn't just fought a hard bout. Then she looked back at Aevar, and his attention lingered on her a moment more before he turned to see who would take up the challenge.

Braan slapped Erik on the back. "Get in there, big brother, and show us how it's done."

Erik's eyes narrowed. "Planning to bet against me too?"

"Nah. I made my money. Besides, I like your odds."

Erik shook his head at him but stepped into the ring with eagerness in his movements. Aevar handed him the sword and shield.

This match was fast and hard-hitting like before, but this time, Erik claimed victory, and the huskarls roared their approval. After that, the Essian guards took turns against Runar's warriors. Most of them lost, but they took it well enough. Despite the struggle with communication, they exchanged plenty of jokes and laughter, as well as enough bruises to last a week.

Eadlyn stood on the edge of the crowd, watching the result of the alliance she had helped forge with a quiet joy.

Once the men had grown tired of beating on each other and worked up a healthy sweat in the sun, both Nords and Essians headed down to the fjord in a noisy pack, eager to cool off and clean up. Laughter trailed behind them like banners in the breeze.

Eadlyn fell in step beside Ranvi as she, Inga, and the children walked back toward the longhouse. The morning heat was lifting mist from the fields, and she welcomed the gentle breeze that tugged at the edges of her dress.

Ranvi glanced over, her eyes bright. "While the men are occupied, we should see what your merchants have brought."

Eadlyn liked the sound of that.

Back at the longhouse, Ranvi and Inga gathered items from the storage shelves—woven trim, an extra tunic, a pair of fine wool dresses to trade. Eadlyn added a few of her own pieces, though she suspected they were worth less than the others. She also took a small pouch of coins from what Edward had sent.

With the children in tow, they made their way to the open field, the sun beating down as they approached the circle of merchant wagons. Other women and children already milled about, their voices overlapping in a cheerful buzz. Trygg shot ahead like a streak of chaos and joy, darting between legs and barrels with gleeful shrieks as he joined his friends.

At the first wagon, they browsed an assortment of utensils, iron pots, polished goblets that gleamed in the sun, and various other household goods. At the next, foreign spices hung thick in the air. Eadlyn leaned in to sniff one jar, savoring the warmth of clove and cinnamon. She sampled a pinch of something sharp and smoky that brought tears to her eyes and forced her to press her fingers to her mouth to stifle a cough. Inga laughed, patting her back and purchasing a selection for special occasions.

The third wagon displayed a wide variety of fabrics. Piles of soft wool, bleached linen, and exotic furs sat in generous stacks. Eadlyn lingered at a bolt of vibrant red silk, brushing her fingers over the smooth, delicate cloth. Back in Essix she may have bought it, but here it was far too fine and costly for her needs.

A bundle of pale blue linen drew her next. Light as a breeze, it would make the perfect summer dress. Something simple and airy, edged with the delicate tablet-woven trim she'd been working on. She held a corner between her fingers, imagining it swaying in the wind near the fjord.

Ranvi appeared beside her. "That color would look lovely on you."

Eadlyn admired the fabric a moment longer but then set it down. "Aevar has already given me more than enough dresses."

"You should still get it."

She hesitated, weighing the pouch on her belt. "Maybe I'll think about it."

As she stepped away, Ranvi's voice rose behind her. "Will you take this dress and this trim for the linen?"

Ranvi still stood at the merchant's table, holding out a green wool gown and two lengths of tablet-woven trim. The merchant studied her offer and gave a sharp nod.

Gathering the linen, Ranvi turned and pressed it into Eadlyn's hands. "Now you don't need to think about it."

"You didn't have to do that." Eadlyn clutched the fabric, both grateful and flustered. "I could have paid for it myself."

"I know." Ranvi grinned wide and unrepentant.

"*Tahk fyr*. For this, I'll give you one of the dresses Edward sent. Any one you like."

"I'm not sure what I'd do with an Essian dress."

"You could use the fabric for something else." Eadlyn lowered her voice. "Or wear it to see how Erik reacts."

Inga laughed.

"That could be fun," Ranvi admitted, mischief dancing in her eyes.

They moved on to the next wagon, where wide tables displayed a variety of trinkets and small wares. One in particular caught Eadlyn's eye. Baskets and bowls overflowed with beads—wood, horn, glass, polished stones—some strung in strands, others scattered across rough cloth like treasure spilled from a broken pouch.

A cluster of Camrian glass beads drew her like a lodestone. They gleamed in deep blues and stormy blacks, flecked with silver and gold. She reached out, letting them slide through her fingers. They were perfectly smooth, catching the light as they moved.

Ranvi reached her side again. "Those are beautiful."

"They are," Eadlyn murmured. "My mother used to have beads like these…part of a necklace with a silver cross. I don't know what happened to it after she died."

The memory arose, no longer sharp but still aching. She would have loved to carry that piece of her mother with her. It was probably locked away in a monastery vault now, forgotten among other treasures that once meant everything to someone.

She turned to the merchant. "How much for a strand?"

The man, heavyset and flushed from the sun, faced her. "You are Princess Eadlyn."

She nodded.

He looked her over with thinly veiled interest, gaze lingering where it shouldn't. She lifted the blue linen higher, shielding herself as she straightened her spine. His smile turned oily as he named the price, which was high as expected.

She considered it but then set the beads back. She wouldn't spend Edward's silver on a whim. Especially not on something this trivial. She had necklaces among the things Galen had brought. She'd repurpose one of those. And she didn't care to reward the merchant's attention, either.

Aevar was beginning to like Galen.

The man didn't pretend to be anything other than what he was—blunt, loyal, and fiercely protective. Aevar didn't doubt for a moment that if he ever hurt Eadlyn, Galen would kill him without hesitation. And somehow, that made Aevar like him all the more. His father and brothers seemed to enjoy the man's company as well. Even Braan, usually skeptical, had laughed more than once at Galen's dry commentary.

After their swim in the fjord, they returned to the longhouse. The place was quiet, the women and children gone, save for the thralls, who greeted them with pitchers of mead and drinking horns. Aevar took one and sank onto a shaded bench outside. The others sprawled along the wall, stretching and lounging. Green grass, fjord water, and warm earth mingled with the honeyed sweetness of the mead.

Galen drank deeply and gave a grunt of approval. "That's good."

"Thank you," Fathir said. "My wife and Ranvi oversee the brewing."

They talked of village routines and longhouse life. The mood was relaxed, edges smoothed by sun and drink.

"You know," Erik said, turning to Galen, "it's a shame you weren't here a few days ago. You could've joined us for *knattleikr*."

"Knatt-what?" Galen raised a brow.

"A ball game," Aevar said, grinning.

Kian downed a gulp of mead. "And not for the faint of heart. We've still got two men limping."

He launched into a dramatic retelling of the match and how he and Aevar had triumphed despite the odds. Galen listened with amusement that soon gave way to shaking his head.

"Do all your pastimes involve bloodshed?"

There was a collective shrug and a rumble of laughter from the group.

Aevar tipped his horn toward him. "Eadlyn enjoyed watching."

"Did she?"

Aevar nodded. "I heard her cheering for me louder than any-one."

"Huh." Galen seemed to chew on that, the corners of his mouth twitching.

Not long after, the sound of returning voices floated on the breeze, light and familiar. The women and children approached from the market, baskets under arms. The children ran ahead, laughing and shouting. Aevar spotted Eadlyn right away, drawn to her smile. She was glowing. Galen's visit clearly meant more than a simple check-in. He was family, not just a guard. Aevar hated to think of the ache that might follow when he left. But that was not today.

"Find anything worth the walk?" Fathir asked.

"A few things." Móthir lifted a bundle of herbs Aevar did not recognize.

His gaze returned to Eadlyn, noting the blue linen in her arms. He imagined her in a dress of that color, and the thought lingered.

Setting his mead aside and pushing to his feet, Galen folded his arms. "What's this I hear about you cheering for some bloody ball sport?"

Eadlyn froze mid-step, eyes wide like Trygg caught sneaking honey. Aevar bit back a laugh.

She recovered and lifted her chin. "I was supporting my hus-band."

"Is that what we're calling it?" Galen chuckled. "Wait until Edward hears."

"No! He can't keep a secret to save his life. If the nobles find out, they'll think I've turned savage."

"Well…" Galen gestured to her attire.

She smacked his arm. "We are *not* savages in Fjellheim."

Laughter rippled again. Aevar watched her, unable to tear his eyes from the joy on her face.

Ranvi stepped beside him, her voice low. "One merchant had a strand of beads Eadlyn liked. She said her mother used to have a necklace with similar ones and a silver cross. I think she would have liked to buy them but put them back."

Aevar's attention sharpened, though he continued to watch Eadlyn.

Ranvi hesitated, then added, "One other thing. The merchant had very hungry eyes. Remember that when negotiating."

That snapped his focus to her. "Which merchant?"

She described him and the beads. Eadlyn still chatted with Galen, unaware. Without a word, Aevar ducked into the long-house. He retrieved his silver and strode down to the field where the merchant wagons sat.

It didn't take long to find the man. Thick through the middle. Grinning too eagerly at the women who passed by. When Aevar approached, the merchant straightened, butchering a Nord greeting. He probably knew just enough to greet customers and negotiate prices.

Aevar responded with a simple, curt, "Hello."

"Ah, you speak Aerlish. Excellent! Is there something specific you seek?"

"Princess Eadlyn was here earlier. Do you still have the beads she was interested in?"

"Yes, yes. Beautiful Camrian glass. Very rare." He scrambled to retrieve them.

Aevar took the beads, turning them in his fingers. Deep blues and jet black, just like Ranvi had described. In another bowl, he spotted a second strand and picked it up too.

The merchant's tone shifted. "Are you the princess's husband?"

"I am."

"You are a lucky man. The princess is *quite* lovely."

His voice was far too appreciative, and Aevar shot him a withering look.

The merchant shifted. "It was an innocent observation."

Aevar didn't blink. The silence stretched, making the man squirm and sweat more.

"I-I can offer a very reasonable price."

Aevar spoke, keeping his voice calm but cold. "How much for both? And I suggest you take your unwelcome interest in my wife into account when you name your price."

The merchant paled and stammered an acceptable offer. Aevar laid the silver down, took the beads, and walked away without another word.

He already knew how he would give them to her. Not today, but soon.

Eadlyn sighed as she slipped from beneath the covers, the soft sounds of morning greeting her. Under the hum of life in Fjellheim, something heavier tugged at her.

Galen was leaving today.

Though happy here—undeniably so—the ache of those she'd left behind would always linger. There was no telling how long it would be before she saw him again. Despite his promises to return, the road between kingdoms was long and often treacherous.

Aevar shifted near the door, preparing to leave the room. "Is everything all right?"

"It's hard to think of saying goodbye. I don't know when or if I'll see Galen again."

He leaned a shoulder against the doorframe, arms crossed, studying her. "I think he'd still rather kill me than see me married to you, but we've all liked having him here."

Eadlyn snorted softly. "I don't think he wants to kill you. Maybe see you vanish mysteriously into the woods."

Aevar's laugh rumbled through the room, low and warm, and for a moment the weight in her chest eased.

"Don't worry," he said, his voice softening. "He'll be back. A man doesn't stay away when he cares that deeply. And he'll always be welcome here."

She appreciated his confidence.

Once he left, she dressed quickly, not wanting to miss a moment of Galen's last morning in Fjellheim. By the time she stepped into the hall, the warmth of fresh bread and milk clung to the air. Galen stood with the other men as Trygg rattled off a tale about a giant. Erik translated bits here and there while Galen listened solemnly as if Trygg were delivering a military briefing. A week ago, the image seemed impossible. But somewhere between the sparring matches, meals, and fireside stories, Galen had carved a space for himself here. Even Trygg had decided he was interesting enough to keep around.

They lingered longer over breakfast than usual, laughter easing the sadness none of them spoke aloud. When the dishes were cleared and the moment could stretch no longer, Eadlyn caught Galen's eye and tilted her head toward the door.

"One more walk?"

"Of course."

They slipped outside, walking at an unhurried pace through the village. The sun had already begun its climb, casting long streaks of gold across the rooftops. Dust stirred around their feet.

As they passed one of the nearby houses, Galen asked, "You're absolutely sure you wish to remain here?"

Eadlyn looked up at him with a smile. "Are you trying to talk me into returning to Essix?"

He shrugged. "Maybe."

There was no weight behind the word, but Eadlyn answered seriously anyway. "I'm sure. This is my home. And you may not want to admit it, but I know you've seen how good Aevar and his family are to me."

He exhaled. "I have."

Just two words, but they meant everything.

They passed a woman brushing out a rug, her children chasing a goat nearby. A man hauling a basket of kindling waved at them, and Galen gave a small nod. The village had folded him into its ways without asking.

"Jarl Runar is a good leader," he said after a moment. "His people respect him. I wasn't sure we could trust him with this alliance…but I see now the choice was a wise one."

Satisfaction swelled within Eadlyn.

His tone shifted, faintly rough. "As for your husband…I still reserve judgment. He'd better behave until my next visit."

Eadlyn laughed. "I'm sure he will. He's earned my trust."

Galen grunted, the closest he'd come to agreement.

When they reached the fjord, their steps slowed. The lapping of water against the shore filled the silence. No one else was in sight. For a breathless stretch of time, it was just them. A question stirred inside her, one that had rested in silence for years, buried deep, waiting for the right moment.

She fidgeted with the edge of her sleeve, steadying herself. "There's something I've been meaning to ask you."

His brows lifted, calm but alert.

"I never dared bring it up in Kenwich. Too many ears. But here…I think it's safe." She drew a breath, slow and deliberate. Her heart beat hard, as though it already knew what the answer might mean. It could change everything. The way she saw her past.

The way she remembered her father. What she thought she knew about herself. "I know there were rumors. About you and my mother. About my birth. Is there any truth to them?"

Galen stilled. For a long moment, he didn't answer. His gaze drifted across the fjord, far away as if haunted, maybe, by a version of the past that might have been.

"I loved your mother," he said at last. "I believe she felt the same." He paused. "But we never acted on it."

Her chest constricted. She had imagined this moment more times than she could remember. Rehearsed his answers, feared them, hoped for them. But nothing prepared her for the ache of hearing it aloud.

"So the rumors about me…"

"Just rumors." His voice carried a sigh, tinged with regret. "I know it would've been wrong, but part of me has always wished they weren't."

A lump formed in her throat. For years she had carried a desperate hope that the one man who had always stood between her and the cruelty of her father *was* her father. The ache of that hope swelled and ebbed all at once.

"You've always been the only true father I've ever known. Blood or no blood. It makes no difference."

Something both gentle and fierce filled his eyes. "No. It doesn't." He reached out, placing a hand on her shoulder. "And you've always been like a daughter to me."

Her vision blurred, but she blinked the tears back. "Thank you. For everything."

He nodded once, and no more needed to be said. They stood together a little longer, the fjord stretching out before them, until the wind shifted and the moment faded. Then they turned back toward the longhouse, their silence filled with quiet understanding.

After instructing Edgar and the other stable thralls to prepare the Essians' horses for departure, Aevar walked the line of stalls, his boots thudding against the packed dirt. He stopped at Vega and Eydis's stall. The filly whinnied when she spotted him, ears flicking, nose nudging at the wooden door. Aevar scratched her forehead, brushing his fingers over her soft coat. She was growing fast.

He still hadn't taken Eadlyn riding like they'd talked about. A certain place came to mind, drawing a smile to his face. Maybe it was too soon… But things were progressing between them.

Heavy footsteps drew his attention. Galen approached, clad in mail like when he arrived, his expression unreadable. He paused at the stall. His attention settled first on the horses, then shifted to Aevar, measured and unflinching.

"Eadlyn seems genuinely happy here. And she cares for you."

It wasn't a compliment, but it wasn't an accusation either. Just a truth he seemed to wrestle with aloud.

Aevar leaned back against the stall door, meeting the older man's gaze. He didn't respond. Not yet. He could sense more coming.

Galen's jaw tightened. "She's endured much hurt and mistreatment in her life. I'm warning you; do not add to that hurt."

The threat carried weight, but Aevar didn't take offense. Instead, something flared inside him, resolute and protective. "I won't. You have my word. She told me about her father. Were he still alive, I might've broken the alliance to see him answer for it."

That earned him the faintest twitch of a grim smirk. "I may end up liking you yet."

Aevar gave a huff. "You've already threatened to kill me less than I expected. That's progress."

Galen didn't laugh, but the stiffness in his posture eased. He looked at Aevar again, not like he saw him as a threat, but as someone who might understand the weight of what he was being entrusted with.

"Just take care of her." This time, his voice wasn't hard. It was quiet. Almost a plea.

Aevar nodded firmly. "I will."

They held each other's gaze. No more words, just silent accord.

Galen turned to leave. He took a few steps before glancing back over his shoulder. "If you ever take her riding and she insists on racing you, don't take the bait. You'll lose, and she'll never let you forget it."

Aevar chuckled. "Duly warned."

The stable fell still again, save for the shift of hooves and the soft creak of old wood. Vega butted her head against his arm, insistent. Aevar rubbed her ears, letting his attention linger on the empty doorway.

"I will take care of her," he murmured, more to himself than anyone.

And he would.

The yard outside the longhouse bustled with motion as the Essians prepared to depart. Eadlyn waited as Galen moved from person to person, offering parting words. His posture was relaxed now, no longer rigid with suspicion. He even joked with Braan, who laughed and clapped him on the shoulder.

And then he turned to her.

For a breath, neither of them moved. The reluctance on his face mirrored her own. But she smiled, even though her throat ached with the weight of unshed tears. She refused to let them fall. Tears would only make him worry, and he didn't need to. Not anymore.

"Thank you for coming to check on me." She kept her voice light despite the pain.

"I promised I'd get you out if I had to." He glanced back toward the longhouse, to the people standing behind her. "But I'm glad you're happy...even if it means leaving you here."

A thousand memories passed between them. Lazy afternoons of *tafl*, walks through the city when she needed an escape, his steady hand shielding her from the worst of her father. She stepped forward and wrapped her arms around him, hugging him with all her strength.

"I'll return as often as I can," he promised as they pulled apart. With the smallest smirk, he added, "I actually think I might like it here."

"Good."

He lingered a heartbeat more before turning to mount his horse. From the saddle, he gave her a final nod. A wordless farewell. Before he turned toward the road, his attention shifted past her, straight to Aevar. They shared a brief look, heavy with unspoken meaning. Then he gave the order to move, and the group rode out.

Eadlyn stood motionless, watching them go. The pain swelled in her chest, but not as paralyzing as the first time. As the sound of hooves and wheels faded down the road, she pressed her hands together and prayed—for Galen's safety, for Essix, and for the day he might return.

She sensed Aevar join her. The gravity of his presence beside her was unmistakable. When she turned, he was already watching her.

"Do you wish you were going back with him?"

His voice was calm, but beneath it, something heavy rested. He was offering her a choice. No resistance. No persuasion. If she said yes, if she so much as hinted at wanting to leave, he would not stop her. He would let her go.

She looked once more at the empty road, dust still floating in the morning light, and turned back to him.

"No. I wish he could stay, but I have no desire to return to Essix." She reached for his hand, slipping her fingers into his. "My place is here. With you."

The truth of it settled over him, easing his posture, and the uncertainty in his eyes gave way to something deeper. Something a lot like hope.

adlyn smiled to herself as she gathered her clothing for the day. She thought of her new blue dress, but it still needed more stitching for the trim. She hoped to have it ready in time for the Midsummer celebration everyone had been buzzing about all week. It would be a perfect opportunity to wear something new.

Yet, a different dress was bound to turn heads today.

"What's that look for?"

She snapped her head up. Aevar stood near the door, watching her. So much for stealth.

"Nothing." She answered too quickly.

He peered at her. "You're hiding something."

"*I* am not hiding anything." But the smile tugging at her lips betrayed her.

He tilted his head skeptically.

She lifted her brows. "Are you going to leave so I can get dressed, or just stand there?"

A slow, roguish grin curved his mouth as his gaze flicked to the clothes in her arms before meeting her eyes again. He probably would stand there if she let him. A little heat crept up her neck.

"Will leaving get me answers any faster?" he asked.

"Maybe."

"Then I guess I'll leave."

He took his time, letting his attention linger on her one final moment before slipping out. As soon as the latch shut, she fanned her cheeks. If he kept looking at her like that, she would melt faster than butter left near the hearth.

When she stepped into the hall, she found no sign of Ranvi or the children besides Trygg, who was already bouncing between the benches like a rabbit. Aevar stood with his brothers and Kian, but the moment she entered, his attention locked on her. She kept her face neutral, doing her best not to react under his scrutiny.

A few minutes passed before anyone else noticed Ranvi's absence.

"Is Ranvi feeling all right?" Runar asked.

Erik shrugged. "She was fine when we got up. Maybe Alvir is fussing."

A moment later, the bedroom door opened. Ranvi emerged with Alvir toddling beside her and Katla close behind. She wore the deep green gown she had chosen from Eadlyn's collection, trimmed in black and gold silk, with a matching sash. Her hair was styled in the Essian fashion Eadlyn had taught her yesterday.

Erik glanced at her and looked again. "What's this?"

She crossed the hall with graceful ease. "A new dress. From Eadlyn. What do you think?"

A slow grin claimed Erik's face. "I think if a stranger walked in right now, they would mistake you for an Essian princess." He wrapped an arm around her waist, voice dropping as he leaned close. "Will you wear it all day?"

"Would you like me to?"

"I would."

"Then I will."

He bent to kiss her, and Eadlyn smiled, pleased with the result.

"So, you and Ranvi like to scheme."

She jumped, Aevar's voice brushing her ear. He stood beside her, one brow lifted.

"I wouldn't call it scheming. Just a little fun."

"How many dresses like that do you have?"

"Why?" She tilted her head. "Would you like me to wear them?"

His eyes dipped to the pale green linen she wore before rising to meet hers again. "I like seeing you dressed like a Nord," he said, his voice low and rough around the edges. "But I'd also like to see you dressed like a princess sometimes. Like when we met."

The way he stared at her, as if he wanted to close the space between them, left her breathless.

"I'm starving!" Trygg's voice cracked through the moment like the collision of training swords.

Everyone moved toward the table. But before Aevar stepped away, he reached out and brushed his fingers over hers in a brief, meaningful touch that lingered like a promise. Eadlyn pressed her hand to her stomach, trying to calm the flurry of nerves and hope blooming there. She had married him for duty.

And yet…the idea of his kiss stirred something deeper than she'd ever expected.

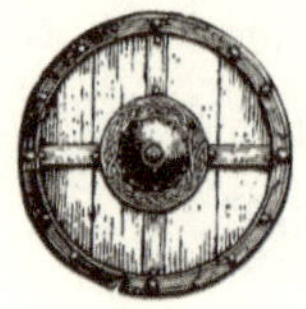

Eadlyn lifted her head as Aevar left their room without a word, and her heart sank. Since the day she thought he might kiss her, she'd been waiting—*hoping*—for him to try again. But something had shifted yesterday out of nowhere. While he wasn't cold or distant as he'd once been, he'd gone quiet and reserved. She'd noticed it last night when he'd hardly spoken before bed. And now, this morning. No lingering glances, no teasing comments. Just a silent exit.

She sat up, blinking against the rising tide of emotion. Disappointment twisted with confusion. And then something sharper flickered to life. Hurt. And anger. She couldn't do this. She could not go one day thinking he might want a life with her, only to question it all the next. Her heart would never survive that. She would rather they remain only friends.

Tears slid down her cheeks. She scrubbed them away, furious with herself for being this vulnerable. She should have been more careful.

"I don't know what I'm supposed to do, Lord," she whispered. "He's my husband, but…"

She let her voice trail off. Shaking her head, she got out of bed, forcing herself to move. She would not wallow.

Once dressed, she paused at the door to gather her strength and hide her emotions behind the mask she'd perfected over her life. When she stepped out into the hall, she expected to find Aevar with the others, but he was absent.

She approached Inga and Ranvi. "Where is Aevar?"

Inga's expression softened. "He left as soon as he got up. Today marks three years since he lost Thora and the baby."

Oh.

The realization sank in, followed by a sharp pang of guilt. Her anger withered. Compassion bloomed in its place, aching in her chest. Yet, beneath the sympathy, a thorn still pressed. Would she always be second to a memory? She had accepted that when she'd first learned of Thora, but now, after everything, she'd let herself hope for more, and that hope hurt.

"I'm sorry," she murmured. "For all of you."

Breakfast passed in unusual quiet. They spoke of Thora in soft tones, recalling memories and small details. Eadlyn listened and allowed herself to learn more about the woman Aevar had once loved. She had no right to envy her. The woman was gone, but her memory was honored here. That was something Eadlyn had to respect.

Still, when the meal ended and Aevar had not come back, the ache inside her returned. After helping clear the table, she slipped back into their room and buckled the knife Heida had given her to her belt.

"I'm going for a walk," she told Inga. Though she spoke calmly, her thoughts churned.

She hadn't gone out alone since Sig's threats, but today she needed space to think, and pray, and search for something she couldn't name. Apprehension prickled along her skin at first, but she walked with confidence. The village and its people were familiar now. People she trusted and who cared about her wellbeing.

When she reached the fjord, part of her hoped to find Aevar there.

But he wasn't.

Only fishermen, their nets catching the morning light.

She walked to the edge and stood in silence, letting the lapping water soothe her. Here, she prayed for strength, for peace, and for wisdom. She didn't want their slow-blooming closeness to slip through her fingers. But she also didn't know how to reach him through the weight he carried.

After a while, she turned back toward the village. She could return to the longhouse and wait for him to show up. Go about her day as if nothing was wrong. But her heart resisted. He was her husband. His burdens were hers now, whether he saw it that way or not. If they could not face things together, their marriage would always be strained and lacking anything more than the surface-level interest that had been growing between them.

With another whispered prayer, she veered toward the far edge of the village. Since he wasn't at the fjord, she had one other guess where he might be. She slowed when she reached the stable but gathered her courage and walked inside. The familiar and comforting musk of straw and horses greeted her. Sure enough, halfway down the center aisle, Aevar stood at Vega's stall, leaning against the door.

As she approached, he looked up. No tears streaked his face, but they glinted in his eyes, and the pain behind them stole her breath. Her earlier frustrations melted. He was the one who had lost. She could not blame him for his pain. And he had not asked to marry her. She had sought this marriage, and she had to accept whatever came with that.

"I'm very sorry about Thora and your daughter."

His jaw flexed. "Her name was Brenna."

"It's a beautiful name."

Silence fell again. He stared at the stall door, unmoving. Then his gaze lifted, hard now, and laden with grief.

"You say your God is loving and merciful. If that's true, why did He kill them?" Anger and aching loss gave his voice a harsh edge.

Eadlyn swallowed past the lump welling in her throat.

"We live in a world that's been broken by sin. God didn't create it to be this way, but it is, and death is part of that." She paused, searching for the right words. How did one comfort someone who did not have the hope of salvation to cling to in tragedy? "I don't know why He allowed them to die. I don't have the answer. But I believe He holds all things, even the ones that break us. Like a child trusting a good father, even when they don't understand...I trust Him."

Aevar scoffed and turned away. The sound of it cracked something inside her.

Her words didn't matter.

Her faith didn't matter.

And maybe...*she* didn't matter.

The thought struck like a stone, crushing her breath before she even braced for the impact. Maybe it had been wishful thinking. The walks, the soft glances, the gentle touches. They'd meant something to her, but perhaps to him, they had been no more than a passing fancy or obligation. Because that's what she was, wasn't she? A duty. A burden forced on him in place of the woman he'd loved.

Tears blurred her vision. She had offered the deepest part of herself—her belief, her comfort, her heart—and he had turned his back without even looking. She blinked the tears away with desperate force, angry with herself for letting them come.

"I'm sorry you're stuck with me." Her voice trembled. "I know you'd rather have Thora and Brenna. If there were a way I could give that back to you, I would."

She hung her head and turned to leave, her heart breaking piece by piece. Maybe she'd been wrong to think she could stand beside him in his grief. Maybe she didn't belong in this part of his life.

"Eadlyn."

His voice stopped her, softer now. She hesitated but turned back. Gone was the anger. Only grief remained. He approached, his expression full of sorrow but no longer closed off.

"I am not stuck with you." His hands found her waist, gentle and sure. "I chose to marry you. I do not regret it."

Her breath caught. She grasped his arms, clinging to the truth in his eyes. "Neither do I."

He sighed, remorse thickening his voice. "I didn't mean to make you feel unwanted. I do want you. But sometimes… remembering what I lost…I fear living through that again."

The words pierced deep. It wasn't the past he was clinging to. It was the fear of losing what he had now. Losing her.

She held his gaze steadily. "I understand. And you can tell me when you're hurting. Or afraid. Whatever it looks like, I'm your wife. I'm here to help you carry it."

His eyes shone, and he pulled her close, resting his forehead against hers. She felt his breath ease and the tremor fade in his chest.

When he raised his head, his lips brushed her forehead so lightly she almost wondered if she imagined it, but the heaviness she'd carried all morning lifted. He slipped his hand into hers as they stepped out of the stable, into the sunlight.

Here, Aevar spoke again, something in his voice searching. "Do babies go to your heaven when they die?"

She studied him for a moment. "Yes. They do."

He nodded, his eyes distant but thoughtful. Though he said nothing more, it was enough. It meant he had been listening.

And maybe—just maybe—her faith meant something to him after all.

adlyn attached two round silver brooches to the dark blue apron dress layered over her new lighter blue one. They were more ornate than the other pairs in Thora's clothing chest. Pieces she'd long admired but hesitated to wear until today. The Midsummer festival was the perfect occasion. She strung a strand of red beads between them, the rich color striking against the blue, and gave her hair one final brush before leaving it loose for Ranvi to arrange.

The hall was already bustling when she entered. Trygg dashed around, shrieking with excitement, while little Alvir toddled after him, clapping and laughing, oblivious to the day's meaning, but delighted by the joy clinging to the air.

Eadlyn scanned the room and found Aevar's attention already locked on her. His eyes traveled from the beads at her chest to the fall of her unbound hair and back to her face. A smile curved his lips, slow and intent. Her heart skipped.

The last few days had deepened something between them. Since their honest conversation in the stable, Aevar had been more present. More open. Like something inside him had finally freed. Today, a quiet awareness pulsed between them as if something was building with each shared glance.

When she reached him, he leaned in, voice pitched low and private. "The new dress is beautiful."

Heat bloomed in her cheeks. "Thank you. I had a lot of help from Ranvi."

Before anything else passed between them, a wild battle cry rang out. Trygg sprang from a bench and launched himself at Aevar's back. Aevar caught him with a laugh, steadying the boy as he shouted and wriggled. He had a particular knack for interrupting their moments. Aevar flashed her one last meaningful glance before surrendering to his nephew's chaos.

Still smiling, Eadlyn found a seat for Ranvi to do her hair. Her sister-in-law took her time this morning, weaving in beads that matched her dress and tucking in small wildflowers they'd picked yesterday. A few times, she caught Aevar watching her with appreciation even as Trygg continued to chatter and climb over him like one of the small monkeys a traveling merchant had once brought to the palace.

As the family gathered for breakfast, Eadlyn leaned closer to Aevar. "Will Kian stay with me again during the sacrifices?"

She'd overheard Runar and Erik discussing the animals set aside—offerings for a bountiful harvest—and the memory of the last sacrifice lingered in her mind.

Aevar shook his head, and for a heartbeat she worried he would require her to attend this time. But then he said, "I will stay with you."

"You won't go?"

"I don't think it's necessary."

He spoke it so simply, but it echoed with significance. What it meant, she couldn't say and didn't want to get her hopes up, but she prayed it might mean a subtle shift in his beliefs.

As soon as breakfast ended, the others gathered at the door, their voices rising with the day's excitement. It took only a moment for them to realize Aevar had not joined them. Runar looked over his shoulder but made no comment. Kian, however, grinned as he backed toward the exit. "Well, I suppose I'll go make myself useful. Someone's got to make sure things are in order."

With a wink, he vanished outside, leaving Eadlyn and Aevar alone.

Aevar turned to her. "Shall we take our walk?"

Eadlyn nodded, something in his eyes causing anticipation to grow inside her.

He reached for her hand, and they stepped out into the clear midsummer morning. Most of the village was empty, voices distant now. The path stretched before them, quiet and sunlit. Wreaths of greenery and flower garlands adorned the houses they passed, done to ward off evil spirits, according to Ranvi. Eadlyn had helped hang many of them the day before, praying as she did so that God's love and light would shine through.

They wound along the silent road toward the fjord, walking side by side with fingers intertwined. As they neared the beach, she noticed the piles of wood stacked for the evening bonfires. They walked between them, and Aevar let her have her few minutes to pray as he always did. But she found it hard to focus when she sensed his gaze on her, warm and unrelenting.

She cracked an eye open. "Your staring is very distracting, you know."

A slow grin spread across his face. "Would it help if I turned my back?"

She laughed. "Not really."

He stepped closer, something new stirring in the air between them. He reached into his belt pouch and held out a small linen bundle.

"I have something for you."

She took it, unwrapping the layers with care. Her breath caught. Two strands of the blue and black beads she'd admired on the Essian merchant's table rested in her palm. At the center of one strand hung a delicate silver cross adorned with graceful knotwork.

"How—?"

His smile grew. "Ranvi mentioned the beads. And your mother's necklace."

Of course she did, and Aevar had made this happen.

He took the strands from her and fastened them to her brooches. The beads nestled against her apron dress. Eadlyn stared down at the gift and brushed her fingers over the smooth glass and the shining cross. Though not her mother's necklace, it was as if a piece of her had been returned. Something to honor the life she had lived despite its tragedy and hardship.

An unexpected wave of emotion welled up, and a tear slipped free. "Thank you," she whispered.

She reached to wipe it away, but Aevar beat her to it. His thumb brushed over her cheek, sweeping away the moisture. It lingered, trailing down over the scar on her lips, and his eyes seemed to memorize every little detail of her face. Then his hand slid into her hair, his fingers resting at the nape of her neck. And when he bent his head, stopping just shy of her lips, she saw it in his face. He wouldn't take what wasn't freely given.

She leaned in, closing the breath of space between them.

His mouth met hers in a kiss that was tender and reverent. No urgency, no rush. Just the soft press of lips, the warmth of his breath, and the stillness of a moment that had been building since the first time they met on that open plain in Essix. His arm wrapped around her back, drawing her in, and she pressed her palms to his chest, the rapid beat of his heart echoing her own.

When they parted, his hands remained at her waist, his gaze soft and dazzled. The world seemed to sway, and it took a long moment before her thoughts settled into place again.

"Was this your plan when you chose not to attend the sacrifices?" she teased, breathless.

"Not really a plan. More of a hope."

Eadlyn studied his face the way he had hers, taking in the blue of his eyes that was the first thing she had noticed about him. Emboldened, she reached up and skimmed her fingers along the cropped side of his head, marveling again at how much the style appealed to her.

His eyes closed at her touch. Then he turned his head and kissed her arm where her sleeve had slipped. Her skin sparked. Catching her hand in his, he brought it to his chest, holding it over his heart. He kissed her again, this time deeper, and she melted into it, the world narrowing once more to just them.

She wasn't sure how long they stood there in each other's embrace. Time blurred until the faint sound of voices tugged at the edges of her awareness, and they parted reluctantly. It must be the thralls returning from the sacrifice to finish preparations before the villagers arrived.

Aevar sighed, though one of contentment. "I suppose we should head back."

Fingers still entwined, they turned from the fjord and walked toward home.

The village came alive with Midsummer cheer. Like during the Gathering, contests sprung up on the edges—footraces, spear throwing, archery, and several informal challenges that seemed to invent new rules as they went. Children ran wild, faces sticky with honey cakes, and laughter rolled across the fields. At the edge of the commotion, thralls bustled, hard at work to prepare food and refreshments. Smoke and sizzling meat curled through the air, blending with the sweetness of mead and fresh bread that made Eadlyn's mouth water.

She walked alongside Aevar as they moved between events, brushing shoulders. Sometimes his hand linked with hers; at other times it rested against her back. After watching Kian and Braan battle to see who could throw a large stone the farthest, they wandered to the grappling ring, where a crowd was forming. Eadlyn edged toward the front with Ranvi, weaving her way through the onlookers as Aevar prepared to step in. The press of people around her was nothing compared to the thrum in her chest.

Since their kiss this morning, everything was heightened between them, including her anticipation to see him compete again. She spotted the same awareness in his eyes as he approached her and tugged off his tunic.

"Hold this for me?" He handed it to her with a knowing smile.

The breath she'd just taken forgot how to leave her lungs. "Of course."

She draped the fabric over her arm. He didn't move right away. His gaze lingered on her mouth, and she was suddenly hyperaware of the surrounding crowd. She wanted to kiss him. Badly. Especially remembering how she wished he'd taken a kiss for good luck before *knattleikr*. But her courage faltered at the last moment, and he didn't press. Before she could change her mind, he turned and walked into the ring. She bit her lip, frustration bubbling. She should have kissed him.

Across the ring, Ingvald stepped in as his opponent. The two of them clasped forearms before falling back into defensive stances. A low horn sounded. Eadlyn flinched as they collided. They grappled hard and fast, the match more brutal than she expected. Their bodies slammed together, each straining to over-power the other. Aevar hooked his arm under Ingvald's, trying to pivot and drive him off balance. Ingvald braced, almost lifting him off the ground.

Eadlyn clenched Aevar's tunic.

He twisted free before Ingvald could slam him down, muscles flexing as he wrestled for another hold. Their boots dug grooves in the ground as they grappled, spun, and crashed to their knees only to rise again in the same breath. Someone behind Eadlyn shouted encouragement. She couldn't hear the words, only the heartbeat in her ears.

Ingvald hooked Aevar's leg and nearly took him down again. Murmurs spread through the crowd. Aevar caught himself and locked Ingvald in a tight hold around the shoulders, dragging him to the ground. Ingvald writhed, refusing to yield. He jammed an elbow into Aevar's ribs and tried to roll them. Aevar grunted and dug deep, using his weight and strength to hold Ingvald down for several moments.

The horn sounded again. Victory.

The crowd cheered, not for one or the other but in appreciation of a good match. For the glorious mess of it all. Eadlyn pressed her hand to her chest and laughed breathlessly, her whole body buzzing with something bright and unstoppable. Aevar pushed to his feet, grinning, dirt and sweat streaking across his skin. Clapping Ingvald on the back, he turned and walked back toward her with a face of pure triumph.

Eadlyn didn't hesitate this time. She reached for him, curling her hand behind his neck, and rising on her toes as she pulled him down into a kiss. For a heartbeat, it was just the two of them, but the crowd howled with approval, hoots and whistles breaking through the quiet. She was pretty sure Kian yelled, "Finally!" and Aevar chuckled against her lips as they parted.

He blinked at her, dazed but delighted. "If that's the prize for winning, I might have to challenge someone else."

She laughed, her cheeks burning with a mix of joy and embarrassment. "Don't push your luck."

He leaned in again, pressing his forehead to hers. Just for a moment. Just long enough to make the noise of the crowd fall away again.

Eadlyn was breathtaking.

Aevar didn't know how he'd been fortunate enough to have married two such amazing women in one lifetime, but tonight, in the fire-lit summer dusk, he couldn't take his eyes off her. The blaze of orange and purple across the sky cast a soft glow against her dark hair, while the bonfires scattered along the beach made the beads on her chest shimmer like the stars above them. Her smile, bright and unguarded, outshone them all.

She was radiant. Not just beautiful. Radiant in a way that had nothing to do with her dress or the way the firelight played along her skin. It was the way she laughed, the way she tilted her head while listening to the village women, the way her eyes searched for him when she thought he wasn't watching.

He looked forward to more time alone with her, whatever that looked like. He would not rush her. Not now when things were so good between them. But after a full day of feasting, games, dancing, and merriment, even a quiet repeat of their time this morning would be welcome.

She caught him watching again.

Her cheeks, already rosy from the heat of the fires, deepened in color. Aevar's pulse quickened, thinking of how she had kissed him after the grappling match earlier, right there in front of every-one. Though her shyness had been plain, her boldness had been just as real.

She ducked her head, tucking a stray hair behind her ear, but not before her smile carved itself into his chest.

"Good for you," Braan's voice cut through his thoughts like an elbow to the ribs, "following my advice."

Aevar raised a brow. "Who said it was your advice I was following?"

Braan smirked. "She looks happy."

"I believe she is."

"And you look happy."

Aevar didn't hesitate. "I am."

His brother clapped a hand on his shoulder, heavy with approval. "Then go dance with your wife before someone else does."

Aevar chuckled and downed his mead—the second and last cup he would have tonight—and motioned toward Heida. Braan wasn't fond of dancing, but he would not let his brother get out of it.

"Your woman's waiting too."

Braan's eyes found her. Tonight was one of the rare occasions Heida wore a dress, and she even had flowers in her hair. Despite how long they had known each other, Braan's expression softened with the intensity of a man deeply in love. That was the kind of relationship Aevar hoped he was building with Eadlyn. The kind he'd shared with Thora. It seemed almost foolish to hope he would find that twice, but he was willing to do his part to make it happen.

He worked his way through the crowd. The other women parted for him without question, and Eadlyn turned as he reached her.

"Would you like to dance again?" he asked.

Her eyes sparkled. "I would."

He took her hand and led her toward the circle of dancers, where the rhythm was lively and quick. Her laughter rang out as they joined in, her skirts spinning, her gaze never straying far from his. It was everything he needed to know he'd made the right choice in letting the past go and focusing on building the future.

As Erik had counseled, he would not waste this second chance. A second chance he did not believe the gods had granted him…but maybe Eadlyn's God had.

Later, as the dance slowed and others broke away to catch their breath or refill their cups, Aevar pulled her just beyond the circle of firelight. Stars dusted the sky above them like silver sparks, echoing the ones drifting up from the fires.

Eadlyn leaned into his side, breathless and happy, and tipped her face toward the night sky. Aevar wrapped his arm around her. When she looked up at him, it wasn't with hesitation. Only trust. He lowered his head and kissed her once more.

The crowd might as well have vanished. She sank into his arms, her lips soft beneath his. He didn't know how long the kiss lasted, only that it was wholehearted and certain. A few shrill whistles and intoxicated hoots rose from nearby, and someone shouted something unintelligible. Aevar just grinned into the kiss. He had never cared who saw him loving his wife.

A scream tore through the night.

They broke apart. Eadlyn turned toward the sound, tensing against him. He was about to reassure her that someone had probably just fallen from too much mead, but another cry split the air. This one sharp with panic. Voices erupted in a sudden flurry. He tried to find the cause in the darkness, but saw nothing past the rings of firelight.

Then someone shouted, "Raiders!" and his blood, which had flowed so warmly a moment ago, turned to ice.

adlyn couldn't move.

For several frantic heartbeats, her body refused to obey her. One moment, she was standing by Aevar, still tasting his kiss on her lips. The next, she was drowning in a roar of panic so sudden it seemed the world had turned inside out.

She didn't even know where to go, what to do, until Aevar's hand gripped her arm, yanking her from the mire of shock. He shoved her forward. Her feet stumbled in the sand as screams ripped across the beach, high-pitched and panicked. Then came the brutal clang of metal on metal, an awful, grating sound that made her teeth ache. The din of battle swelled like a tide, swallowing the laughter and music that had filled the air only moments before. Somewhere in the chaos, Runar's voice thundered commands, rising above the terror.

They wove through the frantic crowd as men grabbed for weapons from the racks, torches flared, and children wailed. Eadlyn struggled to keep her balance. The world tilted, every shadow full of threat. Ahead she caught sight of Ranvi holding Alvir, who screamed with wide, terrified eyes. Trygg clung to her skirts. Inga stood nearby with Katla in her arms, the girl's tear-streaked face pale as bone.

Aevar released her arm.

The sudden loss of his steady hand left her floundering as though she were adrift in a raging storm. She spun around. Their eyes met, but only for a moment. Long enough for her to see the turmoil in his expression before he turned and disappeared into the chaos.

"Women and children to the longhouse!" Runar shouted over the clamor.

Her legs refused to move again, but she forced her limbs to obey, each step a war against the terror clawing its way up her throat. She moved closer to Ranvi and Inga, helping to keep the children sheltered between them, and gasped a prayer for protection, barely aware of her own voice.

Aevar reappeared, this time with Kian, both armed with sword and shield. They took up positions beside Runar, Erik, Braan, and Heida, closing in around the women and children like a wall of flesh and iron. Their presence was a shield of its own, but it didn't stop the pressure building inside Eadlyn. A tight, choking ache that constricted her ribcage.

They moved as one toward the longhouse, the path darker now without the bonfires to light the way. Every shadow seemed to lurch forward. Eadlyn kept looking over her shoulder, heart pounding like a drumbeat in her skull. Still, she saw nothing of their attackers. Only the crashing, shouting, and screaming told her the danger was very real. Aevar remained behind her, standing between her and whatever horror lurked in the darkness.

A sound pierced the air. A cry, unnatural and cold as a grave. Two figures exploded from the shadows like specters, their faces white in the moonlight. Black circles ringed their eyes, and jagged streaks ran down their cheeks like blood. One lunged straight for her.

Eadlyn's scream caught, strangled in her throat.

Aevar was there in an instant, shield raised. The raider's blade struck with a crack so close it thudded in her chest. Swords met, ringing in her ears. Aevar's blade flashed, and the attacker dropped with a gurgle. To Aevar's left, Kian felled the second man, and they were moving again.

Eadlyn couldn't tell how far they had left. The path she had walked so many times in daylight now stretched endlessly in the dark. But then they reached the longhouse. She darted past the doors with Ranvi and Inga. Inside, the air was no less tense. Women and children poured in, some crying, others wide-eyed with shock. Eadlyn turned back toward Aevar. His face was hard, set in the same fierce lines she'd seen the day he faced down Sig. Yet something else lurked in his eyes when he looked at her. Fear.

Not for himself. For her.

"Stay here," he said, his voice rough.

Before she could speak, he turned and joined Runar and Kian at the door. A few more women rushed past them. Braan paused at the threshold and turned to Heida. "Guard the door."

There was a beat of hesitation. A war raged in Heida's posture and her white-knuckled grip on her axe, but duty won, and she nodded. Braan turned to join his father and brothers. A moment later, the door slammed shut, muffling the chaos outside. Heida dropped the bar across it, and Eadlyn flinched at the heavy thud.

Dread settled like a smothering blanket over the longhouse. Children sobbed. Mothers clutched them tightly, whispering trembling words. Eadlyn's hands wouldn't stop shaking, and her thoughts spiraled. The thick door was the only thing separating them from the horrors that raged outside. Heida paced in front of it like a caged predator, constantly readjusting her grip on her axe. If their enemies breached that door, she was their last defense.

A hand on Eadlyn's shoulder made her jump. Inga stood beside her, Katla pressed to her side. Her face was calm and resolute. She said nothing, just gave Eadlyn a nod. The simple gesture almost undid her. Unshed tears stung like smoke behind her eyes, but she wouldn't cry. Tears wouldn't stop the blades.

Only One could.

So, once again, she lifted her prayers. For the women. For the children. For the warriors outside the doors.

And most of all, for the man who had slammed his shield between her and death.

A Kalgoran almost twice Aevar's size charged with a guttural roar, his blade catching the light of the torches as it slashed toward Aevar's skull. He raised his shield just in time. The blow struck like a falling tree, splintering the wood and rattling his bones. The edge of the blade sliced into the shield's grain inches from his hand.

Aevar grunted and shoved upward, throwing the man's sword wide. He countered with his own, but the Kalgoran dodged, agile for his size, and the blade only grazed his side. Snarling, the raider attacked again. Aevar ducked the next swing and lunged low, driving his sword deep into the man's leg. The Kalgoran howled and dropped to his knees, trying to raise his shield, but Aevar was faster. He swung, and his blade bit into the man's neck. The body crumpled and twitched as it hit the dirt.

Aevar scanned the battlefield. Smoke curled from torches, mixing with the copper stench of blood. Screams and metal rang through the night. The Kalgorans had spread like rot, fast and choking.

A shout drew his attention. Ingvald.

Aevar turned as a Kalgoran dropped from a rooftop like a demon from the sky, crashing into the huskarl and dragging him to the ground. The two struggled, fists pounding, weapons lost in the dirt. A dagger glinted in the Kalgoran's hand, rising above Ingvald.

Aevar sprinted as the blade fell.

He kicked the raider to the side, sending him sprawling. Aevar didn't hesitate. He plunged his sword straight into the man's chest, and the resistance gave way as it sank deep. The man thrashed once and stilled. Aevar grabbed Ingvald's arm and hauled him to his feet.

Ingvald gave a sharp nod, blood streaking his face like war paint. They both turned and ran to meet the next threat. Kian appeared, locked in combat with two more Kalgorans. Aevar joined him, slicing down one while Kian disarmed the other and buried his sword in the raider's side.

A third figure lunged from the dark, blade sweeping fast. Aevar parried, but the angle was awkward. He braced and slammed his shield into the man, sending him reeling back. The raider coughed violently and gasped for breath. Aevar didn't give him time to recover. His sword flashed again, and the Kalgoran collapsed, choking on blood.

"Behind!"

Kian's warning rang in his ears. Aevar spun as a battle axe flew toward his neck. He ducked, avoiding decapitation. The blade hissed through the air again. It slammed into his shield and embedded with a crack. The force just about tore the shield from his hand.

Aevar didn't yank it free. Instead, he let go, and the Kalgoran staggered as the weight of the lodged axe pulled him off balance. Aevar charged and drove his sword up beneath the man's ribcage. The raider seized and went limp, sliding from the blade.

There was no time to breathe. A new attacker leapt forward, invisible until the last moment. Aevar turned too late. Pain ripped across his arm as the blade sliced through his sleeve. He gasped, twisting away, and narrowly avoided a second attack.

The Kalgoran pressed hard, slashing with one blade while drawing a dagger. They came in tandem, too fast to separate. Aevar blocked the sword but missed the knife. It slashed across his side. Pain flared in his ribs.

He hissed in breath, but the heat of battle dulled the edge. He dodged another swing and struck low, knocking the man's knife aside. Striking again, he brought his sword down hard on the raider's wrist, severing the man's hand. The Kalgoran screamed, but Aevar didn't let him finish. One final attack silenced him.

Aevar staggered back, his chest heaving. He looked around and raised his sword in preparation, but no more raiders appeared. Stillness spread across the village. The screams and clang of battle had faded. Only the soft moans of the dying and the barking of dogs remained.

He straightened, forcing air into his burning lungs. Pain flared in his side, and he glanced down with a wince. Blood soaked his tunic, black in the moonlight. He pressed his hand tight against the wound. The blood oozed hot between his fingers. Deep but not fatal.

Kian appeared at his side, his face spattered. His gaze dropped to Aevar's side, then snapped up again. "How bad?"

Aevar gritted his teeth. "Flesh wound, I think. "

He turned, sweeping the road. Dark forms lay strewn across the dirt, some Kalgoran, some Nord. Huskarls moved between them, blades still drawn, finishing what needed to be finished.

"I think we got them all," Kian said, his breath ragged. "Hard to say in the dark."

Aevar nodded. The heat of battle was fading fast now, leaving only ache and blood and cold reality along with one burning thought that pushed through everything else.

Eadlyn.

adlyn hunched on the bench, fingers knotted white in her lap. She pressed harder until a dull tingling crawled up her arms. It was the only way to keep them from shaking. She prayed—fervently—but still the fear coiled inside her, burning like acid.

She had never known terror like this. Not even under her father's wrath. That fear had been close and cutting, aimed straight at her. This was colder. Feral. It grabbed at her with icy claws. Not the fear of pain—of cuts or bruises—but the gnawing dread of the unknown.

She lifted her head slowly, as though moving through water. The air tasted of stale sweat and panic. Next to her, Ranvi sat with Alvir in her lap, the child limp with sleep or exhaustion. Trygg nestled beside her, his small hands gripping her waist. Inga cradled Katla on the other side, the girl's face hidden in her shoulder.

Eadlyn watched them, envy cutting through her. Ranvi stroked Alvir's hair as she rocked him, and Inga's calm seemed unshakable. How could they appear so composed? So strong amidst the chaos?

She wiped her sticky palms against her skirt and scanned the longhouse. A hush pressed in from all sides. Women huddled with their children in tight knots, some whispering, others staring at the door as though death might walk in at any moment.

Heida still stood at her post, no longer pacing, but her axe tapped against her leg in a restless beat. Though the sounds of battle had faded some time ago, the silence that followed was worse.

What if it meant defeat?

What if the next face through the door was an enemy?

A muffled voice echoed outside. Eadlyn's heart slammed against her ribs. Murmurs swept through the women as they stood, eyes wide, but Heida didn't hesitate. She threw the bar aside and yanked the door open.

Braan stepped in. Blood splattered his tunic, a fresh stream cutting down the side of his face. He barely made it through the door before Heida caught him in a fierce embrace. Relief rolled through the room like a wave, loosening the tension in the air, but not in Eadlyn's chest. She focused on the doorway, still open.

One by one, the others entered. Runar. Erik. Kian…

And then Aevar.

Her breath caught. At first glance, he appeared whole, but blood, bright and glaring, seized her attention. It soaked one side of his tunic, trailing down his leg. His sleeve was torn, the skin beneath smeared with red. Her vision narrowed, black prickling at the edges.

So much blood.

Around her, the women rushed to meet their men, blocking her view. Eadlyn pressed forward and wove her way to the front with Inga and Ranvi. When they broke through the crowd, Aevar's gaze met hers. His expression softened for a heartbeat, but the haze of battle and pain in his eyes dulled everything.

"You're wounded," she said, not even aware she'd spoken until the words reached her ears.

He shifted, wincing. "Not mortally."

Kian appeared and guided Aevar toward a bench. "Let's have a look."

Eadlyn followed, her legs numb. She snatched a towel from a nearby basket and handed it to Kian. Aevar sat stiffly, bracing himself as Kian pressed the cloth against his side. He groaned, his head dropping forward, jaw locked.

Inga joined them a few minutes later with a basket and a bucket of water. Kian pulled back the towel that was now soaked with Aevar's blood and stepped aside for her. Eadlyn moved closer to help. As they peeled away his tunic, the gash across his ribs came into view, deep and angry. Too close to things that mattered. She looked away before her knees gave out.

Inga motioned to the table. "Sit up here where I can see better." She gestured to Kian. "And bring a lamp closer."

Aevar climbed up with a hiss, his knuckles white against the edge of the wood. Kian fetched the lamp, setting it nearby. The light illuminated the torn skin and muscle. Inga dipped a cloth in water and cleaned around the wound.

As she prepared to stitch it closed, Erik handed Aevar a horn of ale. Aevar caught eyes with Eadlyn before tipping it back. She said nothing. If it dulled his pain, she welcomed it. She stayed close, ready if Inga needed help, but when she began stitching, Eadlyn found herself unable to watch for long. Not the bite of the needle. Not Aevar's flinch. Not the way his hand gripped the wood.

He had almost been killed.

For her.

For all of them.

When Inga finished, she wrapped his wounds in clean bandages and passed Eadlyn a fresh cloth. "Here. Clean the rest. I need to tend to the others."

Eadlyn hesitated, clutching the cloth, but then took Inga's place. She caught Kian giving her a questioning look.

"You got this?"

No. Not even close.

But she nodded anyway. "Yes."

Kian shifted his attention to Aevar. "I'm going to find Ingvald and see if anyone needs help."

As he strode away, Eadlyn wet the cloth, wiping blood from Aevar's arm. Then she moved to his face and the blood that wasn't even his. Her hand trembled as she reached to rinse the rag.

Aevar caught her wrist. "You're safe now. No one will harm you here."

His touch helped still the tremor. She licked her dry lips, resuming her task and gathering her resolve one breath at a time.

When she finished, she scanned the hall. Inga and Ranvi moved between the men, tending wounds and giving orders to the thralls. Several men still waited for care. The tang of blood coated the air, thick and coppery. Nausea bubbled, but Eadlyn pushed through, grabbing a fresh basin to help.

Time blurred. An hour passed. Maybe more. Eadlyn's head throbbed and pounded in her temples. She set down a bowl of pink-tinged water and rubbed her forehead with the back of her hand, blinking away dizziness.

Most of the men had left, though several huskarls lingered just outside. Aevar now wore clean clothes, standing with his father and brothers in low conversation. A fierce, irresistible pull tugged at her. She washed her stained hands and crossed the room.

He noticed her right away and reached for her arm. "Are you all right?"

The contact warmed her chilled skin. She nodded now that she was beside him.

Runar placed a hand on Aevar's shoulder. "You and Eadlyn, go to your room and try to rest."

Aevar motioned toward the door. "I can stand guard."

"We have men for that. You're wounded." Runar glanced meaningfully at Eadlyn before giving Aevar a prodding look.

With an understanding nod, Aevar turned to her and ushered her toward their room. But after only a few steps, her insides lurched, and her head grew light. She stopped, swallowing hard as her heartbeat elevated.

"Eadlyn?"

"I need…" She couldn't finish. She bolted for the door.

Outside, she stumbled past the threshold and doubled over. Her stomach convulsed and emptied itself onto the grass. Spasms racked her body, her muscles wringing themselves out. The night air was cool, but the stench of battle clung even here. Her knees wobbled. She braced a hand against the longhouse wall, trying not to retch again.

She sensed Aevar behind her. His hand pressed against her back, rubbing slow circles. She sighed at the soothing motion, but shame pricked at her.

"I'm sorry," she whispered.

"For what?"

She straightened away from the wall and peeked up at him. "For being so weak."

"What makes you think you're weak?"

"I don't see your mother or Ranvi out here emptying their stomachs."

Aevar reached out, cupping her face and tilting her chin until she looked at him. "You're not weak. This was your first battle. Your body reacts. It's not something you can fight." He gave her a crooked smile. "After my first battle, I didn't even make it to a tree. I ended up spilling my guts all over Braan's shield."

A weak laugh cracked from her lips and helped ease the tension in her body.

His thumb brushed her cheek. "No one here thinks you're weak."

"Except maybe Oda."

He smirked at her attempt at humor.

Footsteps approached. Kian handed Eadlyn a cup of water with an expression that conveyed understanding. She thanked him and tried not to think of how many had seen her get sick. Maybe they'd all done the same at some point.

She rinsed her mouth and took a careful sip. Her stomach still rolled, but it no longer revolted. She drew a fortifying breath. "Do attacks like this happen often?"

"Not here. Raiders rarely make it this far south, and never in numbers like this."

She looked towards the village. "Do you think there are more?"

Aevar followed her gaze. "It's hard to say. We'll search at first light. But if any survived, they've likely fled."

A evar sat up, careful not to pull at the stitches in his side, but the pain sliced through him like a freshly honed blade. He clenched his jaw, hissing through his teeth as the muscles around the wound protested. Still, lying in bed while others combed the village or counted the dead was worse.

He pushed to his feet and his attention pulled towards the bed. Eadlyn still slept, or at least she appeared to be. She lay curled on her side, arms wrapped around the pillow, knees drawn up tight like someone who'd fought for every moment of sleep. Her hair was tangled, and the flowers that had adorned it now lay crushed and wilted among the strands. A sad remnant of what had begun as a perfect day.

The lamp on the table near the bed flickered low. She'd asked if they could keep it burning through the night. He'd already relit it once when the flame had sputtered, but now, with dawn's haze creeping through the window, he blew it out.

Her lashes fluttered, but she didn't stir. He watched her a moment longer, the image of her in last night's chaos etched into his memory. He would never be able to forget the moment the raider lunged at her. She could have been taken from him. In an instant.

The urge to lie beside her, to hold her and feel her breathe against him, almost broke his resolve. But he wouldn't risk startling her. Wouldn't invade her space without an invitation. So he turned from her, gathered his sword and knife, and slipped out of the room.

The longhouse was nearly silent. Just the soft rustle of the thralls near the hearth and Móthir's quiet instructions. She appeared calm and collected despite the turmoil of last night. She'd always been a pillar of steadfastness and strength. Now that he thought about it, he didn't remember ever seeing her cry. Perhaps his father might say differently. He had no knowledge of what emotions his mother allowed to break through in the privacy of their bedroom.

He thought of Eadlyn's words the night before. "Weak," she'd said. She couldn't have been more wrong. She had faced blood, death, and terror, and had still helped. Still served. Her hands had trembled, but they'd moved anyway. That was strength.

Móthir turned when she noticed him. "How are you feeling?"

Aevar touched his side, ignoring the way it throbbed. "Fine."

She gave him the same look she had when he was five and tried to convince her that he hadn't nicked himself with Erik's knife.

"Alys, boil water for tea," she said over her shoulder. Then she turned back to him. "Sit. Let me see."

He laid his sword belt on the table and grunted as he pulled off his tunic before sitting on the bench. Cool air filtered through the open door and drifted toward him, but it didn't quite wash away the hint of blood. Voices from outside drew his attention. Fathir entered with Erik and Kian, their faces worn with fatigue.

"Where's Braan?" Aevar asked.

"Searching the village," Fathir said. "Jorund found tracks heading north along the river. At least six men. Possibly more. I've sent a raven to Halbjorn alerting them to be on the lookout. I'll send more once we have a better idea of what happened."

Pain flared as the bandage pulled away, and Aevar gritted his teeth.

Móthir's lips thinned. "It's inflamed. You need to rest, or it could worsen."

Rest. A luxury he didn't have.

But her expression sharpened. "I mean it."

Kian leaned against the table, arms crossed. "I'll make sure he does."

His raised brow dared Aevar to argue, but he didn't rise to the bait.

"How many did we lose?" he asked his father.

Fathir's face was like stone, but his eyes revealed the pain of a leader who hadn't been able to fully defend his people. "Seventeen. Five in the first strike. Twelve more in the defense. Eleven men, six women. Another dozen wounded. Some may not last the day."

Aevar swore under his breath, squeezing his fists. Almost twenty dead in one night. Fjellheim hadn't seen such loss since the winter sickness several years ago. And the attack made little sense. Kalgoran raiders rarely ventured so deep into Nordra unless…

Ice spread through Aevar's veins. "Do you think they were after Eadlyn?"

"It's possible. She's the only thing that makes this worth the risk. They might have been trying to break the alliance."

Aevar gripped the hilt of his sword. "So what are we going to do about it?"

"I'll send a message north to King Drocca. If he tries to claim ignorance, fine. But another attack, and it's war. We'll call for aid from Talta and Essix if needed. I'll have Gudrik place more men along the border. Maybe send some to help him."

Aevar's blood urged him to ride north himself, to strike now and strike hard. They had tried to kill his wife. But that would take him away from her, and he did not want to see Nordra thrown back into war if avoidable. Especially when Drocca would deny any direct involvement in the attack.

Móthir finished binding his wound as Ingvald walked in.

"My lord, we found a wounded Kalgoran."

Fathir straightened. "Where is he?"

"*She* is in the guardhouse. Braan and Heida are questioning her."

Aevar pushed himself up and tugged his tunic on, ignoring the way his side protested and his body moved sluggishly with the lack of sleep and blood loss. He grabbed his sword, but his mother blocked him with a mug of tea.

"Drink this first."

He downed it in a couple of gulps. Hot and bitter, it tasted of willow bark and other painkilling herbs. He handed it back, and she gave him a look piercing enough to stitch a wound on its own.

"Take it easy."

"I will."

He moved to catch up with his father and Erik.

Kian waited at the door and pointed a warning finger at him. "After this, you're eating. And resting."

Aevar rolled his eyes. "I'd forgotten how insufferable you and my mother are when you join forces."

Kian chuckled.

They crossed the village toward the guardhouse, where huskarls stepped aside to let them through. Inside, the prisoner sat in chains, a crusted gash cutting across her forehead. She was young—barely a woman—with raven-dark hair, kohl-smeared eyes, and jagged runes inked across her cheeks. Heida stood before her, speaking Goric in low, firm tones. The girl only sneered in reply.

Fathir gestured at her. "What has she said?"

Heida turned to face them, planting her hands on her hips. "Other than cursing us all? Nothing useful."

Aevar regarded the woman warily. While he didn't really believe the curses held any weight, Kalgoran women were feared for a reason. Said to carry the favor of their gods, they were more than warriors; they were vessels. But in the back of his mind, he heard Eadlyn telling him there was only one God, and he found an odd amount of comfort in that.

Fathir stepped forward, looming over the girl. She didn't flinch. Just stared back, small and furious. But that was what made her so dangerous. The small ones could slip through shadows un-noticed. Quick. Silent. Deadly. And you'd never know it until your blood was soaking the ground.

"Have you asked what their purpose was here in Fjellheim and why they traveled so far south?"

Heida nodded and held the girl's stare without wavering, reminding Aevar she was one of them. Had she not grown up in

Nordra, she might have been the one in chains. But no, Heida never would have been caught.

"She refuses to answer. We may get something from her with time, but Kalgorans are as unyielding as Nords."

Fathir considered the girl for a long moment. "Normally, I'd say keep trying and then get rid of her, but she can carry my message to Drocca."

Heida's expression didn't change. "You want her patched up?"

"Enough to travel. Feed her. Dress her wounds. Give her supplies. I'll write the warning, and you can translate it."

"Gladly."

After painstakingly untangling the crushed flowers from her hair, Eadlyn brushed out the snarls and worked it into a simple braid. Her shoulders ached, and her stomach pinched. Last night's memories clung to her like cold fog. It was a miracle she'd slept, but even rest hadn't dulled the exhaustion pressed into her entire being.

She turned to leave the room and paused. The furs where Aevar had slept were rumpled and empty. There had been moments in the darkest stretch of night where she'd almost asked him to join her in bed. Just for his nearness and safety. Yet she'd held back for reasons she couldn't fully grasp.

She stepped into the hall, and the hush struck her. The air felt wrong. Too quiet. Ranvi and Inga sat by the hearth with Alys and Nesta. Katla pressed in tight against her mother, silent, while

Trygg stacked wooden blocks with Alvir. No usual mischief or uncontained energy. The subdued atmosphere sat heavily on the vibrant hall.

She looked around. "Where is everyone?"

Inga's face turned solemn. "A wounded Kalgoran was found. They're questioning her now."

That news settled uneasily in Eadlyn's stomach, though not with the sharp fear of last night. Just a deeper kind of wariness.

"How is Aevar?"

Inga sighed. "He should be resting, but stubborn men never do." She softened the words with a smile. "We'll see he sits when he returns."

Before long, voices stirred at the door, and the rest of the household entered, their faces stony. Eadlyn immediately sought Aevar. He was pale this morning, hints of weariness and pain tugging at his taut expression. However, when he met her eyes, his face relaxed, and she sensed his relief at seeing her. The attack last night had surely awakened his fear of loss.

He came straight to her, scanning her face as if daylight might reveal something he'd missed. Once near enough, he reached for her, drawing her close.

"Are you well this morning?"

She would need time to recover a sense of safety and peace, but it would come. "I am. And you?"

"I'm fine." He leaned down and pressed a kiss to her forehead.

Eadlyn soaked in the warmth of it, then tipped her chin up in silent invitation. His tired face crinkled in a smile, and he kissed her again, this time on the lips. A quiet assurance that they were both still here.

adlyn took a steaming mug of tea from Alys, cradling it in both hands. Chamomile and willow bark wafted into the air, comforting but slightly bitter. She carried it to where Aevar sat near the central hearth. The glow of the fire wavered across his face, casting shadows that exaggerated the pallor of his skin. He shifted at her approach, a grimace tightening his features. This was not the first time she'd caught him wincing today. *Lord, let this bring him relief.*

She held out the mug. He accepted it, a whisper of gratitude softening the fatigue in his eyes. "*Tahk.*"

He took a sip and released a slow breath. Eadlyn settled into the chair beside him and gathered the remaining pages of Scripture she'd been reading aloud. She'd offered it as a distraction from the pain and the heaviness that had settled over the household like a veil. For two hours, they'd read together in quiet companionship. She hoped some words had reached Inga and Ranvi too.

"Would you like me to read more?" she asked, eyeing how he clutched the mug. They were just about through the collection she had brought with her from Essix. She hoped to write to Edward as soon as possible and ask for the missing books. Anything to continue what had become a cherished ritual between them.

"It will soon be time to eat…and then we must gather to light the first pyres." He offered a wan smile, but pain left grooves in his forehead. "Perhaps later."

She gathered the pages, a knot forming in her throat. As she carried them back to their room, the longhouse pressed in around her, heavier than it had all day. As if the weight of the dead hung in the beams and rafters.

Dinner passed in subdued murmurs. Aevar only picked at his food. Eadlyn watched from the corner of her eye, her own appetite waning with every shallow breath he took.

Dusk had draped itself over the village by the time they gathered at the forest's edge. The huskarls flanked them in silence, torchlight flickering on grim faces. Villagers followed in a solemn procession. Six pyres stood waiting with the bodies of the fallen laid atop them and surrounded by tokens of their lives. Blades rested in the hands of the warriors, polished one last time. Aevar had explained that, once burned, the ashes would be scattered over the fjord or buried in memorial mounds.

Runar stepped forward, his voice low and reverent. He praised the fallen, calling them brave, worthy, and welcomed by the gods into Valhalla. But Eadlyn's heart pained to hear it. She bowed her head and prayed. For the souls of the living. For the lost to find the truth. And for God to provide the opportunity for her to be a light to them.

When Runar finished, the families stepped forward, torches trembling in their hands. Flames touched the edges of the pyres and then rose in a consuming roar. Burning wood and cloth filled the damp night air, the acrid heat brushing Eadlyn's skin and clogging her lungs. Sobs rose around her. Her chest ached at the sound. It could have been Aevar lying on one of those pyres or someone else from her family.

She turned to take his hand, but her breath caught.

Aevar was swaying.

Before she could reach for him, he staggered. Kian caught his arm just in time to keep him from collapsing.

"I'm all right," Aevar muttered, his breath uneven.

"You're not." Kian pressed the back of his hand to Aevar's forehead. His expression darkened. "You're burning up."

"It's the fires." Aevar tried to shrug him off.

Kian snorted, though the sound lacked humor. "Not unless you've been roasting your brain over one."

Aevar didn't argue further. He just closed his eyes as if even staying upright was more than he could manage.

Inga stepped in with firm guidance. "Let's get you back to the longhouse."

He gave a weak protest before stumbling again. Erik moved to his other side, and together he and Kian half-carried him away from the pyres. Eadlyn followed close, her heart pounding at a frantic pace against her ribs.

Halfway there, Aevar lurched forward and vomited into the dirt. The harsh sound tore through Eadlyn, and she clutched her stomach, bile rising in sympathy. *Lord, I don't know what is wrong, but please let him be all right.* No one spoke, but Eadlyn sensed the growing fear surrounding her.

Back at the longhouse, she rushed ahead to their room, flinging back the bedding with shaking hands. She turned as they brought him in.

Aevar tried to resist. "No. It's your bed."

She ignored him, and Kian and Erik eased him down, guiding his sagging form to the edge of the mattress.

"I need to see the wound," Inga said, her voice clipped but steady.

Eadlyn stepped in to help, peeling away his damp tunic. Her breath caught when the bandages fell. The wound was inflamed, angry red streaks spreading far beyond the original cut.

Inga's gaze flicked to her, then to the others. "We need the healer. Now."

"I'll get her," Braan said, already moving.

They lowered Aevar back against the pillows. Sweat beaded on his skin.

"How did it get bad so quickly?" Eadlyn whispered against the dryness in her throat.

She didn't like the grim look on Inga's face.

"Some Kalgorans poison their blades."

The word struck Eadlyn like a blow. *Poison.* "Is there anything that can be done?"

"We'll see what the healer says." But Inga's eyes gave her away, dark with concern and something far too close to fear.

Minutes crawled by before Braan returned. The woman who stepped in behind him was older than Inga, her face deeply lined and her hair entirely gray. A basket hung from the crook of her arm, the air around her thick with crushed herbs.

Eadlyn stepped aside, though her attention never left Aevar. The rest of the family lingered near the door as the healer worked, but Aevar's eyes kept drifting closed. His strength seemed to bleed away with every passing moment.

When the healer finished, she handed Inga a small pot and a pouch. "Salve for the wound. Tea to cool the fever. As much as he can drink. I'll return in the morning."

Eadlyn stepped forward, desperate for hope. "Will he be all right?"

The healer paused, her attention lingering on Aevar's pale, sweat-drenched face.

"He is strong," she said at last. "The gods will decide."

Eadlyn clenched her hands.

No. Not the gods.

God would decide.

Eadlyn slumped in the chair beside Aevar's bed, her spine stiff with fatigue and her hands chilled despite the fever heat that poured off him in relentless waves. The air was thick with the sour stench of sweat and sickness, like something that didn't belong in the world of the living.

He hadn't spoken for hours. They'd managed to get a little of the healer's tea into him, coaxing his lips to part while he drifted somewhere far beyond reach. But nothing stayed down. Every attempt had ended in gut-wrenching heaving—violent, wracking tremors that left him gasping and the wound bleeding again. The sight of fresh blood had turned Eadlyn's stomach.

The last time his eyes opened, they'd been glassy and unfocused. Before that, the fevered muttering had turned into restless thrashing. He'd called out names—Thora's at first, and then hers.

When she had taken his hand and whispered she was there, he had quieted.

Now he lay still. Too still.

His skin burned beneath her fingers, the heat of his fever seeping into her like a wildfire she couldn't smother. Her prayers had long since turned from murmured words to silent, breathless pleading, repeated again and again in her mind.

Please, God. Please. Don't take him. Not like this. Not now.

Beside her, Inga moved with purpose, dipping a cloth into the basin and pressing it to Aevar's forehead. They had taken turns through the night, replacing that cloth and whispering encouragements that felt like lies. It was like trying to douse a blaze with a thimble.

The hours blurred together. By the time the light of morning crept into the room, Eadlyn's body ached as if she'd sat vigil for many days already. Voices stirred outside the room. A moment later, Runar appeared in the doorway.

Sleeplessness shadowed his eyes as he stood at the foot of the bed, staring down at his son in silence before turning to Inga. "Any improvement?"

She shook her head, yet her voice carried a brittle hope. "No. But he kept down a little of the tea."

Runar gave a single, curt nod. "Good."

Inga rose, stretching her back with a groan. "I will see to breakfast." She rested her weary gaze on Eadlyn. "I'll bring you something when it is finished."

Eadlyn glanced up at her. "Thank you, but I don't think I can eat right now."

The fear that had taken root inside her the moment Aevar stumbled at the funeral still hadn't let go. It left no space for hunger.

Inga laid a comforting hand on her shoulder. "I will return shortly."

One by one, the daylight hours dragged by. With each, Eadlyn prayed for the fever to break, but it remained high. Aevar grew restless again at times, and at others he shivered uncontrollably. Though various members of the family took turns sitting with him, Eadlyn only left his side to see to her most pressing needs. She dreaded another long night but had no power to stop the day from passing. When Inga left again for the evening meal, Eadlyn still declined food.

Alone once more, she slid her chair closer to the bed. She took his hand, threading her fingers through his, aching for a response. Even the slightest twitch.

None came.

Tears blurred her vision. She blinked hard, fighting for hope, but dark thoughts were quick to invade. If Aevar died now, he'd be lost forever. Her throat constricted, and she choked out a whispered prayer. "Please, God, we need more time. He needs more time."

A couple of tears escaped despite her efforts to stop them. She kissed his fingers and rested her forehead against their joined hands as she continued to pray for his healing.

Footsteps drew her attention. Kian stood in the doorway with a plate in hand, his expression pale and strained. He stared at Aevar, frozen in the unbearable reality of helplessness.

When at last his gaze met hers, a flicker of his usual self returned but didn't quite reach his eyes. "I brought food. And before you say you're not hungry, I know. But if you keel over, he'll be furious when he wakes. You'll never hear the end of it."

Her lips twitched, but no actual smile came. Still, she took the plate with numb fingers and whispered, "*Tahk fyr.*"

The savory herb chicken and warm bread made her stomach turn, then growl. Her body at least remembered it was alive. Bite by bite, the trembling in her limbs eased.

Kian sank down in the chair beside her and leaned back, stretching his legs out with a long breath. For a while, silence pressed between them.

Then his voice came, low and rough. "I should've gotten there first. I saw the Kalgoran going for him, but I was too slow."

Eadlyn lifted her eyes from the plate. "No one was fast enough for all of them. It's not your fault."

His jaw tightened. "Feels like it is. I've seen him take hits before. But…" His voice trailed off.

She followed his gaze to Aevar's sweat-slick face. His chest rose and fell with shallow, uneven breaths. Alive, but only just.

Kian scrubbed his hands over his face and braced his elbows on his knees. But then he straightened again, squaring his shoulders.

"He's too stubborn to die," he muttered. "He'll wake up."

A tight breath broke from Eadlyn's lips—half laugh, half sob. "I hope so."

"He *will.*" Kian's voice hardened to iron. "If he doesn't, I'll chase him into the afterlife and drag him back myself."

That earned a real, if weak, smile from Eadlyn. She reached for Aevar's hand again, holding tight as if she could anchor him to this world with nothing more than touch and prayer.

The hall had grown silent with the stillness of the night, the children tucked away into their beds. Inga sat beside Eadlyn once more like an anchor in the weary hours. They passed the time in murmured conversation. Inga was just finishing a tale of Aevar as a child, stealing honey cakes meant for a feast and blaming the dog, when Runar entered the room.

Unlike Inga, who held onto hope like a banner, Runar wore his worry plain. The lamplight etched deep lines into his face, aging him further. He didn't speak. He just stood at the bed looking… lost. A man who had fought countless battles utterly helpless in this one.

His gaze shifted to Eadlyn, carrying a weight that made her sit straighter.

"If something should happen to Aevar," he said, his voice quiet but firm, "your place here is safe. The alliance will stand. You are family now. Even if you choose to return to your brother, you will always have a home here."

His tone held no hesitation. No diplomatic obligation. Only truth. She was family. The words hit hard. They were a gift, yet she couldn't imagine this place without Aevar.

She swallowed the ache that swelled in her throat and drew a deep breath to fortify herself. "Thank you. But he will recover, and I will not be leaving."

Runar met her eyes. Something softened on his face, and a dozen emotions warred behind his calm. He nodded. One sharp, silent agreement. He, too, would not accept the alternative.

He left a few minutes later, his footsteps fading into the stillness of the longhouse. Eadlyn turned her focus back to Aevar, unable to keep from pondering what Runar had said. What would her life look like if the worst should happen? Would she return home if Aevar died? Would she even want to?

That the answer didn't come easily surprised her. *Home* had shifted since coming here. It wore new faces now. It sounded like Kian's teasing and Inga's practical affection. Like Aevar's smiles and fierce protectiveness…

No. She couldn't think of losing it all. Not now. Not while his heart still beat.

Time passed in thick silence. The world had grown very small, Eadlyn realized. Just this room and each moment of waiting.

Ranvi appeared in the doorway some time later. She observed Aevar first, then Inga, her face softening with concern.

"You should get some sleep," she said gently. "I will sit with him tonight."

Inga hesitated, but after a long look at Aevar, she relented. "Just for a few hours. If there's any change—"

"I'll wake you." Ranvi stepped aside to let her pass, and Inga offered Eadlyn a reassuring squeeze of the shoulder before she slipped out.

Then Ranvi turned to her. "You too. You need rest."

Eadlyn wanted to refuse, but Ranvi was right, just like Kian earlier with the food. She could not tend Aevar if she collapsed from hunger or exhaustion.

Still, the idea of sleeping terrified her. Her mother had died while she slept. One moment she had gone to bed, and the next morning, everything had changed. She still remembered the cold press of her governess's hands and the hush in the room when she was told.

Please, God. Not like that again. Don't let him slip away while I rest.

She drew in a breath that stung. "All right."

Her limbs dragged as if being pulled down by invisible chains as she stepped away from the bed. She peered at the corner where Aevar had made his place each night since they married. Always a respectful distance. But tonight, that distance felt unbearable. He was her husband. Her home. She did not have to leave his side.

Quietly and decisively, she turned back and climbed into bed. The blankets shifted beneath her as she lay down beside him. Searing heat pulsed from his skin like a forge. She rested her hand on his chest. His heart beat beneath her palm, faint but there, and she prayed for it to keep beating.

adlyn craned her head to each side, a dull pop sounding in her neck as she tried to loosen the ache that had settled deep into her muscles. Four days of sitting at Aevar's bedside had left her stiff and wrung out in body and soul. Her fingers, raw and reddened from the endless wringing of wet cloth, trembled in her lap. A yawn threatened to escape her, but she swallowed it down and rubbed at her burning eyes.

The breakfast Inga had brought sat mostly untouched on the table beside her—the bread had gone tough, and the fish curled at the edges. But she couldn't summon the will to eat. Not while Aevar still lay unmoving.

She stared at him, and a chill spread through her limbs. The fever had cooled in the last two days, no longer burning as it once had, but it still clung to him with greedy fingers. His skin had taken on a pallid tone, and his face, usually so full of fierce life, had gone slack. Even when she laid the damp cloth on his brow, he didn't stir.

He looked like he was slipping away.

She reached for her spindle to distract herself. The familiar sensation of wool and wood steadied her—somewhat. Inga had taught her to spin not long ago, and in these quiet moments it had become a small mercy. The rhythm. The control. But now, the fibers caught and tangled between her fingers. Her vision wavered again. She blinked furiously, dragging her sleeve across her cheeks.

From out in the hall, Trygg laughed, young and blissfully unaware. A blade of longing twisted inside her. The sound was like a memory from a life she'd once lived. The sound of a world before this waiting and fear. She bowed her head. Another prayer. Another plea. Her voice remained silent, but her soul ached for God to move.

Footsteps neared, and she lifted her head to find Braan in the doorway. He looked first at Aevar, and worry pulled at the corners of his mouth. When he turned to her, something gentler touched his face.

"You need fresh air." It wasn't a suggestion. More like an order cloaked in concern. "Come. Just a short walk. You've been in this room too long."

Eadlyn hesitated, tightening her grip on the twisted yarn. Of all people, Braan wasn't the one she expected such insistence from. Perhaps that's why it worked. After a pause, she set the spindle down in resignation.

She stared at Aevar once more. Was it foolish to leave, even for a moment? But she knew she needed to breathe something other than fever-stale air. She rose, though her legs protested, stiff and unwilling. With one last look, she followed Braan out of the longhouse.

The sun struck her like a blow, bright and startling. She winced, squinting. The heat on her skin seared after the dim chill of the sickroom, and the world outside seemed too alive. Around them, the village bustled. People worked, tended to animals, and hung fresh herbs to dry. Life hadn't stopped. Her chest tightened at the contrast, but she clung to the hope that she might find renewed strength to endure in this respite.

Neither she nor Braan said much as they passed through the village, though she found comfort in his presence. When they reached the beach, she stood at the water's edge and drew in the fjord air as if she had not fully breathed since the attack. Letting it refresh her mind, she closed her eyes and prayed for Aevar's healing and for a return to the normalcy she had come to love so much. It was as though both rested right on the edge of a steep cliff, and only God had the power to keep them from toppling over and falling away from her. Her world had been shattered once before. Her heart ached at the possibility of it happening again, weighing on her chest.

She drew a hard breath as memories seeped into her mind. "I was very young when she died, but I still remember sitting on my mother's bed when she was sick, asking God to heal her." She wiped the tears that had run down her face. "I never thought I'd have to relive that with Aevar."

Braan's eyes met hers with shared concern, but resolve sparked within them. "Don't lose hope yet. He is stubborn, and he has something to live for."

Darkness wrapped around Aevar like sea-fog, dense and suffocating. His mind drifted beneath it, thoughts scattered and half-formed. Somewhere in the murk, hazy memories surfaced. An attack. Injury. Pain. He tried to open his eyes, but they wouldn't respond. Was this death? Had he been denied the warrior's end?

However, after some time of drifting, sounds crept in, very faint at first. A faraway voice. A rooster. A giggle. Each one pulled him closer to consciousness, like a wayward boat drawn to shore. Sensation followed. His body seemed distant. Weak. But still his.

Finally, he pried his eyelids open, blinking to bring his surroundings into focus. Morning light spilled from the window above him. The door out into the hall stood open, but he couldn't lift his head to see beyond it. His limbs ached under their own weight, but he could still feel them. That counted for something.

Air brushed his shoulder, and he caught the whisper of a quiet breath. Gathering what strength he could scrape together, he turned his head to find Eadlyn curled up beside him. Her hand wrapped around his arm, her breath warm on his skin. The sight of her lying there chased away the last remnants of the fog. Not only did it show how deeply she cared, but it also revealed her level of concern. Just how close had he come to death? Considering the weakness clinging to him, he'd been on the brink.

For a long few moments, he studied her face—every curve, each scar. The shadows beneath her eyes told him she hadn't rested well in days. He wanted to reach out, brush her hair back, and draw her near, but he had no strength for even that.

She must have sensed his gaze, because she stirred. Her eyes fluttered open. They held his for a moment before she gasped and sat up.

"You're awake!"

"I am." The words scratched against his dry throat, and he winced.

Eadlyn scrambled out of bed. Had he the strength to reach out and keep her there, he would have. She grabbed a cup from the table and turned back to him. He tried to sit up, but his body resisted as though a waterlogged blanket weighed it down.

"Here, let me." She slipped her hand beneath his head and tilted it up as she put the cup to his lips. Her touch was even more soothing than the cool water.

After he'd taken a long drink, she set the cup aside and sat down on the edge of the bed beside him. He lifted his hand enough to find hers.

"How long has it been?"

"You were unconscious for five days. Your fever broke last night. We weren't sure when you would wake."

Or if he would wake, judging by the signs of distress on her face. He rubbed his thumb over the soft skin on the back of her hand. Making her fear for his life was the last thing he'd wanted to do.

"I'll be fine." Though the weakness may take time to leave him, he was sure his body was on the mend.

She nodded, relief easing some of the worry from her face. Still, she clutched his hand tighter, as if she were afraid to let go.

A grin came to his lips as he thought of waking up with her next to him. "So I had to be injured for you to share your bed with me?"

Eadlyn's brows shot up before she ducked her head. Dusty pink flushed her pale cheeks. "Well, I had to stay close to make sure you didn't die on me in the night."

As much as he enjoyed seeing her a little flustered, he didn't want to push it too far. "I'm teasing. The bed is yours once I'm strong enough to move."

Her gaze returned to his. "You will stay right where you are until you've healed. I am perfectly able to sleep on the floor."

He didn't want her to sleep on the floor. He wanted her here with him. But he kept his thoughts to himself. They could see about that once they'd both recovered from this ordeal.

adlyn whispered her thanks to God as she and Aevar concluded their morning walk, her heart lifted by the return of ordinary peace. Life, at long last, had settled back into the comfortable pattern it once knew before the attack. Aevar's strength had returned little by little, and with it, so had the ease between them.

They paused in front of the longhouse, and Aevar's hands slipped around her waist, his fingers settling with familiar comfort. That easy, lopsided smile curved his mouth. The one that still fluttered her breath no matter how many times he offered it.

Then came the kiss, gentle and unhurried. She leaned into it without hesitation, treasuring the open affection. In Kenwich, most noblemen treated their wives with cold reserve in public. But Aevar kissed her like the world wasn't watching, and even if it was, he didn't care.

He pulled back only a little, and his breath warmed her cheek. "I should find my father and brothers," he murmured, the reluctance in his voice soft but unmistakable.

She let her hands linger on his chest. "I'll see you later."

He pressed one more kiss to her lips and turned, striding toward the training field. She stood for a moment longer, watching him go, a smile still clinging. In her heart, she whispered another thanks that his health had returned and for their growing relationship. Things had changed the morning of the Midsummer festival when he'd first kissed her, but it was more than that now. His near death had grown something even deeper between them.

When he disappeared, she turned and entered the longhouse. The heat of the summer sun had left sweat tickling her neck, and she welcomed the cool shade inside. Inga and Ranvi stood at one of the long tables, smoothing out a swath of yellow wool. Eadlyn joined them, letting her fingers drift across the fabric, admiring the color.

When she looked up, both women watched her with knowing smiles.

"What?"

Inga's eyes twinkled. "We just enjoy seeing you and Aevar so happy. It was hard won."

Hard won. The words echoed in her mind. Yes, it had been. She and Aevar could have remained cordial strangers, bound only by duty. Instead, they had broken through pain and fear to find something real.

Her deepest prayer now was for his salvation. In that, they were not yet united. But she had increased hope. Though they'd finished her small collection of Scripture, Aevar had agreed to start again from the beginning. He seemed more invested this time, his questions more frequent and deeper. Perhaps almost dying had him thinking about his eternal future.

After helping to cut pieces of the yellow fabric for the new dress, Eadlyn went to work at the loom, while Inga and Ranvi worked on their own projects. Nearby, Alys and Nesta spun wool. Soon Nesta entertained them with a tale she must have picked up while still living in Waelon. When she finished with one, it left Eadlyn with the perfect opportunity to offer to tell a story from Scripture. Switching to spinning, she sat down and began the story of Joseph.

She had just reached the part where Joseph forgave his brothers when the muted sound of hooves drew everyone's attention. A moment later, Aevar rode through the open doors. He came straight toward the raised platform where the women sat, causing Alvir to squeal and babble in delight.

Inga arched a brow. "Aevar, what are you doing bringing that beast into my hall?"

"I came to ask if Eadlyn wants to ride with me." His attention landed on her with a boyish grin.

Eadlyn broke into a smile as well. "I would."

He tipped his head. "I have Hiroc waiting outside."

She shared an amused look with Inga and Ranvi and set her spindle aside to follow Aevar. Out in the sun-drenched yard, she spotted one of the stable thralls holding Hiroc by the reins. He was already saddled and pawed at the dirt in impatience. After giving him a pat on the neck, she mounted, the saddle creaking under her and warmed by the sun.

Moving up alongside Aevar, they rode through the village, following the same path they'd taken when she had first arrived. As they reached the outskirts and turned toward the forest, she glanced back, gripping the reins more tightly.

"Are you sure it's safe to leave the village?"

Aevar's sword and seax hung from his belt, their presence both comforting and ominous. What if raiders were still nearby?

But he sat easily in the saddle, his posture relaxed. "It's been a month since the attack. We've doubled our patrols, but none of them have found any sign of raiders. By now, King Drocca should have received Fathir's message. I don't believe there is any danger of another attack." He shifted to face her. "Besides, I've learned that if we let fear dictate how we live, it's not really living."

She couldn't hold back a smile.

They rode on, the trail winding upward through the hills, toward the plateau above the village. As they crested the rise, Eadlyn's breath caught, just like on the very first day. But now, this place was not foreign. It was hers. The fjord shimmered below with the mountains towering behind it like guardians. The green of summer painted everything with life, and the breeze touched her skin like a blessing. She closed her eyes and offered thanks for the mercies God had showered on her these past months.

Then she looked over at Aevar, and her heart filled to bursting. He sat watching her take it in before motioning for her to follow.

"Come. There's more to see."

They turned from the overlook, following an unseen trail that wound higher into the mountains. The trees thickened around them, towering pines whose needles seemed to brush the sky. Soon the forest opened again, and they entered a hidden meadow.

Flowers blanketed the ground in every shade of gold, violet, and white. Bees hummed nearby. Higher up the slope, mountain sheep picked their way along narrow outcroppings and bounded from rock to rock. On a plateau across the valley, a brown bear ambled through the grass, massive and calm and entirely disinterested in them. Everything breathed with life, untamed and vibrant.

They rode together in comfortable silence, the meadow giving way to a shaded path that wound down the mountainside again. Aevar led the way, the trail dappled with sunlight and shadow. Eadlyn breathed in the sweetness of pine and wildflowers. None of the rides she had taken in Essix had ever soothed her soul quite like this.

As they passed beneath a stand of ancient firs, the sound of flowing water caught her attention, soft at first, but growing steadily louder. The trees opened, revealing a hollow wrapped in green. A narrow waterfall spilled over mossy rocks into a crystal-clear pool, the water catching slants of sunlight and scattering golden mist into the air. Willow branches trailed like curtains across the banks, and the whole place exuded peace.

Eadlyn drew a soft breath. "It's beautiful."

Aevar slid off his horse in one effortless motion. "I thought you'd like it."

He tugged his belt free and slung it over the saddle.

She narrowed her eyes in playful suspicion. "What are you doing?"

"Going swimming," he said, as if it were the most obvious thing in the world. His hands were already at his tunic.

"What about your wound?"

He shrugged one shoulder, the fabric slipping away to reveal the noticeable line of pink, puckered skin that curved along his ribs and would turn into a scar. "It's nearly healed. It'll be fine. Come on."

Eadlyn eyed the calm, inviting water but wasn't fooled. "I don't know how to swim, remember?"

"That's why I'm going to teach you."

She hesitated. The only experience she had in water was when Brother Winstan had baptized her in the river outside Kenwich. There it had been shallow enough to stand. Here, the thought of the pool rising over her head left an unpleasant swell of apprehension.

Aevar walked over to Hiroc and rested his hand on her knee. "You live beside the water now. You should know how. You never know when it might save your life."

His hand was warm through the fabric of her dress, and so were his eyes. Firm but not forceful.

She nodded and dismounted. He was right. She should know how in case she was ever out on a boat.

"You will enjoy learning here better than in the fjord. It's warmer." He waded into the shallows.

Eadlyn peered down at her dress. She wouldn't be able to swim well fully clothed. She'd have to shed some of it. With a breath, she unfastened the brooches at her shoulders and eased off her dresses, draping them over her saddle. Then she kicked off her shoes, the soft grass cool beneath her bare feet.

Down to her shift, she approached the water and crossed her arms, nerves prickling under her skin. "You swear to me you won't let me drown?"

His answering grin was full of mischief. "You have my solemn oath; I will not let you drown. I have an alliance to protect."

"Oh, is that all it is?"

He shrugged, though his smile grew deeper. "There may be other reasons."

Insides fluttering, she followed him into the pool. The water was cool, but pleasantly so. Aevar reached for her hand, steadying her as he explained the motions of swimming. No pressure. Just calm instruction. His fingers remained firm around hers until she gained confidence. She splashed a little at first, ungraceful, but laughed. The water held a refreshing joy. No wonder the men liked to swim after sparring.

As she grew more comfortable, Aevar drew her in deeper. When he let go so she could try it on her own, she treaded water for a few glorious moments before she sank. Her head dipped toward the water, and panic spiked. She reached out blindly. His arms wrapped around her, lifting her above the water. She clung to him as he drew her back into a shallower area of the pond.

Her heart thudded in her ears, but his voice was close and calm. "I told you I wouldn't let you drown."

Eadlyn released a breathless laugh, the burst of fear draining, and she tilted her head back to look up at him. Immediately, she found herself held by his eyes. Something unspoken passed between them. Something deeper than teasing, and his gaze softened. He bent, and his lips touched hers. The kiss began slow and gentle as the water around them. But it deepened, like a current pulling her under, steady and consuming and yet safe. While she had feared drowning, she did not fear this. His strong arms pulled her closer, and she let herself sink further into his embrace, everything else fading.

A sudden flurry of birds took flight, their wings slicing through the quiet. Eadlyn gasped and pulled back, her pulse skipping. On the far side of the pond, the horses stamped, their ears perked and alert. Memories of the attack leapt into Eadlyn's mind.

Aevar's face shifted, calm vanishing. Gripping her arm, he guided her to shore. As soon as they reached the horses, he yanked out his sword and pushed her behind him. For a long moment they stood in tense silence, Eadlyn's breaths coming rapidly. She tried to slow them down, but the fear only grew. All was silent, yet the horses did not relax, and neither did Aevar.

Finally, he called out, "Show yourself!"

The silence stretched like a taut bowstring. Eadlyn's skin prickled, every nerve alert. Was it Kalgorans? A bear?

The brush rustled, and a rider emerged.

Oda.

Relief hit Eadlyn first, followed by a hot flush of humiliation. She crossed her arms over her shift, the fabric soaked and clinging. Aevar's sword did not lower.

"What are you doing here?" he demanded.

Oda didn't answer, her attention lingering on Eadlyn with open disdain.

"Were you spying on us?"

She gave a derisive snort. "You don't own the forest. I can ride where I please."

He pointed the sword at her. The sharpness of his voice revealed barely contained fury. "Leave. Now."

Her lip curled, but after a tense beat, she turned her horse and disappeared into the trees. The silence she left in her wake was deafening.

Eadlyn exhaled a shaky breath and wrapped her arms tighter around herself, the wet fabric chilly against her skin and leaving her feeling exposed. Not because of Aevar, but she prickled with the uncomfortable sensation of more eyes watching them. Surely Oda was the only one around, but now every bush and shadow seemed to hide onlookers.

Aevar turned to her, his jaw clenched. "I'm sorry. I didn't know she was out here."

She nodded, trying to calm her breathing.

He seemed to sense her discomfort, and the regret increased. "Let's go back to the village."

They dressed and mounted their horses. Neither spoke much on the way back. The ride was different from earlier, shadowed with unease and watchfulness. At the longhouse, they dismounted.

"I'll take care of Hiroc for you." Aevar took the horse's reins but did not walk away. Instead, he searched her face. "Are you all right?"

Eadlyn drew a deep breath. Though her emotions had settled, discomfort still lingered. "Yes, it was just…a lot. First thinking we were in danger, and then her. Watching us."

Her skin crawled to think of Oda creeping in the bushes, especially in a moment that had been more intimate than any she and Aevar had shared previously. What if they'd never realized she was there? It felt like a violation.

Anger still simmered in his expression. "It won't happen again."

Eadlyn wasn't sure what he planned to do and didn't ask, but she didn't want their time together today to end on such a note. She reached for his hand, hoping to reclaim what had been stolen from them. "The pond and waterfall were beautiful. I loved being out there with you. I hope we can go again sometime."

This pulled a warm smile to his face. "We will."

Aevar strode away from the stable, leaving the horses with Edgar. Anger burned in his gut like hot coals that refused to go out. He thought about stopping by the training field and working off the fury on a target or a man with a blade, but no. This wasn't something to be hammered out with a sword. This had to be dealt with. Now. He would not be looking over his shoulder and eyeing the shadows every time he left the longhouse with Eadlyn. Nor would he have it for her.

Halfway through the village, Kian called to him.

"So, did you take her to the waterfall?"

His friend shot him a sly look. Everyone had been teasing him about it as soon as he'd mentioned taking her out for a ride. The waterfall was all but sacred to the couples of the village.

But the grin vanished as soon as Kian saw his face. "What happened?"

Aevar gritted his teeth. "We caught Oda spying on us. I doubt it's the first time."

She had to have been watching and following them to know they'd gone for a ride.

Kian's brows furrowed. "Are you going to talk to her?"

Aevar nodded sharply as Kian fell into step beside him. They said nothing more as they marched toward Oda's house.

Her horse stood out front when they arrived. Good. That meant he didn't have to hunt her down elsewhere.

"Oda!" He did not keep the ice from his voice.

A moment later, she stepped outside, chin high with the same defiance she'd worn back at the waterfall. Always her face was unpleasant. He didn't remember a time she'd ever smiled, at least not with any true joy or kindness. She and Thora had always been opposites in that way, just like their mothers. Perhaps because Oda's mother had been a thrall, though that had never affected Oda's standing.

Aevar closed the distance in a few long strides. "Have you been spying on us?"

She remained stubbornly silent. He took a step closer, his shadow falling over her. He wasn't in the habit of intimidating women, but Oda was different. She'd pushed this too far.

She did not cower, but her gaze faltered. Though she still refused to respond, her silence was answer enough. When she did speak, her voice was low and biting. "I'm not the one embarrassing myself all over the forest."

He almost laughed. "No, you're the one hiding in the bushes like a coward."

She bristled, jaw taut.

Aevar shook his head in frustration. "Why can't you leave it alone? What could you hope to gain?"

Now she looked up, eyes blazing. "Because I know you deserve more than some little foreign princess foisted on you, but you're too blinded to see it. She doesn't belong here."

This again. Aevar was tired of it. "She belongs with me. I chose her."

"You chose wrong."

His temper flared white-hot. "I would choose her again a hundred times over."

Oda scoffed.

He balled his fists. If she had been a man, he'd have broken her nose by now. "Why can't you accept my choices? You act like Thora—and now Eadlyn—stole something from you."

Her eyes flashed with dangerous intensity. "Thora *did* steal you from me."

Aevar blinked, stunned for half a breath. "What are you talking about?"

"Don't you remember all the time we spent together? Sparring and fishing and wandering the woods?"

He frowned. Of course he remembered. Oda had been around—loud, relentless, always tagging along. But that was her choice. He'd tolerated her. Nothing more.

"Oda, we were children. I loved Thora. I always did. It was never you."

Something on her face cracked. For a moment, Aevar thought there were tears in her eyes. He wasn't sure if it was grief or humiliation, but she blinked and they were gone, buried under the ice she wore like armor.

Still not convinced she accepted the truth even now, he lowered his voice, deadly serious. "This ends here. Spy on us again or go anywhere near Eadlyn, and I will have you banished from Fjellheim."

Her brows shot up. "You'd banish me from my home?"

"I will do whatever I must to protect my wife."

Eadlyn sat beside Aevar at the table, the comfort of the evening meal and the laughter of family weaving together. The weight of the day—of that moment in the woods and eyes watching when they shouldn't have faded as the hours passed. It helped to know Aevar had taken action. Firm action. The kind that made her feel safe like she never had before her life here.

What lingered in her mind now were the moments before Oda's intrusion and what might have been if they'd not been interrupted. She caught herself blushing and ducked her head. However, the move must have drawn Aevar's attention because he looked over at her. His brows wrinkled in question, but she just smiled, leaning into his shoulder.

Later, after a few rounds of *tafl* and a round of goodnights, the family retired to their rooms. The longhouse settled into its nighttime hush, and Eadlyn and Aevar moved through their evening routine with the same practiced rhythm they'd adopted months ago. She was once more in the bed while he'd returned to sleeping on the floor, but it hadn't felt right since he'd been ill. She hadn't admitted it to anyone, but she missed sleeping beside him.

As she changed into her sleep shift, she glanced over her shoulder to where he prepared for bed and caught sight of his healing scar again. She paused. She didn't see the wound; she saw the man who had shielded her with his own body during danger. Who had clung to life while she prayed at his side. Who had fought the pain and grief of his past to give her a place in his heart. Who had come to mean *everything*. The realization hit her now with such incredible force and clarity it knocked the air from her lungs.

She loved him.

Not just as the man she now trusted or as the husband she had vowed to honor. But deeply. Fiercely.

She took a step toward him. "Aevar."

He turned to her and stilled. She held his gaze with purpose, her heart beating against her ribs as if trying to proclaim her thoughts faster than she could put them into words.

"I love you." The declaration broke from her chest. "I will choose to love you for the rest of our lives. Not because of the alliance, or because it's expected. I want to be your wife and for you to be my husband for no other reason than that we love each other. I want to live out every word of the vows we both took until death do—"

His lips against hers cut off her words, and he kissed her like he'd been waiting his entire life for this moment. Wrapping her arms around his neck, she kissed him back, sensing a shift in their relationship that would begin the rest of their lives together.

Morning nudged at Eadlyn's senses, but she lingered in the space between sleep and waking, unwilling to leave the surrounding warmth. Yet as she drifted, she became aware of Aevar's arm draped over her waist, solid and reassuring. She let her fingers trace over his. He responded by pulling her closer, and his chest pressed against her back, rising and falling with each steady breath. This was right.

For several peaceful minutes, they lay there in stillness, listening to the subtle creaks of the longhouse and the birdsong beyond the window. Then he shifted. A breath of air brushed past her ear, and a moment later, a kiss landed just beneath it.

She squirmed, laughing as his beard prickled her skin. "That tickles."

He chuckled low in his chest. Fully awake now, she rolled over to face him. He was propped up on one elbow, staring at her as if content to lie there and watch her forever.

"*Góthan morgin,*" he murmured.

She echoed the words before he leaned in and kissed her, slow and lingering. The kind of kiss that made the rest of the world distant and unimportant. By the time they parted, sunlight streamed through the window. Eadlyn sighed, brushing her thumb along his jaw. "It's late. If we don't move soon, we'll miss breakfast."

Aevar didn't appear even slightly concerned. "We could stay here all day."

She raised a brow, though her smile betrayed her amusement. "Someone will come looking for us."

"Let them," he said, shifting closer. "I'll send them away. Tell them you've been kidnapped by your husband and negotiations are ongoing."

She laughed and sat up. "Tempting, but we both have work to do."

He groaned and flopped back against the pillow. "You're a princess. You shouldn't want to work."

"Are you saying I should be lazy?"

"I'm saying you've earned a slow morning."

She leaned over and gave him one more quick kiss. "We've already had one."

Grumbling good-naturedly, Aevar sat up and swung his legs over the side of the bed. She followed, and they both dressed for the day.

After brushing out her hair, she settled at the table in the corner and tried to twist it up the way Ranvi had shown her. But the braid slipped through her fingers again, unraveling for the third time.

With a frustrated huff, she muttered, "I do not know how your mother and Ranvi manage this. I'm not sure I'll ever learn."

Aevar came up behind her. "Let me."

She froze as his hands combed through her hair and gathered the strands with unexpected ease.

"How did you learn to do this?"

"Thora wasn't good at it either. Móthir and Ranvi used to do it for her, and I watched."

Eadlyn blinked, struck by the simple honesty of it. He hadn't needed to explain, but he had. And that, more than anything, told her what she needed to know. He wasn't erasing the past or avoiding it. He was offering her a place within it.

Curiosity sparked within her. "What was she like?"

A beat of silence passed before he answered softly. "She was fierce. She could give Heida a challenge and even bested my brothers in a bout or two. But she was also kind and loved deeply." He finished the braid and tied it off before resting a hand on her shoulder. "All qualities you share."

Eadlyn smiled, though something uncertain tugged at her heart. "I'm not a warrior."

He moved to her side to see her face. "You don't need to be. There are many other ways to fight that do not involve a weapon. You fought for your people by coming here when you did not know what awaited you. That took a warrior's courage."

The tiny bit of insecurity faded. "*Tahk fyr.*"

They left their room, and the hall was already full and lively, as expected. Runar had Trygg slung over his shoulder, threatening to feed him to the frost giants. The little boy squealed in mock terror, kicking his feet while Katla shrieked with laughter at their grandfather's side. Everyone else, save for Inga and Ranvi, was already seated at the table.

As Aevar and Eadlyn approached, he rested a hand at the small of her back, guiding her with comfortable familiarity. Before they sat down, he leaned in and pressed a light kiss to the base of her neck, but the moment was short-lived. From across the table came a voice that was far too casual.

"Sleep well last night?"

Eadlyn found Braan watching them. His expression was all innocent curiosity, but the twinkle in his eyes gave him away. A beat passed, and realization dawned. This was the first morning she and Aevar had left their room together. And her hair braided in a way she hadn't mastered on her own. A style Thora had worn.

Oh no.

Flames lit her cheeks. She ducked her head, trying not to meet anyone's eyes. Across the table, Heida smacked Braan's shoulder and leveled him with a glare that promised violence. Next to her, Kian appeared to be trying mightily to hold back a grin as if he'd incur her wrath as well.

Aevar didn't miss a beat. "We slept very well, thank you."

The smug humor in his voice made Eadlyn want to sink under the table. She wasn't sure whether she wanted to kick him or kiss him.

Ranvi appeared and set a bowl of fresh berries down. "What did I miss?"

Eadlyn peeked up as she glanced between them. Ranvi took in every detail before her expression turned to one of accusation she pinned on Erik.

"Ignore them, Eadlyn. They are children."

Erik raised his hands. "What? I've said nothing."

A low chuckle rumbled from Aevar, and it was impossible not to smile. Even with the embarrassment, something warm and wonderful permeated this moment. These people—this family— were hers now. She'd never belonged more than she did right here, heat still rising in her cheeks, laughter on her lips, and Aevar grinning beside her.

The forest was quiet. Peaceful.

Slowly, Aevar followed the path he hadn't been able to bring himself to walk in the last three years. But after last night and Eadlyn's declaration, it was time. A few months ago, before everything had changed—before Eadlyn—he wouldn't have made it this far. The weight would have crushed him. Now, as the clearing opened before him, he paused. Emotion swelled, pressing heavy against his chest, but not unbearable.

Grass-covered mounds and memorial stones stretched out across the glade, nestled among the roots of ancient trees. Generations of Fjellheim's dead laid to rest here, their names carved into stone, their stories remembered. He took a deep breath and moved forward, weaving between the mounds until he reached the one near an ash tree. His gaze landed on the runes etched into the stone.

Thora.

Brenna.

His vision blurred.

Memories surfaced unbidden. The weight of Thora's body in his arms as he'd laid her on the pyre. The small bundle holding their daughter as his mother had passed her to him. So tiny and perfect, her downy wisps of hair golden like her mother's.

He knelt beside the mound where he'd buried their ashes. His breath shuddered in his lungs, but after a moment, he could breathe again. For a long time, he sat in the silence, letting his mind wander the past. The memories, the love, the loss would always be a part of him. Nothing would ever take that away, but what he hadn't realized until Eadlyn was that there was room for more.

He reached for his seax knife and dug a small hole in the earth. Then he sheathed the blade again and unfastened the pouch at his belt. From it, he withdrew a silver arm ring. The sun caught on the polished metal, highlighting the twin horse heads that adorned the ends. He traced the familiar pattern with his thumb and had to clear his throat to work his voice past the knot there.

"I kept my promise to you. Now I intend to give it to another. This time I hope I am the one who takes it to the grave."

He placed the ring into the hollow and covered it with care. A couple of tears rolled down his face, but he brushed them away and pushed to his feet. His old life was behind him. His new one was just beginning.

Back at the village, Aevar stepped into the smith's shop, greeted by the familiar scent of scorched leather, oil, and smoke. Tallak turned from his workbench, sweat beading at his brow. He swiped an arm across his forehead.

"Let me guess. A gift for Eadlyn?"

Aevar smiled. Apparently, he was becoming predictable. "Yes."

"You're going to single-handedly keep me in business buying things for your wife."

"Then I will happily keep you in business."

Tallak chuckled and set his tools aside. "What'll it be this time?"

Aevar set a leather pouch onto the bench. It clinked heavily. Though he knew how much the cross necklace meant to Eadlyn, to him, this had greater meaning.

Tallak picked up the pouch, his brows lifting at the weight. "Must be something special." He opened it and looked inside, the beginnings of a grin spreading across his face. "Ah. I think I know what you want."

The afternoon sun beat down on Fjellheim, filling the air with the earthy aroma of herbs. Eadlyn brushed stray wisps of hair from her forehead, sweat clinging to her temples. She tied off a bundle of sage stems with a strip of leather and crossed to the drying rack, the heat-dried grass crunching beneath her feet.

Ranvi passed her with a handful of thyme. Gathering for the upcoming winter would soon begin in earnest now that summer waned. Eadlyn found a deep sense of purpose and belonging in being part of it. As a princess in Essix, she'd often felt useless much of the time, especially when her father had ruled and prevented her from seeking more ways to be of use to Essian citizens. But here, the simple act of gathering for her family filled her with contentment.

She returned to the table. As she reached for another bundle, strong arms slipped around her waist from behind. Her breath caught, but she relaxed into the familiar embrace as Aevar pressed a kiss to the back of her neck.

She leaned into him. "You scared me."

"Sorry," he murmured in her ear. "Walk with me."

She hesitated, glancing at the mound of herbs on the table. But then she looked back, meeting his eyes, and whatever resolve she had melted. Work could wait.

His fingers laced through hers. She caught Ranvi's smile as they passed. Though she had never questioned her position here, truly being Aevar's wife seemed to have deepened her camaraderie with her sister-in-law and permanently secured her place in the family.

They followed a narrower path than usual, one that wound toward the southern edge of the village, beyond the docks and the noise. The beach here was quiet and untouched. Only gull tracks and driftwood marked the sand.

Eadlyn turned to him, curious. "So why did you bring me out here?"

His lips lifted. "Do I need a reason?"

"No reason at all, but I think you have one."

He chuckled. "You're right."

Something in his expression changed subtly. He reached into the pouch and withdrew a round silver object—an arm ring like she'd seen others wear, including Ranvi. Her heart thudded as he took her hand, his thumb brushing across her wrist as he slipped the ring up her arm to rest snugly above her elbow.

His eyes found hers again, more serious now, and she knew this was more than a piece of jewelry or symbol of status or wealth. This meant something. She could hear it in his voice.

"When I married Thora, I swore to her there would be no one else. That I would remain faithful to her and her alone. Even after she died, I felt bound to that oath. But I've come to realize I buried that promise with her, unbroken. I now give you the same oath. For as long as we both draw breath, there will be none but you."

Eadlyn didn't try to stop the tears from welling. They burned but were full of something too deep for words.

"You have the same oath from me," she whispered.

He leaned in and kissed her. The kind of kiss that sealed vows.

When they parted, she studied the ring on her arm. Intricate knotwork wove around its surface. And there, at the very center, so subtle she almost missed it, was a cross. Her throat tightened again, and her fingers brushed it with wonder. All this time, he could have tried to forbid her from practicing her faith. It was what she had expected before meeting him and his family. Instead, he'd shown her nothing but respect and acceptance.

She exhaled, letting the wave of emotion wash through her and settle. "It's beautiful." She looked up at him. "Your mother and Ranvi, were their arm rings given with the same oath?"

"Yes." His hand caressed her arm. "My father taught us that we should cherish our women. He believes that if a man cannot honor one woman for a lifetime, he has no business taking a wife."

"Your father is a good man. And he raised good men. Even in Essix, most do not hold their marriage vows in such high esteem."

"Some have mocked us for it, but it's important to us."

"I'm sure their marriages are much less pleasant."

He nodded and reached up, cradling her face and skimming his thumb over the scars on her cheek. Drawing her closer, he pressed a kiss to her forehead and murmured, "*Ást mín.*"

She repeated the phrase. "My love."

Though his actions had already made it clear, this was the first time he'd uttered the word.

He drew back to look her in the eyes. "Yes. My love."

"Trygg, don't run so far ahead," Ranvi called as they walked along the forest path.

Even from a distance, they heard his dramatic sigh and saw the slump of his little shoulders, as if obedience were a burden too great to bear. Eadlyn laughed at the display, and Inga joined her. Ranvi shook her head with a long-suffering smile.

"I don't know what I'll do with him once he gets older."

Inga smirked. "When he's older, he'll be off with the men, and Erik will have to deal with him. Then you'll be chasing after Alvir instead."

They laughed again, the sound floating through the trees. Eadlyn's thoughts turned inward. What would her future children be like? Before the alliance, she never imagined raising a child somewhere like Nordra in a culture so different from her own. Uncertainty came with that. Sons raised to be warriors. Daughters taught to bear hardship with strength. Life here would not be easy. But the hesitancy didn't last long. She would raise her children with Aevar, and she knew without question he would be a good father, just like Runar and Erik.

As for the rest? She breathed out and peered up at the trees. The dangers they might face were not hers to control. They were in God's hands.

Some ways from the village, they reached a spot lush with bilberry bushes and found where they had been picking yesterday. They'd spent three days collecting the dark berries to dry for the winter. Unlike when they'd picked strawberries, Aevar had not joined them—something that stirred a little disappointment—but the men were busy with the hay, an equally essential task before the season changed.

Still, they weren't alone. Heida had accompanied them, axes strapped to her hips, sharp eyes sweeping the tree line for any sign of danger, be it beast or man.

The bilberry bushes were dense and low, only reaching Eadlyn's knees, but thick with dark fruit. She knelt to fill her basket, the sweetness of ripened berries plump under her fingers. Katla joined her, eager and bright-eyed. Ranvi and Inga picked nearby, keeping half an eye on little Alvir as he toddled between the shrubs, occasionally plopping down with a giggle. Trygg, meanwhile, had taken up his usual role as defender of the patch, swinging his wooden sword at invisible enemies, leaping from logs, and narrating imaginary battles with great enthusiasm along the forest's edge.

Not long after, he shouted, "I found mushrooms!"

Heida strode over to inspect them and gave an approving nod. "These will be good for tonight's stew."

She dropped the mushrooms into his outstretched hands, and he tore off toward Eadlyn, who was closest.

"Here!" He dumped the handful into her basket among the berries.

"Excellent find," she said, ruffling his hair. He grinned and dashed away again, sword already back in hand.

Eadlyn exchanged an amused look with Ranvi. That boy never slowed down. She hoped she'd have the energy for that kind of wildness when her time came. Knowing Aevar and his brothers, there was no doubt. She would have sons just as adventurous.

For the next hour, they worked steadily. Trygg brought back various finds—rocks, moss, more mushrooms—each one earning him praise. After picking all she could reach in one area, Eadlyn rose to straighten her back. Stretching, she noticed Heida staring into the trees. Something in her alert posture sent a chill crawling along Eadlyn's skin.

Still keeping an eye on the forest, Heida walked over to where Trygg was playing. "Let's go look over here."

Her tone remained calm, but she rested her hands on her weapons as Trygg followed her into the bilberry patch to Ranvi. Eadlyn tried to convince herself she was just paranoid, but then Heida murmured something too quiet to hear. Ranvi's expression tensed, and she nodded as she rose and reached for Alvir.

"All right, I think it's time to head back now." She caught Eadlyn's gaze, confirming her suspicion that something wasn't quite right.

"But the baskets aren't full!" Trygg protested.

Ranvi kept her voice light. "They are full enough. If we put much more in, we'd be spilling bilberries all the way back to the village."

Eadlyn wove through the bushes, trying to swallow the apprehension rising in her throat. When she reached her, Ranvi leaned in close and whispered, "Heida thinks she saw someone in the trees."

The words tightened around Eadlyn like a rope. Inga had joined them, taking Katla's hand, and together they left the bilberry patch. Eadlyn glanced over her shoulder as they followed the trail back toward the village. Heida had taken up the rear, walking stiffly and scanning every shadow. Eadlyn prayed she'd only seen a glimpse of a deer or other harmless animal.

A sharp snap broke through the stillness, too loud and crisp.

Eadlyn froze mid-step. All around them, the forest hushed, and the silence rang in her ears. She drew a shallow breath and shifted closer to Inga and Ranvi.

Two figures exploded from the trees. One wore a black leather mask that wrapped over his face, only the whites of his eyes visible. The other was a woman, her face deathly pale beneath war paint, black streaks smeared like claws across her cheeks. The sun caught the metal in their hands.

Kalgorans.

"Run!" Heida's voice rang out as her axes flashed.

Iron met iron with a clang that echoed through the trees. Inga lunged for Katla, sweeping her up into her arms, and Ranvi clutched Alvir, her voice trembling as she called for Trygg. Eadlyn's hands went slack, the basket dropping from her fingers. Then they ran.

Clashes erupted behind them, and Eadlyn darted a look back. Could Heida hold off two attackers by herself? But what could Eadlyn even do to help? She had the knife Heida had given her, but even with some training, she could not—

A scream echoed as another dark shape burst from the bushes. In one swift, monstrous motion, a man snatched Trygg off his feet, clamping a thick arm around the boy's chest and raising a blade to his neck.

"*No!*" Ranvi cried, raw panic splitting her voice.

Inga spun, thrusting Katla into Eadlyn's arms. Eadlyn staggered under the weight of the girl. Trygg's face went white as the burly Kalgoran adjusted his grip on him. His lip trembled, but he didn't cry out.

"Let him go!" Inga demanded, stepping forward, knife drawn.

Heida appeared moments later, panting, with blood staining her arm. Her axes were still in hand, her expression murderous. She flanked Inga and faced the three Kalgorans now gathered before them. Her voice rang out, harsh and demanding, with words Eadlyn did not understand. The man eyed them before responding in the same coarse language. Though Eadlyn failed to decipher anything he said, she was almost certain she heard her name in the jumble of words.

A tense silence followed, but something in Heida's posture changed.

Eadlyn's legs went cold. "What did he say?"

Heida shifted, flexing her hands around her axes. "He said… they'll let Trygg and the rest of us go…if they take you instead."

The world tilted. Eadlyn fixed her attention on Trygg. His chin quivered, and his eyes, wide and scared, met hers. He whimpered as the man's blade pressed harder against his throat.

Heida gestured at her own chest with her axe, and Eadlyn's stomach sank. But the man shook his head and spoke shortly. Heida's voice rose, yet Eadlyn read the hard resolve in the man's black-rimmed eyes. Either they got what they wanted or they would kill Trygg and anyone who stood between them and her. There wasn't time to think.

"I'll go."

Heida's expression flashed with protest, but no words came. They had no other choice.

Eadlyn set Katla down beside Ranvi and locked eyes with Heida again, finding her expression twisted into a sort of grim admiration.

In a low voice, she said, "We will come for you."

Eadlyn dipped her chin and then met the gaze of the masked man. Moving slowly, she pulled out the knife on her belt and let it drop. It landed in the dirt with a soft thud. She took another step forward, and the man seized her. His grip was cruel, yanking her into place. A blade scraped against her neck. She sucked in a breath and fought the swell of panic clawing at her throat.

But the other man released Trygg. His little legs scrambled as he ran to Ranvi, who fell to her knees and swept him into her arms. She looked at Eadlyn over the boy's head, her eyes swimming with tears and a wordless mix of gratitude and grief.

Eadlyn tried to smile, but another jolt of panic raced through her as the raiders backed away, dragging her along with them. *Lord, please protect me.*

Heida sent the captors a glare, speaking what sounded like a threat.

None of the three responded. Before another word could be spoken, the man holding Eadlyn turned and shoved her ahead of him, deeper into the woods. She didn't dare look back with his sword still hovering dangerously close to her neck, but she heard the other two following. Hurried footsteps and Inga's urgent voice told Eadlyn they were on their way back to the village, and relief cut through the fear. The raiders had gotten what they wanted and let everyone else go. If sacrificing herself meant they lived, then she'd done the right thing in surrendering.

After a ways, the Kalgoran removed the blade from her throat, allowing her to breathe a little easier. His grip, however, remained crushing around her arm as he forced her ahead of him at a fast pace. They hurried through the forest for about a mile before reaching a small creek. At the bank, they paused, scanning the trees as if making sure they had not been followed. Eadlyn wouldn't put it past Heida to do that, though she hoped she'd seen the others safely back to Fjellheim. She could not take on three warriors by herself.

While the other two were preoccupied, Eadlyn's captor pulled her back against him, pressing a hand to her middle and sliding it upward. Revulsion swelled in her throat. Eadlyn spun and slapped him away, her breath ragged. His grip tightened, and pain flared in her arm.

"Enough," the woman snapped. "We keep moving."

Her voice was low, clipped, and in Nordric.

It made no sense, but Eadlyn did not have time to ponder it before they continued on through the forest.

Despite the heat of the day and the fast pace building up sweat under her dress, Eadlyn's whole body flushed with ice. She would likely die at the hands of these people if God did not provide rescue, but she hadn't had a chance until a moment ago to consider what might happen to her in the meantime.

They traveled another mile at least before they broke into a small clearing. Here, four horses waited, guarded by one lone figure.

Eadlyn gasped. "Oda?"

The woman glared at her, all her loathing unmasked. She strode toward them, focusing on the man behind Eadlyn.

"Did you have any trouble?"

"None at all."

The familiar voice of the man who had dragged Eadlyn through the forest shot dread straight into her core. She looked over her shoulder as Sig yanked off the mask, and a fresh wave of panic almost upended her stomach. This could not be happening. She could not be left at Sig's mercy. Death would likely be a kinder fate than what he planned to do to her if rescue did not come soon.

"They were exactly where you said they'd be."

Eadlyn breathed harder. Oda wasn't just watching their horses; she'd been part of their plan. Spying again, telling Sig exactly where they had been picking berries.

"If you value your lives, you'll let me go." Eadlyn spoke in Aerlish. Some whisper in the back of her mind told her it might be wise to conceal her understanding of Nordric for the time being.

Oda sneered at her. "You think we're afraid of a spoiled little princess?"

Eadlyn held her gaze, trying to keep her voice even. "If you do this, Aevar will hunt you down and kill you. You know he will."

Right or wrong, the moment he found out she'd been abducted, he would do anything within his power to find her and exact vengeance on all involved. She had not forgotten how much effort it had taken for him not to kill Sig the first time he'd put his hands on her.

Oda snorted. "You'll be long dead before he ever gets close to finding you."

The ice in her voice chilled Eadlyn's blood. She'd known Oda hated her, but not to this extreme.

The woman drew closer and pulled out a narrow dagger. Eadlyn's heart missed a beat, but she forced herself to breathe evenly. Oda assessed her with a scowl.

"I'll never understand what he sees in you." She placed the tip of her knife against Eadlyn's cheek right where two scars marred the skin, courtesy of her father's ringed fist. Perhaps she was thinking of adding another as if it would lessen her worth.

Though every instinct screamed at Eadlyn to pull away, she refused to move. She may have been born an Essian princess, but she was a Nord now.

"We don't have time for this," the other woman's voice broke into the stare down. "The king's men will be after us soon if they aren't already."

Oda scowled but backed away and snapped her knife into the sheath. She glanced at the other woman before turning to Eadlyn again and speaking in Aerlish.

"Make sure she suffers. If I can't have what I want, then neither can Aevar."

evar rested his scythe on the ground and dragged a forearm across his brow. The sun bore down, heavy and unrelenting, wrapping the field in a haze of heat and dust. His shoulders ached, and every breath tasted of hay and sweat. Nearby, his father, brothers, and Kian worked alongside the thralls, their blades sweeping through the tall grass. The sharp swish of metal as it sliced through stalks blended with the low drone of insects.

Another day nearly done. They'd finish this field by nightfall. Then, after a dip in the fjord, he could go home to supper. To Eadlyn.

He reached for the waterskin offered by one of the older thrall women, nodded his thanks, and drank. Cool water cut through the heat in his throat. He hadn't realized how thirsty he was until now. When he handed it back and bent to retrieve his scythe, movement caught the edge of his vision. A lone figure running. Fast. He shaded his eyes and recognized Ingvald. The huskarl's full sprint soured the water in Aevar's stomach and turned the sweat clinging to his back to ice. Something was wrong.

Ingvald didn't veer toward Fathir. Instead, he came straight toward Aevar.

Aevar's pulse stuttered, then slammed into a faster rhythm. "What happened?"

"The women," Ingvald gasped. "They were ambushed. Eadlyn was taken."

Aevar didn't even feel the scythe slip from his fingers. He only heard it hit the ground with a dull thud that echoed through the hollow in his chest.

"What?" he choked.

"I don't know more. I came straight here."

The rest died away beneath the sudden, rushing roar in Aevar's ears. *Eadlyn. Taken.* The two words didn't belong in the same breath. Fathir's commanding voice cut through the fog, but Aevar barely heard it. The others converged, questions flying, but it didn't matter. None of it mattered. He turned and ran.

The children's cries met him before he even reached the longhouse. Their wails echoed off the timber walls, and as he burst inside, he found them clinging to Ranvi, whose face stretched tight with worry. Heida sat on the edge of the table, Móthir working in front of her.

But no Eadlyn.

The breath died in his lungs. Some part of him had refused to believe she was gone, but her absence struck like a blow to the ribs.

The women turned toward him. First came his mother's pained regret. A look far too reminiscent of the one she'd given him the day Thora died. He dropped his gaze to the blood on

Heida's sleeve. When their eyes met, hers roiled with both remorse and anger.

"Aevar, I'm sorry. I tried…" She shook her head.

He crossed the space in long strides, the rest of the men piling in behind him. "What happened?" His voice cracked. "Who was it? Where is she?"

"Three of them. They looked Kalgoran, but—" A deep groan that Heida forced through her teeth like more of a growl cut her off as Móthir applied pressure to the wound.

The couple of heartbeats of waiting—the couple of heartbeats he did not know where Eadlyn was or if she was even still alive—almost broke Aevar. "But what?"

She sucked in a hard breath. "But they fought like Nords. And the one I spoke to was fluent in Goric, but there was something off about it, like it was not his native tongue."

Aevar's mind spun, but the only clear thought was Eadlyn. Getting to her. Now. "Where did they attack?"

"Northeast. Near the old bilberry patch."

Behind him, Fathir gave orders to Ingvald to gather men and horses. He then stood at Aevar's side and focused on Heida.

"You're sure they were Nords?"

Heida winced. "No, but I don't believe they were typical Kalgoran raiders either."

If it was Nords, who would dress up like Kalgorans and take Eadlyn? They would have to have a reason. A move like that could start a war. Aevar's thoughts scrambled until one name launched itself into the forefront of his mind.

"Staegar." He spun toward his father. "It must be him. Who else would target her like this?"

Fathir did not speak, but his grim expression was answer enough.

Fire ignited in Aevar's blood, and he curled his fists. He was going to kill Staegar. And the three who'd taken Eadlyn and anyone else who laid a finger on her. But first he had to find her.

He turned and almost crashed into Kian, who held out his sword.

"You forgot something."

Aevar grabbed it and snatched a shield from the wall on his way outside.

At the stable, a dozen huskarls rushed to saddle horses. Fathir shouted orders, selecting six riders to accompany them. He dispatched the rest to patrol the village borders in case more trouble lurked nearby. Within moments, they had mounted, and Heida took the lead, riding hard toward the forest trail. Aevar's heart pounded in time with his horse's hooves, a brutal drumbeat driving him forward. He gripped the reins tighter, clenching his jaw against the images trying to claw their way into his mind. Eadlyn in enemy hands. Afraid. Bleeding. Or worse.

Branches whipped past in a blur of green and shadow as they rode deeper into the woods. At last, Heida slowed. The trail ahead bore signs of struggle. Baskets lay overturned, deep blue bilberries scattered across the grass.

She turned in the saddle and pointed into the dense cluster of trees to the north. "This is where they attacked. They took Eadlyn that way."

Aevar didn't wait. He turned his horse, ready to charge in, but Fathir's voice broke through the haze of desperation driving him forward.

"Erik, take the lead. You're the best at tracking."

Erik moved ahead at a slower, more deliberate pace.

Aevar ground his teeth. His mount, as restless as he was, tossed its head and snorted. The horse wanted to run. To storm through the forest with Aevar. By the time they reached a clearing and paused, he, like his horse, was about to crawl out of his skin.

Erik looked around. "They stopped here." He dismounted to better survey the ground. "Horses. Four of them, I think."

Aevar squeezed the reins until his knuckles ached. That proved Heida was right. Kalgorans didn't use horses for anything but food and sacrifices. It must be Nords.

"They continued north from here?"

"Looks like it."

They pressed on, and Aevar found himself praying. To the gods. To God. To the wind. He wasn't even sure. He didn't care who answered, so long as *someone* heard him. The trail narrowed, winding through trees and uneven rock. Pine sap and damp soil thickened the air as they rode deeper into the forest. Branches clawed low, and every hoofbeat thudded against the growing dread in Aevar's chest.

Eventually, Erik reined in and dismounted again, frowning at the rocky ground ahead of them. He moved carefully and crouched low over a patch of disturbed moss and gravel. Long minutes passed. Aevar held his horse steady as it pawed at the ground, ears twitching. Tension burned beneath his skin in a slow-rising fire, crawling into his throat.

Erik straightened and turned back to them, his expression grim. "I've lost the trail."

The words hit like a hammer.

"What? They were heading north. Shouldn't we keep going?"

"They chose this spot for a reason. It's rocky and hard to track through. They were trying to cover their trail. They could have turned aside at any point. We can't be sure where they went from here."

Aevar scanned the trees as though they might offer an answer. The forest stared back in silence. "Then what do we do?" He turned to his father. "Do we gather the men and go to Ormvik?"

He had no doubt Staegar was behind this, and he was ready to fight the entire clan to find Eadlyn.

Fathir didn't answer right away, and Aevar could see his mind turning.

"Staegar will deny knowing anything," he said at last.

"We can make him talk," Braan growled, his voice full of heat.

Fathir frowned. "Perhaps. But it would take time."

Time they didn't have. Every moment wasted left Eadlyn at the mercy of her captors. Who knew what they were doing to her?

"Then we'll tear Ormvik apart." Aevar gripped his sword hilt and peered back toward the fjord.

Fathir shook his head. "Staegar wouldn't risk keeping her in the village. Too many eyes. Too much risk."

"One of his other settlements then. We'll start with the closest and work our way through them."

War might follow, but he didn't care.

"He wouldn't risk that either. He would take her somewhere isolated. Somewhere we wouldn't think to look and won't draw attention from anyone less than loyal to him."

Aevar's pulse thundered in frustration. "Then what? We go back and do nothing?"

"We go back for Jorund."

The silence that followed was deafening. Even the horses seemed to still.

"He's the best tracker we have," Fathir went on. "He'll be able to find the trail again. If we press forward now, blind, we might lose more time. Or lose her entirely."

Aevar struggled to breathe. It would take an hour to return to the village. More to get back here. Jorund then needed time to track. "They already have the lead. And now we're going to give them more?"

Fathir's voice softened. "I know it's not what you want to hear, but it's the best chance we have. And once we do find her, we could be outnumbered. We need to prepare for a fight now that they've had time to gather more men."

Every part of Aevar resisted. Rage, fear, and helplessness twisted in his gut. But Fathir was right. Charging in half-armed when the captors could have met up with reinforcements was a quick way to fail. He forced himself to nod, though everything in him screamed to press on.

Back at the longhouse, Aevar marched straight to his room and threw open the old chest where he kept his armor. He yanked off his sweat-soaked tunic and pulled on a clean one, the cool fabric clinging to skin still hot from the ride. Then came the reinforced leather jerkin, scarred and worn with the memory of past battles. The motions were familiar, muscle memory guiding him.

His gaze slipped to the bed.

Still. Undisturbed.

The room pressed in without her presence. Silence wrapped around him, bringing ghosts in its wake. The emptiness after Thora's death. Nights that didn't end. Days that bled together. The part of him that had so recently healed now throbbed like an old wound ripped open. He dragged a breath into lungs that refused to expand.

He would find her. Or die trying.

Strapping on his sword and seax, he returned to the hall where his father, brothers, and Kian had already donned their own armor. Fathir wore the chain mail passed down through generations, its links darkened with time. Heida entered a moment later, dressed for battle despite the fresh bandage on her arm.

Braan eyed her. "You should stay here. You're wounded."

Her voice was quiet but lined with iron. "I'm going."

"And what if they actually were Kalgorans and the blade was poisoned?" Braan pressed. "What if you fall ill?"

Heida turned to face him. "Then you leave me behind."

They stared each other down, the air thick between them, until she sighed.

"I couldn't stop them from taking her. I need to help bring her back."

Braan's expression softened as he relented.

Móthir approached. Her face was set and grim with purpose, but Aevar caught the fear in her eyes. The same fear she'd worn before they'd lost Thora. She loved Eadlyn. They all did.

"We packed provisions. Enough for a few days. Gods willing, you won't need them." She gestured to the packs laid out on the table.

They gathered the supplies and carried them out to the horses.

Here, Fathir faced Móthir and set his hands on her shoulders. "Keep an eye out for trouble, especially from Ormvik. If you suspect anything, send for more men from our other villages and to Halbjorn. And send ravens to the other jarls. Don't mention

Staegar, only that Kalgorans took Eadlyn, and everyone should be on the lookout for her in case we don't find her right away."

She nodded. "Be careful."

"We will." He drew her close and kissed her.

A short distance away, Erik exchanged parting words with Ranvi. Aevar couldn't help but watch. The pain in his chest stabbed deeper. He should've been holding Eadlyn. He should've had her beside him, safe, whole. Her absence screamed in the spaces she used to fill. Standing here alone brought the agony of the past roaring back.

As Erik turned to mount, Ranvi caught Aevar's eye, her expression somber.

"One of them grabbed Trygg," she said. "They were going to kill him if Eadlyn didn't surrender. She gave herself up willingly."

Aevar looked at the boy. Pressure choked his throat, and his vision blurred. She had sacrificed herself for Trygg. Just as she had once sacrificed herself for her people. His brave, selfless wife.

A hand gripped his arm. He turned to find Móthir beside him. She pulled him into a fierce embrace. "You *will* get her back."

He nodded against her shoulder, unable to speak, but he had to believe it.

He *would* believe it.

With final goodbyes exchanged, they mounted again, this time with several more riders in tow. At the village's edge, Jorund waited, his dark braids matching the color of the winding tattoos across his forehead. Some said he could track a bird through the sky. Exaggeration or not, Aevar was willing to believe it. They needed every bit of the man's skill, real or imagined.

Night was falling. The warm light of the sun dimmed above the treetops, giving way to the long shadows of dusk. They crept between the trees, pooling beneath ferns and wrapping around the narrow game trail the riders followed. Eadlyn craned her neck for the hundredth time, scanning the forest behind her, willing Aevar to appear. To hear the pounding of hooves. To see the flash of a sword raised in fury.

But the path remained empty and quiet. Only the thud of the horse beneath her, and the soft jingle of tack from the others. Her hands, bound at the wrists with rough rope, ached from the pressure. The cord bit into her skin with every jostling movement, and her arms had gone half-numb. Sweat clung to the hollow of her back, but it cooled now in the evening air, sending shivers through her body.

Lord, please bring rescue.

She had whispered the same plea so many times it had worn thin. It continued to beat in her heart, tethering her to hope, but with every fading glimmer of daylight, hopelessness sank deeper.

What if they didn't find her? The forest was vast, and her captors had made careful efforts to hide their trail, doubling back, crossing creeks, and weaving through thickets and rocky plateaus.

She glanced to her left where Sig rode beside her, slouched comfortably in the saddle and unbothered by the weight of the day. But his attention had been on her all afternoon. Measuring her. Waiting. She turned away, bile rising in her throat. Her whole body tensed with the certainty that the moment they stopped, he would make his move.

She looked to her right for an escape, but found only thick, tangled brush. Nowhere to run. Even if her hands were free and she had control of the horse's reins, she'd crash headlong into roots and undergrowth.

All too soon, the woman—Asfrid, she had learned—drew to a halt. They had reached a patch of open earth beneath a cluster of firs where the ground sloped toward a stream. The canopy above hung like a thick curtain, blotting out most of the sun's last light.

She turned to them, tall and broad-shouldered for a woman. Clearly a warrior like Heida. She addressed Sig and the other man, Dagr, in Nordric. "We should camp here tonight."

Eadlyn's heart pounded harder. The moment she had been dreading. Sig dismounted first. She braced herself, but a tremble ran through her limbs as he stalked toward her. His hand clamped around her arm and yanked her from the saddle. She hit the ground unsteadily, and he pinned her against him.

"Aevar's not around to interrupt this time." His sour breath hit her in the face.

Panic surged. She struggled, and he laughed, but she wouldn't make this easy for him. The moment he leaned in, she spat in his face.

For a moment, everything froze. Then pain cracked across her cheek. His open palm slapped her so hard she stumbled. Tears sprang up, but she blinked them back and straightened. She'd been hit harder before. She locked eyes with him. No pleading or fear. Just fire.

His brows twitched, something unreadable in his expression. No doubt he'd expected her to cower and cry and beg for mercy. Wanted it. But she refused to give him that. His expression hardened to match hers. He reached for her again, but another hand seized her arm first and wrenched her backward. Eadlyn stumbled again, catching herself as Asfrid dragged her away from Sig's grasp. The painted warrior woman's expression was like stone, her black-marked face unreadable.

Sig snarled. "What are you doing?"

Asfrid didn't even flinch. "My job is to deliver her to Kalgora. Not watch you toy with her."

"I can do whatever I want."

"That was not part of your uncle's orders."

Sig stepped toward her, puffed with self-importance. "I am his heir. You will do as I command." He leered now. "Or I'll take what I want from both of you."

From somewhere behind Eadlyn, Dagr swore. "That's my sister you're talking to."

He was beside Asfrid in a breath, his face flinty.

Sig sneered. "Then maybe you should teach her to obey."

Eadlyn held her breath as they glared at each other. Would Asfrid and her brother decide it wasn't worth it and let Sig have her? Would they bow to his position and stand aside to let him do whatever he pleased?

Asfrid didn't move. She didn't even raise her voice. "We were commanded to take her north. That is what we are doing. If you want our help to communicate with the Kalgorans when we get there, you will keep your hands off. Otherwise, we walk away. You can travel with your sword and your title. I'm sure the Kalgorans will welcome you with open arms."

They continued to stare at each other in an intense, silent battle of wills.

Sig broke first.

With a muttered curse, he stormed into the trees, a string of angry threats and obscenities trailing behind him. Eadlyn couldn't help praying he'd meet a bear. Or something worse.

Now that he was gone, the heaviness of the encounter and the information she'd learned descended. They were taking her to Kalgora. The thought of that left her legs wobbly, but it did give Aevar time to find her if Asfrid kept Sig at bay.

The woman dragged her over to a tree and sat her down none-too-gently. While Asfrid seemed happy to protect her from Sig, they were far from friends. Even so, Eadlyn caught her eye and murmured, "Thank you."

She stuck to Aerlish. Even if Asfrid didn't understand the words, the meaning was clear. The woman paused before turning toward the horses. Dagr joined her, glancing first at Eadlyn and then into the trees where Sig had disappeared.

"You're playing with fire."

Asfrid tugged at the straps of a rolled-up blanket and sheepskin on her saddle. "I won't stand by and watch that pig assault a bound woman. We're delivering her. That's all."

Dagr followed as she walked back over to a spot near Eadlyn and laid out the bedding. "He'll have you punished when we return to Ormvik. He won't let it go."

"I don't intend to give him the chance. We will do as ordered and disappear. I'm tired of being treated like a stray dog. We are not Staegar's thralls just because Móthir was. We should have left Ormvik a long time ago."

"You don't think Staegar will come after us?"

"He's got bigger things on his mind. As long as we deliver the princess, he'll forget about us. Sig can whine all he wants, but he needs us."

That ended the discussion. Dagr grunted and laid out his own bedding beside his sister's. Eadlyn looked at the horse she had ridden. No blanket. No comforts.

Sig returned eventually, prowling the edge of the camp. As darkness fell in full, they shared provisions. Asfrid gave Eadlyn only a handful of berries. Though she wasn't hungry, Eadlyn needed her strength and tipped the berries into her mouth. To her dismay, no one started a fire. It would have made finding her easier in the dark.

Not long after they ate, they decided the watch order. Dagr went first, and Asfrid settled down on her bedroll, while Sig lay down several feet away. With a tight cramp in her middle, Eadlyn curled up, the grass damp beneath her cheek, and stones biting into her hip. She tried not to think. Thinking hurt. But she ached for Aevar's arms around her, holding her close. She fought to push it down, to stay strong, but a tear rolled over the bridge of her nose. She bit her lip hard as pain swelled, forcing more tears to rise, and prayed for rescue.

Eadlyn jolted awake with a gasp. Cool, damp air filled her lungs, and the forest greeted her with a heavy silence cloaked in predawn shadows. She blinked, trying to shake the fog of half-sleep. For a fleeting moment, she had believed she was home. Safe. But no soft bed or tender arms cradled her now. Only cold earth, aching bones, and the ropes that still bit into her wrists.

It wasn't a dream.

She was still a captive.

A rustle made her flinch. Asfrid knelt, rolling her blankets and securing the straps. Nearby, Dagr moved through the gloom, brushing pine needles off his cloak and cinching saddles. A few feet away, Sig still lay sprawled on the ground and snored like a beast, far too comfortable for someone so cruel.

Eadlyn's whole body ached. Her back was sore from the hours in the saddle the day before, and her hips throbbed from sleeping on knotted roots and uneven stones. But worse than anything was the hollow space in her chest. An ache carved by fear and longing.

Asfrid stood, brushed her hands on her trousers, and walked toward her. Without a word, she gripped Eadlyn's arm and tugged her to her feet. Her fingers were firm, not unkind, but gave no room for resistance. Eadlyn followed, her legs unsteady beneath her as they moved deeper into the forest. A cool breeze swept through the trees, stirring the underbrush.

They stopped near a fallen tree, its trunk stripped bare and damp with dew. Asfrid said nothing, but the implication was clear enough. She was giving Eadlyn the chance to relieve herself away from the men. Eadlyn should be grateful, but all it did was remind her of the first night with Aevar on the journey to Fjellheim. How frightening it had been. So much had changed. This was the first time they'd been apart since they'd married.

Unlike Aevar, Asfrid didn't give her the courtesy of walking away or even turning her back, though she didn't seem inclined to watch. Instead, she swept the trees like she expected Aevar to come tearing through them any moment. Eadlyn begged God that he would.

But after a few heavy heartbeats, the forest remained empty. Swallowing her disappointment and pride, she turned to take care of her business. Then she gathered her courage and faced Asfrid once more. This might be her only chance while Sig wasn't nearby. Asfrid clearly had no affection or loyalty to him or Staegar. Perhaps Eadlyn could persuade her to help.

She breathed a prayer, pressing hope into every word that followed. "I heard what you said to your brother," she spoke in Nordric. "If you take me back to Fjellheim, the king will protect you from Staegar."

Asfrid's head whipped toward her. Her eyes narrowed, flashing in the gray light with the revelation that Eadlyn had understood them this whole time. "You really think they'd forgive us? For abducting you?" Her tone was flat and skeptical. "You think your husband would?"

It wouldn't be easy, but Eadlyn nodded. "They will if I ask them to."

Asfrid snorted. "I like my plan better."

She grabbed Eadlyn's arm again and led her back toward camp. Brush snagged Eadlyn's skirt, the forest cold and unkind around them. Each step bit harder at her resolve. If she didn't get out of this soon… If Aevar didn't come…

Back in camp, Sig was awake and saddling his horse. His mouth contorted in a sneer as he watched them. When the others began eating, Eadlyn wasn't sure she would receive anything until Asfrid passed her a handful of wrinkled berries and a strip of salted meat.

Between bites, she eyed Sig as she debated. Now that Asfrid knew she understood Nordric, it probably wouldn't take long for the others to find out. Might as well learn what she could.

"Why take me to Kalgora?" she asked no one in particular

Sig's head shot up. "So the princess has been listening." His grin was all teeth. "As much as I wanted to keep you for myself, my uncle had other plans. You're to be a gift. A peace offering to the Kalgorans so when he becomes king, they'll support him."

"And what makes him think he'll ever be king? Even if he manages to defeat Runar, the other jarls won't just fall in line."

Sig shrugged. "Nordra needs strength. The alliance was weakness. Eventually, the others will see that."

She shook her head. "I think he underestimates the respect Runar has from the other clans. It takes more than strength or force to rule. A good leader has both strength and humility. He understands the wisdom of cultivating relationships with those around him. He thinks of his people and not only of his own power. Things neither you nor your uncle seem to understand."

Sig's smirk didn't fade. "Well, once Runar's dealt with and my uncle has the support of Kalgora, there won't be much choice but to follow him."

His words oozed with arrogant certainty. Was there already a plan in place to kill Runar? An assassination rather than an honorable challenge? "So murder Runar, ally with Kalgora, and threaten the other jarls into obedience. That's your uncle's plan?"

"Pretty much."

Asfrid and Dagr rolled their eyes. Either they didn't think too much of this plan or were annoyed over his blabbing about it so freely.

Eadlyn barely had time to think before Sig leaned closer, his voice like venom. "And once the king is dead, I'll take your beloved Aevar as my prisoner. He'll beg for death before I give it to him."

Her stomach recoiled, but she didn't flinch. Didn't look away. She finished the last of her berries, eyes locked with his. Little by little, his grin faded.

Finally, she said, "You talk a lot for someone half the man Aevar is and who shamed himself in front of the other jarls."

Color flooded Sig's face. He lunged at her, the back of his hand striking her hard across her face. Her knees buckled, and the earth rushed up to meet her. Shouting and a scuffle rose over the ringing in her ears. When she regained her senses, Dagr was restraining Sig.

Asfrid grabbed Eadlyn's arm and yanked her upright, dragging her toward her horse with a muttered curse. "You'd do well not to provoke him if you want me to keep him away from you." But, just for a moment, she glanced at Eadlyn with something like grudging respect. "Not that he doesn't deserve it."

Something wet trickled down Eadlyn's chin from her stinging lip. When she touched the back of her hand to it, it came away smeared with blood.

Asfrid sighed and dug a cloth out of her pack, handing it to Eadlyn.

"*Tahk*," Eadlyn murmured and used it to slow the bleeding.

Over by his own horse, Sig fumed, still uttering curses. Dagr shook his head, shooting Asfrid a sharp glance, but said nothing as he checked their gear.

After a tense few minutes, they all mounted. Asfrid kept Eadlyn's horse close to hers and turned to her brother. "Hang back and cover our trail."

Dagr gave Sig a wary look before nodding, and Asfrid led them deeper into the forest.

Her face throbbing, Eadlyn peered over her shoulder. The trees blurred behind her, but no rescue came. Where was Aevar, and how long would it take him to find her?

evar stared into the forest as dusk closed around them like a tightening fist. Shadows stretched long across the undergrowth, cloaking the trees in smoky gray and silencing the birds one by one. The wind had stilled, and all that remained was the faint rustle of leaves overhead and the slow, steady crush of hopelessness settling deeper into his being.

So many trees. So many endless, indifferent trees. And still no sign of Eadlyn beyond the occasional hoofprint or broken twig. None of it enough to say she was even alive or chase away the haunting thought that she might already be lost to him forever.

Nine days.

Nine days they had been on the trail. Every day they rode farther north, closer to Kalgora, and still she remained just out of reach. It was like running toward a star that never got any closer. The weight that had been pressing down on him descended with such force he struggled to breathe.

He closed his eyes against the burn behind them. Would he ever see his wife again? Would her voice and laughter become only a memory like Thora's? Would he have to carve her name into stone beside Thora and Brenna and grieve for another life lost too soon?

The ache in his chest was sharp now. His throat thickened with it, each breath a battle. The grief he'd kept at bay all these days roared to the surface, threatening to break him wide open. His life teetered on the brink of shattering once again, and he didn't think he could survive it this time. Not again.

Behind him, the soft clatter of gear and murmur of men told him the others were settling in for another night. He caught snatches of voices—grim, weary, and too quiet. He didn't need to hear the words to know what they were saying. The pity had grown more visible each day. Some of the men had begun to speak in the abstract now. *If* they found her. *When* they reached Kalgora. *What next*, in case the worst had already happened. His brothers and Kian never spoke like that, but Aevar read the worry in their faces, the weight of time pressing on all of them.

Footsteps approached. Aevar turned his head as Fathir came to stand beside him. The older man's face was lined with weariness and years of hard leadership, but his eyes still held strength and something akin to hope.

"We will get her back."

Aevar looked away, blinking. Each day made that harder and harder to believe. "It's been over a week. We still haven't caught up."

"They're growing careless. Jorund believes we can overtake them tomorrow."

Tomorrow.

Another night Eadlyn was at the whims and mercy of whoever had taken her. And if not tomorrow, they were running out of time. In two days, they'd reach the border of Kalgora. He would march straight to King Drocca's throne if he had to, but even then, would she survive long enough to be found?

Fathir must have sensed the doubts. He put his hand on Aevar's shoulder, squeezing it firmly. "You will not lose another wife."

He wanted to believe that, but what if tomorrow was too late? What if tonight was the last she had? And even if they got her back, would things ever be the same? He dug his fingers into his belt, trying to anchor himself to something solid.

"What if they've already hurt her? What if…" He couldn't finish the thought. The words tasted like blood in his mouth.

"Then you will love her. And we will help her heal. Whatever has been done can be endured. But we are not too late. Not yet." He stared out into the gloom, his voice quieter now. "And perhaps her God will protect her."

Aevar stood motionless, pierced by those words.

Her God.

The One she read to him about at night. The One she prayed to at the fjord's edge every morning.

For days now, his heart had been a battlefield. Half cursing the gods who had failed him, half whispering desperate prayers to the One Eadlyn called Father. And somewhere along the road, between hoofbeats and unanswered prayers, his loyalty to the old gods had died. Maybe it had been dying for years.

He couldn't take another breath in the camp. Not under the weight of so many eyes. Not with the war in his mind.

"I'll be back," he muttered, turning.

Fathir didn't stop him.

He walked with no direction, no plan. The forest stretched before him, darker now, the trunks blurring together. The farther he went, the more his thoughts surged, questions, fears, and guilt crashing against each other like waves in a storm.

Would he ever find her?

Would he even recognize her when he did?

Would she still be his?

The forest opened to a narrow river, dark and glassy under the half-hidden moon. Aevar stopped at the edge, breath ragged, limbs trembling, not from exhaustion, but from holding everything in.

Memories clawed their way forward. Thora's body in his arms, her soul slipping into silence. Brenna, so small and still. Prayers offered to Odin and Freyja and anyone who might listen. Pleas made with blood and sacrifice and tears.

Nothing had come.

No signs. No answers. Just silence.

He reached for the pendant around his neck, the one he'd worn since childhood. Thor's hammer. The old symbol of strength and storm and fury. He closed his fingers around the cool metal, but there was no strength in it. No fury that could help him now.

He yanked it off, the leather cord snapping with a soft pop. The pendant sat heavy in his palm. Lifeless. A lie. If Eadlyn and her Holy Book were right, then all the prayers he'd offered to the gods in his lifetime had been empty requests thrown into the wind. Pleas that went unheard by creations of men. Words that accomplished nothing and saved no one.

He didn't even know when or how he had truly started listening those nights Eadlyn had read to him, but the realization struck him like lightning from heaven. He believed it. He believed her.

The gods were not real. They could not help him, and they could not help Eadlyn.

Aevar looked at the pendant one more time and flung it into the river. The silver arc caught the last light and vanished beneath the black surface with a small splash. He stood motionless for a moment before sinking to his knees on the damp earth.

His voice broke the stillness. "God… Lord…" He struggled to shape the words. "Only You can save her. Only You can save me. Please. I can't lose her too."

Tears slid down his cheeks unchecked, and he bowed his head. There in the dark he knelt, caught between belief and fear. Faith and anguish. Wrestling not just for Eadlyn's life, but for something deeper. Would this God hear him? Would He answer?

Finally, the tempest in Aevar's mind quieted. Not vanish or fade entirely but settle. For the first time in his life, he didn't feel as though his fate was governed by chance or by whim but by purpose.

Dawn streaked across the treetops in soft gold and pink. Eadlyn blinked herself awake, flinching at the dull throb that pulsed behind her brows. Every muscle groaned as she pushed herself upright, the cold ground leeching heat from her bones.

Ten days. Or eleven. Maybe twelve.

She'd lost count. The blur of hunger, exhaustion, and constant vigilance had swallowed time whole. Her limbs were leaden, her breath shallow. When she drew her knees to her chest, she winced, and a shiver rippled through her. The early morning chill clung to her like wet linen, seeping beneath her skin. Tears prickled, and she blinked hard, but the ache inside her burned fiercer than ever.

Where are You, Lord?

The voice in her head barely sounded like her own anymore. Not even during her darkest nights in Kenwich had God felt so far away. Did He even hear her anymore? The hollow distance between herself and hope echoed inside her. And yet, in the very next breath, she murmured, "*Thou art my refuge and my portion in the land of the living.*"

Footsteps broke the stillness.

Eadlyn rubbed her eyes and forced her head up. Asfrid stood there, face unreadable as always. She extended the usual meager offering—dried berries and a tough strip of meat. Though Eadlyn hadn't been full in days, exhaustion had robbed her of appetite. Still, she took it with numb fingers and forced herself to eat.

After she finished, Asfrid led her into the woods, away from the others. The trees stood tall and still, heavy with silence, as if holding their breath. The forest was beautiful in a strange, solemn way, but even its majesty couldn't touch the dread curdling in Eadlyn's belly.

On the way back, Sig brushed past her. His fingers slid against her hip like grease. A shudder of revulsion cut through her. Asfrid had protected her from assault, but not from the lingering touches whenever she wasn't looking. Eadlyn jerked away from him, and he chuckled under his breath. He'd made tormenting her his daily entertainment.

Once she was on her horse, she exhaled. At least here, he couldn't touch her, though it only meant they were continuing deeper into the north. Farther from hope. Farther from Aevar.

And now Dagr no longer hung back to obscure their trail. Either they believed no one was following, or they were so deep into Kalgoran territory it no longer mattered.

On they rode, following no discernible path, but ever heading north as far as Eadlyn could tell. As the miles passed, she drifted in and out of prayer, clutching verses like lifelines despite how fragile her grip felt. *My times are in thy hand: deliver me from the hand of mine enemies, and from them that persecute me.*

Asfrid halted.

Eadlyn snapped to attention.

Something had shifted. The stillness was different now. Watchful. The birds had gone quiet. Eadlyn held her breath and dared to hope. *Please, God…*

Figures lunged from the trees, swift and dark. The horses shrieked as the forest erupted in chaos. A dozen Kalgoran warriors encircled them in an instant. Eadlyn's horse half-reared, stamping and snorting. She clung to the saddle, panic and despair swelling like a rising tide. All around her, foreign voices barked orders. The unmistakable harshness of Goric made her head spin.

Asfrid raised her hand and spoke rapidly to the one who appeared to be in charge—a towering man with a bald head and a forked beard like twisted rope. When she gestured to Eadlyn, her stomach dropped.

The Kalgoran gave a grunt.

Asfrid dismounted and strode over to Eadlyn, dragging her down from the saddle. The Kalgoran commander studied her and exchanged more clipped words with Asfrid.

Tremors threatened to seize Eadlyn, but she stood straight. She wouldn't cower.

Movement drew her attention beyond the commander. Another figure appeared, and the hair on the back of Eadlyn's neck rose. A woman only about her age, draped in fur, bones, and feathers, approached. Her long blond hair was almost as white as the paint that covered her face, though black ringed her eyes. Dark runes inked her cheeks and brow. The strange charms sewn to her dress rattled as she moved. This must be a seer like Heida talked about.

She paused in front of Eadlyn and stared, long and unblinking, like she was reading her soul. Even Asfrid shifted, giving the seer a wide berth. Eadlyn stood frozen under her scrutiny.

Words passed between the seer and Asfrid. Eadlyn caught none of it, but she didn't need to. She knew. A deal was being made, and she was the price. Again. Another alliance, another transaction, but this time, against her will.

A curt nod from the seer ended the conversation and seemed to all but seal Eadlyn's fate. The woman turned and motioned to the man behind her, who stepped forward and reached for Eadlyn.

"Wait."

The man paused as Sig approached. He glanced warily at the seer before turning his full, undesired attention on Eadlyn. She tensed as he drew near and leaned in close.

"I didn't get what I wanted…" he said, voice low and oozing, "but I'll not go away empty-handed."

He seized her arm, his fingers crushing her skin, and slid her arm ring off before she could stop him. The polished silver—Aevar's promise to her—flashed in the morning light and vanished into his hand.

"No!" The word tore from her throat. She lunged for it, but he stepped back, grinning.

She stood helpless as he rolled it between his fingers, studying it like a prize. It wasn't just a ring. It was *Aevar*. His oath. His love. Everything they'd fought for reduced to a trinket in Sig's filthy hand. Tears blurred her vision. She wanted to scream. To claw it back.

But the Kalgoran grabbed her by the arm. His grip was harsh and unyielding, and she stumbled as he dragged her away. She caught Asfrid's gaze. Something like regret or pity softened her expression, but then it hardened. She, Dagr, and Sig turned for their horses, leaving Eadlyn alone at the mercy of her new captors.

evar held his breath as Jorund knelt again, fingers skimming over the turned-up soil. The silence was thick with expectation. Even the trees seemed to lean in, waiting. For a moment, no one moved.

Then Jorund straightened. "Very fresh. An hour old. Maybe less."

Finally. Ten days of chasing shadows. Ten days where every heartbeat hammered his chest like a countdown to the worst. But Aevar could feel it. She was near. So close he swore the air still carried her scent. The need to reach her roared through his veins.

Fathir raised his voice. "We don't know what we're riding into. Ingvald, take Njal and flank left through the trees. Kodran, Brodir, go right. Stay hidden. Cut off any escape when we engage."

The men melted into the forest.

Jorund returned to his horse and was about to swing into his saddle when he froze. His head tipped toward the wind. Everyone went still, listening, and Aevar caught a faint thudding echo. Hoofbeats. He tensed. This far north, one wasn't likely to come across any but enemies unless some of Jarl Gudrik's men were on patrol or hunting. Everyone waited in silence as the horses drew closer. Aevar leaned to the side, straining to see through the trees. Movement flashed through the brush ahead, and the riders appeared. Three of them. The leader jerked his reins, pulling up short. The others skidded to a halt behind him.

Aevar's heart turned to fire in his chest.

Recognition struck them both at once. Aevar caught the flicker in Sig's eyes, first of shock, then calculation. The two riders behind him stiffened in their saddles, but Aevar only spared them a glance. He kept his gaze fixed on Sig as every instinct screamed at him to ride over and rip him off his horse. He had no doubt in his mind Sig was part of Eadlyn's abduction. Had probably led it. But where was she then? Why was she not with them?

Sig's attention darted to Fathir, mockery dripping from his voice. "Quite a ways from Fjellheim, my lord."

"Where is she?" Aevar demanded before his father could respond.

Sig eyed him, something cruel and twisted in the way he smiled. "Who? Have you lost someone?"

Heida rode up beside Aevar, her voice sharp as a blade. "They're the ones. I recognize them. That one grabbed Trygg—" she pointed her axe at the man to Sig's left, "—and she cut me." Her weapon turned toward the woman. "And now we know who wore the mask."

Sig's smirk vanished. For a moment, fear cracked across his face. Then he wheeled his horse around, back to the north. But it was too late. From both flanks, Fathir's men burst from the trees, blocking the path.

"Drop your weapons and dismount," Fathir ordered.

The three riders eyed the men surrounding them as if contemplating whether to comply or try to fight their way through. But at three against more than a dozen, they didn't stand a chance.

Even so, Sig turned his horse toward Aevar again, and that was when the mask fell. A feral look claimed his expression. He bared his teeth like a beast and yanked his sword free, spurring his horse forward in a reckless, furious charge.

Straight at Aevar.

Aevar moved on instinct. He threw himself from his horse as Sig's blade carved through the air, slicing a whisper from where his head had been. His feet hit the forest floor with a jarring thud, and he bent his knees to absorb the shock. Sig's horse screamed and reared, almost crashing into Erik's. Sig toppled from the saddle, slamming to the ground with a crunch. But he was up again in a blink, eyes blazing. Aevar yanked out his sword and stepped forward to meet him.

Sig fought like a man possessed, each strike brutal and wild as if his blade had no edge and only blunt force would work. He didn't block or counter. Just swung with both hands, overhead chops and wide, sweeping arcs meant to cut Aevar in half. He fought with the fury of one who knew he was a dead man and had nothing left to lose.

Aevar gritted his teeth and met the onslaught. With each blow his arms numbed, the clang of iron ringing in his ears. But he moved with purpose, striking back with tight, focused slashes, using Sig's recklessness against him. The circle of onlookers blurred at the edges of his vision. Nothing existed but Sig. Sig, who had taken Eadlyn. Who might have harmed her. Might have killed her. This was no heated competition. This time they were out for blood.

Sig's sword whipped low and narrowly missed Aevar's leg. He staggered back. Sig lunged, grinning, and drove a horizontal strike toward Aevar's shoulder. Aevar shifted, and the blow glanced off his jerkin. He turned the momentum into a brutal counter, hammering his blade down onto Sig's wrist. Sig cried out, but then bared his teeth like a rabid dog and switched his sword to his left hand, slashing blindly.

Aevar growled and struck again, once to Sig's ribs, slicing through his tunic. Sig stumbled, panting, eyes manic. Blood ran down his side, wetting his trousers. Still, he fought.

They clashed again, harder. Aevar met him shoulder to shoulder, sword to sword. The impact jarred them both, and for a moment they grappled, faces inches apart, sweat and blood and hatred between them.

"You'll lose her," Sig spat. "Just like the last one."

Aevar slammed his forehead into Sig's with a crack. Sig reeled back, dazed, and Aevar kicked his leg out from under him, driving him to the ground. However, Sig rolled, scrambling to his feet, sword raised high for an overhead strike.

But he was too slow.

Aevar saw the opening—Sig's exposed belly, wide and vulnerable. He stepped in and swung. The blade tore through wool, skin, and muscle. Sig gasped. His sword slipped from his fingers, clattering on the ground. He bent forward, hands flying to his adomen, trying to hold his insides in. Blood gushed between his fingers in dark streams. Staggering, he bumped into a tree and slid to the ground with a hissed breath and a curse.

Aevar stalked toward him. Blood roared in his ears. He yanked Sig's seax knife from his belt and tossed it aside. Then he seized him by the front of his tunic and hauled him upright.

"Where is she?"

Sig laughed, a wet, choking sound. "She's gone."

The heat of battle evaporated into ice. Aevar's heart failed to beat for a moment.

"I very much enjoyed her company…"

The filth that came out of Sig's mouth burned through everything inside Aevar. He couldn't even understand the words. Just the sound of his own blood rushing with the urge to kill him. To kill him right now. His vision darkened. He gripped his sword tighter, one heartbeat from plunging it straight through Sig's throat.

"He's lying."

A woman's voice sliced through the haze.

Aevar spun. The woman they had captured knelt beside her fellow prisoner, flanked by Braan and Heida.

"He didn't touch her," she said flatly. "He tried. I didn't let him."

Sig hurled a curse at her, but Aevar barely heard it.

"Where is she?" he demanded.

The woman hesitated. "We handed her off to a group of Kalgorans. Less than an hour ago."

The earth seemed to tip beneath Aevar's feet. Every muscle in his body locked into place.

Heida yanked the woman to her feet. "You'd better show us."

Aevar shook himself loose and turned toward his horse. They had to move. *Now.*

But the woman called out again. "Wait. Check his pouch."

Aevar stopped and turned back to Sig, ripping the pouch from his belt. He dumped its contents into his hand. Eadlyn's silver arm ring fell into his palm. His breath left him as if he'd taken a blow to the gut. The symbol of his vow. Stolen from her.

"What about him?"

Aevar tore his gaze from the arm ring to see Ingvald motioning at Sig. Everyone looked at Aevar. Anyone else would have killed Sig right then and there. The urge seethed inside him, but he remembered something Eadlyn had read in Scripture. Something that had made no sense to him but now echoed in his mind.

Vengeance is mine, I will repay, saith the Lord.

Indecision held him in place, rage and uncertainty wrestling inside him. He turned to his father as if he might find an answer there. Though his father couldn't know what he was thinking, he seemed to understand Aevar faced some sort of dilemma.

Shifting his attention to Sig, Fathir eyed him with contempt. "Leave him to the wolves."

Sig made a strangled noise. In the end, whatever they chose, he was a dead man. Not even a skilled healer could have done anything for him in this condition. His fate was sealed. He might last an hour or two, but eventually he'd bleed out if a wild animal didn't finish him first. This far north, wolves and predators were plentiful and always hungry. They'd find him before nightfall.

For perhaps the first time, the arrogance drained from Sig's face. He looked around frantically until his gaze settled on something behind Aevar.

"Give me my sword. Or my knife. Something." His voice trembled with desperation.

To die without a weapon was to be denied Valhalla. A Nord warrior's greatest fear. Aevar didn't move. Worthless as the peace was, he couldn't find it in himself to give that to Sig. Not after all he had done.

When Sig shifted as if to crawl toward his weapons, Braan snatched them from the ground. Sig reached out with one bloodied hand, but Braan just glared at him.

"I think I'll give these to Eadlyn when we rescue her." He turned and carried them to his horse.

Sig howled as they mounted. Curses. Pleas. Cries for mercy. But no one looked back. With Heida, Jorund, and the captured woman in the lead, they rode on as Sig's final screams faded behind them.

Aevar soon forgot him, his mind centering only on Eadlyn. At least with her initial captors, she'd been relatively safe if the woman could be believed. The thought of her now in the hands of Kalgorans left him struggling to breathe. He gripped the reins tighter, whispering prayers for her safety and for success in finding her and freeing her. It would not be easy. The Kalgorans would fight and be more bent on killing their prey than allowing her to be rescued.

A few miles from where they had left Sig, the woman called them to a halt in a small clearing. "This is where we met the Kalgorans."

Aevar searched the trees for any sign Eadlyn was near. Jorund jumped down from his horse to study the ground. They waited anxiously as he searched the perimeter and deeper into the forest. Finally, he jogged back.

"It looks like they turned west here. Not north."

Aevar noticed Heida stiffen. "What is it?"

She glanced at him, her face pale. "They're not taking her to Kalgora. They're taking her to the Stone. They are going to sacrifice her."

Eadlyn stumbled over a branch, and her foot twisted beneath her. Pain flared in her ankle, but the massive Kalgoran brute did not slow. He yanked the rope at her wrists, dragging her forward with such force she almost dropped to her knees. Her lungs burned from the exertion, and her head pounded, sweat rolling down her back and dripping from her temples. Ten days of riding, hardly any food, constant fear, and now this. Every step was a battle. Her legs shook beneath her, muscles spent.

Ahead of her, the seer walked with an unsettling grace, her long limbs moving smoothly through the forest brush. She never stumbled, never faltered. It was as if even the trees dared not touch her.

Eadlyn's chest ached with every ragged breath. If they expected her to walk all the way into the heart of Kalgora, she wouldn't survive it. But worse than the exhaustion was the heaviness, the weight of hopelessness pressing against her ribs. Her eyes stung with tears she refused to let fall, but she was so tired. So ready for it to end. Whatever fate they had in store for her, let it come. She couldn't keep waiting for the inevitable.

Yet even as the despair threatened to consume her and make her question everything she believed, something deep inside clung to hope. She was not alone. God had kept her this far. He would not abandon her now. She had to believe that.

The trees thinned, the canopy giving way to sunlight. She squinted against the glare as they stepped into a clearing. In the center rose a tall, jagged stone, its surface covered with deep, sharp-edged runes. Next to it lay a second stone, flatter and wider, about waist high. It, too, bore runes carved along its edges. Moss clung to the cracks in the rock. A rusty red stain marred one corner.

The sight hollowed out Eadlyn's stomach. It far too closely resembled how she imagined the pagan altars in Scripture. The hair along her arms lifted. A few feet from it, they stopped, and the seer turned to face her. Though her eyes were pale blue, something dark and menacing lived in their depths. The air around Eadlyn grew thick and oppressive, pressing on her chest and makng her skin crawl, as if Satan's influence were particularly strong here.

Fear clawed up her throat like invisible fingers and dried out her tongue. Her heart beat so hard it ached, but she swallowed against the rising panic and took a shaky breath. If this was where she was to die, she would do so with God's Word in her mouth. Her voice wavered at first, but she clung to the verses with every bit of strength she had left.

"I love thee, O Lord, my strength. The Lord is my rock, and my fortress, and my deliverer; My God, my strength, in whom I will trust; My buckler and the horn of my salvation, and my high tower. I will call upon the Lord, who is worthy to be praised: So shall I be saved from mine enemies."

The seer's expression shifted, first confused, then wary, then angry. She snapped something to the men behind Eadlyn. A moment later, something flashed in front of Eadlyn's face. A thick, scratchy strip of cloth yanked into her mouth, stealing her voice. Even so, she continued to recite verses in her mind, not giving in to the way fear tried to take control of her body.

The seer grabbed the rope at her wrists and yanked, dragging her to the altar. The already raw flesh around her wrists flared in agony, and she gasped against the gag. At the stone, the seer drew a long, thin knife, its hilt polished bone. A lump lodged in Eadlyn's throat. She flinched as the seer reached out and cut the sleeves from her dress and shift, baring her arms and shoulders. Though the air was warm, a shiver spread across Eadlyn's skin, trembling through her body in waves.

Then came the pouch, black and cracked, filled with the same tar-like substance the seer wore on her own skin. With a stained finger, she traced symbols on Eadlyn's arms. Thick, sticky, ice-cold ink slid across her skin, leaving behind jagged runes. She couldn't move. Couldn't breathe. Could only endure it.

The seer moved to her face, marking her cheeks, forehead, and the base of her throat. Eadlyn turned away, but it didn't matter. When the seer finished, the Kalgoran brute behind Eadlyn knelt and tied her ankles. A fresh wave of panic flooded her.

Then he lifted her up. The gag smothered any sound, swallowing her gasp as the man laid her on the stone. The rough suface scraped against her shoulders. *No. Please, no.* She tried to gulp in a breath, but the gag suffocated her. *Lord, please, I don't want to die like this!* She pulled against her bonds and tried to get up, but the Kalgoran shoved her back down. She was going to die here, so far from home and family. Tears leaked out, leaving hot streaks as they rolled down her temples.

The seer stood over her, the knife glinting in her hand. Eadlyn squeezed her eyes shut and cried out to God as she waited for the blade to plunge into her heart or slice across her throat.

A roar shattered the air.

Eadlyn flinched, expecting pain. Expecting the end. It took a moment to hear anything past the pounding of blood in her head, but when death didn't come, she opened her eyes. The seer no longer stood over her. Movement blurred at the corner of her eye. The sounds of battle arose, screams, clashing metal, and war cries echoing all around her.

She bolted upright, tearing the gag from her mouth, and gulped air like she'd been drowning. Reaching for the rope around her ankles, she clawed at the knot. Her fingers slipped, but finally it loosened. She pulled the rope away, swinging her legs over the edge of the altar.

And froze.

The seer stood right in front of her. Their eyes locked. Dark fury poured from the woman's face, and the blade slashed. Searing pain tore across Eadlyn's chest. She stumbled back, hitting the altar stone with a cry. Blood welled, hot and fast. The seer lunged again, blade raised to finish the job.

Eadlyn threw her hands up, catching the woman's wrist. The knife hovered inches from her throat. But she had no strength left. Her arms gave way, the blade dropping lower.

A choked gasp escaped the seer. Her body went rigid. The pressure behind the dagger eased, and Eadlyn just stared, unable to process what was happening until the woman toppled sideways to the ground. Aevar stood behind her, his seax knife dripping red.

Eadlyn's vision swam.

"Aevar." His name left her lips in a half-choked sob.

He wrapped his arm around her, pulling her close as he turned to guard her, knife still raised. She pressed herself against his side, her entire body collapsing with relief. Nearby, Erik and Ingvald finished off the remaining Kalgorans. Several others lay scattered around the clearing. Within moments, the sounds of fighting fell silent, and Aevar turned to her. His eyes scoured her face before dropping lower, and his expression pulled tight.

Somewhere amidst the shock, pain broke through. Eadlyn looked down. Blood soaked the left side of her bodice around a slit in the fabric, starting at her shoulder and going up toward her neck. She winced, the pain sharpening. The blade must have just missed her throat.

"Sit down."

His voice sounded distant through the buzzing in her ears. She took a shaky step back, and her legs gave out. Aevar's hold tightened around her arms, lowering her to the ground. After wiping his seax knife in the grass, he cut the ropes from her wrists. Grabbing one of her sleeves that had been discarded nearby, he pressed it to the wound. She sucked in a breath, a groan rising in her throat.

Once the sharp stab of pain lessened, she settled back against the stone and met his gaze, afraid she was dreaming. "You're here."

He reached up and rested his hand against her cheek. "Yes."

She leaned into it, and tears leaked out as the reality sank in. She was safe.

Ævar's heart thundered, the heat of battle still pulsing in his veins. He kept his hand pressed against Eadlyn's wounded shoulder, but he eyed her face in mounting horror. She looked thinner, fragile in a way he had never seen before. Her lip had split and begun to heal. Faded bruising colored one cheekbone in a sickly yellow beneath streaks of rune paint. Her wrists, free of the ropes, were worn raw. These weren't just signs of captivity. They were signs of suffering.

Rage flared anew, burning up his throat. If he hadn't known Sig was probably already dead, he might have ridden back to finish him. But the anger faltered the moment he spied the tears. They trailed silently down her cheeks. Not sobs or weeping, but slow, steady tracks. She didn't even seem to notice them. Her face was frozen, caught somewhere between relief and utter exhaustion.

He brushed his fingers along her cheek, smearing away one of the inky runes. "Are you all right?"

She nodded against his hand. "I am now."

A rustle made him turn. Heida approached, almost silent on the blood-spattered grass. She stepped over the seer's body and picked up the knife that had cut Eadlyn. Aevar's lungs seized. What if the blade was poisoned? *No, please.*

Heida turned the blade in her hand and rubbed the edge with her thumb. At last, she shook her head. "It doesn't appear poisoned."

Relief crashed over him so fast it made him dizzy. *Thank you.*

Fathir knelt beside them. He set down a small bag of supplies and pulled out a roll of linen. "We'll wrap the wound and take her to Kjolur. There will be a healer there."

Aevar shifted Eadlyn to sit straighter so they could wrap the wound more easily. She winced, her breath hitching, and he tightened his hold on her. His father peeled back the makeshift cloth Aevar had used, and the sight of the wound robbed him of breath. The gash traced a deep line below her collarbone, curving dangerously toward her neck. Another inch higher and she might have bled out before he'd been able to reach her.

His hands trembled as he helped his father wind the bandage around her shoulder, binding it tight to stop the bleeding. He could hear every shallow rise and fall of her breath and the tremor in it.

He had almost lost her.

When they finished, Aevar reached for her and gathered her into his arms. She gave a soft gasp as the motion jarred her wound but then sagged against him. Her body, light and far too thin, curled toward his chest, and she rested her head in the crook of his neck. The familiar scent of her hair reached him—earthy and faintly sweet despite the dirt and blood—and something about it nearly broke him.

He swallowed hard and whispered, "I've got you."

She didn't respond in words, but the way she tucked herself more fully against him said enough.

He carried her to his horse. Though she tried to help as he lifted her into the saddle, her limbs trembled too badly to hold her own weight. She sagged once more, breath catching in pain. Aevar climbed up behind her and settled himself so her back rested against him. He slid his arm around her waist, anchoring her there. She leaned into him as if she had no strength left to do anything else.

He pressed his lips to her hair. "I will never let them take you again."

Her hand found his and clutched it. Together, they turned from the blood and horror of the clearing and rode into the trees.

Kjolur, the place where Heida had grown up, unfolded along the slope of a rugged hill, overlooking a wide, lush valley streaked gold and rust with late-summer grass. In the distance, the river shimmered like molten copper beneath the lowering sun, its rippling surface catching every last shard of daylight. Smoke drifted from thatched rooftops as Aevar and the others approached, the horses' hooves crunching on packed earth as they followed the winding path through the village. He hadn't been here in years. Not since their last battle against Kalgora. It felt like a different life now.

As they approached the great longhouse at the center of the settlement, its carved doors swung open. Jarl Gudrik walked out, flanked by his wife, Jodis, and Heida's brothers.

Gudrik was not a large man—shorter and leaner than Fathir or Erik—but he carried a fierce, untamed energy. Gray streaked his dark hair, his wiry frame hardened by decades of defending the northern border and surviving. Jodis stood beside him, tall and composed, with her silver-threaded braid resting over her shoulder. She was the only one capable of tempering Gudrik's recklessness when necessary.

While Heida greeted her family, Aevar slid from his horse and turned to Eadlyn. Her face pinched in pain, but before he could lift her, she laid a hand on his arm.

"I think I can walk now."

He hesitated. Her color was still too pale, the painted runes on her face stark against skin that had lost its summer warmth. She looked like a ghost of her former self. But she was trying to stand. Trying to reclaim even the smallest shred of independence after everything she'd endured. He could honor that.

He helped her down, supporting her when her legs trembled under her. She stood, barely, and he kept his arm around her as they walked toward the jarl and his family.

Gudrik stepped forward, eyes sweeping over Eadlyn with open concern. "Princess Eadlyn. Praise the gods you survived."

Praise God. Aevar startled at how natural that thought felt. Not only to think it, but to mean it.

Eadlyn offered a faint smile, and Gudrik and Jodis led them inside the longhouse, its warm interior lit with lamps and flicker-ing firelight. One of Heida's brothers hurried off to fetch the healer while Jodis guided them through the central hall to a quiet room off the corridor.

"The healer will be here shortly," she said. "I'll bring fresh clothes."

Once the door shut behind her, Aevar helped Eadlyn sit on the edge of the bed. She sank down, stiff with pain. He knelt before her and gathered her hands in his, seeing again how raw her wrists were. The sight of them reignited the fury simmering in his chest, but he forced it down. She didn't need his anger right now.

"Is there anything you need me to do?"

She nodded, but all she said was, "Just stay with me."

"I'm not going anywhere." He tightened his grip around her hands to prove it.

Tears rose too quickly for her to hide. She blinked them back, but the effort cost her. She darted a look toward the door, her voice low and wary. "Where is Sig? He was one of the three who took me, but I didn't see him."

"He's dead."

She exhaled a long, trembling breath, and her shoulders sagged. The relief on her face was immediate, but it only made Aevar's own tension return.

"Did he hurt you?"

She met his gaze, pain behind her eyes. "He hit me a couple of times…kept putting his hands on me, but nothing more."

The breath rushed out of Aevar's lungs. It wasn't good, but it could have been so much worse. That woman had told the truth.

"Oda was in on it too," Eadlyn whispered. "She told them where to find me."

Aevar fought to quell the anger that kept being fueled. He should have suspected that. "We'll deal with her when we get back."

Footsteps approached, and Jodis returned, bringing the healer and Heida. The healer, a stooped woman with a kind manner, began working without fuss. As she helped Eadlyn ease out of her ruined dress and shift, Aevar remained beside her on the bed, letting her lean into him as he kept his arm secure around her back. When the woman peeled the stiffened fabric from the wound, Eadlyn turned her face into Aevar's shoulder with a shudder. She didn't cry out, but he tightened his arm around her.

As the healer threaded her needle, he murmured words of comfort to Eadlyn to remind her he was there. After stitching the wound, the healer applied salve and wrapped it, then moved to her wrists, bandaging those too.

She then handed Aevar a fresh cloth and poured another bowl of clean water. "I'll let you finish," she said, motioning to the marks on Eadlyn's face. "And she should wear a sling for a few days. It will help with the pain. I'll come back to check her wound in the morning."

Aevar thanked her, and the healer departed with Jodis, but Heida lingered.

"Do you need anything?" she asked.

Aevar glanced at Eadlyn, noticing the way her cheeks were hollowed. "Yes. Food."

Heida nodded and left.

Now that they were alone again, Aevar dipped the cloth in the water and washed the black death runes from Eadlyn's skin. The ink had dried and crusted, and he worked gently, though his hands shook as he revealed every new bruise and scratch beneath the marks. Each one was a record of his failure to protect her.

Yet also proof she had survived.

Afterward, he helped her into the clean shift Jodis had left. A few minutes later, Heida returned with a tray of meat, cheese, soft bread, and a pitcher of water. She didn't speak as she set it down, but Aevar caught the look she gave Eadlyn and the flicker of guilt buried beneath the usual calm. She turned and left without a word.

At first, Eadlyn only picked at the food, her face drawn with exhaustion, but Aevar coaxed her to eat. Once she began, her appetite returned, and it became clear how little she'd been given. She finished most of what he placed before her, and he was glad for it. By the time she set the last bite aside, her head drooped, and the shadows under her eyes darkened.

"You need to rest."

She nodded and shifted carefully, lowering herself back against the pillows without jarring her shoulder. Her gaze found his, soft and pleading.

"Do you have to leave? Or can you stay with me?"

"I'm staying." No force on this earth could take him away from her.

He stripped off his boots and armor and slid in beside her. She turned to him, and he reached out, brushing his thumb across the fading bruise on her cheek. Though he believed he'd done the right thing in not finishing Sig off, part of him still itched to have put his sword through the man's heart for what he'd done.

Eadlyn's voice came in a hush, shaky at the edges. "I didn't think I'd ever see you again."

A ragged breath escaped him. "Neither did I."

Tears dribbled from the corners of her eyes, and she whispered, "Kiss me so I know you're really here."

He did.

The kiss was soft at first, careful. Then deeper and fuller until the horror of the last ten days blurred. She gripped his tunic, drawing herself to him, and he wrapped his arm around her, mindful of her wounds. He stroked her hair, his breath mingling with hers, and a steady calm settled over him, tension melting for the first time since she'd vanished from his life.

A dull, persistent ache tugged Eadlyn toward waking, but it wasn't the pain that drew her fully to consciousness. It was the warmth. The familiar safety of solid arms wrapped around her. She was lying on his chest, his breaths slow and even beneath her, the sound of his strong heartbeat in her ear. For a moment she feared it might be a dream, but the comfort was too real.

She sighed, sinking deeper into his hold. She didn't want to move. Didn't want to let go. Not yet. Not while this fragile peace still held. Yet memories pressed in, as creeping as shadows. The seer's dark eyes. The blade glinting above her. The rough stone at her back. Panic had overwhelmed her so utterly that, even now, she tensed as though she were still tied there, waiting to die.

She curled closer, gripping Aevar's tunic. His arms pulled her in, holding her securely as his thumb traced slow circles against her arm. Each pass of his touch soothed something frayed within her, and the tightness in her chest loosened.

She was safe. She was alive. God had not abandoned her. He had protected her in the direst of circumstances and brought Aevar and the others to her right when they were most needed.

Thank you.

For a while, she drifted in and out of the edge of sleep. Outside, the warble of birdsong rose with the waking village. Beyond the door, voices murmured. She shifted, trying to sit up, but a sharp lance of pain shot through her shoulder. She gasped, squeezing her eyes shut.

"Let me help you."

Aevar's voice came low and immediate. He shifted beneath her, easing her upright and bracing her as the world tipped. Dizziness wrapped around her. His palm smoothed over her back in wide, reassuring strokes. "It will be sore for a few days."

She breathed through her nose as the pain subsided from blinding to tolerable. His fingers brushed the hair from her face, lingering at her brow and her cheek as if checking for fever. Then he slipped out of the bed and lit a few lamps. They chased away the cool shadows, filling the room with a gentle glow.

"I'll see if the healer is nearby to check your wound," he said over his shoulder. "I'll be right back."

When the door closed behind him, she let her gaze wander around the little room. The space was smaller than their chamber at home. Homesickness nudged her, but she offered silent thanks she *would* return home. That she'd survived to experience that longing again.

Aevar returned not long after with the healer from yesterday at his side. Her hands were gentle and capable as she peeled back the bandage and examined the wound.

"It looks like it will heal well," she murmured. "No swelling or signs of fever."

She cleaned the area and re-wrapped it with fresh linen. The tugging of the bandage and the exposure of tender skin made Eadlyn wince, but Aevar was there, holding her hand the whole time. When it was over, he helped her dress, his hands gentle as he eased the sleeve over her injured arm and secured the sling. He found a comb and sat beside her again, working through the tangles in her hair. The rhythmic pull of the comb lulled her, each stroke smoothing more than just knots.

"There," he said, finishing a braid and tucking it over her shoulder.

Eadlyn sighed. It felt good to be clean and dressed, but she touched the empty space where her arm ring had once rested. It was only silver, yes, but she hadn't realized how much the weight of it had comforted her.

Aevar stood and crossed the room, picking up something from among his things on the table. As he turned, an object caught the light.

Eadlyn gasped. "You found it!"

He nodded and returned to her side. With the same care as when he'd first given it to her, he slid the ring back up her arm, settling it into place.

"The woman told me Sig had it." Though his voice was calm, his shoulders remained stiff, and fire lingered behind his eyes as he studied her face. He leaned in and kissed her, tender and full of emotion. Then he drew back, his voice low but intense. "I love you."

The words weren't new, but they were different somehow. They carried urgency, as if it were imperative he say them in case he somehow lost the chance.

Eadlyn slid her hand into his and squeezed it. "I love you too."

Aevar let out a breath like a weight leaving his chest. He stood, brushing her hair with his fingers one last time before saying, "I'll wash up, and we'll go have breakfast. Jodis is making tea to help with your pain."

The idea of food made her stomach growl, the first pangs of hunger cutting through her fatigue.

As Aevar stripped off his tunic and washed with the rag from the basin, Eadlyn watched him, taking in every familiar line of him. Her mind wandered, still dazed from exhaustion, until she blinked and realized something was missing.

"Where is your pendant?" From the time she'd met him, she had never seen him without it for long. He even wore it to bed most nights, but she had not seen it since he'd rescued her.

Aevar looked over his shoulder, then turned to her with a slow, meaningful smile. "At the bottom of a river somewhere southeast of here."

"Why?"

He came to sit beside her again and took her hand, his gaze unwavering. "Because I don't need it. My faith is in God now."

The weight of his words washed over her, stealing her breath. Tears sprang up so fast she couldn't even wipe them away. "Truly?"

He nodded, the truth shining in his eyes. "Yes."

Eadlyn leaned into him, resting her forehead against his as the tears kept flowing with emotion too vast to name. They were truly one now. Not just in body or vow but in faith. No more fearing for his soul. No more begging God to reach him. He had come of his own free will. And now she understood the purpose behind their pain and the waiting.

They had come through the fire and were still standing. Together.

Though the pain lingered, as Aevar had predicted, each day brought Eadlyn more relief. The healer's tea dulled the ache in her shoulder enough to allow her to sleep at night, and with food, shelter, and Aevar never far from her side, her strength returned. The weight of captivity fell away piece by piece, like the remnants of a nightmare chased away by morning light.

By the fourth morning in Kjolur, her steps were steady, no longer dragged down by exhaustion. When Aevar helped her tie the sling around her arm, she caught the small smile on his face.

"What is it?" she asked.

His smile deepened. "It's just good to see you recovering and doing well."

For a heartbeat they were silent, savoring each other's presence. Then he kissed her forehead, and they left the room.

In the hall, Aevar's father turned to meet them, and his weathered face softened. Like Aevar, Eadlyn read the relief in his expression.

"Gudrik is preparing us a ship to return to Fjellheim," he said.

They had decided the river was the best route home, faster and less taxing than the long, rough ride by land. Ingvald and a few of the huskarls would take the horses south, but the rest would travel with her and Aevar downriver.

Runar held her gaze. "Are you up for traveling?"

"Yes," she answered at once.

Though Kjolur had offered peace and safety, her heart longed for home. For the comfort of Inga's mothering and Ranvi's sisterly affection. For the children's laughter. In Fjellheim, the last remnants of this ordeal could finally heal.

"Good," Runar said. "We will leave once we've eaten."

Across the hall, Heida lingered by the hearth where Jodis oversaw breakfast. She had been quieter than usual since they'd arrived, even here, in the place where she grew up.

Eadlyn touched Aevar's arm. "I'll be right back."

Heida straightened as she approached. Ready to help. Ready to act. She'd been like that ever since the rescue, always making sure Eadlyn had what she needed. Food. A cup of tea. A place to rest.

But Eadlyn had no need of anything right now, except to share what was on her mind. "I know you feel guilty I was taken."

Heida's mouth twitched, half grimace, half confession, and her eyes dropped.

"It wasn't your fault," Eadlyn assured her. "You couldn't take on all three of them yourself."

Heida sighed, and her shoulders slumped enough to betray the weight she carried. "I know. I just wish I'd seen it coming and could have prevented all this." She looked at the sling around Eadlyn's arm. "I should've been able to protect you. That's why I was there."

The words were quiet but carried iron. She felt she'd failed, but Eadlyn did not want her carrying that burden.

"It wasn't about what you could or couldn't do. I gave myself up to save Trygg. That was my decision. And I would make it again."

For a moment, Heida said nothing, her jaw taut. Then her face softened. Though she'd never been as affectionate as Ranvi, Eadlyn saw how much she cared.

"That was very brave of you."

Eadlyn shrugged her good shoulder. "That's what family does. They sacrifice for each other."

Heida smiled, and they turned toward the breakfast table together.

Their last meal in the longhouse was unhurried, the mood light despite the looming departure. They had come here on the edge of death and fear, and to leave now in peace was worth savoring. When they finished, the men busied themselves with supplies, while Jodis directed thralls to carry food and furs down to the river. Eadlyn reached for a bundle to help only to have Kian all but bat her hand away.

"Not you." He wagged a finger at her. "Your only job is staying on your feet."

Eadlyn laughed and shook her head at him.

Even Braan fussed, handing her a soft cloak he must have gotten from Jodis and muttering something about keeping warm while they were still so far north. Aevar said little, but she noticed how he lingered at her side, his body always angled protectively, even here where no danger lurked.

Belongings in tow, they gathered near the entrance of the longhouse. Here, Gudrik and his youngest son waited, packs slung over their shoulders. During Eadlyn's time in Kjolur, Gudrik had been surprisingly gentle, offering not just quiet kindness but respect. He never hovered or coddled like the others, but he always made sure her needs were met. Now, however, the warrior broke through. Fierce, ready, and unmistakably dangerous as he faced Runar.

"Bard and Sven will remain here to guard the border and make sure Drocca stays where he belongs, but Viljar and I and some of my men will join you. If Staegar wants to fight, I mean to be there."

His words fell heavily, stripping away the fragile peace of the moment. Despite Eadlyn's rescue, the whole ordeal that had brought her here was not yet resolved. Staegar remained a threat that must be addressed. He had betrayed his king, tried to destroy the alliance with Essix by having her kidnapped, and sought to form his own connection with an enemy kingdom. On a political level, the offense could not be forgiven or allowed to go unpunished. Blood would be shed, and all Eadlyn could do was pray that only the guilty would suffer for his crimes.

One by one, they exchanged farewells with Gudrik's family. Jodis hugged Eadlyn gently, and Heida's brothers offered respectful nods, their expressions solemn but kind. Despite the pain that had brought them together, Eadlyn was grateful for them.

They made their way down the slope to the river. The air was crisp up here in the far mountains. Below them, the water glimmered under the morning sunlight. Aevar kept his hand pressed to her back on the way down as if he feared she might stumble, though the path was not steep.

At the docks, two ships waited, both long and sleek. A canopy stretched over the stern of one, sheltering a bed of furs Eadlyn guessed was meant for her. In the other vessel, Asfrid and Dagr sat bound near the bow. Their expressions were blank and unreadable. Eadlyn tried not to look too long. She didn't know what she felt toward them. She was thankful for how they had protected her from Sig, but they had still handed her over to the Kalgorans.

Erik reached the gangplank first and turned to help Eadlyn across. Aevar was right behind her, keeping his hand at her elbow. As the rest of the party climbed aboard, the men settled at the oars, their movements fluid and practiced. With a call from Gudrik, the longships pushed off, the water parting beneath the hulls.

Eadlyn stood in the center of the ship, Aevar beside her. The wind tugged at her braid, and the fresh smell of river and pine filled her lungs. As the land slipped by with the rhythm of oars, she leaned into Aevar's side and his arm curved around her. They were going home.

Eadlyn breathed deeply as the fjord opened before them, its silver-blue surface rippling beneath the light of the late afternoon sun. Fjellheim came into view, the wood-and-thatch buildings nestled along the shore and silhouetted against the forest and hills beyond. The sight pulled a smile to her lips. After almost three weeks away, it soothed something deep inside her. Not even Kenwich had ever filled her heart with such joy and feelings of home.

Their longship glided toward the dock, the creak of timber mingling with the soft splash of oars and the distant cries of gulls overhead. As the ship slowed, ropes sailed through the air, caught by waiting hands along the dock. Once secured, Aevar took her hand and helped her out of the boat. When her feet touched solid ground again, a strange mix of relief and unreality washed over her. This was home, and yet she was no longer quite the woman who had left it.

The others came ashore, and a group of huskarls met them, greeting Eadlyn with warm welcomes.

One of them turned to Runar and bowed. "Jarl. We received your message about Oda."

"And?" Runar asked, his voice clipped.

The huskarl shook his head. "Gone. When we went to arrest her, she was not at her house. Shortly after, her horse went missing. It seems she caught wind of our plans and fled the village."

Braan's face twisted in a scowl. "Ran to Staegar, no doubt."

A knot tightened in Eadlyn's stomach. The thought of Oda still out there, free and unrepentant, slithered through her mind like a snake.

Runar cast a dark glance over his shoulder toward Ormvik. "If she's fled, then she knows what will happen if she returns."

He turned back to the huskarl and ordered him and a couple of others to secure Asfrid and Dagr while they awaited his final judgment. A judgment that would no doubt be severe, probably fatal. If only Asfrid had listened to Eadlyn and brought her back to Fjellheim.

Then they trekked through the village. All the familiar sights wrapped around Eadlyn, drawing her in like a quiet embrace. Near the longhouse, a sound broke through the shuffle of boots and low chatter—children's laughter and hurried footsteps. Eadlyn looked up as Ranvi, Inga, and the children rushed toward them.

She had little time to brace herself before Trygg barreled into her and threw his arms around her waist. Katla was right behind him, clutching her good arm fiercely. Emotion swelled, and all the pain and terror Eadlyn had experienced melted in the light of their joy. She blinked hard, but couldn't hold back tears. A couple slipped down her cheeks, but these were tears of return and re-union.

Ranvi reached her next, arms wrapping around her, careful but strong, and filled with the depth of the bond they had formed.

"I'm so glad you're safe," she whispered, her voice cracking.

Eadlyn nodded against her shoulder. "So am I."

They pulled apart, and she found her own tears mirrored in Ranvi's eyes. Inga stepped in, embracing Eadlyn with all the warmth of a mother. As the others shared greetings, Eadlyn spotted two familiar figures among the growing crowd. Halbjorn and Gorum. But she knew they had not come simply to celebrate her safe return. They, like Gudrik, were here for what followed.

This wasn't over.

The joy of the moment shifted like a sudden wind. She saw it in Erik's expression as he turned from Ranvi to Runar. "Staegar will know we've returned. He'll have had someone watching the fjord."

The celebration stilled, smiles and laughter fading.

Runar's gaze cut toward the shore. "Then we move now. He's had too much time already. If he knows we found Eadlyn, he'll be prepared for us."

Gorum stepped up beside him, quiet but firm. "You will not face him alone. We came to stand with you."

Halbjorn strode forward, his tone thunderous. "Aye, and to see justice done!" He ran his thumb along the edge of the large battle axe he carried as if testing to make sure it was sharp enough to cleave Staegar's skull.

"Staegar will not stand down without a fight," Runar warned.

"Good," Gudrik growled. "Then we can just kill him."

They stood together, four of the ten jarls united to oppose Staegar.

But Eadlyn's heart sank as her gaze found Aevar. The strength of him. The steady weight of his presence. The love in his eyes that had helped sustain her through her recovery. And now he had to leave again. She wanted to cling to him and refuse to let him go, but she could not do that. He was a warrior, and this must be done.

All at once, the men moved with swift purpose, gathering their weapons and sending for their warriors. It all happened so fast. Eadlyn's steps carried her to Aevar as if drawn by a string. He already held his shield in one hand, the other resting near his sword. His face was the mask of a warrior, focused and resolved, but it changed for her, his expression softening.

She put her hand on his chest. "I know when you see him you will remember everything that has happened to me, but don't let it drive you to do anything you'll regret. Justice must be done, but please, let it be justice and not vengeance."

They'd fought so hard to get to where they were, and his faith was so new. She wanted to protect it if she could.

His jaw clenched, and his throat worked. "I will do my best."

Heaviness pressed on Eadlyn with the weight of everything she wished to say, but no words were enough. Not when he might not come back.

Aevar reached for her, pulling her close. His mouth found hers, the kiss deep, slow, and desperate. When they parted, he pressed his forehead to hers and whispered, "I love you."

"I love you," she breathed. Tears burned, and she blinked them back. She would not send him away with the memory of her crying. She swallowed hard, fighting to keep her voice from wavering. "Please come back to me."

"I will."

With that promise, he turned to join the others. Eadlyn stood with Ranvi and Inga at her sides, the children watching from behind them as the men marched away. She knew he needed to go, and she needed to stay, but her prayers went with him.

Please, God. Bring him back. Bring him home.

The keels of the two ships ground against the shore with the sound of wood scraping sand. The men disembarked into the shallows in a wave of splashing boots and bristling weapons. Aevar dropped into the knee-deep water beside the hull and cast one final look back across the fjord. Fjellheim was a dim smudge on the far horizon. Home. Where Eadlyn waited. Watching. Praying.

His ribs pressed against his lungs, but he turned back toward the tree line ahead. The forest swallowed the road to Ormvik in thick, shadowed silence. Nothing moved. No smoke or banners. No eyes watching from the trees. It was almost as if Staegar didn't know they were coming, but Aevar knew better.

He fell into step beside his father and brothers as they entered the woods, shields and swords at the ready for anything. His heart pounded, the blood in his veins already running hot. It had been years since he'd marched to true war, but never had a battle felt so personal. He prayed silently. Not for blood or vengeance as he might have once, but for strength and for justice. For the lives of the men beside him.

They marched in grim silence until the trees thinned and gave way to a clearing. There, across the open field, a line of warriors waited. Blades gleamed. Red and black shields blazed in the afternoon sun. Right in the center of it stood Staegar. His hatred scorched even at a distance, and Aevar's stomach turned at the sight of him. He scanned their number. Seventy, maybe eighty. About the same as their own force.

They halted thirty feet from the enemy line, the air between them pulsing with a long-brewing fury. The silence stretched out until Fathir stepped forward, his voice clear and powerful.

"As king, I command you to throw down your weapons and surrender."

Staegar's lip curled. "You bring an army onto my land, making demands. For what purpose do you march against your own people and dare to threaten me?"

"For having Princess Eadlyn kidnapped, for planning to trade her to the Kalgorans to gain their favor, and for plotting to make yourself king, though we both know if you ever clawed your way to the position, you'd never hold the title. Not even with Kalgora backing you. The other jarls would never be satisfied, and they know you can be beaten because I've done it. Twice. I will do it again today if need be."

Staegar shot a fiery glare at Halbjorn and the others before returning it to Fathir. "You make many accusations. What proof do you have?"

"We have witnesses to your treachery. The words of your own heir condemned you."

"And where is he?" Staegar snapped, glancing past them. "I don't see him supporting your claims."

"In the bellies of wolves up north."

A flicker of something passed over Staegar's face. Fury or shame. Perhaps both.

"Nords have not fought each other for generations. You would come here and start a war all for an Essian princess and an unnecessary alliance? You would divide Nordra over a woman not even of our people?"

Aevar stepped forward, flames rising in his chest. "Eadlyn is *my wife*. And she is more Nord than you'll ever be. You are the coward scheming behind the backs of all Nords, letting others do your dirty work instead of issuing an honorable challenge."

Staegar bared his teeth, his sword twitching as though he were thinking of calling the charge right then and there.

Fathir looked past Staegar to the men flanking him. "We have no quarrel with you. This is not your war. You need not follow him."

The line stirred. Some exchanged glances. A few shifted their weapons as though reconsidering.

Staegar shot a death glare down the line. "Cowards! Anyone who stands down today forfeits the right to call himself a warrior."

When his gaze swung back to them, Aevar knew it was over. There would be no negotiating.

"Shields up!" Staegar roared.

The clamor of wood snapped into position all down the line. "Attack!"

Staegar's men surged forward like a wave of iron and fury, battle cries tearing the air. The thunder of boots tremored in the ground. Aevar slammed his shield into place and braced for impact. They met in a crash, metal on metal, wood on wood. The force drove through Aevar's bones, almost buckling his knees. A blade scraped against the rim of his shield, just missing his face.

He shoved hard, ramming his sword into the man's belly. The warrior dropped with a strangled cry, swallowed by the churn of bodies.

Another came fast, swinging high. Aevar ducked and smashed his shield upward. The rim caught the man's jaw with a crunch. Aevar didn't wait. He thrust low, his sword biting into flesh. The warrior collapsed at his feet.

But there was no pause. A third man rushed him, roaring. Aevar turned the strike with his shield. He slammed his shoulder forward, driving the warrior back, then cut deep into his thigh. The man fell, clutching at his wound, and Aevar dragged in a breath as sweat stung his eyes.

A shadow loomed.

Aevar spun, ducking as a sword whistled past his head. His shield came up by instinct. Staegar stood before him. Eadlyn's face flashed in his mind, and what she had suffered, but his focus narrowed to survival. Blood and iron choked the air. Staegar's face twisted with loathing, his eyes ablaze. With a snarl, he charged, hacking at Aevar's defenses. His attacks were relentless and brutal, but not wild like Sig's. Each swing was honed by years of experience and battles. Aevar blocked one attack after another. His shield rattled under the strain, and one savage strike splintered its edge.

He struck back, low and swift, but Staegar pivoted and slammed his shield into Aevar's ribs. The force jolted through his leather armor, and pain lanced his side. Aevar gritted his teeth, sweeping his blade up, but Staegar slipped away. With a savage roar, he drove his shield straight into Aevar's face.

The world snapped white. Aevar stumbled and dropped to one knee, blood filling his mouth. He lashed out blindly. Staegar kicked him hard in the chest, knocking him into the dirt. Aevar caught himself with one hand, teeth bared. He lunged, blade carving a line across Staegar's knee. Staegar cursed and brought his sword down, but Aevar rolled and came up inside his guard. He drove his shoulder into the man's gut. They staggered together in a knot of limbs, slipping in blood and gore. Staegar's elbow cracked against Aevar's skull.

He hit the ground hard, the air punching from his lungs. Everything blurred as the world tilted beneath him. Blood roared in his ears, drowning out the battle. Faint and distant, someone screamed his name. He groped for his weapons and found his sword. He wrapped his fingers around the hilt, which was slick with blood or sweat, but his shield was gone. Staegar loomed above him, shadowed against the sky.

Aevar fought to stand, his vision swimming. The clouds wheeled as he forced his legs beneath him. He raised his sword. Eadlyn's face came again. Her smile. Her tears. He would not break his promise.

He reached for his seax as Staegar lifted his sword, but a voice shouted Staegar's name. Staegar hesitated and looked back. Silver flashed. He jolted, and Aevar caught a gurgling sound as Staegar stumbled backward. Fathir stood just beyond him, the edge of his sword stained crimson. Swaying, Staegar dropped to his knees and then toppled face first into the dirt at Fathir's feet.

Aevar gasped for air, blinking the world back into focus. Around him, the battlefield grew quiet. The clang of iron gave way to groans of the wounded, shuffling feet, and the heavy silence of death. Some of Staegar's men retreated toward the settlement in the distance. Others dropped their swords and shields with a hollow clatter of surrender.

He turned in place as his heart thumped his battered ribcage. His brothers, Kian, and Heida all still stood, streaked with sweat and blood but alive. So did the other jarls. Viljar walked with a limp, his pant leg bloodied, but he waved off help from Heida.

Then Aevar faced his father again. Their eyes met, and he gave him a grateful nod. As Fathir turned to give orders, Aevar closed his eyes and breathed another ragged breath, savoring it after how close he'd come to never taking another. How close he'd come to breaking his promise to Eadlyn. Tipping his head toward the sky, he whispered, "Thank you."

Night had settled like a heavy blanket over the longhouse, quiet but oppressive. The fire in the hearth burned low. Eadlyn sat near it, staring at the embers. The warmth of roasted meat and fresh bread lingered from earlier, tempting and comforting, yet her appetite recoiled.

The hours since the men had marched off to confront Staegar had stretched like years. Every minute passed with the weight of uncertainty pressing down on her, imagined horrors attacking her mind. What if they had walked into a trap? What if Staegar had prepared more than anyone had guessed? What if Aevar was dead?

She breathed through her nose, forcing those thoughts away, and reached up to grasp the cross necklace she'd put on right after Aevar left. But even when met with faith, the fear was hard to silence.

A gentle hand settled on her shoulder. Eadlyn looked up into Ranvi's kind eyes. Worry lived there too, beneath the calm surface, but so did strength. Ranvi gave her a soft, reassuring smile and set a steaming cup of tea on the table beside her. "Drink this. It will help calm your nerves."

Eadlyn took the mug gratefully. The sweet scent of honey and chamomile floated upward, soothing her. She sipped slowly.

"I suppose this isn't the first time you've had to wait like this."

Ranvi sat beside her. "No."

"Is there anything that helps?"

Ranvi considered the question for a moment. "Only the understanding that they go because they must. And they go for us. It's not just battle they face. It's the burden of protecting those they love."

Eadlyn wrapped her fingers around the cross again. *Please, Lord. Bring them back to us.* At least she had the certainty God was with Aevar.

The door creaked open.

She turned with a start. Light from the lamps spilled over the threshold, catching the figures that stepped inside. Runar entered first. Then Aevar. A sharp gasp tore from Eadlyn's chest, and she shot to her feet. Her knees almost gave beneath her from sheer relief, but she didn't care. He was here. He was alive.

She hurried from the table, and he met her halfway. Dried blood flaked around his nose and brow and streaked his jaw, but he moved under his own strength. She looked him over, searching for deeper wounds or signs of pain. She spied bruises and scrapes, but his eyes, when they met hers, were clear and filled with warmth. His hands found her arms and drew her in. She stepped into his hold without hesitation.

"Are you all right?"

"I'm fine," he said, quiet but steady.

"What happened?"

"Staegar chose to fight. He attacked me during the battle, no doubt hoping to break the alliance with my death."

Eadlyn held his gaze unwaveringly. "And you killed him?"

Aevar shook his head. "No. My father struck the final blow." His hand rose, thumb brushing her cheek. "I thought of you when I faced him, like you said. But my only desire in that moment was staying alive so that I could return to you."

Eadlyn smiled and melted into him as he drew her in for a soft kiss.

As they parted, she searched his face. "So it's over now?"

"It's over. One of Staegar's cousins is now jarl and has already sworn fealty to my father. He seems to be a much more reasonable man. With Staegar and Sig gone, there will be no more threats from Ormvik."

"And Oda?"

"No one in Ormvik has seen her. We will keep searching, but no doubt she has fled far from here where she thinks her actions won't catch up to her. She has no allies left. You do not need to worry."

A deep breath eased from Eadlyn's lungs, and for the first time in days, all the tension left her body.

He was home.

They both were.

The morning air cooled Eadlyn's face, crisp and carrying the mustiness of dry leaves and smoke from morning hearths. Autumn would soon take hold of the land. Though the afternoons remained warm, the nights and mornings had grown chilly. The harvest was being gathered in earnest, along with preparations for Braan and Heida's wedding to take place in only a few days' time. Eadlyn looked forward to the celebration and to seeing the two of them finally united. A perfect way to put the last lingering shadows of the trouble with Staegar behind all of them.

Behind her, the longhouse door shut. Aevar stepped out, his sword belted at his side, though she hoped he wouldn't have need of it again anytime soon. His boots crunched as he crossed to her. He didn't speak, just reached for her hand as naturally as breathing. She took it, lacing her fingers with his.

Together they walked, their pace unhurried. The sun rose higher, highlighting the leaves that were turning gold and crimson. The chill nipped at Eadlyn's cheeks and nose, but her heart was warm beneath her shawl, full to bursting. Here, in this place she had once feared, she had found a life that was hers.

She leaned into Aevar, wrapping her free hand around his arm. Though he was gone most of the day to help with the harvest, every moment together was a blessing she cherished. While winter would bring its own challenges, it would allow them extra time to share with each other.

At the shoreline, they stopped. The fjord stretched out before them in perfect stillness, a mirror of the sky and flame-colored leaves. Quiet wrapped around them, not heavy, but something almost sacred. They bowed their heads in prayer.

Eadlyn closed her eyes, and the words poured from her heart. Thankfulness for safety, healing, and for the husband beside her.

She prayed for the future, for wisdom, for grace, and for strength in whatever storms might still come. Beside her, Aevar's voice murmured. His prayer was almost inaudible, but the fact that it existed at all still made her soul lift with wonder.

When the silence stretched long enough, she turned to him. Nerves twinged in her belly, and she touched her hand to it. She'd suspected for a week now. Inga and Ranvi had confirmed it yesterday, and she'd waited for the right moment to tell him. Now, standing here, it was time.

Aevar smiled at her but seemed to sense she had something on her mind. "What is it?"

"I have something to tell you. I think it may cause some fear, but I hope it brings more joy." She reached for his hand and placed it against her stomach. "I'm with child."

Aevar stilled, his eyes widening. He dropped his gaze to her belly, where his hand rested as if he might feel the truth through her skin. His fingers twitched, and his throat worked as he swallowed. Emotion bloomed across his face in layers—shock, fear…and then something so deep it stole her breath.

He exhaled as though it was the first time he'd breathed in full since she'd spoken. "You're certain?"

"Yes." She blinked at the sting of tears. "I am."

His hand stayed on her belly as he leaned forward to press his lips to her forehead.

"It does bring me joy," he whispered.

Relief cascaded through her, loosening the tightness in her chest. She had known he would love this child—she had never doubted that—but she'd feared the pain of the past would overshadow the miracle of the present. Instead, his eyes held hope.

"I know it might not be easy," she said, "but I want you to remember everything God has already done for us. How He carried us through every dark moment. How He brought us together. He's with us now too."

Memories flowed through her mind. The first time she'd seen him, the long road to trust, the aching fear of being taken from him, and the unshakable strength of his arms when he had found her again.

"I was so afraid to come here, but God did so much more than I ever could have imagined. He didn't just give me the security I sought for Essix, He gave me a home and a family and a husband I love dearly. He has also given us this child and a new path to walk together. But, above all, He has given us life beyond this one no matter what happens."

She reached into the small pouch on her belt and pulled out a simple leather cord. "This is to help you always remember and take comfort in that." She opened her hand. A silver cross pendant rested there. "I had Tallak make it for you."

Aevar took it reverently, turning it over in his fingers. The corners of his mouth lifted. "Between the two of us, he'll never lack for work."

Eadlyn laughed. "He said much the same."

Aevar slipped the cord over his head, the cross settling against his chest. It looked right there, contrasting so brightly against his dark tunic. He reached for her, drawing her into his arms with care that was fierce and tender all at once. His voice was rough when he whispered in her ear.

"*Tahk fyr, ást mín.*"

Epilogue

An unexpected spring blizzard raged outside, the wind howling and pelting the longhouse with ice and snow. Before Eadlyn had introduced him to God, Aevar would have seen it as a bad omen. Even now, he struggled not to let those feelings take hold. He sat unmoving at the center of it all, hunched forward at the main table, hands clasped before him. He stared at the flames in the hearth, but he wasn't really seeing them.

Eadlyn had gone into labor just after dawn. Now the sun had long since vanished behind storm-darkened clouds, and it had to be well past midnight. Her cries echoed from their room in waves, every one of them striking Aevar like a blade to the gut. He could not ignore them, and yet they were agony to hear.

Around him, his father and brothers, Kian, and Heida sat in uneasy silence. They spoke occasionally in hushed tones, but every time a cry came, the words died on their tongues. Their faces were drawn and subdued. Even Braan sat with his fingers laced, bouncing one knee in a tense rhythm.

Aevar struggled to breathe and tried to pray instead. He had whispered more prayers since this morning than he could count, but his thoughts kept slipping back into old, familiar darkness. The day he had lost Thora and Brenna. The silence. The grief. The shattering.

He clenched his jaw and reached up to grab the silver cross at his neck, pressing it hard into his palm. *Please. Spare her. Spare our child. Let this time be different.*

Footsteps approached. Aevar looked up as his father crossed the floor, a mug in one hand. He offered it without a word. Steam curled from the warm ale. Aevar accepted it out of habit more than want, took a sip, and set it aside. His father didn't speak, just placed a firm hand on his shoulder and gave it a squeeze. The weight steadied him.

Another cry came from beyond the door, this one longer and harsher. Aevar gripped the edge of the table hard. He bowed his head, forcing himself to breathe, to trust. A moment passed. Then another sound—piercing and unfamiliar. A cry, but not Eadlyn's.

Aevar froze. The world narrowed to that sound alone. Thin and new but powerful. A baby's cry. It came again, more forcefully now. Not the weak, fading whimper Brenna had made before the silence. No. This was a shout to the world that life had arrived.

Aevar pushed to his feet, barely able to stand under the weight of hope swelling in his chest. Around him, the others broke into smiles and muted cheers, but Aevar couldn't celebrate yet. Not until he saw them both. Not until he knew.

The minutes that followed were a blur of pacing, heart-thundering silence, and unanswered questions. He kept his attention always on the door.

Finally, it opened.

Móthir stood there, her face aglow. She motioned to him. "Come."

Aevar didn't hesitate. He rushed across the hall and followed her into the room. Immediately, he found Eadlyn. She lay propped against a pile of pillows, her skin pale and glistening with sweat, strands of hair clinging to her face. She looked spent. Fragile. His heart nearly stopped, but her eyes met his, and in them he saw strength. And joy.

"I'm all right." Her voice was soft and full of everything words could never say.

Aevar crossed the room in two strides. The fear in him hadn't released until this moment. He sank down beside her on the bed, and for a breath he just stared at her, drinking in her smile. Then he looked down.

Wrapped in soft linens and cradled in her arms was a tiny, perfect face with a dark crown of downy hair. The baby's eyes were closed, cheeks flushed from the effort of birth, a tiny fist pressed near its mouth. Wonder struck him as if it were the first time all over again.

He reached out with trembling hands, and Eadlyn passed the child into his arms.

"Meet your daughter. Eliana. 'My God has answered'."

They had decided on the name months ago, choosing to trust God would indeed answer their prayers for a healthy child and safe delivery, and He had.

The weight of her, so small, yet so real, stole Aevar's breath away. Tears caught in his throat, and he swallowed them down hard as he pressed a kiss to his daughter's brow. She shifted in his arms and let out a soft, sleepy murmur before settling back into stillness. Eadlyn reached for his hand, and he took it, their fingers knotting together like the final thread in a tapestry only God could have woven. Together, they sat there in the lamplight, the blizzard raging beyond the walls, but within this room was only warmth. Only love.

Only answered prayers.

Thank you for joining me on Eadlyn and Aevar's journey!
If you found hope or joy in these pages, would you consider
leaving a review on retailer websites and Goodreads? Even a
few words can help other readers discover the story and
mean more to me than you know.

- Jaye

About the Author

JAYE L. KNIGHT is a hopeless romantic with an active imagination and an AuDHD brain that fuels her stories with twists, adventure, and heart. She weaves tales of faith, courage, happily-ever-afters, and the power of God's love to light the way even in the deepest darkness. When she's not crafting fantasy, she dabbles in contemporary romance as Jaye Elliot.

www.jayelknight.com

Also by Jaye

ILYON CHRONICLES
A Completed Six Book Series

Half-Blood (Prequel Novella)
Resistance
The King's Scrolls
Samara's Peril
Exiles
Bitter Winter
Lacy (Novella)
Daican's Heir

CONTEMPORARY NOVELS
(Written as Jaye Elliot)

No Chance Meeting
Safe With You

www.ingramcontent.com/pod-product-compliance
Lightning Source LLC
Chambersburg PA
CBHW022255310726
48973CB00001B/75